GAME OVER

SILICON BILLIONAIRES

ALEXIS KNIGHTLY

Game Over

Editor: Mackenzie at Nice Girl, Naughty Edits

Cover Designer: Ashley at Book Cover Couture

Photographer: Wander Aguiar

Model: Chris Lynch

Proofreaders: Ashley Boyle, Brooklyn Messer, Catherine P., Madison Barnes, Sutton Landavazo, Tammy Jordan Wagner

For Derek,

My beloved cornerstone.

CONTENT WARNINGS

This book contains a morally-grey hero, sexually explicit content, profanity, and topics that may be sensitive to some readers. For a list of content warnings, please visit:

alexisknightly.com / content-warnings

The Playlist

Lose Control - Teddy Swims

Too Sweet - Hozier

On Your knees - Ex Habit

Cruel Summer - Taylor Swift

I Wanna Be Yours - Arctic Monkeys

Favorite - Isabel Larosa

Guilty As Sin - Taylor Swift

If u Think I'm Pretty - Artemas

The Color Violet - Tory Lanez

Belong Together - Mark Ambor

PROLOGUE

15 YEARS AGO

"Never tell anyone what you saw."

Mama shoves the camcorder into her purse.

Clutching my arm, she guides us down the hallway, setting a pace that leaves my short legs struggling to keep up. She banks a left, her breath waning above me as we bound across the kitchen. Moonlight streams through the windows, illuminating stainless steel appliances and marble counter-tops that stand taller than my pigtails.

Her modest heels *click-clack* their way across Mr. Kingston's rolling estate, room after room, corridor through corridor, until she stops suddenly, dropping to one knee. Now at eye level, Mama shakes my shoulders, earning my full attention.

"Juliana," she rasps. "You can *never* speak of this. Not with your friends. Not at school or even with your brother. Do you understand me?"

I stare into her pupils, transfixed by their intensity. Usually, they're soft and inviting. Glinting with a warmth I can't seem to find. Now, only fear shines in them, amplified by the smudge of charcoal liner around her waterline. And the frazzled state of her hair and miss-buttoned leopard blouse.

Biting my trembling lip, I nod without a word.

"Good... good..." Her voice wanders, as does her stare.

Time wanes on a slow breath, before I break the silence. "C-can I go back and play with Jer now?"

Snapping into focus, she bursts to her feet. Then we're on the move again, leaving my lingering question in our wake. Anxiety crawls up my throat, tripping my heels, but Mama keeps me upright by my arm. Her hold is tight. Too tight. Like the suffocating squeeze of a python in the throes of fight-or-flight. I'm about to protest, when the playroom door sweeps into view, releasing a heap of tension off my shoulders.

I nearly giggle. *Phew-ee! She* did *listen.*

I'll just go back to playing with Jer and Hayden and forget all about what happened—*whatever-it-was that I saw.* But, on second thought, why *should* I forget? Mama really is acting strange for no good reason. What's the big deal? She and Mr. Kingston were only playing. Rather *loudly,* I'll say, with an array of noises I've certainly never heard come from Mama's lips...

But still.

Adults have playtime, too—right?

No matter what *it* was, the instant Mama flings the door wide, unveiling my favorite room inside Mr. Kingston's humongous house, all memory of the incident fades to black. My attention stolen by yellow Tonka trucks, Lincoln Logs, fuzzy sock puppets, and Jer and Hayden sitting crisscross on the carpet, their focus conducted by Thomas the Tank Engine steaming across miniature railroad tracks.

On the same breath, their eyes meet mine, Jer's brimmed with wonder and Hayden's above a rosy blush slowly staining his chubby cheeks. Jitters erupt in my insides—a funny sensation I can't quite explain, but never fail to feel whenever I'm around Mr. Kingston's youngest son. It's as if my stomach decides to do a cartwheel, then a somersault *and* a belly flop, all on its own, without my body ever being in motion.

A high-pitched whistle zips through the air as Thomas rolls past the train station, flickering lights celebrating his arrival. Returning Hayden a toothy grin, excitement propels my feet forward—

"Jeremy."

I freeze, not having ventured more than a couple of steps, as all the hairs on my arms stand on end. *Mama never says his name like that...*

"We're leaving... *Now.*"

Jer's expression falters. But he hasn't the time to argue, not when Mama lifts his skinny frame off the carpet, standing him on his feet, then treats his arm much like mine moments ago.

"You too, Juliana."

"Can't Hayden come along?" I whine.

On their rushed exit out the door, she shoots me a stern look. I huff a grand sigh and fall into step behind them. But before I leave the room, I pivot on my heel. Hayden sits amongst the toys, his eyebrows knotted in confusion. I wish to tell him everything I saw. To explain that it's my fault we're leaving.

Instead, I brush a lock behind one ear, my toes curling when his ocean-blue eyes find mine. "S-sorry, Hayden."

"That's okay!" he chirps, an abundance of energy rolling

off him in waves, as usual. "Next time, we can build the tracks together. I promise!"

Then that inexplicable feeling washes over me once more. And it lingers... Lingers through our departing glance. On my way out the door. And as I trail Mama's hasty steps atop checkered tile and polished mahogany. Until we're beneath the umbrella of a cloudless night.

Cobblestone lines the long driveway, our path lit by floodlights peeking between pristine hedges.

"We still had more time. I just know we did!" Jer wriggles in Mama's grasp, blabbering on, his voice like a squeaky mouse in the calm air. "We hadn't made it to the Legos yet. Or added other cars to our tracks. Not even—"

"Shhh," Mama hushes him.

Noting me lagging behind, she grabs my hand, forcing me to keep up. Her heels clack against the driveway, piercing through the silence, as she guides us hand-in-hand down a row of cars, all neatly parked along the sidewalk. They're always here. Mama once said they all belong to Mr. Kingston, but I don't think I believe her.

Nonetheless, I run my fingertips across their shiny exteriors like always.

First, they glide along a car that gleams like snowy pearls, the surface so clean my reflection gazes curiously back at me. Until my fingers slip off into thin air... and connect with another shade. This time, a deep onyx with athletic grooves and chrome rims. Next up, a vibrant azure... then another midnight black. Specs of white offset the dark color perfectly, as if a masterful painter flicked her wrist in just the right ways, her brush emulating tiny diamonds...

Next is orange. But the tinge is... *off,* sporting random splotches. Somehow dull and dingy, yet offensively bright, all at the same time. Then there's the mismatched door—a cherry red. The whole thing's like the same painter did away with her careful strokes and opted for a brasher technique. Hasty, sloppy. Possibly discarding her brush altogether, using her hands to smear along the bottom side of the—

Oh. Oops.

My hand falls to my side.

That's our car.

"Mama's Trusty Steed," she often calls it. Or *"The Rust Bucket,"* depending on her mood. I smirk at that, hearing her sassy voice recite the nickname in my head—until I hear Mama's actual voice. Frazzled and panting. My smile fades as she rummages through her tote frantically, retrieving a pair of keys.

A car door clicks open nearby.

"Shit," Mama breathes out, a rare curse slipping from her lips. And out walks Mr. Kingston from the beautiful vehicle parked directly in front of ours. He rises to his impressive height, clad in a navy suit, a phone pressed to his ear.

Our car *beeps,* its headlights flashing. "Get inside," Mama hisses, tossing us into the backseat. "And don't move."

"I'll call you right back," Mr. Kingston says in the distance, closing his door simultaneously with ours. Through the window, my gaze connects with Mama's. For a brief moment, the whites around her pupils widen like saucers. Then they blink slowly, exuding a shocking confidence. Plastering on a calm expression, Mama turns, facing Mr. Kingston.

My left pigtail jerks backwards.

"Ow!" I screech as Jer crawls over the top of me. Shifting in protest, I exhale sharply, as he steals the window seat. "What're you doing?! Mama said not to move."

"I'm not," he lies. "Don't you want to listen?"

Not waiting for my answer, he works the manual window crank, dropping the glass an inch. Just enough to pick up Mama's heels halting atop the driveway. Jer sucks in a breath at the same time I do, going deathly silent. Like one whisper might betray our eavesdropping as we shuffle closer, huddling against the window.

Mr. Kingston sinks his hands into his pants pockets, sporting a playful grin. "Where do you think you're running off to, baby? You still got another hour of watching Hayden."

Baby? Jer and I exchange a look. *He never calls her that.* I nibble on my lip, thinking. Well, I guess he did a few times. When he and Mama were playing earlier...

"Oh, uhm..." She shuffles, drawing her purse close to her side. "Didn't I tell you? We have to get home early tonight."

Cocking his head, he eyes her bag. "Do you now?"

"Yes. We have plans in the morning."

"Well, then, if it's so urgent, I'll drive you. Or"—he takes a step closer, hunger flashing in his eyes—"even better, you can stay the night here."

"Why, that's very kind of you, Mr. Kingston." Her tone is sweet, but his name sounds strained on her tongue, as she gestures toward us. Gasping, we duck low, just enough to still peek through the bottom of the glass. "But I've already got them buckled up. We'll manage just fine."

He doesn't look our way. Not even a glance, as his smile grows. "I know when you're lying, Amber."

She squirms under his scrutiny. "I'm not lying."

"Yes, you are." He takes another step, which prompts her to take one back. "You want to know why? Because you're terrible at it." Flicking his chin, he eyes her purse again. "Are you going to tell me what you got in there?"

She doesn't say a word.

"God, I love when you play hard to get." He wets his lips. "Does my little mistress need another round—so soon?"

"N-no."

"Another lie." He clicks his tongue. "Or else you wouldn't have stolen something to get my attention. What is it, then? Jewelry? Shoes?"

Another step backward.

With a dark chuckle, he watches her movements with a predatory gaze. "I'd buy all those things for you, baby. I'm sure a smart girl like yourself knows a few ways to convince me."

Fists clenching, Mama wills strength into her voice. "I didn't want to have to do this here."

"Show me."

As he inches forward, she reaches into her bag...

"That's it," he coos, his voice like gravel.

... and pulls out the camcorder.

He stops dead in his tracks, that wicked smile falling flat.

"It's over, Warren."

He blinks slowly... then blinks again... as the gears grind inside his brain. Ominous shadows form along his features. "You know the first thing that would happen if you released those tapes."

"You're right—*I do.* Sylvia would divorce you. She'd take you to the cleaners. I'm sure of that. And I can't imagine the shitstorm the media would make of it."

His jaw ticks. "How much?"

"What?"

"Money. How much money do you want?"

She laughs a wretched sound. "Are you serious? You think this is about money? You're delusional."

"Am I?" He nods toward our car. "Looks like you need

some. I'm sure you're hardly making ends meet with that teacher's salary. Raising them all on your own, too, after what happened to poor D—"

"Fuck. You," Mama spits, churning my stomach. "You don't have the right to speak his name. He was ten times the man you'll ever be, and I couldn't care less about your money. Care to know what I really want? No—what I *demand?* You're going to stay the *hell* out of my life and away from my family. Or else I'll ensure we make headlines."

"Enough with the empty threats, Amber. You wouldn't do it. You don't have the gall. Besides, there's probably nothing on that camera."

"Try me."

Uncertainty flickers in his lethal gaze. Taking a considerable step, his voice lowers. "I'll never allow such a tape to exist."

Shying away, Mama buries the camera into her bag. Adrenaline spikes through my blood, tears welling in my eyes as I spot the fear emerging in hers.

"Hand it over, girl. If you know what's good for you."

He closes in faster, rolling up his sleeves, flashing muscled forearms and the sheer size he has over her. When she freezes in terror, a tear gliding down her cheek, he smirks and goes to grab the bag—

In a flash, Mama whips her hand from the tote, revealing a bright-green tube.

"Ahh!" Mr. Kingston cries out, stumbling backwards as liquid squirts across his eyes in a plume of mist. He hits the pavement—*hard*—before Mama races to the driver's seat.

Jer gasps beside me, cranking the window shut. We rush back to our seats, buckling ourselves in, and plaster bored expressions on our faces. Whether our act is believable doesn't seem to matter, because Mama bursts into the car on a crazed whirlwind, not uttering a single word. In seconds, we're speeding down the driveway.

And then I'm staring out the window with that inexplicable feeling in my gut. Thinking of Hayden—and his promise about next time. Wondering if this means I'll have to wait longer to visit the Kingstons again...

But there was never a next time.

ONE

HAYDEN

SIX MONTHS AGO, my buzzkill of a father gave me an ultimatum. Clean up my act or kiss my trust fund goodbye. Let's just say...

My act could go for some bleach.

A perky blonde stands between my legs, clad in fishnet stockings and seven-inch, clear platform heels. She bends over in a way that honestly has me questioning if she has a backbone. But before I decipher my answer, she pops back up, long locks cascading down her bare shoulders.

Taking another drag of my cigarette, I let the nicotine cloud my brain, draping an arm over the backside of the couch. When dollface twists and faces me, flaunting the Benjamins dangling off her G-string, whistles and hollers erupt in the private room. A rowdy concoction of raging testosterone, silver spoons, and self-proclaimed fuckboys, all brought to you by ten of my Sigma Alpha Epsilon alumni brothers.

One of them being Jeremy, who sits to my left in a similar,

relaxed state, as another stripper sways her hips over his lap in a serenading dance. Through the red haze in the air, he eyes me above the rim of his Whiskey Coke.

"You got that look again," he says, his voice hardly audible over the R&B thumping throughout the room.

"What look?"

"Like your dick's here, but your head isn't. And not in a good way. Got something on your mind?"

Christ, am I really such an easy read for him? Well, we *have* known each other our entire lives. Since first grade, to be exact.

I shrug, smoke pluming past my lips. "Ol' Pops has caught on that I'm not actually getting my real estate license."

He snorts into his drink. "You don't say."

I shoot him a look.

"Sorry, sorry." He clears his throat, suddenly wearing a serious expression. "What makes you think he knows? Aside from the fact that it's two months past the date when your alleged class should've finished."

I roll my eyes.

Jeremy fucking Brooks. Even though we're both the ripe age of twenty-four, literally born two days apart, he's always been like the older brother between us. The wiser of the two. Maybe it's because he has his life in order and his shit figured out. While I... well... *don't.*

Dollface—Candy, is her stage name—runs a hand down my chest. When she notes my lack of interest, she struts over to the pole positioned in the center of the room, earning another round of cheers and tips. Seeing the commotion, Jeremy's lady follows suit.

"Oh, come on, Hayden. You knew he wasn't going to fall for that. You'll have to be a bit more convincing."

I exhale sharply. "And how the hell am I going to do that?"

"For starters, maybe don't host orgies at his house."

"That was *one time*."

And the main reason for my intervention six months ago, I don't add. Jeremy's already well aware.

My father's reaction to the whole thing was completely excessive. It was just one party. So what, I and a couple dozen of New York City's top models and A-listers banged on the couches, the guest beds, the kitchen counters, the dining table and... other places... and the cops were called... *and* the whole thing ended up plastered all over popular gossip sites...

Big deal. Boo-fuckin'-hoo. The way I see it, he should thank me. That party was the most interesting thing that's happened in his and his dull business friends' lives in the past decade or three—and they weren't even in attendance.

But, there's no matter. Sex party or not. I'm still the shame of the Kingston family—his words, not mine. Guess I'm just doing my job by living up to the hype.

"I don't know, man..." Jeremy rubs his chin, pondering. "Oh! I got it—maybe you can start attending church."

What the fu —

My head snaps to him, prepared to berate him for his outlandish joke. But I find his eyes unwavering. I blink, waiting for a smirk, the *gotcha*. Then blink again... He's... serious? From the corner of my eye, I catch a self-identifying "frat lord" wielding a money gun, raining an unknown sum of cash over Candy's head. Knowing this crowd, it's probably in the thousands.

Meanwhile, Jeremy thinks I—admittedly, the worst of us all—should go to *church?* Confine myself between the four walls of a confession booth? That's like asking a fox to guard the henhouse, then acting surprised when the hens wind up nestled between my sheets.

I'm irredeemable.

"Dude, you can't be seriou—"

Jeremy busts up laughing, and that's all it takes for the butt end of my dead cigarette to go flying his way. He topples over in a fit of hysterics, shoving my shoulder playfully. Tears brim the corners of his eyes, the whiskey on his breath potent.

"Oh! You should've seen the look on your face. Bro, come on. You? Hayden Kingston—the most infamous Casanova in Princeton's Greek life history, maybe in all of New York City —in a *church?*" He pries a devilish grin from me. "What're you gonna do, take a vow of celibacy? Settle down while you're in your prime? Your father would have an easier time believing you were struck by lightning on your way to cash in a winning Powerball ticket."

"Alright, alright," I silence him, downing half of my mojito in two gulps, hoping the vodka will ease the sense of dread trickling into my veins. If Jeremy can't come up with a solid solution on how to dupe my father, then I might be shit out of luck.

"I'm sure you'll figure something out."

He folds his arms across his chest, leaning back into the couch, his eyes gravitating to a new lady entering our private room. Skimpy black leather adorns her figure, bunny ears protrude past her locks, and diamond beads sway along her thighs as she struts. Like a siren's call to a ship of drunken sailors, she steals the attention of every man in the room.

Yet, I still can't curb the feeling of impending doom.

With a sigh, I pull out my phone, letting muscle memory take over. It doesn't long before I'm swiping left and right on my favorite app, Charmr. The best part about this particular online dating app is you really don't have to charm *anyone*, as the name might suggest. Not when it's flooded with singles who want nothing more than casual hookups and no-strings-attached relationships.

So, in such a playing field, my strategy is simple.

If my dick likes what it sees, swipe right.

Otherwise, swipe left.

Propping an ankle over my knee, I click the large button in the center of my screen: *See Singles Near You.* After a couple of spins of the loading symbol, I'm met with a long-haired brunette.

From the snapshot of her profile, her name is Leona. She's a twenty-two-year-old yoga instructor. And is, by mere coincidence, twenty-two miles away from my current location. Her bio reads *Roses are red, lemons are sour, spread my legs and I'll give you an hour.* I snort, even though I've encountered the exact same bio about a hundred times.

Nursing my drink, I study her selfie. She stares straight into the lens, pouting her red-stained lips. My gaze inches down the screen. With her elbows drawn inward, she pushes her breasts together, accentuating them beneath her low-cut top.

I swipe right.

Only to meet Jordan, who's twenty-four years old. Works as a social media manager. Is fifteen miles away. And has the bio *My tits and I have one thing in common. And that is, we're a lot to handle.* My eyes descend once more, confirming her words.

Another right swipe.

Alessandra. Studies biology and nursing. Twenty-one.

Forty miles away. And apparently, she *really likes pizza and anal.*

Right. Fucking. Swipe.

Kourtney. Single mom. Thirty-three. Works as a—

"Hunting your next conquest, aye?" a drunken Kyle slurs behind me and grabs my shoulders with vigor. His eyes squint into slits as he peers over, smelling of aftershave and expensive cologne. "Ohh, man, she's hot! And a cougar, too? Fuck..."

Nodding in agreement, I chuckle. Kyle hoots and hollers in tune with each swipe, every new profile showing more skin than before.

Christie... Right. Addison... Right. Naomi... Right. Lucy... Right. Juliana—

My heart stops.

Plunged into a state of disbelief, I stare into a pair of familiar eyes. Round glasses shield their unique shade of green, a captivating blend of emerald and juniper, with golden flecks dotted around her pupils. A rare combination I've seen only on one other person—Jeremy. *My best friend.* And this is his little sister.

Who he's *very* protective of.

I eye him over my phone, watching him tilt his whiskey glass skyward. Every internal instinct screams at me to sink low into my chair, in hopes the fabric might swallow me whole. I should lower my brightness, switch to the Bible app, or slip my phone between a stripper's ass cheeks and call it a tipsy donation, just to rid myself of the evidence.

Because here's the thing about Jeremy Brooks.

Don't let that freshly pressed polo and those Prada boat shoes fool you. Jeremy's not like the rest of these clowns— myself included in said group. No silver spoon fed him. Nor did familial donations grant him acceptance to Princeton University. Meaning, my boy's scary smart. Like, *works-on-Silicon-Avenue-fresh-out-of-university-as-an-electrical-engineer* kind of smart.

But that's not what has my pulse racing. The dude was an all-state *and* division one tight end, who might as well sleep on a bench press and probably seasons his four-daily chicken breasts with protein powder. Which is a whole lot of words to say... Jeremy would kick. My. Ass. If he suspected I was pursuing his sister. Hell, if I even looked at her for too long.

To him, I'm a serial playboy. An all-male dog with only one thing on my mind. The womanizer who plucks upon women's heartstrings, until they're offering themselves up like a three-course meal to my insatiable ego, oblivious to the wreckage I leave behind. Their names forgotten the next morning.

What can I say? He knows me better than anyone.

Wetting my lips, I return to my phone. To innocent... nerdy... Juliana. The most forbidden of fruit.

Wearing a basic white tee beneath an apron labeled *The Caffeine Cove,* Juliana smiles shyly at the camera in the midst of coffee machines and bakery sweets. Aside from a modest coat of mascara, she doesn't wear a lick of makeup. Wispy bangs frame her soft features, while the rest of her dark hair flows from a ponytail.

I stifle a groan, my boxers suddenly suffocating. Then all I can smell is her rosy perfume. A scent I can't seem to forget, one that should be left five years in the past. From the last time we were truly alone and—

"Borrrinnggggg." Kyle yawns in my ear, pulling me from my near out-of-body experience. "She'd have your kids named by the end of the first date."

Coming to my senses, I slip on a fully fledged poker face and read her bio. Juliana. Part-time barista. Twenty-three. Fifteen miles away. With a bio of... *No,* I blink away, unable to read whatever bullshit, suggestive play on words she has readily available for any fuckboy who stumbles upon her profile.

I mean, look at her.

Why the fuck is she on this type of app?

I'm seconds from snitching to her older brother, only so he'd blow a fuse and make her delete the profile, until I'm struck with a realization. Struck *hard.* I didn't just find the Charmr profile of my best friend's younger sister... I found the solution to my problem.

Jeremy's words replay in my ear. *You'll have to be a bit more convincing...*

And here lies my golden ticket: Juliana Brooks.

Sweet, sweet Jules.

For as long as I've known her—which is, well, her entire life—she's been the furthest from my type of girl as she could possibly be. Introverted. An overachiever. The classic teacher's pet, with her head chronically buried in a computer screen. No one in a million years would pair her with someone like me, the last on that list being my father. While he was listening to Jeremy's valedictorian speech and then Juliana's the following year, he was simultaneously praising my older brother for merely existing and naming me the pit stain of our family.

But if he thought I was serious with someone like *her?* That she was mine? Then I'd wager that stain might lift.

So, in the throes of half-naked strippers, bachelors with pockets brimmed with cash, and lines of suspicious white substances decorating our tables, I swipe right. A sliver of my soul aches as I anticipate her rejection. But much to my surprise, I receive an immediate match, with a message already sitting in my inbox.

A message that has me questioning everything I thought I knew about innocent Juliana...

TWO

JULIANA

"YOU WHAT NOW?!"

My palm shoots to my lips, far too late to stop my shriek now echoing through the little coffee shop. Fortunately, The Caffeine Cove is well past its morning rush, leaving the judgment of two side-glancing customers as my only consequence. Although they're seated on the farside of the store, it's enough to set my cheeks aflame, since the shop's the size of a shoebox.

That's The Big Apple, for ya.

Sporting a matching apron, Mei smirks from across the table, noting my blush. "Juliana—*Juliana.* Girl, breathe. It's seriously not that big of a deal."

"Not a big deal?" I hiss under my breath. "Since when is signing your best friend up for online dating in secret—and against her will, might I add—not a *big deal?* Here I was, thinking that pic you took of me yesterday was for one of your cutesy scrapbooks. You know how I feel about those apps. I'm not trying to meet a guy that way. Besides, I'm too —"

I stop my rant short, as a sticky gooeyness clings to my skin. My head snaps downward, to my poor ham-and-cheese sub I'm squeezing to death. Sighing heavily, I release the mutilated sandwich, snatching some napkins with aggression.

So much for my peaceful lunch break.

"Busy?" Mei finishes my point with pursed lips, her lash extensions somehow amplifying her sass tenfold. "Yeah, you always say that, Miss No Time For A Relationship. Which is why you should entertain something fun. Keep things light. Flirty. Spontaneous. No commitments..." She leans closer with each buzzword, her eyebrows raising higher and higher, like they're reeling me in on a fishing line. When I don't bite, she shrugs, flashing her signature dragon shoulder tattoo. "I mean, everyone needs a quickie now and then."

My face scrunches up.

I don't do quickies. In fact, I don't *do* anyone. Mei knows that, always has since we met years ago at Columbia University, but that's never hindered her efforts. See, Mei doesn't judge my virginal status. Instead, she takes it as a challenge, a problem in need of fixing, as if ignoring my V-card may just *poof* it from existence.

Not that I can blame her determination—Mei *is* the older, more edgy sister I wish I had. But she's never gone *this* far.

"Thanks, but... I think I'm good for now."

I avoid her stare and retrieve a hefty laptop from my backpack. The beast takes up half our bistro table, and with one press of the power button, fans roar beneath the keyboard, loud and wheezing, the sound as familiar as it is cringy. Look, I wouldn't call my laptop a hunk of junk; it's just the cheapest model that can do what I need it to do. Which is allowing me to program and manage the most important project of my life

—my second source of income, the leech of all my free time, and the culprit of my non-existent social life:

Cosmic Kitty Defense.

Yes, you read that right. No need to pass over a second time. It won't prove any more enlightening than the first.

From the corner of my vision, Mei folds her arms as I shift into autopilot mode and boot up my necessary programs. The notorious indie game developer trifecta—Github, Visual Studio Code, and Unreal Engine.

The first to track changes and backup my code to the cloud, so five years' worth of blood, sweat, and tears isn't lost when this baby inevitably dies on me. The second to, well, *code*. And the third allows access to a massive toolbox of game dev features, all of which help make Cosmic Kitty Defense—or CKD, for short—the mobile app that it is today.

Initializing the testing environment, I switch to the mobile viewer and click play...

Take, for example, the graphics rendering feature, which loads up the visuals at the start of each match. A pixelated grassy field, a cute farm in the center bustling with dozens of kitty cats, and a frazzled grandma in her nightgown, encircling her home with a pitchfork. In seconds, the scheduler kicks in, spawning a wave of alien foot soldiers around the perimeter, who all begin creeping toward the farm, with the horrendous intentions of—*audible gasp*—abducting kitties.

And they will, one by one. Unless Granny Mabel, controlled by the player, stops them. But don't fret over dearest Mabel. Although she may appear outmatched against the ever-growing wave of alien kitty-nappers, she possesses an arsenal of her own, one that expands with every extraterrestrial she foils. Granting her—and her beloved kitties—

weapons like the paw-some plasma cannon, the catnip cluster bomb, the purr-fect laser pointer, and soon, the new feature my small-yet-devoted fanbase has been waiting weeks for...

The kitty litter sand trap.

Excitement sings through me as I pull up the code responsible for the sand trap. I've been testing it over the last week or so, tweaking and making minor adjustments, and I'd say it's about ready for—

"Aren't you the least bit curious about who you matched with?"

My fingers stall, hovering over the keyboard. *Matched...?* My head snaps up. "I thought you only made my profile."

A mischievous grin blooms across her lips—she's got me hooked. Another shrug. "Let's just say, I vetted your playing field."

More bait.

I bury my head once more. "Not interested."

"No? Not even about..." she hums, her acrylic nails tapping against her phone screen. "Hunter?" She whistles— actually *whistles*—at the sight of him. "Wow, look at that hair. And those *forearms.* Bet he could really throw you around..."

I grind my teeth, all but failing to tune her out.

"Then there's Sean. He's got that tall, dark, and handsome vibe going for him. With that bone structure, he might as well be a young Henry Cavill..."

Curiosity sparks in my gut, but I keep typing.

Mei rests her chin in her palm as her nails tap dance once again. "Next up is Lucas." She sighs longingly, and it takes every fiber of my being to stare straight ahead, my lines of code slowly turning into gibberish. "Then Lamar... And, oh my, how could I have forgotten Xavier? One look at him and you'd be sprawled between his bed sheets after half a glass of wine—"

"Alright, fine." I abandon my work, finding Mei's eyes sparkling with delight. "I'll take your word for it. I matched with some hot people." The notion tastes sour on my tongue, as I'm ninety-nine percent positive Mei's over-exaggerating the quality of my matches. "So what? It's not like I'm going out with any of them. You might as well—"

"Yes, you are."

I blink. "Huh?"

"You're going on a date, Juliana."

My heart thumps anxiously. "No, I'm not—"

"Tonight."

"What?" My cry echoes through the café yet again—that's to my luck, now empty—as my chest heaves up and down. "That's not possible. I haven't messaged a single one of them."

"You're right. But I did."

My jaw drops, threatening to slap against my keyboard.

"Oh, come on. Don't give me that face. Like you would've ever messaged them."

My lips purse. "You're right. I wouldn't have. Maybe because I *never would've been on the site in the first place.* Let me reiterate—I want to meet someone the old-fashioned way."

Her hand lands on her hip, signaling the onset of one of our customary bouts of wit. "Sure, sure. Keep spouting that nonsense. What about that guy who gave you his number while we were on shift last month?"

Oh, boy. Not this again...

I refrain from rolling my eyes, even though, deep down, I sense the tsunami of truth that's moments from crashing over me. Because I *did* receive a customer's phone number—a really attractive customer, too—on a napkin he slid across the counter before exiting The Caffeine Cove with a wink.

My latte flower was cute, the note read, *but the barista who brewed it is even cuter. Call me, if you'd like to share another.*

Maybe the whole pickup line on a napkin thing was a little silly. But it worked. I wanted to call him—and I almost did that same night. Had his number dialed and everything. Until those slimy, intrusive thoughts came rushing in, right on queue, and convinced me otherwise.

He only wants one thing from you, they said, like little devils on my shoulder with no angels to match. *An attractive guy like him, with the way he made the first move so confidently? He's definitely had practice. And you have none.*

I brushed their words off with a forced laugh. *I have too much on my plate right now, anyway,* I told them, before the napkin—and the potential of a new connection—was lost in my wastebasket.

Mei seizes my hesitation, using it to push her point further. Humming, she taps her chin. "Braxton was his name, yes? He *was* a bit older, but what's not to like when he was so easy on the eyes? And even better, a spur-of-the-moment meet-cute in a cozy coffee shop, with a sweet napkin icebreaker that's straight out of a Hallmark movie? Well, I couldn't conjure up a more old-fashioned scenario for you, unless I had the producers right here next to me."

My mouth opens on a retort... then snaps shut. *Dammit.* "Okay, I know when to admit defeat—but that doesn't mean I'm going on a date tonight."

"Oh, you're going." She rests an arm across the backside of her chair, wearing an expression that says her queen is already in checkmate. "Or else."

My eyes narrow. "Or else, what?"

"Or else I'm not covering any more shifts for you."

I audibly gasp. *Now that's playing dirty.*

And Mei knows it, too, because she quickly adds, "Not until you go on some sort of date. You don't have to bag the guy, but at least make an effort to advance your love life. Or give Braxton a call. One or the other."

I don't have the heart to tell her where his number ended up, but that doesn't simmer the annoyance splintering across my skin. "This is getting ridiculous. I don't have to—"

"What do you think you two are doing?" A hiss sounds behind me, the shrill voice raking up my spine. Mei's eyelids droop slightly, her face flatlining in the presence of our manager, Meghan, whose presence alone rolls in a dense smog, clouding the joy of those caught up in it. She stops two inches from our table, crossing her arms.

Even though I'm not doing anything wrong—I still have another ten minutes of my lunch break—my blood pressure spikes. I hate confrontation. Always have, always will.

With my gaze downcast, I watch her kitten heels tap impatiently. "I'm taking my lunch break," I mumble.

"Are you now? Well, I would've never guessed. To me, it looks like you're working on that stupid game again."

My eyes flicker from Mei, who's silently debating whether to throw hands, to our manager. Only two years our senior, Meghan really is an attractive girl—or would be—if it wasn't for the scowl permanently marking her lips.

Lifting my head, I hold her stare as my small act of defiance. A fire ignites within me, begging me to go on the offense for once. But it's unwise to pick a fight with my boss, so I hold my tongue. When in reality, it's just cowardness, a lack of guts. In my fuming silence, I anticipate her next round of insults. Something along the lines of *you're only wasting your time,* or *who would play something so childish?* Or, her personal favorite, *you'll work here forever...*

When I break her stare, she smirks. "People come here to enjoy a cup of coffee, Juliana. Not to watch some astro cat disaster." Snickering, she flicks her head toward Mei. "And is this where you're supposed to be? Your break isn't for another hour."

Mei surveys the room, her gaze wandering between the clusters of vacant chairs and barstools. "Sorry, Meghan," she murmurs, but her apology lacks any genuine remorse. "I was just—"

"No. I'll stop you right there. If you have time to chitchat, you have time to clean. Now get back to work." The second she twists on her short heels, Mei scowls, flipping her the bird until she disappears into the backroom—where she'll do short of nothing. Unfortunately, Meghan's laziness will never be reprimanded, not when her parents bought out the place and let her run it the way she sees fit. Must be nice.

Standing, Mei rolls her eyes. "You really want to spend more time with *her?*"

I nibble on my lower lip. *Hell no.*

"Fine. I'll go."

She smiles brightly. "Good."

Sighing, I outstretch my hand. "Let me see who I'm going with."

But Mei whips her phone to her chest, hiding the screen like it's some precious relic. "No can do. That's the best part. It's a blind date."

"I'm going on a *blind date?*" I ball my hands into fists beneath the table, stilling their nervous tremble. One thing I hate more than confrontation? *Surprises.*

"Well, a one-sided blind date," she corrects, as if that does anything at all to calm my anxiety. "I *did* say I vetted your playing field, didn't I? Just think of me as your personal matchmaking service." She winks, tapping on her screen. "Let's just say, out of all the hot guys you matched with, none of them came close. And I got a suspicious hunch he's rich— you know how fine-tuned my radar is with that kinda thing. You'll thank me later."

I scoff. I couldn't care less about what this mystery man has in his pockets, but curiosity gets the better of me. "And what makes you say that?"

She twirls a strand of hair, clearly loving that she's landed me in such a predicament. It's been her number one goal for years. "Well, for starters, most matches on this particular app choose casual first date spots. Grab coffee at a café, take a walk in Central Park, meet up at a bar, that kind of thing. But your match must really want to impress you—he's taking you out to a restaurant, a nice-ass looking one, too." Her gaze turns dreamy. "Can't say I'm not a twinge bit jealous.

I'm going to throw up.

"Can I at least know his name?"

"Hayden."

My stomach drops. "Uh... Hayden-who?"

"The app doesn't show last names, for obvious reasons." She gives me a puzzled look. "Why? Do you know a Hayden?"

"Oh, no," I lie, concealing the truth that I spent my childhood alongside the son of one of the wealthiest families in the country. "I was just curious."

Well, that's an odd coincidence, I think, as a swarm of images flood my brain, all replaying the last time I was alone with Hayden Kingston. My brother's best friend. Who certainly has more experience than the charming man who slipped me a napkin, maybe more than anyone in this entire city. But luckily, common sense swoops in, banishing the thoughts at their root. Because, in a city of over eight million strong, that's all it is.

A coincidence.

THREE

HAYDEN

BEING a playboy is an art form with a strict set of rules.

Rule #1: A playboy must always show up late on the first date.

Why, you ask?

While pissing off my date before I've even sat down at the dinner table *seems* counterintuitive, a playboy must never appear overeager. Because his time is valuable, and this is just another date for him. Which is exactly why it's seven o'clock on the dot, the time when my date with Juliana should've begun, and I'm here, seated behind a bar, sipping a gin and tonic.

Cherry oak and chesterfield sofas dominate the moody lounge, located in the lobby of the Mandarin Oriental hotel. Soft chatter trickles in through the double doors, which allows for a perfect view of the well-dressed guests who pass through. Not only do rooms here fetch well over two-grand a night, their list of amenities is nothing to scoff at. Including a spa and wellness facility, high-end shops and designer boutiques, as well as a Michelin-star rooftop steakhouse with panoramic views.

A view Juliana is certainly enjoying. Alone.

Unbuttoning my suit jacket, I pull out my phone, intending to re-read the bizarre text conversation I had with Juliana last night. Or, should I say, with the person who I *thought* was Juliana. My jaw ticks at the sight of the first message that was in the preview box the moment we matched.

Juliana: *I shouldn't share these pics, but I'm having a hard time choosing between red or black ;) ...*

Even though this time I know what to expect when I click into the messages, blood rushes to my groin all the same.

Juliana: *Gotcha! Goodness, what kinda girl do you think I am?*

Me: *The kind who deserves a spanking.*

I was just asking for a verbal lashing—she *is* my best friend's little sister, after all, who has always been the reluctant recipient of my most crude comments. I spare her no mercy, only so I can savor her incredulous reactions. And highly sought-after attention.

But before her next text arrived, I had countless questions and zero answers. First and foremost, why did we match in the first place? That would mean she had already right-swiped on me, after seeing my profile. And given how things left off the last time we interacted, I'd wager that was a very low chance. Which could only leave one possibility...

She was right-swiping every guy without looking.

To put it plainly, once I had that realization, I was no more fun at that strip club. Until I received the next text.

Juliana: *Duly noted. Before we chat more, I should let you know that this isn't really Juliana. This is Mei, her best friend. I manage her account and set up blind dates for her.*

See what I mean? Bizarre.

Bizarre, but... *the miracle I needed.*

A way of trapping Juliana into actually speaking with me —in person. All I needed to do was convince this Mei character that I was the right guy for Juliana. And I did, easily. Went above and beyond. Why? Because I know everything there is to know about Juliana Brooks. Her taste in music. Her hobbies. What makes her tick. What makes her laugh or cry or roll her eyes. And the kind of guy she *thinks* she's interested in. So, I cherry-picked my answers accordingly, assuming her friend would connect the dots.

I landed a blind date within the hour.

It's only now that I'm starting to wonder how many *other* blind dates she has planned... Breathing sharply through my nostrils, I force down the rest of my drink, noting the leggy blonde approaching the bar. When she sits two seats down from mine, offering me a side glance, I decide to familiarize myself with her.

In less than five minutes, she's halfway in my lap on one of the sofas.

"I'm a model and a part-time actress," she says, running a manicured hand down the front of my suit. When I answer with an uninterested *mhmm*, she inches closer, the hem of her dress scooting higher up her thighs. "What about you?"

Thinking of a response, I sip my second gin and tonic, the alcohol warming my insides. Knowing I don't intend on entertaining her—or any woman—long enough for them to sniff out my falseness, I lie through my teeth, keeping things vague. "I work in finance. Trading crypto, primarily. I'm a numbers guy."

She sighs in my ear. "Wow, you must be really successful."

I graze a finger along her thigh, earning a shiver. "Tell me more about yourself."

She lights up at the attention—and away she goes. "Well, I was scouted in my hometown when I was fifteen at a fair. I started out locally, doing smaller print shoots and catalogs. Then I moved to New York and began walking in runway shows..."

Her voice drifts off into the background of my consciousness, which is too preoccupied with Juliana. I imagine her sitting at our table, dressed in her best, waiting anxiously, debating whether she's been stood up. *No, no, he'll show,* she tells herself, her knee bouncing restlessly, but with every passing minute, that confidence wanes. So much so, that when I *do* finally show and provide no explanation for my lateness, she'll realize I have the upper hand and that she'll need to work harder to earn my attention.

I check my watch. Eight minutes past seven. I'll give it another five. I really want her to be—

Like a sixth sense, my gaze gravitates toward the exit. Through the double doors, I spot a striking woman in blue. Subtle hints of auburn mark her otherwise dark locks. Her dress is modest, but with fabric tight enough to reveal a figure I'd undoubtedly drop to my knees for. Unable to tear my eyes from her, I watch her march across the marble, powerful and full of determination. But then... disbelief holds me hostage, her every step sinking my backside farther and farther into the couch.

"...my agency booked me a suite for the night. I have a shoot nearby. Buy me another drink, and I may just invite you to join me..."

Juliana passes by the double doors, aiming for the hotel entrance, oblivious to my existence. My heart contracts... stuttering in its rhythm... then springs back to life, like the first breath following an electric shock. I shoot to my feet, practically dumping the blonde onto the ground.

"Ow!" she grunts. "No need to be a jer—"

Without so much as an apology—not even a glance in her direction—I bolt after Juliana, the rest of the woman's remark drowned out by the blood raging in my ears.

I weave between sofas and dining tables and bargoers, nearly tripping over my two feet out the double doors. Like the release of a bucket of water over my head, the lobby's brightness blasts through my senses, sobering me up the instant my vision refocuses. Only to watch the revolving doors swallow up my temptress in blue.

Shit.

More than a few finely dressed business types shoot me strange looks as I book it across the polished marble. Alone in the achingly slow revolver, my breath puffs among the silence. I swipe a quick hand through my locks and button my suit jacket, searching for Juliana through the glass, to no avail. And once I'm out on the sidewalk, it's even worse.

Much the typical Friday night in The City That Never Sleeps, hordes of people bustle to and from, creating for me a maze in which Juliana—the solution to all my misfortunes—resides. Reckless, I dive nose first into the sea, swimming with and then against the current, my head bobbing and turning like some aimless plank of driftwood. Until I spot my life raft, one street over, crossing an intersection with her hands tucked beneath her armpits.

My heart jumps to my throat, propelling my legs forward in a mad dash. In mere seconds, I've crossed the walk at the last possible moment, narrowly missing a collision with a passing taxi. "Juliana, wait!"

She freezes, her shoulders going rigid. I gain more ground, coming right up behind her, embarrassment nipping at me as I huff and puff in her ear. "Jul—" Her legs snap into motion, resuming her purposeful pace.

Seriously? She didn't even look at me. Heaving a sigh, I chase her bouncy curls once more.

"Oh, Jules, I wasn't even—"

She twists on her heel, a deadly whirlwind of contempt and hostility. Closing the distance between us, she jabs a finger into my chest. And *God*, I can't help but love the way she tilts her head back—and back some more—to meet my eyes, even when there's hate swirling in hers.

"Don't call me that."

I don't hide my grin, taking her hand in mine. "Oh, *Jules."* I repeat her nickname slowly, like I'm melting a delectable chocolate on my tongue, something savage in me laughing when her pupils visibly dilate. "No need to be like that. Don't tell me you're still mad about—"

She rips her hand away. *"I'm not."*

Clearly.

"You don't look surprised to see me."

She scoffs. "Want to know why?"

"Enlighten me," I purr, still close enough to smell the mint on her breath.

"I knew the instant my date was a no-show, that it could only be you."

"I was running late."

"Sure, you were." She rolls her eyes, returning an appropriate amount of distance between us. "Why trick me into a date, just to show me you're the exact same guy you've always been? You could've saved me a trip and called instead."

Ouch. Seems someone's grown some teeth.

"Don't act like you haven't been ignoring my calls for..." I tap my chin, feigning as if I'm lost in thought. Even though I know the answer by heart, maybe down to the exact day. "About five years."

She looks me dead in the eye. "Why would I pick up? I have nothing to say."

Genuine hurt nips at me. The size of a sliver, but it's there. Only for my self-importance to stride in like a smooth storm, who yearns to inform my best friend's little sister of her newfound importance to me. One that's greater than inflating my ego—although, a much-welcomed by-product—but of the freedom she can provide me. Of our symbiotic relationship she doesn't know she'll soon enter into willingly.

Sinking my hands into my pant pockets, I hit her with my trademark, smoldering gaze. The kind that would have ninety-nine percent of New York City's female population's knees trembling. "Let me take you back to our table, and I'll buy you a drink."

But, as I've always known, my dearest Jules is the one percent.

"Un-be-lievable." She enunciates each syllable, then twists, intending to leave me in the dust.

Now, for my trump card. My Ace in the hole. The wildcard on the flop that'll have her eating out of the palm of my hand...

"Don't you want your little game to land a feature in this year's DreamScape?"

FOUR

HAYDEN

RULE #2: **A playboy must maintain an air of mystery.**

He never reveals too much about himself, and his secrets are always under wraps. Secrets like how I knew about Juliana's little mobile app. A question she's surely trying to find the puzzle pieces for as we *don't* speak.

Sitting across from me, nibbling her lower lip in the most distracting way, she re-reads her menu for what has to be the twentieth time. A tall candle crackles between us, casting a moody glow, while the lights of the cityscape twinkle in the distance like stars reflecting off still water.

Unbeknownst to my begrudging date, tables here require a two-month reservation—*minimum.* My name alone warranted an exception, granting us the best seat in the house on less than a twenty-four-hour's notice.

I scored the epitome of romantic date nights.

Minus the romance.

"You're really not going to drink anything?"

Her gaze flickers over the top of her menu shyly, before darting back between the pages. "Water's fine."

Jesus. I stifle a groan. *I'm really about to subject myself to a fake relationship with the most vanilla girl on this planet.*

Silence grows between us, forming an awkwardness that's a living, breathing thing, which I'm frankly not accustomed to and is slowly seeping the oxygen from my bloodstream. In short, I'd rather have my sex tapes leaked than bear another second.

"You reading a book in there?"

"Mhmm," she hums sweetly, flipping a page. "It's titled *Seven Signs Your Date is a Sociopath.*"

"A sociopath, huh?" I swirl my drink with a smirk, watching flecks of mint dance by like a flurry of snow. "I'm not one for labels, Jules. I like to think of myself as having a flexible moral compass."

She snaps her menu down—*thank God.*

"Why am I here?" she asks, annoyance written across her pretty features.

Her tone may be blunt, but she could never foresee the bomb coming her way. One that, upon detonation, will ruin what miniscule connection we have going for us right now. Which is why I intend on toying with her while I still can, before all words cease to fail her—or she's hurling her five-star meal across the table.

"Well, you see..." I twiddle my thumbs as I let the tension grow between us, humor bubbling in my gut when serious-ness marks her expression. Reeling her in further, I clear my throat, pleased when it comes out hoarse. "The other night..." I sigh deeply, avoiding her worried stare... then shoot her a sparkling smile. "I was scrolling on Charmr, when I came across *quite* a shock..."

With an irritated scoff, she lurches back into her chair. I soldier on, weathering her frown.

"My homeboy's ex girl, Alison!" Feigning second-hand offense, my palm shoots to my twitching lips, a laugh lodged in my throat as Juliana's head shakes disapprovingly, duped not once, but twice. "The thing is, they had just broken up. Not even two weeks ago. And there she was, out scouting for her next hookup. Can you believe that?" I allow for a pause, soaking in her murderous gaze like whispers to a nosy socialite. "I know, I know. Heartless. Absolutely horrible. Well, I didn't want to hurt his feelings—so, let's keep this between the two of us, okay?—but..." I swallow, seconds from some life-altering confession:

"I swiped right."

Juliana rolls her eyes, so far back I think she might lose them. Then she's collecting her things—her phone, her purse, certainly her better judgment or dignity or both— moments from ditching my ass before we've even seen our appetizers.

"Then there was this barista." She freezes, halfway out of her chair. "Far from the typical girl you'd find on that site..." When a blush stains her cheeks, and she's inching back down to her seat, I wink. "So, I swiped... *and swiped and swiped and swiped*. What can I say? It's simple, really. The bigger the tits, the faster I—"

She throws—*literally chucks,* amidst upper societal elites— her napkin across the table at full force. I catch it mid-air, unable to contain my laughter. Sure, what I said about her is true. But the playboy in me can't have her thinking that.

"You haven't matured a day in five years," she hisses low as a few heads turn in our direction, embarrassment hot on her cheeks. "You should really consider growing up."

"And you should *lighten* up, dollface."

Satisfaction burns in my middle when her lips part

slightly, too long to go unnoticed, before her face scrunches like a raisin. "You're a walking cliché."

"Am I?" I chuckle, deep and rich, leaning closer, entering her space across the intimate table. Shamelessly, I let my gaze wander, taking my time appraising her silky hair and tight dress. Surprised when my voice comes out thick. "Do tell."

She wets her lips. "I-I'm sure it's not hard to guess."

Fuckkk.

My jaw ticks in restraint, noting her subtle signs of submission as if they're written boldly on a billboard solely for my viewing. The waver in her voice. The flush on her chest against the candlelight. The caution swirling in her green eyes, twisted in anger yet pleading for more...

"Enlighten me, Jules."

Her pet name comes out like sweet honey, sending a shiver clattering across her skin. But a fire trails shortly behind, as she bares her teeth. *"Fine,"* she huffs, expelling the tension in the air. "Aside from your permanent grin, bulky Rolex, and douche-bag hairdo..."

OUCH. When I flinch ever-so slightly, I swear her eyes twinkle. *She had that locked and loaded.*

"You *tricked* me into this date, after I made it crystal clear that I never wanted to see you again. Then, you had the audacity to show up late to said date. *Then,* when I left—as I rightfully should've—you baited me back in here with veiled promises."

"Hmmm..." I tap my chin. "Veiled promises, you say?"

"Yes," she snaps, done with my bullshit. "You haven't even told me how you know about my mobile game."

Rule two strikes red-hot.

The real answer?

Her brother blabs about everything, including his nerdy

sister, who has been attached to her computer since high school, programming indiscernible lines of gibberish and playing cozy, pixelated video games that would put me to sleep. So, it comes as no shock, when Jeremy, out of love and admiration, as well a genuine interest, being the fellow techie he is, spouts off about his little sister's accomplishments.

That, and it's kinda hard to forget a name like Cosmic Kitty Defense. No, seriously. What was she on when she came up with that...?

I run a hand through my *douche-bag hair.* Wavy, blond, short enough to be masculine, yet long enough to scream generational wealth. "Ohh, I'd tell you, but where's the fun in that?"

Her eyes narrow.

You see? *Poof.*

Just like that, I'm pure mystery. How *did* I know she's an indie game dev? Surely, she doesn't shout her true identity down the digital ether for all to hear, linking reality with her online persona... Her assumptions will range far beyond the simple explanation, unwittingly painting me an enigma in her mind, an alluring challenge, someone she'd like to impress and gain attention fro—

She grabs her purse again, chipping a shard off the colossal statue that is my ego—toned, porcelain, and gloriously tall like David, obviously hand-crafted by Michelangelo himself.

I digress.

"Wait."

"For what, exactly?" Her brows tick when I remain silent. "That's what I thought. I guess I shouldn't be surprised that you'd dangle something as important as DreamScape in front of my nose, only to get me back inside. Like I said—empty promises." She twists in her chair.

"Are you so sure?"

Stilling, her eyes meet mine. "About what?"

"That I couldn't land Cosmic Kitty Defense a feature?" *God*, does that name taste ludicrous on my tongue.

"... Yes."

Leaning back in my chair, I sigh, opening my menu nonchalantly. "Bummer. Well... if you're so sure."

"I *am* sure," she repeats.

I peek at her. She may sound confident, but her body language is anything but, as if there are sudden weights tied to her ankles.

"Because..."

"Oh, no need to explain yourself." I flip to the next page. "I understand."

"Because you would've said something by now."

"Or perhaps, I like to wine and dine before talking business."

"Business?" She doesn't hide her amusement, laughing genuinely for the first time all night, the sound a sweet chorus in my ears. "You—talking business? Now I've heard it all."

I resist the tug on the corners of my lips. The idea *is* ridiculous, but I'm going to have to play along if I stand any chance of pulling this off. So, I slip on a mask of seriousness, hoping it resonates in my tone. "A lot can change in five years."

She hesitates, searching my gaze. When her shoulders finally relax and she sets her purse back on the table, a part of me aches. That's what wins her attention—the idea that I've changed? Well, the notion couldn't be further from the truth, seeing as my bachelor lifestyle hangs in the balance of whether I can or cannot convince her of such a blatant lie.

"Fine. One meal, then you'll tell me why I'm here." She skims through her menu once again, suddenly unable to meet my stare. "But don't pull any of that *Kingston-charm* crap on me. Changed or not, I'm not your next *conquest*—or whatever it is you idiots say. So, get that thought out of your head."

"It wasn't there to begin with. I would never cross such a boundary," I say smoothly. The lies keep piling on and on...

FIVE
JULIANA

NEVER WOULD I have thought a dessert menu could insult my social class.

Squinting, my eyes drag down the list. With each name, I'm wondering more and more whether I missed out on French tutoring lessons in my adolescence, while simultaneously accepting I couldn't possibly pronounce a single dish to our waiter. But it's worse than that. Because the parts that I *can* read are even worse—the prices.

Even though I should be accustomed to them by now, having already devoured our eighty-dollar lobster tail appetizer and my three-hundred-and-fifty-dollar Wagyu ribeye, my stomach drops all the same. Especially when I come across the only item I recognize.

"There sure is a lot of scowling going on over there."

If Hayden's deep tenor wasn't enough to redirect my thoughts back to him, then one look across the candle-lit table does the trick. As our eyes connect, my pulse flutters.

Even though it shouldn't, I remind myself.

This whole night, I've done nothing but wonder when the

sensation would subside, when his appearance would lose its effect. But, just like this expensive menu, Hayden Kingston is a conundrum of two degrees. Not only is he the epitome of an upper-class heartthrob, with crystal-blue eyes, perfectly tousled hair, straight teeth, a jawline destined for the cover of GQ, and a wardrobe that certainly costs more than I'll make in my lifetime. But he's actually charming and makes great conversation, when he wants to.

He smirks, and I instantly realize I've been staring. *Again.*

My head snaps back down to the menu. A fire blazes along my cheeks as I recall the most dangerous of all his qualities.

I'm an open book to him.

His warm chuckle simmers across our space, leaving it crackling with tension. My thighs move of their own accord, pressing together tightly, causing a sensation that does little to help my case. And like the mind reader he is, Hayden teases, "Stare all you want, Jules. Take a picture, if you like."

Jules.

In an instant, I'm bombarded with a barrage of unwelcome images. Like the slide of an old film reel, yet more vivid and enchanting, each scene soaring by at warped speeds.

Anticipation, teenage angst, and Green Day's *"21 Guns"* float through the tiny room. His lips are on mine. One hand on the nape of my neck, the other drawing circles on my thigh. For a moment, I'm captured by the lust of it all, reveling beneath a touch so experienced, a touch that rarely lands on someone like me. Until reality dumps an ice-cold bucket over my head, washing all but my sizzling anger.

They always come, these images, at the sound of that nickname. Jules. *His* nickname for me. And his only. The name he once laid claim to, before he—

No, I stop myself, stuffing the memories right back where they belong, where they've remained for five years:

In the past.

Ignoring his taunt, I face the desserts once more, lips curling in disapproval. "Who in their right mind would pay fifty-nine dollars for tiramisu?" Despite my words, saliva coats my tongue as I picture the delicate layers of chocolatey goodness.

"Is that what's got you dissin' the desserts, the cost? Well, choose whatever you like. I thought it'd be obvious, but I don't believe in fifty-fifty."

I quirk an eyebrow. "What on earth does that mean?"

"I don't believe in splitting the bill. Ever."

I blink, letting his words sink in.

If I'm being honest, I assumed he *was* paying for the meal, seeing as I sure as hell couldn't. Not at a place like this. I'd have to roll up my sleeves for the dishes in the back—for weeks—and cough up rent money I can't spare. Hayden's on a level of wealth I can't fathom, even having grown up beside him. So, accepting the notion is easy. But... it's the way he said it.

He doesn't believe in splitting the bill. He doesn't *believe* in letting me pay for myself, as if the idea itself offends him.

Reading my reaction, Hayden shoots me a cocky grin, adjusting his long sleeves and flashing the band of his gold Rolex. I stare at the watch, which probably costs more than what I make in a year, and his smile only widens.

My toes curl in my heels. *Curse my fleeting feminism.*

"Come on." He winks. "I know tiramisu is your favorite."

Gosh, does he really have to know everything?

"No need. I'm pretty full, anyway."

"Take one bite, then."

"One bite?"

He nods. Plain and simple.

"Yeah, right. Like you'd pay sixty dollars for me to take a single bite of my dessert."

He looks me dead in the eye with not an ounce of humor. "No, I'd pay sixty dollars for you to just *look* at it."

I nearly choke on my water. Exhaling calmly through my nostrils, I swallow the burn. *Keep it together,* I scold myself. *He's rich. You knew that already. Get over it. At this point, you've done nothing but inflate his ego more than it already was.*

Clearing my throat, I shrug. "It's okay, really. I'm not a fan of tiramisu for leftovers."

I expect another round of persistence from him, but instead, all I receive is the oddest expression. One I'd earn if I said the Yankees were from Philly or the Empire State was in Seattle. Utter. Confusion.

"Leftovers?" He says the word as if it's got a bad taste.

Now it's my turn to nod, my brows cinching in confusion.

"Why would you take leftovers?"

What is this, some foreign concept to the guy???

"So I can eat it tomorrow...? Duh."

"Wouldn't you rather just go out again?"

Case in point. Unfathomable wealth.

Who can afford going out to eat *every* night? Especially to a place like this. I skip the small talk. "How many times have you been here, to this steakhouse?" Waiting for his reply, my stomach twists uncomfortably, for a reason I can't quite pinpoint.

"Hmmm..." He sweeps his thumb and forefinger across his jaw in the most distracting way. "This has to be probably my twelfth visit." My gut drops, immediately identifying the source of my queasiness.

Jealousy.

Suppressing any and all emotions that may surface, I scan the restaurant's spacious layout for perhaps the tenth time tonight. But with a new perspective.

Intimate tables line the perimeter, cloaked in white clothes and accented by spotless silverware and wine glasses. Ambient lighting glows from low-hanging, modern chandeliers, flickering candles, and the spectacular view, casting smooth shadows along the faces of affluent men in suits and women donning cocktail dresses. Dresses that, upon a closer look, trump mine in every sense. They sparkle a little brighter. Drape a little smoother. Accentuate their curves a little more seductively.

This is obviously a date night hotspot. And to Hayden, I'm his *twelfth.*

The number stings in my headspace, but I quickly bat it away. "Wow..." is all I say, returning to his confident self, surprised when my voice comes out even. Rid of all that pesky—*pointless*—jealousy, because there's nothing dumber than being hung up on a playboy. A man who made his rounds through my entire high school, then graduated to Princeton's sorority sisters, and is now on the prowl amidst New York City's upper elite.

You're nothing special to him, Juliana, those little devils whisper. *How many times does he have to remind you?*

When he counters with another flirtatious remark, I stop our conversation in its tracks, and with it, killing off any unwanted feelings toward my brother's best friend. Then I resort to my favorite form of deflection—insulting him.

I roll my eyes. "You're insufferable."

～

"AND WHAT WILL YOU HAVE, MISS?" the bartender asks. Cleanly shaven and wearing a professional vest with the Mandarin Oriental's crest, he complements the bar's gentlemen-esque vibe.

"I'll take a Shirley Temple, please."

Seated beside me on a leather-backed barstool, Hayden grumbles curses under his breath. The bartender nods, not the least bit offended by my non-alcoholic choice, *like some people*, then disappears down the wall lined with top-shelf liquors. None of which are required for my fruity refresher.

I swivel on my stool to find Hayden pinching the bridge of his nose, as if he's physically in pain. "We're in a *bar*, Jules. What twenty-three-year-old orders a *Shirley fucking Temple* at a bar?"

Pursing my lips, I don't bite the bait, ignoring his taunt that would only lead to more banter and bullshit. Enough is enough. Tonight, I played his stupid games, sat through a date he *tricked me* into attending, then lured me into staying. I even let him walk us straight into a lounge once our elevator opened to the lobby floor, when the last thing I want is to share a drink with him. But no more. Now, I want what he promised.

Answers. And answers only.

I cross my legs, neatly intertwining my fingers over my knee. "Tell me how I can land my game a feature at DreamScape."

His face falls, but a smirk still snags the corners of his mouth. "Don't you want to wait for your drink before grilling me?"

"No."

He blinks, presumably waiting for me to lighten up. For a reassuring smile or something. But one never comes.

"Alrighty, then. No waiting." He clears his throat and props an elbow on the bar top. "Kingston Entertainment is sponsoring five games at this year's DreamScape, and one spot for the Indie Creator Showcase."

One sentence. One sentence from his mouth and...

My. Mind. Goes. Fucking. Blank.

Thanks to this barstool, I remain upright.

Dumbfounded isn't really the right word. Neither is stupefied or really *any* single word capable of adequately capturing my reaction. It's more like my entire ribcage catapulted into my windpipe or a boulder the size of the sun splashed down in the pit of my stomach.

Because what he said *can't* be true.

DreamScape is only the largest gaming convention in the country, probably in the whole world. It's *the* way to put your game on the map and in front of the most eyes possible. For years, I've tried to land a feature, since starting Cosmic Kitty Defense during my first year of college. But landing one is nearly impossible. Thousands of indie devs apply each year, all hoping for the same thing.

I stare at him, my brain a vacant slate. "Come again?"

"You heard me right."

When the bartender returns with our drinks, I recollect my thoughts as my mental gears churn. "Why would a film production company involve itself with DreamScape?"

"The company's considered moving into the gaming industry for a while. It's a lucrative sector right now with an expanding market capitalization. Although it hasn't reached public knowledge, the board has decided to pull the trigger."

Lucrative sector...?

Market capitalization...?

... Am I still speaking with the same Hayden who throws

sex parties, frequents the front of gossip news for dating A-listers, and intentionally arrives late to first dates? Or did he and his body double swap places while I was undergoing a mental crisis? My eyes narrow into slits as I judge his straight yet relaxed posture, the controlled gleam in his gaze, and the way he hasn't even glanced at his drink...

The math isn't mathing.

I cross my arms. "And how would you know such an insider secret?"

When he reaches into his pants pocket, I expect some magical paper that'll clear my suspicions, but out comes a box of cigarettes. Anxiety coils around me at the sight of them. *Is smoking allowed in here?* But it seems Silver Spoon here doesn't care for rules, as he plops a white stick between his lips. Flicking his metallic lighter, he eyes me with amusement, smoke billowing from his mouth and nostrils as he says, "My father's taken me under his wing."

My brows shoot to my hairline.

Hayden and Mr. Kingston have always had an estranged relationship, to put it lightly. Growing up, Hayden never explained it so politely, having on many occasions deemed the word *hate* more appropriate. On top of that, he compares corporate life to slavery, so why would he suddenly start working under his father?

A lot can change in five years, he said.

My gears hum once more. *Turning, turning, turning.*

In my silence, he takes another drag. "I could put in a good word with him. Make sure you get a fair shot..."

My knee bounces anxiously.

Kingston Entertainment may be a publicly traded company, with an acting board and a large array of investors, but Warren Kingston is the majority shareholder. He has the final say. In everything. Landing an audience with him, someone who decides whether a game lands a DreamScape feature, is like every game dev's wet dream.

A once in a lifetime opportunity.

An opportunity so rare that I'm tempted by Hayden's words, despite the muddy waters between our two families. Between our parents, specifically.

It wasn't apparent until I got older but, during a short window of my adolescence, my single mother was Warren's mistress. Why the two split is unknown. My mother never speaks of it, I never bring it up, and neither does my brother. As children, all we knew was, one day, we were allowed to sleep over at the Kingston's residence. Then the next, we weren't. A year later, the news buzzed with their divorce, as Hayden's mother, Sylvia, banked over ten billion in the settlement, despite their prenuptial agreement.

My mother has zero comment regarding the matter.

So, if I'm willing to sweep all *that* under the rug...

Hayden taps his cigarette, raining ash onto the polished mahogany, the rebellious act squirming my insides. Giving me a leisurely up and down, his eyes dance with delight. *He's got me wrapped around his finger.*

"Although... my father may need some extra convincing."

Oh, no. Here it comes. The final drop of the hammer, the harsh yank of the rug from under my feet, the reminder that there's a price for everything in life. With a sigh, I bite the bait, and ask the question I've been dreading all night.

"What do you want out of this?"

SIX

HAYDEN

SHE'S EXACTLY how I want her.

Desperate.

Judging from the look in her eyes, Juliana will agree to anything I ask. What a shame she's here, stone-cold sober, furthering her nerdy agenda by tolerating my company, and not trapped in my penthouse apartment, sprawled between Egyptian cotton sheets or lounging in a two-piece beside my private rooftop pool. Because, ohh, that would that be so—

Wrong, my annoying, typically dormant, shard of integrity interjects. *So, so, so wrong. Are you stupid? She's not your little play bunny. She's your best friend's sister. Off-fucking-limits. Do you want Jeremy Brooks to murder you?*

I stifle an eye roll, thoroughly aware I'm conversing with myself. *No...*

Good. Then stick to the scheduled program.

Fine. No matter. I bet Juliana wouldn't be so eager right now if she knew of the trickery I've slipped past my tongue for the past half hour. Since entering this lounge, I wouldn't say I've *lied,* per se. That's quite a strong word. Rather, I've stretched the truth and followed...

Rule #3: A playboy practices selective honesty.

For one, I'm not under my father's wing. I'd rather carve my eyes out with a plastic spoon than spend any more time with the man than absolutely necessary. But I do have plans to make that false statement a—very temporary—reality. Show him I'm *really* turning my life around.

As for the rest of the nonsense and well-rehearsed business jargon, Kingston Entertainment actually *is* moving into the gaming industry. I know this not because of some trade secrets, but because I had the misfortunate pleasure of hearing my older brother, Elias, blab on and on about it to his date during our last family gathering. How he was the *genius* who thought of encroaching on the gaming sector, how he pitched the plan to the board, single-handedly swaying their opinions by ways of tactical and assertive negotiations, bla, bla, bla, blaaa, blaaaaaaaaaa....

Anyhoo.

Point proven. No lies here.

And thanks to the stub of a cigarette left between my fingers, I've managed to keep my nerves in check this far. It's not that I'm a bad truth-stretcher. Quite the contrary, seeing as that's all I did growing up, about where I was and where I wasn't, the type of people I hung around and didn't, that kind of stuff. But this? The conversation I'm intricately weaving under the scrutiny of a woman who knows me better than any other? *That's* pushing it, even for a pro like me.

So, it's time to rip the bandage clean off.

I look Juliana straight in the eye.

"I want you to be my fake girlfriend."

Tension the size of Mount Everest slinks off my shoulders.

Whew, out with it. But despite my sudden courage, my stomach twists in a knot, awaiting what has to be an explosive reaction.

But... it doesn't come. In fact, *no* reaction marks her pretty face. Blinking slowly, Juliana stares at me blankly, as if she's watching paint dry after I wiped her memory, *Men in Black* style. There's just... nothing.

Did she hear me?

If I thought asking such an outlandish question was painful the first time, then I wholly underestimated the second. "Uhh... Jules? I, uh... want you to be my fake girlfriend." *Just kill me already.* I squirm on my barstool, thanking the universe no one's close enough to eavesdrop.

"Ju—"

"So, that's what you brought me here for? The reason you swindled your way into my DMs, impressed my best friend into choosing you for a blind date, reserved a table at the most exclusive steakhouse in New York, chased me down on the streets, and then paid for an eight-hundred-dollar dinner tab. Not win me over or make up for what you did." Her eyebrow lifts, only slightly, but enough to hit me where it hurts. "But to play a prank on me."

A prank?

I shoot to my feet the same moment she does. But instead of running off like at dinner, she cranes her head way back, then shoots me a look so scathing, my words fumble on their exit out my mouth. "I-I... Jules, I'm not playing a prank."

She keeps staring, infusing a little more venom.

"I'm not!" My palms fly up defensively. "I'm being serious."

"About me being your *fake girlfriend?* Okay, sure, Hayden.

I believe you. You're right, that doesn't sound like the most ridiculous thing I've ever heard you say in our entire life."

Fuck, hearing it from her is even worse. What, did I fall and hit my head? Who says shit like that? No... No, *I need this*... I need her to accept this insane proposition, or I'm royally screwed.

"I know it sounds crazy, but I'm telling the truth." She shakes her head. I force a strained laugh, swiping a nervous hand through my locks. "Things have been rough with my dad. I mean... worse than usual. He's threatening to pull my trust fund."

She scoffs. "Are you really so surprised by that? You're not exactly someone I'd call a model citizen or some golden child."

My thoughts instantly go to my brother, a wave of annoyance washing over me. "You'd really go there—"

"What was it, three months ago, you were making headlines? Half of New York knows what kind of parties you throw."

"Oh, so I should act like my brother, is that it? Lock myself in a corporate cage. Strive to be just like our father—"

"No. I'm not saying that. But maybe you could clean your act up a little, so you can leave me out of your BS..."

By now, we're at each other's throats, chests puffed outwards, hands waving with aggression, bickering like a couple of kindergarteners—or a married couple. Over the top of Juliana's dark hair, I spot the bartender inching in our direction, caution swirling in his eyes. Not wanting any trouble, I step back, switching up tactics.

"Do you want the feature or not?"

Her next insult fizzles out on a slow breath. She stays quiet for several seconds, then several more... Avoiding my gaze, she sits back on her barstool, nibbling her lower lip, as a war of mental turmoil rages on in that pretty head of hers.

That's right, dollface. Focus on the prize.

I take a seat myself and light another cigarette, this time purely for pleasure. Propping an ankle atop my knee, I draw in a breath and hold, the smoke warming my lungs. With a smirk, I exhale, my eyes never leaving her sight. Because there's something addicting about Juliana. About someone who's contemplating a deal with the Devil.

"You do, don't you?" I purr.

Her lip plops out from beneath her teeth, the movement rushing blood straight to my groin, before she meets my stare. "I-I..." Wetting her lips with a nervous flick of her tongue, her tiny fist clutches at her skirt fabric absentmindedly. "I..."

"Where else could you land that kind of exposure, hmm?" I stand, noting how her ankles interlock with a slight squirm. She swivels on her stool, staring straight ahead, at the wall lined with liquor she won't drink.

Sweet, innocent Juliana.

I step closer.

There's something else that's addicting. A unique type of hunger, present only when she's near...

I take another step, delighting when her shoulders stiffen in my presence.

... A hunger which silences that pesky, inner voice of reason, igniting in me one single desire...

To get under her skin.

Behind her, I trail a soft finger down her bare arm, eliciting a shiver. "Answer me, *Jules.*"

Looking away, her breathing turns erratic. "I... I don't know," she manages to get out.

"You don't?" I brush her skin once more, this time slower,

while tracing the strap of her dress. When she squeezes her thighs together in response, I muster up every ounce of resistance not to nudge them open, only so I can discover how wet she is between them. Banishing the thoughts, I refocus on the deal, my voice like gravel. "A trailer or a run-through of gameplay, in front of thousands, and all you have to do is act like you're mine, for a time."

You're already doing such a phenomenal job, I don't say.

When she remains quiet, I sweep a lock behind her ear, her soft skin soon touching my lips. "I promise I'll behave."

A breathless moan slips from her mouth, the sound forbidden as it is addictive. When she inches closer to the bar, the movement riding her skirt higher up her thighs, I clutch the backside of her chair in restraint.

"No one would believe us."

"And why do you think that?"

"I couldn't fake the..." She clears her throat, her voice a mere whisper. "The attraction."

I nearly laugh. "Really? But you're so responsive to me."

Her jaw drops slightly, but before she can conjure up some lie, I cup her jaw with one hand, my fingers threading through the hair on her nape. And then she's like putty. Shoulders drooping, thighs parting, I turn her head to face me, angling upwards, not a hint of protest on her tempting lips.

Juliana stares up at me, pupils blown wide, as they flicker from my left and right and to and from my mouth. When her tongue sweeps across her bottom lip, I draw near. She hesitates for a moment, but with one brush of my thumb across her jaw, those eyelids flutter shut.

And she's all mine.

Closer... and closer... until my lips graze hers, ever-so

lightly, like the stroke of a feather. I breathe in her scent, an alluring aroma of roses and cherry, as her breath thunders against my mouth, minty, erratic, and needy, before I—

I pull away.

For several heartbeats, she sits there, frozen in anticipation, eyes closed and lips parted softly. But when she finally does look, her eyebrows pinch. She blinks, as a wave of embarrassment turns her cheeks beat red. Snatching her legs together, she shimmies her dress back to the appropriate length, her head downcast as she fumbles for her words.

With a dark chuckle, I come up behind her, close to her ear once again, freezing her all the same.

"Why don't you think on it?"

SEVEN
JULIANA

I DID THINK ON IT.

Every hour. Minute. Second. Every waking moment, for the past *two days*. His fingers grazing against my shoulder. His touch down my back, on my jaw, applying pressure at the nape of my neck. The way he tilted my chin upwards, his gaze consuming mine. And the kiss we almost—

Almost nothing! a voice roars in my conscious. *That was all an act. Testing the waters of this hypothetical scenario,* it reminds me, for perhaps the fifteenth time. *Hayden Kingston doesn't have that kind of power over you.*

Right... *That's right.* For the past forty-eight hours, I didn't think about that... *little rehearsal* Hayden and I had. But of the lengths I'm willing to go to further my career. Even right now, as I grind a batch of coffee beans for the lady in red's latte, I can't shake the thoughts of my brother's best friend's fake dating proposition. Although, I already made up my mind last night. A decision I know I'll regret.

Slipping into autopilot, I pour the grounds into the portafilter, before securing the metallic handle into the espresso machine. With one press of a button, it whirrs to life, the familiar sound usually fading into the background. But now, the grinder is somehow jarring, disturbing my brain like a shaken beehive, buzzing conspiracies around in my headspace.

Maybe this really *is* an elaborate prank, one he's ultra committed to. Being a billionaire's son, I'm sure he's got time to kill. All his friends must be in on it, too. They've probably been laughing their asses off since the moment I texted him last night, agreeing to such madness. Which would explain why he didn't text me for two straight days. He doesn't actually need this; his father's not *really* threatening his trust fund...

The machine quiets, and a green light flashes with a beep. I snatch the paper cup now filled with espresso, labeled *Heather*, then pour steamed milk from a pitcher. My wrist sways from side to side with precision before bringing a line up the middle, forming a perfect, frothy tulip.

Maybe I just imagined it all.

I swipe a towel around the rim, cleaning up spillage.

Maybe I didn't really go on a date with Hayden.

Armed with a flawless latte, I make for the pickup counter...

Yes. The whole thing was a fever dream. I didn't really—

My toe catches on something hard. I gasp as my world tumbles *down, down, down.* "*Oof!*" I smack against the ground, and brown liquid darts across the checkered tile.

Before I can register what happened, Mei's glittery sneakers stop a hair's breadth from my nose. "Shit, are you okay?"

"Yeah," I croak out. "I'm fine." Rising to my hands and knees, I discover a brown pool dripping down my front.

Luckily, my apron took the brunt of it, or I would've been seriously burned.

An annoyed sigh sounds from over the counter. "Oh, that's just great." Fully aware of who I'll see, I lift my head to a pair of arms looming over the counter, folded across a studious red blazer.

Once Mei helps me to my feet, I note the crowd of customers gathered behind the woman. Humiliation scorches my cheeks as Heather taps her heel, eyeing Mei. "Is she new or something? I have a meeting in fifteen minutes."

Am I new??? I've been working here for two years!

Mei stills beside me, shadows looming across her dark eyes as she stares at the woman. *Oh, no...* In her hand, a metallic pitcher shakes—a pitcher she chucked at the last customer who yelled at me. The incident nearly got us both fired.

But that's the thing. Mei took this part-time job to fill up some of her free time while at university. She comes from money and, frankly, doesn't need a dime. Me, on the other hand? I need every dime I can get, and I can't risk losing this job over one mouthy customer.

"Mei," I hiss under my breath. "It's fine, really."

Her gaze darts to me, the crazy in her eyes dimming slightly.

Heather scoffs, snapping her fingers. "What're you two doing?"—*Oh my god, lady, if you know what's good for you, shut up, shut up*—"Make me another."

Milk splashes next to our feet, joining the coffee still dripping from my apron, as Mei's pitcher now buzzes with hostility, seconds from going airborne. But before she hucks the thing and kisses both our jobs goodbye, I pry the pitcher out of her hands, earning a glare. She's about to argue, when Heather strikes again. This time with a nasally *hellooooo?*

Mei whips her head. "You can take your latte and shove it right up your—"

I yank her hand. *"Coming right up!"*

For a fleeting moment, wariness flashes in Heather's gaze, before her superiority complex returns. "You've wasted enough of my time. I want a refund."

Another retort flies out of Mei's mouth, which I cut off. "Totally understandable—my apologies." I plaster on the fakest smile I can muster. "I'll ring you up over here."

WHEN MRS. ENTITLED is out the door, we've mopped the floors, and I'm wearing a fresh apron, Mei says, "You've been acting strange today."

I freeze, already well-aware of that fact, including the reason *why.*

"And I'm not even saying that because of your fall."

Playing it cool, I lean against the counter. "Have I?"

"Yeah, you have. For a couple days now, actually."

I shrug, avoiding her prying eyes. "Maybe it's the weather." But I want to kick myself the instant the words slip off my tongue. In the same breath, both our eyes flicker toward the bustling streets outside, to the sunrays trickling through the windows, then back to each other. "Uhm... I meant—"

"Oh my god!" Mei squeals. "I knew it! I knew something happened with that guy from Charmr. You just played it off, didn't you? Saying he was boring and all that... Oh, you did!"

An uncontrollable smile spreads across my lips, one I can't decipher is from the good or the bad that occurred that night.

The *good* being the heat, the touching, the—*well, wait, that's bad too!* And the *bad-bad*, being that I agreed to a fake relationship, which Mei can never know about because... *because that's just frickin' weird.*

Seated at the bistro tables lining the windows, customers turn their heads and lift their eyebrows, failing to deter another wave of girlish squeals.

"You *have* to tell me everything!" Mei scampers over. "What does he do? I bet he works on Wall Street, or he's a salesman—or a lawyer. Did he pay the bill? Oh, who am I kidding? By the looks of him, he screamed money. Of course he paid..."

I pinch the bridge of my nose. "Mei."

"Did he take you back to his place after?! I bet that's why you won't fess up—you two totally hooked up—"

"Mei!"

She sucks in a breath. Holding it, she searches my gaze, and suddenly I'm in a police station sporting handcuffs, with a detective angling a bright light in my eyes. Her jaw drops. "You so did! The guilt is written all over your face."

"No, we didn't do anything!" I hiss, dragging her into the backroom, lest people on the sidewalk hear her interrogation.

My nose scrunches. If the harsh smell of coffee grounds didn't tell me that I've entered the cramped storage room, then the annoying flappy door with a little circular window certainly does. With one step, I've abandoned cozy vibes for the stockroom of some rundown kitchen.

Eeeee, errrrr, eeeee, errrrr, the door wails on its hinges, each sway revealing customers who shake their heads, obviously sick and tired of all the girly outbursts, here at The Caffeine Cove. Mei purses her lips like she always does, waiting out the creaks.

Once in silence, she starts back up. "Where was his apartment?! Tell me he lives on The Upper West Side. Did he drive you? *Shit*, did you two even make it to his place before you —"

"Mei!" I scream for what feels like the tenth time. "For criminy sakes, we didn't sleep together. You really think I'd lose my V-card after one dinner?"

She deflates like a balloon. "I guess you're right. I shouldn't get my hopes up over a potential one-night stand."

"Act—" I shut my trap, internally scolding myself. I nearly corrected her, but she doesn't know I grew up with Hayden. *Damn, I gotta get my stories straight!*

Her eyes turn into slits. "But something *did* happen."

It's a statement. Not a question. One I can't steer myself from, not without a sprinkle of truth. Mei knows me too well.

I shrug, even though at just the thought of him, my clothes feel suffocatingly hot, the drawstrings of my apron tied too tight around my nape. "Things may have gotten a little bit... handsy at dinner."

Her eyes alight with excitement, brighter than a child's on Christmas morning. *"Yes, I— "*

"But!" I lift a finger, silencing her. "That was the end of it."

She pouts her full lips, whining. "Whyyyy? He's so easy on the eyes. Seriously, he might be the hottest guy on all of Charmr, and he took you out for *steak."*

"Well, I called things off. I want more than a pretty face. And to be honest, he wasn't as hot in person," I lie through my teeth, hoping it'll resonate with my brain.

"Ohh, no." Her face contorts. "You got catfished?"

Biting down on a laugh, I imagine how furious Hayden would be hearing his name and *catfish* remotely used in the same sentence. Unfortunately for him, he's not here to defend himself.

I sigh, feigning disappointment. "Yep, I guess I did."

"Don't worry, you happen to live in the largest city in the whole country. There are plenty more fish to fry." She pats me on the shoulder, right as I spot our next customer walk in.

My pulse jumps.

Tall, with a gorgeous head of dirty-blond hair, all eyes gravitate to the man who, despite it being summer, wears plaid pants and a stylish long overcoat. A coat I'd recognize anywhere...

Noting my statue-like state, Mei follows the line of my gaze through the small window. With a breathless inhale, she gapes, staring just as shamelessly as I am. "Juliana... that doesn't look like a catfish to me."

EIGHT

HAYDEN

JULIANA IS ANYTHING BUT DISCRETE.

Standing at the empty counter, I check my watch again. I'm just like any regular café customer awaiting service. Aside from the fact that, from the corner of my vision, I make out two heads peering through a little window. Do they not realize how thin that door is? I can hear every word they're saying.

It's him.

No, it's not.

Yes, it is. Look at him! Who else looks like that?

A smile twitches my lips, and when I remove my sunglasses, I earn a squeal.

Go take his order.

What? No way! Why me?!

Because he's obviously here for you.

It's just a coincidence.

Right, right.

I'm serious!

It's going to be fine. Just put your hair down and —

I flick my gaze, catching Juliana's stare. With mortified shrieks, they duck their heads.

Oh my god, oh my god, he totally saw us!

No, he didn't.

Girl, are you blind? He looked right—

I clear my throat loudly.

There's a pause in their discussion. Black hair creeps up the circular window, higher and higher, until I meet a pair of hooded eyes wearing false lashes, who I presume is Mei. With another gasp, she disappears quickly. A girlish pep-talk follows, which Juliana counters with strong objections. Then a decision is made—which Mei makes on her own, by shoving her friend out the door.

Juliana stumbles into the bar area, narrowly tripping over a wet floor sign. Eyes wide like an owl, her hair's a frazzled mess, and her glasses slip half-way down her nose. A snarky comment is seconds from darting out of my mouth, when it's rudely interrupted by the most offensive noise.

EEEEE, ERRRRR, EEEEE, ERRRRR...

We only stare at each other, as the entire café slows to a standstill.

The ambient music fades, transitioning to the next track. Chatter dies out on a whisper. Coffee buffs turn their heads. Even the constant hum of the city outside seems to hush. And in walks that cringe-inducing, socially paralyzing, *skin-crawling* awkwardness. A feeling so suffocating and foreign that I find myself praying the floor turns into quicksand.

The instant the squeaking subsides, I practically choke out my order. "I'll have a vanilla latte with a shot of espresso."

At the edge of my vision, Mei peeks through the window, driving my pulse higher. It's still so fucking quiet, which is no thanks to Juliana, who only looks at me with a million thoughts bombarding her brain. Just... *blank.* I'm on the verge of a heart attack, before the music picks up slowly, as does the chatter.

As if zapped by lightning, Juliana springs into action. She bats her hair and fixes her glasses, suddenly unable to meet my gaze.

"Is it always so hard to get service at The Caffeine Cove?" She glares at me, shooting a thrill down to my bones. "Well hello to you, too."

"Why are you here?" she hisses under her breath, wary of her friend's obvious eavesdropping.

"I was in the area."

She deadpans, to which I reply with a polite smile. Rolling her eyes, she grabs a paper cup off the stack—

"My order's not to go."

Her hand freezes midway. "Why not?" she clips out.

"I'd like to enjoy the atmosphere," I say, my tone oozing sarcasm.

With a bored sigh, I lean against the counter, forcing my head on a swivel, only to come to the horrifying realization that I might actually like what I see. Although it's the polar opposite of my typical scene, The Caffeine Cove has its charm. A vintage charm, to be precise, with a truly impressive attention to detail.

Unique tiles grace the flooring, boasting a black-and-white checkered pattern with streaks of marbled gray, and dark oak woodwork accents the bistro tables, cross-back chairs, and floor-to-ceiling bookshelves that house hundreds of leather-bound novels. The place is like a thousand-piece puzzle—the longer I look, the more discoveries I make. Small knick-knacks, brick accent walls, hanging wall china, taper candles, period artwork, Tiffany lamps, floral curtains...

I manage to pull myself away.

Did I just let some dusty old books win me over...? Shit, I think I need to cleanse my eye sockets at a nightclub.

Clearing my throat once more, I curve my lips back to their permanent smirk with a wink. "And I'm here to enjoy your company, of course."

She huffs in annoyance, selecting a ceramic mug. "Our meeting isn't supposed to be until tomorrow."

"Is that so? Gosh, I think I got the days mixed up."

"Well, maybe you wouldn't have, if you'd actually cared to text me back these past two days."

Guilty as charged. Radio silence is my M.O. Maybe because...

Rule #4: A playboy never texts back.

Poor girl should know that by now.

When I don't reply, she secures some metal thing into the espresso machine, cranking so hard I'm surprised the handle doesn't snap in two. The machine's hum soon masks her voice. "You can't show up unannounced after five years, drop a bomb on me, and then ghost me."

"Woah, woah. I didn't ghost you. I *did* text back."

Her eyelids fall, as she breathes deep. "Oh, you responded alright. To my walls of text with the letter *K.*"

"I neither confirm nor deny such claims."

She mumbles what I presume to be a string of curses, only for the machine to quiet and confirm my assumptions. Rolling my lips, I bite back a laugh at her obvious restraint. She's like a little volcano on the verge of eruption.

I know I probably sound like an asshole—well, I definitely do, seeing as I *am* one, more often than not. And if someone were to overhear, I couldn't deny them my real reason for grabbing a cup of coffee at this particular coffee shop. To fuel my amusing habit of terrorizing Juliana.

Well, at least that's what I told myself on the drive over here, instead of needing to make the photo I've been staring at for two days straight a reality.

As she pours my coffee, I take my time giving her a once-over. Just like her Charmr profile, she wears a modest amount of makeup, glasses, and a basic tee beneath a striped apron. A far cry from how she looked at dinner, but no less distracting.

She twists on her heel, aiming for the back wall, and my lips part. *Those are new.* My gaze falls lower as I appreciate her yoga pants. Tight and gray, they hug her hips and perfect ass, which jiggles with every step. My jaw locks as she stands there, working on something I can't care to look at. By some miracle, I pull myself from my hypnosis, right before she turns back around.

"That'll be seven-fifty." She passes the cup across the counter.

I raise an eyebrow to the perfect white tulip drawn on the surface. "Impressive. That has to be the best coffee art I've seen," I say, and I mean it.

To my surprise, she thanks me with a shy smile, sweeping a loose bang behind her ear. "Cash or card?"

Flipping open my wallet, I offer her a card. Without a glance, she grabs it instinctually, but pauses once she carries its full weight. Her gaze flicks to the card, her arm still outstretched, suspended midair, and when her eyebrows arch upwards, satisfaction pools low in my gut.

Although my family's fortunes are no secret to Juliana, she's been keeping her distance, but a Black Amex is a powerful reminder. You see, when people refer to the status symbol of a black card, they don't mean just any black card, but *the* black card. The American Express Centurion Card. Exclusive and invite-only, the Black Amex is offered to high-net-worth individuals who meet a certain spending and income threshold. A level which isn't actually specified but my trust fund stipend covers.

A modest two-hundred thousand.

Per month.

So, I'm not all that surprised by Juliana's common reaction to seeing a Black Amex in person. But, for some reason... as I cock my head... it looks good between her fingertips.

Snapping out of her daze, she speeds through the payment process, working the tablet in front of her. I watch her intently as she nibbles her lower lip, until the tablet chimes, finishing the transaction.

"I like the sight of that," I murmur.

Peering up at me through her thick lashes, she taps her glasses into place, drawing attention to the freckles dotted along her nose and cheeks. "Of what?"

"You, swiping my card."

She flinches, her mouth plopping open on a silent exclamation. As her jaw snaps shut, my eyes search her green ones, capturing the shock flashing in them. "U-uhm," she stammers. "Here's your check." She slides the paper across the counter, my card placed on top.

"Thank you, Jules."

Turning quickly, she bee-lines straight to that awful door, which still harbors a lurker behind the window.

"Wait." She halts at the sound of my voice. Eyebrows cinching, I inspect the check, then the counter, finding no jar. "Is there nowhere to tip?"

"... No, there's not." There's a hint of ire in her tone.

No tips? At a coffee shop?

"Well, that's kinda odd. Why the hell not?"

She swivels, all remnants of her awkwardness disappearing as she folds her arms. "The owner thinks tips deter customers from returning."

I scowl. *What the fuck???* How does she make any money, then? She's supposed to work retail, in the city, without any tips? "What kind of backwards, twisted shit is that?"

She shrugs, seemingly saying *it is what it is.*

I fish out my wallet again. "Then I'll tip with cash, and tell your punk-ass boss I'm returning with more." I press three bills flat on the counter.

"Thank you, I'll make sure to tell her." She giggles, reaching for them. "But you really don't have to—" She stiffens. "Uhh... did you mean to do that?"

"Do what?"

"Hayden, those aren't singles." She hands them back, a genuine laugh echoing between us. "Seems someone is used to tipping at other *establishments.*"

I look at the bills with confusion. "I don't see the problem."

She blinks. "You tipped me three-hundred dollars, in cash, for making a latte... You're aware I'm not a stripper, right?"

"I am. Because if you were, I'd let you keep my Black Amex instead, only if you promised to leave on your apron."

To say the way she gapes at me is like I hit her with a ton of bricks would be an understatement. More like I threw the entire house. But as much as I'd like to stay around and soak it up a little longer, I need to keep her wanting more.

"Is your lunch break soon?" I ask her stunned expression, taking a sip of my coffee. Slurping sounds bounce between our silence. "Oh, good. Let's bump our meeting to today, then." Another taste test, this one coupled with a smoldering gaze. "I'll be expecting you at my table."

NINE

JULIANA

THANK GOD IT'S TUESDAY, Mei's shortest day of the week.
Which means I won't have to endure her prying gaze during
my lunch break while I'm *negotiating my terms for fake dating
my brother's best friend.*

Yikes. How could I ever say that out loud, especially to
her? She'd check me into a psych ward.

It was bad enough that she yanked me right back into the
storage room the instant Hayden went to his table, then shot
me question after question. *Did he come all this way for you?
Does he work nearby? What did you two talk about? When's your
next date?* I dodged each one, offering vague answers, even
though all I could hear were his words to me.

Sure, the whole comment about the stripper and my apron
was just regular old Hayden Kingston shenanigans. Creative,
straight-forward, and overtly sexual, meant for maximum
shock factor—which he achieved and then some. But that's
not what stuck with me; isn't what's been replaying in my
mind on an endless continuum since and even now, as he sits
across our tiny bistro table, sporting his signature smirk.

I like the sight of that.

You, swiping my card.

Before the butterflies in my stomach flap their wings, I shove the idea of being Hayden's spoiled plaything as far back into my consciousness as humanly possible, instead focusing on how ridiculous he looks in that chair.

While Hayden isn't excessively bulky and tends more toward a lean-muscle physique, he *is* rather tall. Six-foot-three, he'd say, even though I know he's actually six-two and a half. A detail he'll deny to his grave.

I bite back a laugh, noting how far his knees jut upwards, his legs much too long for that chair. But the farther my gaze rises, the more my grin falls and heartbeat escalates. Resting his chin on a clenched fist, he gazes out the window, his hair disheveled and wild yet somehow effortlessly stylish. And worst of all, his coat flaps open, the long fabric kissing the floor while his Rolex peeks out of his sleeve. Looking kind of like—no, exactly like—a model you'd spot on the cover of Men's Vogue or in a mainstream music video.

And he's here. Sitting across from me. The girl with four-day-old hair, chipped nail polish, and a stained apron to show for.

And no experience, that little devil adds.

I clear my throat, hoping to kick it off my shoulder—and curb my distracting thoughts. But when he turns his beautiful head, they come rushing back, anyway. I bury my face in my backpack, rummaging for my notebook.

"Well, dollface, you called for this meeting, so I think it's best you lead."

My cheeks burn. *Does he really have to call me things like that?*

When my nail catches against a dark blue color, I pull out

my notebook, which I now realize looks like it belongs in a middle schooler's backpack—and honestly might've once been in *mine.* Donned in space suits, happy animals with oversized eyes dance across constellations, alongside planets, friendly aliens, colorful spaceships, and a smiling sun.

His eyebrow ticks skyward. "Space shit. Nice."

Could this day get any more humiliating? I zoom to the page I left off on.

"Wait..." Hayden leans over, his face twisting in horror. "You took *notes* for this?"

I raise a quizzical brow. "Yes. And?"

He scans over the words, even though they're upside down to him. When I flip the page, revealing two more, his face contorts in misery. "Gee, Juliana. When you texted me about *establishing ground rules,* I didn't think you'd write a book." He laughs, more to himself than at me. "Pen and paper. I couldn't think of a drier way to start a relationship."

"Fake relationship," I correct him quickly.

"Yeah, yeah." He waves his hand in the air. "You know what I mean."

"You see? This is why we need rules. You're already downplaying the seriousness of this arrangement." I flip through the rest of the pages. Specifically, five more. Seven in total. There would've been more, too, if it weren't for Mr. Show Up Unannounced here. "Unfortunately, I didn't have the time to reach ten."

With each flip, his grimace worsens, as if I'm some vindictive teacher assigning a massive project before winter break.

He whistles low. "Wow, how *terribly* misfortunate."

I shoot him a damning look.

Crossing his arms, he flicks his chin. "Let's get this show on the road, babe."

I huff a breath. "Fine, we'll start with that. Enough with the babe, babydoll, baby-whatever. It's unnecessary—"

His laugh roars across the busy café, the sound swallowed up by loud chatter. Apparently, my first rule is so hilarious, tears brim his eyes, as he slaps his palm down, rattling our table. "Oh! You did *not* just say that, Jules."

Steam shoots from my ears at his defiance. "What's. So. Funny?"

Eyes widening, he zips his lips, before another bark spews through them. "Oh my god, you're serious!" he sputters, slapping some more, until only a few chuckles linger.

"Yes. I am serious," I repeat, my jaw clenching.

"Who in their right mind is going to believe that I don't have pet names for my girlfriend?"

"They're not some dating prerequisite, so—"

"They are with me, *baby girl.*" His voice lowers an octave, sparking a warmth right between my legs.

My breaths grow shallow. "Stop that."

"Stop what?" he murmurs, a tomcat toying with his prey. Beneath our cramped table, his knees graze my chair, and his thighs close in on the outer sides of mine, trapping my legs between his.

"Giving *my girlfriend* affection? Here's a little secret. What I call you should be the least of your concerns, because my favorite place to show off what's mine is in public..." He trails a fingertip up my bare arm, light and teasing, eliciting goosebumps and fanning the fire in my center. "...and I love to play with what's mine."

My legs squirm against the cage his built for mine, prompting a deep chuckle from his chest, as he tightens back against them.

"We don't want anyone thinking our relationship is

anything but real now, would we?" Sweeping back down the length of my arm, his touch grows possessive, and I find myself drawing closer, leaning over the tabletop. "So, you better get used to my attention, baby." Lazily, he fiddles with the front of my apron, lightly tugging the drawstrings under my breasts. "Although, it seems you're already—"

I bolt backwards, my tailbone crashing against my chair, like a man freed from Medusa's seductive stare. My heart palpitates in powerful thumps, seeping the breath from my lungs. I look elsewhere, unable to meet his satisfied grin.

How am I so easy for him? He knows I still can't contend with him, even five years later.

If I take this deal, I'm doomed.

If? that little devil singsongs. *Honey, you already did. You might as well buckle up and enjoy the ride. And by ride, I mean his—*

My eyes dart between customers in the café's nooks and crannies, to the bustling streets outside, *literally anywhere*, desperately needing a distraction. But I come up with no such solace.

"I-I'm, uhm..."

"Mhmmm," he drawls.

Christ! How can a man so good-looking sound that *hot?*

Acting a fool, I dare a peek and regret it immediately. His eyes search mine. No, *ensnare* mine, holding them hostage without a single word. Dunking me in their crystal-blue, oceany depths, a composed dominance lying just beneath the surface, while teetering on a flirtatious edge that may be genuine or all a ruse.

A look I've seen once before...

I spring to my feet, my chair scraping with a harsh grating noise. Whether I draw the attention of nearby customers is news to me. Hell, I don't even know if there *are* customers anymore. "I-I'm g-gonna go get some..." My words taper off, gone with a whisper as I speed-walk toward the coffee bar.

Water... I need. Water.

The Caffeine Cove's newest barista, Rylee, gives me a strange look. I zoom past her without a glance and disappear through that annoyingly talkative door.

TEN MINUTES LATER, I'm back in my seat. Poised, professional, and hydrated as ever.

Fingers folded in his lap, Hayden reclines comfortably, curling his lips in a way that says *I'll behave now.* With a sigh, I trail a finger down the first page of my notes. Business meeting... this is just a business meeting.

I clear my throat. "No one can find out about us."

He rolls his lips together to stifle a chuckle. "The whole reason of a fake relationship—"

"No one unnecessary, I mean."

He blinks.

Oh my god, must I spoon-feed him everything? It's like geometry class all over again.

"No one we grew up with. Not Mei. My co-workers. My mom..." I squirm in my chair at the thought of my mother, the woman who practically raised Hayden, finding out about all of this.

Not only was she Mr. Kingston's nighttime nanny for years, but she taught—and still teaches—second grade at Riverside Prep on the Upper East Side. A private school Jeremy and I would've never attended alongside wealthy kids

like Hayden, if it wasn't for our mother's dedicated involvement in school affairs.

So, while she *does* accept Hayden as one of her own, given
the countless sleepovers he had growing up at our tiny apartment once the Kingston Estate was off the table, that wouldn't
make her discovery of this any less mortifying. Her nickname
for Hayden was *troublemaker*, a label that's still appropriate
today. There'd be no escaping her questions... She'd make
Mei's interrogations sound like small talk.

Steering clear of such a scenario, I add, "And your friends
can't know, either."

He frowns. "That's just great, Jules. Makes total sense. You
don't think my friends talk? Or that their families and mine
aren't part of the same social circles? People talk. There's no
avoiding my friends."

"What about my brother, then?"

"That's... going to have to be carefully managed."

I shrug. "If it's a problem, I know it'd be super weird, but I
could just come clean to him about it. I'm sure he'd under—"

"No, no." He sits up, all the color draining from his face.
"No, that's not a good idea. We'll figure something out. I'll
make sure you're out of my apartment when he comes over.
Maybe hide your things and..." he mumbles to himself.

My lips dry. "Why would you need to hide my things?"

His brows cinch in confusion. "Obviously, because I can't
risk my best friend seeing his sister's toothbrush on my bathroom counter or her shirt in my hamper."

"M-my... What?" I shake my head, grappling for my
words. "I'm not *living* with you."

Amusement flashes in his eyes. When he doesn't respond,
my heart lurches.

He can't seriously think I'm going to *move in* with him. I

get that it would make us appear more serious, but I can hardly withstand his flirtatious remarks in public. What in the world would become of me behind closed doors? My mind wanders, lying me beneath Hayden's masterful touch atop a New York City luxurious apartment, no doubt overlooking some glistening view of Central Park at night. In the main bedroom, there's not a curtain in sight. Same goes with the kitchen, even the living room...

My palm smacks onto the table, yanking myself from that *ridiculous* fantasy. "It's... It's right..." I frantically search through the notebook, my finger dragging across the paper as my words quickly spiral into some chicken-soup mess. *"Here!"* I yelp, then turn the page to him. I double tap the rule written in bold red ink, like it proves anything at all.

Lips pursing, he reads aloud blandly, "During the duration of the arrangement, the two parties will not cohabitate under the same roof." He pinches the bridge of his nose. "Parties...? *Cohabitate...?* What're you, a lawyer now?"

"No, but I mention hiring one in another rule." His eyes bulge. "I can show you. I think it's on the next pa—"

He snatches the book from my hands. *"Give me that."*

"Hey!" I lurch over the table, failing to swipe it back.

"What other nonsense do you have in here?" He flips back and forth between pages, holding the notebook at different depths, squinting like he's deciphering a morse code transcription. One by one, he reads them off, each rule more embarrassing than the last.

"No sleepovers."

My cheeks flame when he snickers.

"No sharing a bed. Ever." His eyes flicker to mine, delight glinting in them. "Very definitive in your statements, aren't you?"

I cross my arms. "With you, I need to be."

"I'll have you know, you'd be *very* comfortable in my bed."

My lips part.

"It's an Alaskan king," he adds quickly.

"An Alaskan king, really?" I drawl. "Don't you think that's a bit overkill? Why would you need a bed that sleeps, like, four pee-oo-pleee....." The word contorts and fizzles out on my tongue, as graphic images flash before me.

His lips curl into a wolfish grin. "Tell me, sweet Jules. Have you slept on Egyptian cotton?"

Lord, help me.

"No. And I don't plan on it."

"Well, seems we're in a bit of a predicament, then."

"How so? I said I'm not moving in. End of discussion."

"Yes, that's *your* non-negotiable. But this is mine."

Now it's my turn to blink. "What's there to negotiate? I'm not moving in, so there's no way I'm sleeping in your bed."

Rubbing his jawline, he hums in thought. "Exactly. Now you're getting it. We're at a standstill. Seems we'll have to..." He lets his sentence drop off open-endedly.

Is this man speaking in riddles? I'm about to make another grab at my journal, lest he continue with my torture, when the answer smacks me upside the head. "Compromise," I whisper, dread pooling in my core. *We'll have to compromise.*

"Ding, ding, ding." He shoots me a wink, full of amusement. "But, don't you worry. Turn that frown upside down, baby. Compromise is the first key to a strong relationship—or so I've heard. I've never actually stuck around long enough to confirm that. You could say I have a slight commitment problem..." His musings drift to the outer regions of my mind, alongside his laughter.

Oh, no. I nibble my lip nervously. *He's making sense. He never does that... Why, why, why, of all the times, is he now making sense?*

What's worse, is a part of me finds itself agreeing with his insanity. If we're really in a believable relationship, one that's serious enough to reveal to his own father, convincing him of Hayden's maturity and commitment, then we *can't* do this halfway. I have to move in. But not into his bed. That's where I draw the line.

Which leaves only one plausible compromise...

I avoid his heavy gaze, aware that my next words will likely book me a one-way ticket to his den of temptation. "I'll move in..."

His ramblings stop, and I can already sense the onset of his smug aura going off like a disco ball, radiating triumphant rays across the table, laughing as they touch my skin.

"...but I'm taking a guest room."

His lights go out.

"That's not the compromise I had in mind."

"Too bad."

"Is it? I don't have a guestroom."

"Are you saying your apartment isn't big enough for one?" I challenge.

He sucks in a breath, charged for another attack, before his lips clamp shut, letting pride get the best of him. "Fine." Nodding toward the notebook, he exhales heavily. "Let's just get through the rest of this garbage..."

"No lovey-dovey social media posts—*yuck,*" he mumbles to himself. "Who does she think I am?"

Flipping to the next page, a quiet laugh escapes him. "No handholding." A knot twists in my stomach, but I let his mumbles continue, something along the lines of *yeah fucking right, has she ever dated before?*

No, I most definitely *don't* say. *No, I have not.*

"No *heated intimacy?"* He rolls his eyes. "It's called *sex,* Jules.

I ignore the burn creeping up my neck. "A lawyer wouldn't write that word on a contract."

That word? I kick myself. *Seriously?*

He gives me a knowing smirk, before returning to my rules. "No falling in love." All the humor slides off his tongue, leaving behind not a single witty remark. Only a confused glance, that I'd say, if I didn't know any better, looks rather forced. "Now *that's* unnecessary."

My heart sinks—*but only a centimeter.*

I laugh awkwardly. "I'm just covering our bases."

"No need. Men like me don't fall in *love."* The word sounds foreign yet definitive on his tongue, sparking a sudden sadness within me. Not *for* me, of course. For Hayden. But maybe I'm too quick to pity, not having been in love myself.

Not true love, anyway.

AFTER AT LEAST twenty more minutes of bickering, confusing innuendos, sideward glances, successfully convincing Rylee to cover for my long lunch break, debating which rules to keep, and going back and forth on whether to call a lawyer, I compromised *yet again.*

Hayden looks over the single piece of college-ruled paper with a permanent scowl. My makeshift contract may be amateur, but it only needs his signature across the dotted line to become legally binding.

. . .

FAKE DATING TERMS & AGREEMENTS
Party 1: Hayden Kingston
Party 2: Juliana Brooks

BOTH PARTIES WILL ENTERTAIN a fake relationship, for the benefit of Party 1, until Party 2's indie game, Cosmic Kitty Defense, is showcased at DreamScape with the help of Party 1's familial connections.

GROUND RULES:

Both parties agree to...

1) Act as a couple around Party 1's friends and family.

2) Keep this a secret from Jeremy Brooks.

3) Not post about the other on social media.

4) Share a residence.

5) Not throw a party or use illegal substances in the shared residence.

6) Sleep in separate beds. Always.

7) Remain romantically exclusive.

8) Practice sexual abstinence. This includes with other people.

"YOU ADDED THINGS," Hayden complains, heaving a massive sigh, exactly how a first grader would when forced to sit for a long period of time.

I hide a smirk. "Oh, did I?"

"Yes. Seven and eight."

"Oopsie." I twirl a loose strand of hair between my fingers. "I wrote them on a whim. Just little additions."

He taps his pen atop the table impatiently. "How is remaining romantically exclusive for a *fake relationship* a little addition?"

I have my answer charged and ready the moment he goes silent. "Well, you said it yourself. You've never entertained anything romantic, including a relationship, before. So, I thought it'd be easy for you."

His jaw ticks. "It would be if I didn't have to refrain from sex, as per your last *little* rule. Please, explain the thought process behind why we can't have sex with *other* people, even though this is all fake."

I shrug. "The thought of not being exclusive makes me... uncomfy." I leave it at that, not wanting to figure out if my real reasoning is more deep-rooted. A long string of curses hisses under his breath, and he looks prepared for another sparring battle, until I say sweetly, "But we can keep negotiating, if you'd like."

In two seconds flat, he scribbles his signature across the dotted line beside mine. And for the first time since Hayden walked back into my life, I feel like I've won. Bested him at *something*.

Maybe this whole thing will be easier than I thought. Hayden will keep his distance. He won't push boundaries, and he'll stick to the contract. Before I know it, my game will be the front of gaming news, at least for a time, gaining me exposure and players and revenue. Hell, I'll be out of this apron in no time and—

Hayden fishes something from his pocket, stopping my thought dead in its tracks. That look in his eyes... satisfaction swirls through them, as if *he* was the one who watched *me* sign the contract, somehow knowing he'd come out on the better side.

Hidden beneath his palm, he pushes something across the table, the sound of metal against metal my only clue. Until he retreats, revealing a single key. It takes me a moment to put two and two together. The key must be for his apartment. A spare key. But...

The initial *J* is already engraved on it.

TEN

HAYDEN

UPHOLDING my trust fund has turned into a game of 3D chess. Too many players sit at the table, all requiring different narratives of what specific details they can and cannot know. My father and Jeremy and my friends and *Juliana's* friends and coworkers and her mother and on and on and onnnnnn...

Luckily, I'm a master at this sort of thing.

Rule #5: A playboy keeps his stories straight.

Which is why I have my plan on lockdown, my mind akin to one of those detective cork boards you'd see while watching *Mindhunter* or *Zodiac,* with the red strings connecting the suspects and pushpins and shit. Not quite on a genius level—because I'm no nerd—but something really, really close.

What impressive dots am I connecting, you ask? Well, let's recap.

Juliana thinks I am under my father's wing, when in fact, I am—and plan to stay—far, far away from its shadow. On the other hand, my father believes I'm pursuing my real estate license. Although, he's starting to have his doubts, which is why I invited him to lunch.

Keyword *I*. Not the other way around, like usual, where he'd take the opportunity to lecture me on my disgraceful lifestyle choices and bleak future. Rather, this time, *I'm* the one who'll do all the talking, by reciting a well-rehearsed elevator pitch. A proposition, one that'll double-down on the two unique truths I'm stretching to him and Juliana, without requiring me to sacrifice my *lifestyle choices.*

Because convincing my father that I've suddenly abandoned my chronic degeneracy will take more than a respectable girlfriend. That's just one piece of the puzzle. In the words of Jeremy Brooks, *you'll have to be more convincing than that...* And I will be, whenever this jackass decides to show up to my favorite sushi joint and hears what I have to say.

I tug at my sleeve, glancing down at my watch.

12:50

Our reservation was for 12:30. He's twenty minutes late to lunch with his own son. That's, on average, five minutes longer than I make all my first dates wait for my arrival.

The audacity of this man.

Heaving a sigh, I rest an elbow atop the sushi bar, finding comfort in the familiar atmosphere.

Metro Maki Lounge has always been my breath of fresh air, with a quaint yet luxurious ambiance. A part of me regrets inviting my father here, as if his presence alone might dull the acacia bar top or wither the faux cherry blossoms weaved in between the birch squares wrapping around the ceiling.

But I was deliberate in my choice, as with my outfit: a pressed pair of navy chinos and a button-down. Formal enough to be taken seriously, but not so much that I come off as some conman. What a shame, really, having taken all this into consideration, only to end up seated beside an empty barstool instead of a perky sidepiece.

"Would you like your usual, Mr. Kingston?" asks the bartender, dressed in a sharp, all-white blazer.

I stifle a sigh, nearly tasting the Sakura martini, if it weren't for the unpleasant grassy flavor already offending my tongue. "That's alright, Kenji. Just matcha today." Don't get me wrong. I'm positive Kenji whips up the perfect matcha latte, but it's far from my usual choice. Look at me, sacrificing my palette for a man who doesn't even bother to—

My back straightens.

Like a sixth sense, I know Warren Kingston has entered the room. Maybe it's the drop in temperature. The flutter in my chest. Or the smog of disappointment radiating from his every pore.

"...a partnership with them would be advantageous, yes, but not the maximum ROI we're looking for..." His voice floats through the air, growing louder and louder. "...leave the option open, until we evaluate other prospects..." I sip on my grassy concoction, as if it contains alcohol that'll soften the anticipation coiling through my blood.

"Talk soon," my father's voice booms behind me. "Good-bye." When his three-piece suit claims the empty seat, I waste no time, clearing my throat, ready to—

He holds up a finger.

My mouth clamps shut. Taking all my effort, I restrain my splintering annoyance, as I stare at the top half of his gray hair and that long digit—a finger I've received since adolescence. With his face buried in his phone, contacts zoom past his screen, until he stops and calls some name I can't read upside down.

And there I sit, thrumming my knuckles against the bar top, picking the sides of my nails, waiting like some forgotten labrador poodle for ten whole minutes. Without so much as a glance in my direction, he spouts off detailed instructions, sprinkling in boring business lingo here and there, effectively shriveling up my ear canals.

Maybe that martini isn't such a bad idea...

"Call me when the bid is finalized. Goodbye."

Finally.

I refocus my attention, finding him pre-occupied yet again. His thumbs tap dance across his screen in a flurry, sending off several texts, before it goes dark. Sinking the phone into his pants pocket, he meets my stare for the first time since arriving.

And says nothing.

My jaw ticks as I search his crystal-blue eyes, which resemble that of a mirror, except the irises in the reflection possess a cold hardness. I let the silence drag on for a few more heartbeats than necessary, while questioning what it is I'm even expecting. An apology? *Sorry* isn't a part of my father's vocabulary—or my brother's, for that matter.

How am I possibly related to this man?

"Hi, Dad," I mumble into my drink.

"Hayden," he says, reaching for his menu. Apparently, a *hello* is too much of an inconvenience for him, too.

"Another round of dumplings is on its way." *Because I ate the first while I was waiting for you,* I don't add.

"Mmm," is all he can muster.

More unbearable silence.

"So, uh... how's work been?"

He flips his menu, eyes roaming down the list of sake rice wines. "You can skip the small talk, Hayden."

"Huh?"

"I presume you didn't ask me to lunch to listen about my work. What is it? Did you overspend your monthly stipend again?"

That was three years ago. Am I never going to hear the end of it?

I loosen some tension, my knuckles leaving behind imprints on my palms. "I just want to catch up with my old pops." His gaze drags onto me, his eyelids heavy. I swallow down a smirk. He hates that nickname.

"Did you, now? Well, if you really must know, Kingston Entertainment received its second quarterly tax return last week. I've outsourced some industry-specialized accountants to move several accounts overseas and expand on our deductions. They've been pouring over federal tax code compliances, looking for loopholes—some even on the state level..."

Oh, GOD. I really shouldn't have asked.

His words drift out into space, as static buzzes throughout my consciousness like an old television. How does he talk like that all day? The man owns a fucking production company, and he'd rather stare at balance sheets than be on movie sets with A-list actors.

I keep a slight smile, nodding every now and then, watching his lips move, until they still into a flat, uninterested line. The buzzing quiets, filled by the soft chatter blanketing the restaurant.

Shit, now it's my turn.

Feeling like some clueless date, I say, "Wow, that's interesting. How do you keep up with all of that?"

He snorts. "By waking up in the a.m."

Dick.

Although it pains me to no end, I continue redirecting the conversation, letting him talk about himself, something he loves to do. While Kenji takes our orders, serves us drinks and appetizers, I suffer through all the details regarding board meetings, annual revenue statements, company stock evaluations, and the latest regulatory changes affecting the entertainment industry. Until Kenji casts me a lifeline, returning with our main course.

My mouth waters at the sight of my impressive dish. California, tiger, and volcano rolls sit artistically in the center beside a colorful assortment of top-grade sashimi. Donning a similar structure, my father's dish favors more tempera and nigiri.

"Enjoy." Kenji nods before disappearing down the bar.

Mixing wasabi into his soy sauce with a pair of chopsticks, my father side-glances my way. "I don't suppose I should ask what you've been up to."

Here comes the bullshit.

I put on a straight face, going straight for a tiger roll. "I've kept busy."

"I bet you have." His tone reeks of sarcasm. "You can spare me the details."

Anger simmers to the surface, enough that I'm surprised my chopsticks don't snap in two. Sure, I'll admit, I'm no shining star in this family, who's never really had his shit figured out. But still... isn't he the least bit curious about my hobbies? My friends? My opinions on, I don't know, *anything?* Of course not. He's never been, so why would he start today?

So, I banish the little kid in me, who still hopes in vain for an ounce of respect from the man who *"raised me"*—slap a pair of serious air quotes around that. Biting down on an extra chewy slice of tuna, I adopt an air of confidence blended with just the right amount of nonchalance, preparing to act out the part I came to play.

I shrug. "There's nothing much to say, anyway. I've been keeping to myself recently. My real estate licensing exam is soon, so I'm making sure to put in a decent amount of time studying."

He freezes. Like full-body-turned-to-stone frozen. Even his mouth stops mid-chew.

Not that I blame him, though. The word *studying* might as well be foreign language on my tongue, never having done the deed for a single minute in my entire academic life. I may have a Business Administration degree sitting inside a glossy Princeton University plaque, but that doesn't mean my name deserves placement across the paper. But hefty checks from esteemed families can buy a lot of things in this world.

The man who writes said checks swallows hard, half-coughing, half-laughing into his napkin. "You expect me to believe that?"

"What's not to believe?"

He rolls his eyes. "You. Studying. Taking an exam. Those three don't mix, and unfortunately for you, I wasn't born yesterday."

My shoulders slouch on a well-practiced sigh, as I push my tiger roll around my plate. "I know, I know. You probably don't believe me, but I'm really trying to apply myself. Granted, I'm not really good at it. I'm thinking of hiring a tutor before I completely flunk the test."

Uncertainty wavers in his eyes, but for the first time in I don't know how long, no scathing comeback slips from his lips. What shocks me even more is when he sets down his chopsticks, leans back, and looks at me. *Really* looks at me. "So, you're actually taking an interest in real estate, then?"

The hope emerging in his tone has my heart contracting,

sparking a sliver of guilt as I shift into the second phase of my grand plan, which I like to call *Even More Lies.*

I shrug. "I'm just as surprised as you. I wasn't at first. The idea of staging and selling properties didn't sound so appealing, but it wasn't until I looked into buying properties that the interest caught on."

He hums, nodding—*nodding,* not shaking. *Toward me.* God, I wish I believed an ounce of what I was saying, that the business of real estate, in any form, wasn't drier than the Sahara in my mind. Then I'd deserve this newfound interest my father's taken in me.

"You're alluding to being a landlord, I presume? Buying up properties and then renting out the spaces."

"Yes, exactly."

Plopping a roll into his mouth, he hums yet again, this time chewing like he actually enjoys the taste. "That's a very lucrative business, especially if you have the capital. And choose the right properties, of course."

"That's what I've been looking into. Familiarizing myself with the city's current market," I say, infusing confidence into my now only partial lies, given my extensive research last night for this very conversation. "I think location matters the most, focusing on up-and-coming areas, like Bushwick in Brooklyn or Astoria in Queens or..."

With every location and minute detail, his eyes sparkle further with what I can only guess to be pride. *Holy shit, he's really buying all this.* I mean, I planned for it, but... I didn't know if he'd take it *this* well.

"I, uh..." I clear my throat, avoiding his gaze, in an almost embarrassed way—embarrassed for my past transgressions, specifically. And he eats it up, his eyebrows raising. "I've started saving up for my first property... I don't know if you'd be open to it, but we could go in on one... together?"

The word floats out between us. *Together.*

The most vital part of my grand scheme, the bridge between the two tales I'm spinning. If I were to go into a property together, then I *would* seem under my father's wing. And, in turn, coupled with the new, responsible girlfriend, he'd think I *had* turned my life around, and I'd soon be off his radar with my trust fund no longer in limbo. All without me having to lift a finger or change my lifestyle, because, as every silver-spooned individual knows, money can fix any problem.

Including having to manage your own real estate.

"I'd run the whole property," I lie. "Make it my first priority. Rent out the rooms. An apartment complex, maybe, or a commercial building. Keep things running smoothly... What do you say?"

Absentmindedly, he taps his fingers atop the table, resting his chin in his palm, contemplating the proposition. My heart somersaults, in light of perhaps the first time my father's ever taken me seriously.

"I think..."

He looks me dead in the eyes, his swirling with a rare delight and acceptance. My blood pressure soars down, my mind finally at ease. I pulled it off. I really, really pulled this off...

"I think you can cut the crap now."

My posture straightens. *Wait, what???*

"Huh?" I feign confusion, frowning deeply.

"*I said,* you can cut the crap. Do you really think I believed a single word you said?"

"But I—"

"God, you really are hopeless." He laughs, cold and vicious. "I checked in on that online school you're supposedly attending. Yeah, they've never heard of you." My mouth springs open, only for him to interject once more, reading my mind as if he's got a key to its door. "And don't waste your breath on some student confidentiality bullshit. A little donation to their fine arts program proved pretty convincing in bending their rules."

Shame burns my cheeks. But also anger, rooted in a long-standing resentment toward the man who made me into the way I am. If he wants someone to blame for the pit stain upon his family, he should look no further than himself.

"Just do it, already."

"Do what?"

"Pull my trust."

He smiles, full of greed. There's nothing Warren Kingston loves more than having power over someone. That's the true reason he hasn't pulled it already. He couldn't dangle the threat in front of my nose anymore.

"Oh, no... I have something much better in store for you. I planned to tell you at our next family dinner, when you two were both together, but now's a good time."

"And what's that?" I ask, wishing now more than ever I'd chosen something stronger than matcha, as if alcohol might soften the blow.

"An internship. With your brother."

ELEVEN

HAYDEN

"CAN'T WE JUST HIRE MOVERS?" I grumble, stepping into the elevator. Cramped and overdue for a cleaning, it hardly fits two people, which could be said about the rest of Juliana's apartment complex—and I've only seen the lobby.

She shakes her head, hitting the third floor. "I'm not paying for that."

Concerned for my designer jeans, I shy away from the dingy wall, brushing up against her. But I regret it immediately, as her rosy shampoo floats through my nostrils, right up to my brain. Who knew a girl in a ponytail, yoga pants, and an oversized *Star Wars* T-shirt could prove so distracting.

When the elevator opens, she practically bolts from my vicinity. Not that I mind, as I trail her down the narrow hallway, appreciating the way her hips sway in her tight pants. Like a man spellbound, I watch shamelessly, until the thought of Jeremy ruins everything, specifically his fist slamming between my eyes. Suddenly, the vinyl flooring and chipped paint on the walls are *really* interesting.

"I could pay for it," I say, when she stops at a door. "Just like I paid for the movers who cleared out your new room, which has an incredible view, by the way." Her brows lift curiously, only to furrow when I mumble, "Though, not as good as *my* room."

She scoffs, sinking her key into the lock. "Even if you did pay, I don't want strangers touching my things. I have valuables, just so you know. Nothing I want broken out of carelessness... Besides, I already rented a U-Haul."

The snarky response I had primed and ready rockets right back down my windpipe. *She's going to drive a U-Haul? In the city?* Knowing I'll likely be her unwilling passenger, dread washes over me, but not as much as when she opens the door, unveiling a nightmare I'm instantly wishing to wake from.

Three words sum it up quite nicely.

Nerd. Shit. EVERYWHERE.

Cyberpunk posters on the walls. Retro gaming consoles that I can't put names to sitting comfortably inside glass cases. A decked-out PC, sporting—

"You gonna help, or just stand there in the doorway?"

Juliana's sass drags me from my fixation, as I note the hand propped on her hip and the heap of empty boxes stacked beside her.

Great.

The door swings shut on my entrance, followed by a loud thud. Blinking, I look past the total nerd haven and take the apartment in as a whole—if I could even call it that. Sure, studios are quite common in dense cities like New York City, but I didn't know they came *this* small.

The whole room is much longer than it is wide and can't be more than a hundred square feet, utilizing the precious space down to the last foot. Floating shelves mark the walls, tiny cabinets stack up to the ceiling, and a two-person couch stands next to a Murphy hideaway bed that folds out *into* the kitchenette.

This place is even tinier than her mom's growing up. Sick bile rises up my throat, full of sympathy and anger, and suddenly I can't move her into my place fast enough.

"Enough with the pitiful looks, Mr. Judgy. I happen to like my apartment just the way it is." Against all odds, pride flows from her, putting a damper on my emotions.

I tilt my head, examining with a new perspective. Aside from the nerdish knickknacks, there's a certain charm to the space, similar to her bedroom back home. A deliberate arrangement of furniture accented by aesthetic blends of pinks and purples, forming a moody vibe with a surprising amount of natural light.

A large bin gets shoved into my hands.

"Chop, chop."

I press my lips into a thin line. *Defiant pride or not, she's still coming home with me.*

FOUR HOURS LATER, I've carried more overly stuffed bins than I cared to count down to the U-Haul, effectively aging my lower back at least thirty years, and we're not even finished yet. *Almost,* but a few stragglers remain.

Her couch. A nightstand. Several lamps. Miscellaneous bathroom and kitchen essentials. And, most notably, the beast that is her computer. To clarify, I don't mean her laptop, although I wish that were the case. I'm referring to the geeky battle station over in the corner, in front of the apartment's only window, fading an array of RBG lights in and out like alluring breath.

"How do we go about packing this monstrosity?"

"Huh...?" Her voice breaks through the clattering of pots and pans. "Oh, that'll go very last."

I approach with caution, as if one misstep might disrupt the quiet hum of the tower, or scrabble the indiscernible lines of code displayed across three monitors. But I quickly think better of it; there's not a wire in sight for me to mess up. With a shrug, I sink into her girly, pink gaming chair, and study the gibberish some more, unable to deduce a splinter of meaning.

"Really? You want to wait? This seems... important."

"It is." Her voice comes up beside me, the sound pleasant in my ears. "It needs to have maximum run-time, so we'll pack it last and set it up first."

I squint, noting a section of green code vertically zooming up the screen, seemingly writing itself. An automation, of some sort. And here I am, Hayden Kingston, player of players, the smooth operator—or *the rake of New York City,* as my friends like to say—debating whether to ask about *code.*

C.O.D.E...

There's no valid explanation, except that I fell on our last trip to the truck. Or that it came from her fingertips, so I have no such restraint.

"This, right here." I point at the moving part. "What in the world is that?"

She sucks in a breath, then hesitates. "You really want to know?"

No! my internal instincts scream in my head, that'd normally steer me into acting unimpressed and subtly demeaning her little project. But instead, like some pussy-whipped amateur, I nod.

Her eyes light up instantly, and when she flashes the most

genuine smile I've seen since storming back into her life, my heart contracts.

"That's a Python script. It handles quite a few things, actually. Namely, running Cosmic Kitty Defense's servers. So, things like user authentication, error handling, ensuring players are on the most up-to-date version, stuff like that."

I nibble on my lower lip, suddenly a clueless date for the second time in twenty-four hours. "So... that's why it's so important?"

"Mhmm," she hums. "Without it running, users couldn't connect and play."

"Which is what moving will do."

"Correct. *But* I have a solution. Which reminds me..." Her hands fly onto the keyboard, her body half-way craning over mine. My teeth sink into my bottom lip on a sharp breath.

Maybe there are *perks to being an amateur...*

"I host my own server because it's cheaper, but I can move it to a cloud hosting service temporarily..." Her nails *click-clack* along the keys, the movement jiggling her ass cheeks ever-so slightly. I don't hear half of what she's saying as the light streaming in through the window illuminates her body like a tempting feast.

"Oh, really?"

She hums again. "I bought cloud space yesterday and even scheduled the code for the move, but the cloud server has lower RAM than my own hosting, so players might experience some lag..."

Whether she notices her compromising position or not, she arches farther, reaching for the mouse. The front of her shirt droops toward the floor, granting a delicious view of her stomach. My lip flops out, my mind turning up utterly blank, when I catch a pair of twin diamond studs sparkling back at me.

Blood rushes straight to my groin. *When did she get her belly button pierced?*

Thick with arousal, I clear my throat, speaking directly to her backside. "How will you deal with that?" I scoot to the edge of the chair, concealing my raging hard-on beneath the table.

She sighs deeply, grazing her thigh against my forearm, which glues to the armrest with an ironclad grip. "There's not much of a fix, aside from sending an email to my newsletter subscribers about it, which is what I need to do now, before we finish packing."

Keep her talking, keep her talking...

"Wow, that's impressive. How many people are on your email?"

"A couple thousand."

Honestly impressed, my eyebrows raise, but not as much as when her shirt slips farther. I cock my head to the side, like a hungry voyeur in a window who finds something he likes with just the right angle. Juliana's bra is lacy and blushy pink, almost as flush as the top half of her breasts spilling out of the fabric.

At this point, I'm ready to drop to my knees before her and beg, if only she asked, seeing as every flick of her wrist, every tap against the keyboard, sends those perfect tits swaying, pressing my cock harder against my zipper. I shift in my chair, relieving some pressure, only for her to laugh about something I can't even register anymore. The convulsions bounce her breasts harder, exposing the slightest sliver of her nipple.

God, help me.

I grind my teeth, all but failing to block out the images running rampant through my mind. Flashes of Juliana bent over this very table, the waistband of her yoga pants cinched around her thighs and ponytail wrapped tightly around my fist. With every thrust, I bury my cock deeper, tug her hair harder, until she's staring wide-eyed at the sky, moaning something precious on her tongue. Something I can't accurately put a sound to and now crave so desperately to hear...

My name.

My name on those sweet lips, overcome with ecstasy. She could name her price—*any price*—and I'd write the check right now to hear it, just this once. All she'd have to do is hand me the pen—

"That should do it."

At the exact moment she pushes off the table, I whip my head back to where it belongs, scoot my chair forward, and sit up straight, hiding my situation from her view. Testosterone still rages through my veins when our eyes connect, hers with a naïve innocence as her shirt falls back into place.

What the hell is going on? Since when has a little cleavage made me as hard as a rock?

Noting my cramped position, she cocks an eyebrow, but before she can question it, I slip on my signature smirk, the one I know gets under her skin.

"I, uh..." She blushes, swiping a lock behind her ear. "Hope I didn't bore you to death."

I wink, holding our eye contact without wavering, a glimpse of my fantasy resurfacing when her blush deepens. "Not at all."

～

I STALLED for ten whole minutes before you-know-what went down, by *rightfully* complaining about my aching joints and muscles. Yet, I'm still rocking a semi-chub and avoiding thinking or looking in Juliana's general direction at all costs, while collecting the final things from her now nearly barren apartment.

Aside from her computer, the final items we've yet to collect lie behind a skinny pantry door, next to the oven. I twist the knob, swing the door open, and—

I freeze midway. *Uh... Okay, not a pantry.*

Creaking the door fully open, that dread pools into me once again, as I stare at no more than twenty shirts hung on a tiny rod. *This is her closet?* Everything she slips onto her back in the morning fits in *here?* I take in the tiny space that can hardly accommodate for my size, noting the mini dresser and the three pairs of shoes slotted underneath.

The longer I look in silence, I expect an oncoming wave of anger. But one never comes. Only sickness. And the insatiable need to wire transfer every last cent from my checking account into hers. I would, right this instant, if I didn't know her so well. Her pride would never allow it, which means I'll have to get crafty.

In due time.

With a solemn expression, I pack her clothes, each *Legend of Zelda, Pokémon,* and *Lord of the Rings* T-shirt lifting the corners of my lips a little higher, until I can't seal them any longer. "Think you need another graphic tee?" I tease.

Her response is immediate. "Only if you buy another pair of yacht shoes to match."

My jaw drops and defenses shackle high. What a garbage stereotype. Does it *look* like I'm on a yacht right now? I'll answer that. No, I'm not, because I'm stuck here breaking my back in a concrete prison. And even though *Daddy's Money* is my sole identifier, that doesn't mean I can't wear something more refined and sophisticated like a pair of...

I look down, finding my feet adorned in navy suede and leather laces.

Shit.

Eyes bulging, I whip a one-eighty. *"Hey,* I didn't pack up your entire apartment on a Friday just to take lip from you."

"Oh my god, Hayden, you're such a girl!" Lips spewing, Juliana laughs contagiously. I turn back toward the empty closet, hiding my smile. "If you're *so* tired, then I'll take the next bin." Her footfalls sound behind me.

A quiet grumble is my only reply, as I stash away her last item, a heavily worn pair of checkered Vans she practically lived in throughout high school.

"But seriously, thanks for finishing up the clo—" Her sentence cuts short, followed by a short silence. "You missed something."

Facing her, I stand to my full height, which is a good full head taller than her. "Did I?"

She looks around my shoulder, pointing. "My apron. It's hanging right there."

I arch an eyebrow, following the direction of her finger, finding *The Caffeine Cove* at the end. "Why would you need that? I'd like to think you don't keep souvenirs of places that don't accept tips."

"Uhh..." She chuckles awkwardly. "I can't go to work without my apron."

"And why would you need to keep working?" I ask, earning a flurry of rapid blinks.

"So I can pay rent."

Ohh, my sweet, silly Jules.

I chuckle. "Come on, now. I'm offended. You really think I'd make you pay rent at my place?

"What?" She shakes her head, her face screwing up like she's getting directions from a toddler. "No, not your place. *Here.* I need to work so I can pay rent here."

My shoulders sag, utterly deflated. "But you're moving out."

"Yes, *temporarily.*"

Wearing a scowl, I look around the tiny space.

She scoffs. "Are you seriously about to ask why?"

"Uhh, yeah. The place is hardly big enough for a bed."

"You're an ass, you know that?" She shoulders past me, snatching her apron off the rack. "I live here because it's *cheap.* And, yes, my part-time day job might be below the likes of someone like *you* and, sure, the owner is a total bitch who's taking advantage of me, but at least she doesn't fire me the second she finds out I'm an entrepreneur during lunch breaks, like my last ten jobs."

Each crack in her voice is another stab to my heart. "Juliana," I say lightly, "I'm—"

"And for the record"—she breezes past me once more, carrying the final bin—"a lot of people would kill for this apartment, even if no one will notice the sudden vacancy, because it's so small I can never host anyone. In this part of the city, micro-studios—especially ones that stick to their monthly rent, year by year—are like striking gold. I had to apply five times before I was accepted, and I don't intend on losing this unit, while I'm off playing your fake girlfriend, only for me to have nowhere to live once I move out of your—"

Unable to stomach another second of her struggles, I grab

her by the arm, halting her a foot from the front door. *"Then don't."*

She inhales a sharp breath, before a silence encroaches between us, until she dares to break it. "Huh?" she breathes.

"I mean..." As the weight of my words finally hit me, I swallow thickly. "Until you're on your feet. After the deal's over with, I wouldn't kick you out right away, not if I knew you'd end up in a place like this."

Meeting my gaze, an incredulous look blooms across her features. "You would..." She jerks her head away. "No, you're talking crazy. I don't need your help. I can make it on my own."

She turns back to the door, grunting as she tries for the door handle with her elbow. When I reach for the bin to offer help, she mumbles, "I got it," and balances it on her knee with one hand and swings open the door with the other.

There's that pride.

I follow her down the hallway. "Jules?" Quickening her steps, she shakes her head in disapproval. "Fine. After the deal, keep your room, and I'll charge you rent. Whatever it is you're paying here." She shakes her head again, and continues to do so, until we reach the elevator. "That sounds fair, right?"

"No. It doesn't. It sounds like charity."

"Not to me."

"Really?" She purses her lips, avoiding my gaze. "I pay six hundred a month here."

I nearly choke on my own saliva, but somehow manage a straight face. *Six hundred dollars? For an apartment in New York City?* I've never heard of such a thing.

When I remain silent, she presses, "Compare that to whatever astronomical rent *you're* paying each month."

Fifty thousand. Easy.

If I were renting it out.

I don't have the heart to tell her the building's one of Kingston Entertainment's many investment properties. My father personally owns every upper-floor unit in the luxurious complex, among others, in his staggering real estate portfolio. He moved me into the penthouse several years ago, which may seem outrageous to someone unaccustomed to such wealth, but it's not in my family.

Besides, my apartment's not much to gawk at. Not when compared to my brother's *estate,* which he inherited from our late-paternal grandfather, after our father passed it straight down to him.

Just to him.

"Is it really so hard for you to accept help?"

"I did today. When I asked you to help pack."

More like told *me,* I keep to myself, rather than throwing off my side of the argument.

She steps into the elevator, which hardly fits herself and the bin. I fold my arms, remaining in the hallway. "That wasn't such a big ask," I lie, as the dull ache in my shoulders intensifies, right on cue.

"No? Like you said, it's Friday. Mid-day, even." Her tone is stubborn, yet she eyes me curiously as the doors begin closing. "Didn't you have work today?" she asks, right before they seal shut. Leaving me in silence, staring back at my metallic reflection, her question hits like a haymaker straight to the ribs.

And a reminder of all the stories I'm juggling.

TWELVE
JULIANA

"IS that what I think it is?"

Hayden scratches his head, lost for words.

"Hayden..." I growl.

"Uhhhhh, no?" He smiles sweetly, as two movers pass us through the doorway, carrying my new mattress Hayden paid for without asking, along with a beautiful white bed frame. He also hired movers the moment I parked our U-Haul in front of his glitzy apartment building, amidst mutters about my horrendous driving and poor decision-making skills, having had his fill of near-death and do-it-yourself experiences for one day.

What a baby. My driving wasn't *that* sketchy. Nobody got hurt. We made it here in one piece. That's what matters. Or it did, until I became the butt-end of a juvenile joke on my first night here.

Lowering my voice, I hiss, "Are you trying to tell me that's *not* a stripper pole in the very *center* of my room?"

"No, uhh..." Collecting himself, he clears his throat, flicking his chin confidently. "That's a detached section of the support wall."

"Ohhh, is it now?"

"Yep. You see how the ceiling slopes slightly there...?"

"Uh, huh. Uh, huh." I nod, my eyes all but slicing him with freshly sharpened daggers.

"...*Very* unstable. Nothing to trifle with. The building's contractor came out and everything, said the place needed a special, reinforced-titanium support beam."

Support. Beam. Did he really just say that stripper pole's a SUPPORT BEAM?!

When the movers turn back around, I suck in a breath, withholding my tongue lashing. My gaze connects with one on his way out, and let's just say, his eyes say all the judgment his mouth doesn't.

Embarrassment burns bright on my cheeks. "And did this fancy support beam come with a disco ball, too?" I jab my finger through the air, pointing to the sparkly glitter bomb spinning circles on the ceiling.

I shoot him a scathing look when a laugh escapes his lips. "Sorry, sorry." He reaches past me, flipping a switch on the wall, putting an end to the light show. "See?"

"Wow, that just makes it all better, doesn't it?" He's about to laugh again, before my hand snaps to my hips. "I'm not playing around." I gesture toward the pole. "You better make them take that *thing* outta here."

"I can't."

"Why the hell not?"

"It's bolted to the ceiling."

I'm gonna rip my frickin' hair out. Pressing both hands to my temples, I pace down the hallway.

It's only for a couple of months, Juliana. It'll pass by quickly, then you'll get your end of the deal, I coach myself, releasing calming breaths. *A few months of immaturity and keeping secrets and faking a connection and re-asserting boundaries and...*

Twisting a one-eighty, I nearly trip.

...and living alone with a roommate who looks like that.

Hayden leans against the doorframe, flashing a feline grin that ignites my core in all the right ways. Tracking my every step with amusement, he sweeps his tongue across his porcelain teeth, as if he knows I'm studying him. He would be correct on that assumption. I mean... how couldn't I? *Look at him.*

Those white chinos paired with that striped polo on *that* body and head of hair are straight out of a Pinterest mood board. Then you couple it with the whole *multi-million-dollar penthouse on Billionaires' Row at the south end of Central Park* thing, and it's all just sickening.

Avoiding his intrusive gaze, I pass him by without a glance, instead focusing on the jaw-dropping view at the end of the hallway. I approach with caution, my stomach flip-flopping on each footfall, until I'm an arm's length from the enormous windows, not daring any closer.

And then I stare...

Out into the open city. Through the unobstructed, bird's eye view of the trees and tiny dots of people walking Central Park. No skyscrapers stand in the way, not that one could, anyway, seeing as we're higher than all of them.

When my heartbeat slows, I brave another step. Only an inch. But enough to crane my head down to the city streets below. Wide-eyed, I gape in wonder, debating if my next blink might poof the little taxi cabs stuck in gridlock into fairy dust, awakening me in my eight-by-twelve-foot apartment.

"You'll get used to it," a voice like velvet murmurs close to my ear.

Too entranced to care with whom I'm conversing, I whisper back, "No, I won't."

"You will," it says. Lips brush against my ear, sending a chill racing up my spine. "You can get closer than that."

I shake my head, transfixed by the scene below, just one step away from fully taking it in.

"Yes, you can," it purrs again, making my toes curl in my sneakers. When I don't budge, a soft touch sweeps down the small of my back, nudging slightly, willing my legs into motion. I take a step, only one, another inch and at a crawling pace, but it's enough to warrant a guttural hum in my ear, teeming with praise.

Absentmindedly, my teeth sink into my lower lip, as tingles bloom between my legs and pulse pounds for a whole new reason.

Another nudge, this time earning an immediate response. My toes bump the base of the window, as I'm suddenly void of fear. I press my forehead to the cool glass and gaze straight down, catching glimpses of the windows below, floor after floor after floor, all reflecting off the setting sun like scattered jewels.

I blink, and they only shine brighter.

"That's it," the voice encourages deeply, as warmth envelops my backside. A strong presence I can't help but sink into, when a careful yet demanding touch grabs my nape, applying noticeable pressure. "You like losing control, don't you?" My legs quiver like molten putty as my eyelids fall. "Yeah, you do. That's my good girl."

I gasp.

As if zapped by a live wire, I jolt backward, only to smack into something hard and immobile. My heart ricochets in fear, as I'm suddenly a bird caught without its wings a hundred stories up, staring down the fall.

Breathe... *Breathe.* You're on even ground. It's just a window. Sturdy, tempered glass, meant for such heights. And look at that, it even comes with two large hands to keep you safe.

Wait, what?

I whirl on my heels, finding myself caged between Hayden's arms. His palms press flat against the glass on either side of my head, even though the shadow of his touch still sends goosebumps along my nape. With a smirk, his eyes rake down my body, leisurely, in a way that makes me feel naked—but just for him.

"You know, Jules, if seeing a stripper pole gets you so worked up, you should think about giving it a spin or two sometime." He winks. "But only if I can watch, of course."

Embarrassment burns my cheeks, setting my whole body aflame. Unable to retort or explain my actions or even look him in the eye, I spring forward, slipping under his arm.

"There's nothing to be ashamed of, dollface. It's great exercise!" His laughter bounces through the air as I flee down the hall, unsure of where I'm headed, but confident my legs won't rest until Hayden Kingston and his twisted games are far, far behind me.

THIRTEEN
JULIANA

"STUPID, STUPID, STUPID," I mumble to myself, ripping the lid off the next bin stuffed with clothes. "Stupid stripper pole..."

Grunting, I heave a large pile of shirts with the hangers still on them, barely able to wrap my arms around the stack. I aim for my closet, passing under the sparkly sphere attached to the ceiling, grumbling some more. "Stupid disco ball nonsense... said it's an expensive light fixture... no way of removing it..." *Grumble, grumble, grumble.*

When I enter the closet, I'm so determined to stay grumpy, I don't stop and stare like the last ten times. Is it the nicest— and largest—closet I've ever seen? With everything a girl would ever dream of? Drawers that stretch to the ceiling. More clothing racks than I can count. Display cases with moody, accent lighting for purses, bags, and jewelry. A marble center island beside a chaise lounge beneath a crystal chandelier...

Sure. It has all those things. But it's also a couple of doors down from a womanizing *pig.*

A pig you sure seem eager to please, a voice interjects inside my head, laughing snarkily.

I huff an irritated breath, slamming the hangers next to the rest of my clothes. My entire wardrobe doesn't fill one-tenth of the space, not to mention how unusual my casual attire looks surrounded by such luxury. Most notably my apron.

On my way back to the boxes, I don't acknowledge the vastness of my new room or the surrealness of my life or gape at the spectacular views, even though the walls of my corner room are a solid sheet of glass. I only give the *support beam* that's smack dab in the center of everything the stink-eye, as if it's some mean girl I'm beefing with in high school.

When Hayden's comment replays in my mind, I can't help but scoff aloud with an annoyed, high-pitched voice. *"You should think about giving it a spin or two sometime—*blegh!" My face screws up like I bit a sizable chunk off a lemon, unsure of who it is I'm more mad at, him or myself.

Knowing the answer, I mumble, "Stupid hormones..." With a sigh, I plop down, criss-cross on the floor beside the final box. "They're always getting me into stupid situations with Mr. Wrong..."

I rip off the lid, only for my anger to subside when I see what lies on top, covered in protective paper. Unwrapping the layers, I pull out the lousiest flower vase Columbia University's pottery club had probably ever seen in its history.

Handcrafted by yours truly.

Lacking any semblance of symmetry, the vase sports uneven bumps and ridges, two mismatched handles, and streaky garnish over a vomit yellowish-green color. Overall, it's similar to a toddler's first attempt at building a sandcastle, except it's not their first time. But their tenth. Maybe even their thirtieth...

Unraveling another, I behold in my hands a vase on a whole other caliber. Polar opposite in every way. Elegant, smooth, and pearly white. Worthy of a mantel place inside some Victorian chateau, where it can boast its graceful curves, having been crafted by—at the time—a second-year Fine Arts student with a focus on sculpting.

My sister from another mister, Mei.

Well, my adopted sister is more accurate. As in, *she* adopted *me,* sophomore year of college in a shared elective class, vowing she was to be my new best friend and I had no choice in the matter. To anyone else, that may sound like strange behavior, but not for socially fearless, hyper-extroverted Mei.

Why she chose me, of all people—the girl with straight As, zero social life, and an obsessive habit of programming her new strange game during lecture—I have no idea. But she sure made it her mission to push me out of my comfort zone, because she immediately began signing us up for workout classes, artsy clubs like pottery and photography, school dances, dragging me to bars, and even tried convincing me to rush her sorority house and go to frat parties.

The latter two she never actually pulled off, maybe because students in video game design and Greek life are like oil and water, but that's not from a lack of her trying. Like I said, the girl's got a vendetta against my V-card.

Frankly, I don't think we would've stayed friends all these years, if we didn't share *something* in common. That something didn't reveal itself until three months into our friendship, when I happened upon her name on the Dean's list, spanning her entire time at Columbia. The little discovery rocked me to my very core.

Sure, it's safe to say that students attending a prestigious university are going to be smart, but it's no secret that those from ultra wealthy families—such as Mei—often gain acceptance through private donations. A.k.a. bribes. An unethical practice that, at the time, had higher correlations with those in Greek life.

So, in the back of my mind, during those early days of our friendship, I put two-and-two together, coupled with Mei's girly exterior—the big lashes, skimpy outfits, dyed hair, acrylic nails, and arm tattoo—her affinity for large parties and living the high life, then *poof.* She was a subpar student from an affluent family who cuts corners, searching for the next geek to do her homework for her, in exchange for an upgraded social life.

I couldn't have been. More. Dead. Wrong.

My girl Mei Nguyen's all smoke and mirrors.

She may drink like she's got no liver to lose and pull the quarterback *and* the captain of the hockey team in one weekend, but she's an academic try-hard, through and through. It *runs through her veins*—her words, not mine—because she's a Vietnamese, first-generation college student and the eldest child of immigrant parents, who struck it big in the manufacturing industry, with all the same pressures and expectations of those who didn't.

Since the very first day I met her, she's never wasted a single minute of her time. Her schedule's fully booked out, like a celebrity hair stylist or some high-profile lawyer.

Even now, she's in the first year of her PhD program and is an adjunct for a lower-level arts class, in hopes to one day become a professor, all while somehow juggling being the president of the pottery club, participating in Greek life as an alum, and working part-time at The Caffeine Cove. A job she took to, *"fill up her free time,"* when I know the girl must hardly have time to sleep.

All of which is a total roundabout way of saying...

Mei is a badass. In every sense of the word.

Sadness ripples through me as I brush my thumb across her vase. *A badass I'm lying to, despite never keeping secrets.* But she can never know the truth about the guy she set me up with or the strange arrangement I now find myself in, because there's no predicting her reaction. Too much is on the line for uncertainty.

What a shame, though. I cross the room with her vase, the city lights like a galaxy of fallen stars as my backdrop. *She'd love the view of my new life, even if it's temporary.*

TURNS OUT, my room doesn't do Mei's vase justice. My nightstand is too small for my new bed and looks like a duck in the desert, surrounded by such luxury. There's no room at my workstation, I don't have an accent table to put near the windows, and my whole closet is off because I have approximately two outfits.

So, I'm on the prowl for the perfect spot, walking the halls all over again, this time quietly in the dark with my fuzzy bunny slippers while still avoiding a certain playboy billionaire. Who I haven't seen since what happened by the—

I shake my head violently, denying the thoughts from taking shape. *Don't go there.*

Slowly but surely, I memorize the penthouse's cavernous layout. Taking a more thorough route than before, I breeze past a dining hall, guest bedrooms, a private workout facility, a state-of-the-art kitchen, a large, empty space—which seems to be for entertaining guests—an exit door labeled *rooftop terrace*, a hallway I avoid because I'm ninety-nine percent sure it leads to the main bedroom, and a surprising amount of paintings on the walls.

Scratch that. A *ton* of paintings—and pastels—most unlike anything I've seen, some even encased in protective glass with overhead, focused spotlights, as if curated for The Louvre. I make mental notes to revisit a few later, which only worsens my guilt. Mei would have much more to say about them than I do.

I bank a left and discover an enormous opening—the main living room, cloaked in metallic grays and modern furniture. My jaw drops as I follow my gaze up a windy floating staircase, which leads up to yet another floor I haven't ventured. Iron rails line the balcony above, and two-story glass encases the one-eighty views of the city, all seemingly centered around one main focal point.

A marble fireplace.

I approach with a smile, having finally found the vase a home—one long slab of oak above a roaring fire that flickers through a bed of glass beads. When the vase sits comfortably off to one side, I backpedal a few paces and rub my jaw with a *hmmmm*, as if I'm some fussy art critic.

My unparalleled, super qualified insight, you ask?

The floral pattern may clash with the modern decor, and this is no Victorian chateau, but anything's better than the second-hand furniture I bought off online marketplaces... Oh, who am I kidding? Screw the chateau. I'm in a twenty-thousand square foot penthouse. I think I did Mei's expert pottery justice. At least now she's here in some capacity.

When I'm not even ten paces into retracing my steps, my phone rings in my pants pocket. *Loudly* echoing through the dark hallway. I curse under my breath, *shut up, shut up, shut up,* only to expand upon my vocabulary when I see the caller I.D.

Mei.

Is she some kind of psychic?!

I silence the ringer, letting out an anxious breath, as I slip it back into my—

RING, RING, RING...

Jolting backwards, I nearly slip on the polished hardwood. When I check the I.D. again, I feel stupid. I nibble my lip, my heart rate skyrocketing as the tone blasts through the penthouse. *Mei's not one to be ignored. She'll keep calling. Shit, shit, shit...*

I whip the phone to my ear, speaking right above a whisper. "Hey."

"Hey, girl!" Mei's voice booms in my ear, doing little to curb my anxiety. "What're you up to?"

"Oh, nothing. Just, uh... working on some features," I lie.

"What...? Hold on, I gotta turn you up. What did you say?"

Like a thief in the night, I tiptoe around a blind corner, eyes squinting in the darkness. "Just working on some features." I brave a little louder.

"Am I crazy, or are you whispering?"

Dammit.

"Yeah, sorry... The, uh... My next-door neighbors, they put in a noise complaint."

The line goes dead for a few moments, and I realize just how stupid that lie was, seeing as I spend all my time on the computer. Alone. Programming. Not uttering a word.

"Really...? That's surprising. Also, it's not even ten o'clock."

I clear my throat, dropping my voice lower as I enter a large corridor. "I think they may have got the wrong room. I don't know. I'm just playing it safe for now."

She hums, feeding into my lie, which only adds another brick onto my pile of guilt. "Makes sense. I was probably too loud last Saturday when we watched *The Shining*. I haven't been able to sleep since... Anyways, my class just got let out, so you know what that means."

Yes, I do. She's going out bar hopping, and I'm semi-obligated to show. "Ohh... I can't tonight, Mei."

"Boooo. That's what you said last Friday."

"The kitty litter sand trap releases next week"—*not a lie* —"and I still got some bugs to work through"—*lie.*

Completely immune to my game's ridiculous diction, Mei doesn't slip a single chuckle through the line, but she does sigh. Heavily. *"Fine.* But you're coming out next weekend. Even if I have to drag you by your feet."

Whew. "You won't have to," I whisper.

"Alright, well, don't work too hard."

Passing the kitchen, I pick up my pace, confident I'm in the clear, making to round another corner. "No promises. Have a good nigh—*Oof."*

I smack into something hard, knocking the wind straight from my lungs and almost dropping my phone. My head rattles in a daze, and I grasp against what I presume to be a wall, except... I explore with my hands... the wall is rather warm... and smells like aftershave... and is *chuckling above my head?*

I gasp, lurching backwards, only to trip over my own feet after I catch a full view of Hayden. Losing balance, the ceiling crosses into my vision as I freefall—

Strong hands catch my arms, tilting my world back to center—and revealing the most mouthwatering sight I've ever beheld with my own two eyes, a vision now etching itself into my consciousness that will surely haunt me forever.

Moonlight washes over Hayden's damp skin, highlighting the defined grooves of his abs and pectorals and brightens the towel wrapped low around his waist. Low enough to see the V pointing down to his...

My mouth dries like I swallowed a ladle of sand as I breathe in his glorious scent that mingles with a citrusy body wash.

"What was that?" a tiny voice asks through the speaker, right when a deeper one purrs above my head. "Did you get lost on the way back to your room, baby? Or were you looking for mine?"

I tilt my head back—and back—until I meet his smoldering eyes. A playfulness churns behind them, exactly like our mishap outside my room earlier. But this time, determined to seem unphased, I hold his gaze tightly, even though every muscle in my being wants to explore his body, to look straight down at his...

He leans forward, his nose nearly touching mine, and chuckles, the sound blasting heat between my thighs. "You can look, Jules," he whispers in the dark. "I won't tell anyone."

I open my mouth, but no words come out, not even a sound, which only satisfies him more. Time slows to a measly crawl as he sweeps a loose bang behind my ear, his touch possessive, and nicks the side of my glasses, before it travels down, down, down, sloping across my sensitive nape, shoulders, then explores the middle of my back.

I suck in a shallow breath, gravitating into him, as—

"O.M.G. Do you have a *boy* over?!"

Mei's quiet screech awakens my common sense. *Girl, what is wrong with you??? Your brother's best friend may look like a snack, but that doesn't mean you need a taste. Hayden Kingston is bad, bad news.*

I jerk back, making the mistake of pushing off his abs, which will surely linger on my fingertips for the rest of the night. He seems to know that, too, as his devilish grin grows wider, along with his already over-inflated ego.

He winks. "I could text you a pic instead."

Gosh!

I dash down another hallway as fast as my bunny slippers can manage, yet again leaving his chuckles in my wake. Huffing and puffing, I take the back roads to my bedroom. In minutes—or maybe hours, not that time is of any concept in my frantic reality—I'm slamming my door closed, then sliding down its wooden frame.

Indescribable sounds spew from my pants pocket, before I remember Mei, who's still on the line. I retrieve my phone and put her on speaker, letting her gibberish ring free across my dim room, lit only by the light trickling in through the windows.

"Did I hear him say you were going back to his bedroom?!" There's no mistaking the joy in her tone.

"N-no..." I gather my breath. "You heard wrong."

"No, I certainly did not!" She laughs, literally *woo-ing* into the microphone, obviously drawing conclusions about my long-lost virginity.

"I'm being serious—"

"Is it that guy you went on a date with? Oh my god, I can't believe you invited him over to your place—what a twenty-first century move..." She blabbers on, bypassing each of my protests. "No, wait. It sounded like you left *him*, not the other way around—so you must be at his place. Holy shit, you did the walk of shame after doing the dirty deed, before the sun even rose?! God, Juliana, I didn't know I created a *heart-breaker!* Did you..."

I rub my palms into my eyelids, vaguely answering her questions as they dart out one after the other. Each of which breathes life into more and more lies, seemingly feeding the rift in my mind between protecting this arrangement and being a good friend, until I'm adrift, lost in my own sea of guilt, and confronted with the truth.

Mei wouldn't jeopardize this arrangement.

Sure, she may freak out and go all *big sister mode* on Hayden, threatening him with a long list of social repercussions if things were to turn sour, but beneath it all... she would listen with open ears and hear out my reasons for signing the contract. Which only leaves one explanation for all my lies.

I'm embarrassed. Afraid of her judgment that may never come. And what a weak reasoning that is, because this deal with Hayden? It's temporary. But my friendship with Mei might span over a lifetime and, frankly, every lie crossing my lips right now is undermining its weight, regardless of my peculiar circumstances.

Because a true friend shouldn't suffer at the helm of your shame.

"Mei..." I whisper, a hush even ghosts couldn't hear.

"... well, it was your first time, so surely not *everything* went perfectly, but *sheesh,* from the outside, he sure looks like he knows what he's doing down there—"

"Mei."

She quiets abruptly. For several heartbeats, there's an aching silence between the phone lines, before worry slithers through her tone. "Yeah?" she says, so soft it grips at my emotions, as if I'm moments from confessing secrets to my own mother.

Picking at the sides of my nails, I take a considerable breath, suddenly glad I'm not looking her in the eye for this. "I need to tell you something." And I do, tell her. Every uncomfortable little detail. Down to the last drop.

FOURTEEN
HAYDEN

I'M a little kid playing dress up at the kiddy table. Who's been instructed to sit still, not touch anything, and keep his lips zipped, or there will be consequences. At least... that's how I'm interpreting my new *internship*, if it's worthy of such a label.

Let me rewind.

Today, on a Saturday—*ahem*, I'll say that one more time. On. A. Sat-ur-day, my brother called me at *seven-thirty* in the morning to meet him at work. I mean, who does he think he is, demanding my presence like I'm some maid at such an hour? It was positively cruel. Inhumane. And I'm still debating whether I should file a complaint with H.R., only so they know that these gorgeous eyes don't open until at least eleven a.m.

Anyways, after that, I was in a near-blinded state, with limited motor coordination without my precious beauty sleep, under-eye bags and all, yet I still somehow managed to get dressed and drive to Kingston Entertainment. *Myself.* Yeah, that's correct. The asshole didn't even have the decency to send a driver, which obviously justified my ten-minute tardiness.

Or so I thought.

The second I stepped into the lobby at the base of the skyscraper, my older brother, Elias, was right there, tapping his foot impatiently and more than happy to chew my ass out in front of each and every corporate drone who strutted by us. *On a fucking Saturday.*

Apparently, according to all high-and-mighty, I was thirty minutes late, not ten. To which I replied *"tomato tomahto"* — no, really, those were my exact words, which were not tolerated well, might I add, and quickly propelled him into his *second* quarrel with me.

My outfit...

I know, *I know*—thank you.

How could anyone possibly think that, right? I'm one of *Cosmopolitan Magazine's Top 10 Sexiest Men Alive* this year... and the last... and the year before that... and the year be—oh, you get the picture. Anyone with a brain half the size of a walnut could realize an impeccable fashion sense comes with that sort of territory.

And, not to mention.

Rule # 6: A playboy always dresses to impress.

Yet somehow, my brother still took issue with my cream chinos, suede loafers, and silky patterned button-down, complete with a pair of Ray-Bans perched at the top button. A look that was refined, casually sophisticated with a slight edge, and honestly impressive, given my unfortunate circumstances this morning.

But Elias had none of it and swiftly sent me off to his office to change into a gray two-piece suit. *His* suit, which hung in a row of several others. I didn't even know offices came with closets—and matching sofa sets—but discovering that his did was both unsurprising and rather sad. For his social life, of course.

And now, for the past four agonizingly long hours, I've sat here. Not in my own office. *Outside his.* Behind a table fit for a glorified assistant—minus the glory.

With Doris.

In my peripheral, she sidelongs me from her considerably larger desk, her wrinkly lips pursing in a frown, the one she's worn since I got here. A stark difference from a few hotties I *have* seen around the office—like this redhead, for instance, coming right toward us.

My gaze pokes above my monitor carefully, watching her hips sway in a tight pencil skirt. A black blazer hangs off her shoulders, and she carries a clipboard beneath a dense textbook. On paper, totally not my type, but well in my range to pull. As she nears closer, I settle back in my chair, propping my chin on my knuckles. Casual yet focused. Mysterious. The new guy in the office she's dying to—

She breezes on by without a glance.

I blink, dumbfounded. *Am I invisible today?*

I glance down, half expecting to find dust gathered on an empty chair. Nope. Just me, wrapped in boring gray.

Is that it?

No. If anything, the suit should make me *more* appealing in a place like this, especially an Armani suit that probably cost my brother a cool five-thousand dollars. One that fits me like a glove, seeing as my brother is nearly my identical carbon copy, in all ways physical.

Then, what is it...?

My eyes flick from my small desk to his impressive office. Curtains draw low across the glass lining the inner wall, shielding him from onlookers, all except one, nearest to my desk. Although his oak door remains shut, his voice drifts past the wood faintly, exuding confidence and prowess as he consults whoever he's taking a meeting with right now. I've lost track at this point.

Elias Kingston, Director of Finance, the door reads in shiny acrylic.

Bingo. There lies the culprit of my ghostliness.

Outside of these walls of corporate hell, I'm the man on the hunt in his own domain. But inside, I'm my brother's bitch lackey, evident from this desk he crammed me behind. The office bombshells must snuff out my inferiority like sharks detect blood in the water.

"Why is that report taking you so long?" Doris sneers, pushing her red cat-eye glasses up her nose. Even *she* won't look in my direction. Not because my brother *and* my father's executive secretary holds any grudge against my lowly status, but because she's too damn busy.

Contrary to her... *aged* appearance, her mind hasn't a day. Her gaze flicks left and right, to the charts and planners and twenty-plus tabs open on her dual monitors, as her short nails skate across her keyboard, seconds from catching flame.

I stare at the documents on my screen, practically hearing a dial-up sound between my own ears. Greeting my poor eyes are a jumble of Excel blocks and flow charts and all the nasty stuff that's stirring memories from my high school math classes. I'm supposed to be making a quarter-one revenue analysis PowerPoint. I'm on slide two.

"Uhh..." I type some nonsense at not even one-tenth her speed, catching my brother's shadow standing behind the window in my peripheral. "There's just a lot of... numbers."

Her typing stops abruptly, and *God* is it not the most

intimidating thing. My brother's muffled tone floats through our silence, his smug smile growing as he converses in his meeting while staring straight down at me, when Doris snaps her head in my direction. Elias sinks his hands into his pockets, resting on the backs of his heels.

Ready to watch me get torn to shreds.

"Too many numbers," she mumbles incredulously. "How far in are you?"

I scratch the back of my head, smacking my knee into the desk with a grimace for perhaps the tenth time today, earning a snort on the opposite side of the glass. "I'm... a good amount of the way through."

Her frown deepens. "Have you even reached out to Katie yet?"

Katie... *Katie, Katie, Katie, Kat*—oh, yeah. The girl in accounting I needed information from. Something about overhead costs and operating expenses, yada, yada. "Yeah, I sent her an email." *But there were twenty-three Katies at Kingston Entertainment,* I neglect to add. *I just picked a few and called it good.*

She sighs heavily. *"And...?"*

"And she hasn't gotten back to me."

Elias snickers again, louder this time. I'd swear he could hear our conversation, if it weren't for the mortification spreading across Doris' features, like a giant billboard of my incompetence, staining her cheeks angrily. "You didn't think to call?"

Now she wants me to call all twenty-three Katies? Well, that doesn't sound very efficient to me.

"I did," I lie. "Went to voicemail."

Her eyes narrow into slits. "Really?"

I nod, humming confidently. Only for the color to drain

from my face when she picks up her phone and starts dialing. *Shit.* "Actually, I meant—"

Doris swivels in her chair, pinning me on the spot. "Why hello, *Katie...* Oh, nothing, just making sure your phone's working." She smiles at me. "My new intern said he couldn't reach you. Seems he has a lot to learn... Mhmm, I know... Sorry to be a bother. Goodbye now." She slaps the phone back on its cradle roughly, her mouth agape on what's surely a promise of endless paperwork and scut, until Elias' door creaks open.

"... and be sure to include a section about their quarterly budget variances. We're encroaching into their market space, so double check everything."

"Yes, Mr. Kingston." A soft voice drifts our way. Doris holds her tongue and swings back toward her desk, plopping a pair of headphones on, before a young woman walks out in tall heels, clad in a matching skirt-blazer combo. "I'll have that report back to you next week."

Elias leans against the doorframe, the spitting image of industry royalty. "I need it by Monday."

Unashamed, his eyes crawl down her body, then flick back up. His appearance is so similar to mine yet colder, harder, and suddenly it's like I'm outside of my own skin, watching me drink in Juliana's presence for the first time and the last.

A nervous chuckle passes her ruby lips as she sweeps a bang behind her ear. "Of course, Mr. Kingston. I'll get it done."

"Good." He smirks, dismissing her with a nod.

After a shy *goodbye,* her heels eat up the carpet past my desk, rendering me invisible once again. Annoyance crackles across my skin as I catch the blush staining her cheeks and the devilish fire raging in Elias's eyes.

I scoff and cross my arms.

"Do you have something you'd like to say, Hayden?" he drawls, fixating on her long legs.

"Seems like we're not so different, are we?"

"Don't answer a question with a question."

Power-tripping maniac.

"Sorry, your highness." I stifle a laugh when his jaw ticks. Finally, his head turns to me. *Down* to me, more like. "Let me rephrase. After watching that, I almost forgot you're engaged."

"Oh, please, like you're one to lecture about monogamy." He gives me a bored look. "If you really care to know, Andrea and I's engagement is strictly business. We opened the relationship up a long time ago. She can mess with whomever she pleases, and same goes with me. As long as we don't end up on some gossip tabloid, there's no problem."

Hmph. That actually makes... an awful lot of sense.

I nearly let him off the hook, until I remember the whole reason for starting this pointless mind game in the first place. *He's a hypocrite,* who never misses an opportunity to bad mouth my promiscuous nature. Yet here he is, surveying the landscape in his own place of work.

"What happened to not shitting where you eat?"

His smile is brash. "She's an intern. She won't be here long."

Gross. What a fantastic loophole.

"Bet the report you assigned her is actually useful," I grumble beneath my breath.

Sure, I haven't put forth an ounce of effort and I'm actively avoiding my own report, but that's because it's pointless. Truly pointless. No one in this company, least of all my brother, will find a use for it, seeing as this particular quarter-one revenue analysis is from *three years back and already exists.* I'm replicating it for absolutely no reason.

Like I said. I'm a little kid who can't touch anything.

Sensing my irritation, Elias creeps toward me, a lion stalking a gazelle. His eyes flick over my shoulder to my monitor, and as he draws closer, the redness in them becomes increasingly noticeable, his pupils dilated to an unnatural size.

Seriously, when's the last time he's slept? I think, but keep my opinion to myself, not wishing to hear about how I've never worked a day in my life.

I shuffle in my small chair, avoiding his intense gaze, and return to my monitor.

"How's that report coming along?" he asks, as if he already knows the answer. *Which he does.* "Ahh," he hums. There's no mistaking the delight in his tone. "And yet you wonder why you were given the easy stuff."

Under the table, my hands clench into fists. What's most infuriating about this whole thing is I don't even *want* a serious assignment. I couldn't care less about Kingston Entertainment, financial records, or stuffy office buildings. But the fact that I wasn't even given a chance...

"Don't act like any part of this internship is real. Dad may have sprung it on you, but you love any chance to gloat."

"Hayden, Hayden..." His tongue clicks sarcastically. "I'm hurt. After all we've been through?" I roll my eyes, only for my stomach to drop at the following silence. He speaks in a near whisper. "Dad sat you in this chair, not me." Pity shines through his words. Only a sliver, but for Elias, it may as well be a mountain.

I swivel in my chair, meaning to say something—what that something is exactly, I don't really know. Maybe a question. An observation. *Anything* at all that would slot his feet into my shoes for once, so he can feel what it's like to be the outcast. The pit stain of the Kingston family.

But that something never comes.

Standing proudly in the doorway, the golden son faces me again, all that pity slicking off him like rain, splashing onto the toes of his Oxfords.

He winks. "Have fun with Doris."

FIFTEEN

HAYDEN

FOR THE NEXT HOUR, I suffer through typing at the speed of a snail, Doris's verbal lashings, judgmental glares, and the absolute shitstorm that is Elias on the phone. Even still, when not a sorry soul remains in the building besides the three of ours, his curtains remain fully drawn in secrecy and his heated negotiations blare through the thin walls, growing louder and more anxious.

It's a miracle he's still got a full head of hair.

I check my watch. *Five o'clock on the dot. Time to get the hell out of Dodge.*

Much to the disapproval of Doris, I flick off my monitor, then kick my shoes up on the desk with an exaggerated groan, not even halfway done with my report. And like the good little assistant I've been forced to play... I wait... *and wait...* for my dismissal. Not from Doris, but Elias, whose arguments show no signs of letting up.

I thrum my knuckles on the side of my chair, flipping a pen between my fingers, and when I start whistling, Doris shakes her head, seething with contempt.

After five minutes of my precious time crawl by, I bolt to my feet, pacing outside his door like a—

A roar erupts from inside Elias's office. *"Well, fuck you too, then!"* The hairs rise on the back of my neck, followed by a sharp slam of what I presume to be his phone. I blink, peeking at Doris, who only click-clacks away on her keyboard, humming.

And, *shit,* am I not the worst brother in New York City when I can't stop a snicker from spewing past my lips. Oh, man... for the guy who always seems to have it all together, this new insight into Elias is quite enlightening, to say the least.

Not wanting him to take another call and leave me twiddling my thumbs, and partly driven by the urge to gloat, I stroll through his office door. "Gee, bro, have you ever tried meditation? It might do you some—"

My snide remark fizzles out into thin air, overpowered by a sharp inhale, a sound I instantly recognize from strip joints or house parties or the bathroom stalls at clubs.

But never from the nostrils of my own brother.

Whether I see the mental image coming or not, doesn't alleviate the surprise that twists my gut when I swing the door open to Elias bent over his oak table, snorting a line of white powder.

"Uhhh," he groans on a curse, stumbling back while pinching his nose. Shaking his head violently, oblivious to my presence, he makes for the wall of floor-to-ceiling windows, before smacking them with vigor. *"Woo!"* he bellows, his hands trembling at his sides.

I'm stuck in the doorway, my ankles deep in a case of cement, when he turns his suit-clad body. "Oh, hey. Didn't see you there." He chuckles with a smile—a real smile—and gestures toward his desk. "You want some?"

His glassy-eyed stare steals the wind from me, closes my throat like a paper straw—tighter than the rolled-up Benjamin on his table and colder than the Black Amex lain beside two more lines. Sorrow pangs in my chest, facing his red stare once more, his pupils blown wide.

Maybe I'm not fit to judge. No, scratch that. I'm definitely *not* fit to judge. If all truth be told, I've partaken in my fair share of drugs, snorted cocaine off hookers' tits, smoked the devil's lettuce, drunk my way down the bottle through every nightclub in Manhattan and Vegas and Ibiza, then *fucked* the bottle service girls.

Okay? Feel slimy about me yet? Good. Sue me, because you won't catch me crying my heart out in some priest's confession booth. What's done is done. Simple as that. I've had my fun—*still* have my fun. But this, this right here?

This is something else entirely.

Yes, everyone and their mother know drugs are bad. They *are* bad, for a myriad of reasons; some I pick and choose, while others I knowingly shove under the rug for the sake of a good time. And call me a delusional hypocrite—quite the theme in my family—but Elias isn't *having* a good time.

He isn't wasted with friends, giving in to peer pressure, making questionable decisions he knows he'll wake up loosely regretting tomorrow morning, all in the name of making memories in his youth that maybe he'll tell his kids one day when they're old enough... only to do it all over again next weekend.

No. None of that is a part of his reality. He's right here. In his bougie corporate office. On a beautiful Saturday. Grappling with mounting pressure by snorting lines of cocaine.

All. Alone.

And if there's anything I know about my older brother... he doesn't do anything halfway. Nothing is *just a phase* for him.

"Don't give me that look."

"I'm not," I lie, closing the door behind me.

He gestures once more as he rounds his desk. "Then you want some?"

"I'm good."

His lips flatten. "Ah. It's like that, huh?"

"Like what?" I ask, already sensing anger boiling in my center.

"You—Hayden, self-identifying playboy and party animal —are too good for me. I never thought I'd see the day."

"That's not what I'm—"

He taps the oak slab, inches from the powder. "I seem to recall the cops confiscating five kilos at that little stunt you threw at Dad's house months back, which ended up all over the tabloids."

It was six kilos, actually... None of which I touched. Not that he'd believe that.

A smirk kisses his lips when I remain silent. "Half of New York City knows you're no saint, so don't pretend to be one."

"Fine." I fold my arms. "But even you can see how this is different."

He's about to hit me with what I'm sure is a clever rebuttal, when the phone on his desk interrupts him. Leaning over, he checks the caller, and there's no missing the way his shoulders tense. He picks up the phone, then slams it back down, whipping his startling gaze onto me.

"Is it so different?" He scrapes his card across the polished oak, collecting white flecks that've gone astray into his second line. "Last I checked, we're snorting the same snow, Brother. Don't believe me? Watch."

Reluctantly, I do, not that a second time eases the queasiness I feel any more than the first.

"Ohh, fuckkk." Grunting, he squeezes his eyes tightly, stumbling backwards like before, nearly smacking into the wall. Urgency blasts through me, and I'm half convinced something's wrong, until he literally *woofs* like a rabid dog—or an overzealous frat guy—and beats his chest with a fist. *"Fuck!* You see that? Don't tell me this is any different, like you haven't felt this *exact* high."

"I have, but—"

"But nothing." He saunters across the room with no destination in sight, mindlessly pacing, the rush shot straight to his brain. "Let me tell you..." he drifts off, heading toward the pull-out couch that's far-too lived in, then swerves my way, pointing a finger.

"Let me tell you the *real* difference between you and me. I keep my shit under lock and key, where it doesn't affect the family. And this?" He nods to the coke. "You *need* that shit, for your little party life. With your little party friends. For your *fun,"* he seethes, and I don't quite believe the twinge of jealousy I hear. "But me? I *utilize* it, for its greatest purpose." He presses a finger to his temple. "To keep me sharp between the ears while I'm negotiating multi-million-dollar deals and running numbers all. Day. Long. And—"

He jolts when the phone rings once more. And *again,* he checks the caller I.D., curses below his breath, and slams the phone in its cage, rougher than before. Then he's eyeing that long third line, an amount I rarely see anyone attempt...

"Who were you on the phone with earlier?" I ask quickly, feeling desperate when his gaze doesn't veer. "You sounded awfully pent up... *Very* unprofessional." I force a chuckle, which earns his attention.

His lips curl in disgust. "A CEO. He's a total jackass."

Keep him talking, keep him talking...

"Oh, yeah? What'd you want with him?"

For a split second, his eyes narrow into slits. *Good,* I think, *he's lucid enough to recognize my trickery.* Until he shrugs, giving me the benefit of the doubt. Very *un-Elias-Kingston* of him.

"Kingston Entertainment wants to buy stock from his company, PixelForge. Gain some capital and market trust in the gaming sector, but he's too stubborn."

"Is that who keeps calling you?"

Sighing, he plops down onto his chair, the movement chipping away at my anxiety. "Yep. He's probably realizing my low-ball numbers weren't really all that low. Or he's putting his assistant up to it, more likely, having her call me with another insultingly high counter offer. But this isn't my first rodeo. I'm putting him on ice. Let him think I've moved on to a different company."

There's the Elias I know.

My pulse calms, but shoots right back up when his head swivels again. It's then I realize I'll do anything, say anything, to keep him from that third line—even bring up Juliana's side of the deal in the worst possible timing. Something I planned for later, once I gained more footing in the company, but now is the least of my concerns.

"So, uh..." I motion toward him, opting to sit in one of the leather chairs in front of his desk. "You're serious about moving into gaming, then?"

His eyes find mine, and their hazy fog lifts a bit. "Definitely. The board's already approved of the strategy, too, and for good reason. The market grew over fifteen percent just last year..."

His voice drifts through my one ear and out the other as he spouts off decimals, floating-point numbers and market share caps, yada, yada, all of which I had the misfortune of overhearing at our last family dinner.

I just nod, until his lips stop moving. "Was it your idea to sponsor games at this year's DreamScape?"

"Yep." He sighs proudly and leans back in his chair, propping an ankle up on his knee. "All me. It's the best way to get consumers' eyes on our company, to be taken seriously in the market. Maybe we'll host our own gaming convention someday, but that's years down the line."

"I see..." I rub my chin, feigning deep thought. "And who gets the final say in which games get picked?"

He cocks his head. "The sudden gaming enthusiast, are you now?"

I fake an awkward laugh. "Just curious, is all."

"Well, if you really must know, I'm picking the games."

My stomach slingshots down to the fucking floor, a cough I somehow stifle rippling up my throat. If my reaction isn't written plainly on my face, he doesn't say. *He's* picking? That can't be right. Because that would mean... *My deal with Juliana is a waste of time.*

Well, not a *complete* waste. I much prefer seeing her sleeping under my roof than her old apartment, even if it's in the guest bedroom and not mine. Especially when she practically lives in skin-tight yoga pants and has the uncanny ability of putting herself in the most tempting situations.

I wet my lips as the scene from last night replays in my mind, when she bumped into me fresh out of the shower, and the mishap by the window... Juliana may roll her eyes and scoff at my dubious remarks, but there's no denying how well she responds to my touch. The way she gravitates toward it, so eager to please me, and loses all control, practically begging for—

Stop it. I grit my teeth. *Now's literally the worst time to pop a boner. Not to mention, it's inappropriate.*

It's not the first time I've thought of her today. Quite the opposite, actually. Earlier, I blamed the recurrence on my boring report, my mind drifting, to no avail, but I'm not at my desk anymore, safe to hide my untimely arousal. I'm in front of *my brother's.*

I stuff down Juliana and her enticing everything, forcing myself to contemplate the *real* reason for my poor reaction. Why having Elias choosing who does and doesn't get a feature is bad news.

Juliana's supposed to have an advantage. Not only because she'll gain a one-on-one audience with whoever's decision it is, but also because that someone should be *our father,* who'll choose her girly kitty game no matter what, once he recognizes how good my new girlfriend is for my reputation. But if that's out the window, then—

"Dad has the final say, as always, though," he says, his tone laden with annoyance.

Air darts back into my lungs.

Thank. God. Couldn't he have just led with that?

"Is that the case with the indie creator feature as well?"

Now he looks *super* suspicious. "You're really beating around the bush here, Hayden. Is there something you'd like to ask me?"

I scratch the back of my head. "Uhh..." *Fuck, this is even weirder than I thought it'd be.* "It's nothing. I just know someone who'd be interested in the spot. A... *friend.*"

"Reaalllyyy?" he drawls, his eyelids drooping. "One of *your* friends created a video game they'd like featured at the nerdiest convention on Earth?"

"Well... not exactly a friend."

Jesus H. Christ. You'd think I'm confessing to murder.

"Today, Hayden." He yawns. "Out with it."

I tug at my collar, which suddenly feels two sizes too small, my entire suit growing heavy and suffocating. "More like my... *girlfriend.*"

The word floats between us, sounding ten different shades of *wrong,* as if I just spoke Mandarin Chinese without possessing the tongue for it. I've never had a girlfriend. *Ever.* Not even in high school.

Elias only stares at me, frozen, one-hundred and ten percent stone-cold sober... In a flash, he doubles over, nearly flopping out of his chair, literally howling at the ground with laughter.

Embarrassment burns my cheeks as I watch him smack the table, gasping for air. "What... what the *fuck* did I just hear?!"

"It's not that big of a—"

"Ahh!" he barks, combusting in another fit. "Who even are you...?" He swipes the tears brimming his eyes. "Who are you, and what have you done with my younger brother?"

I roll my eyes. "Are you done yet?"

"Sorry—sorry!" He breathes, in and out, settling back in his chair. "Come on. You really think I'm buying that? *You,* dating a gamer chick? What, are you attending church on Sundays now, too?"

Again, with the church analogy. Are him and Jeremy passing notes or something?

"Fine, fine," I grumble, looking out the windows. "It's more of an... off-and-on kinda thing."

"You don't say, Mr. Monogamy." A snicker breezes past his lips. "I was two minutes shy of sending you off to get your head checked out."

Could he be any more dramatic?

"Will you consider her game or not?"

His eyebrows lift. "Gosh, Hayden, if I didn't know any better, I'd say you're acting a little defensive over this nerdy girl. Don't tell me—are you catching feelings?"

My face screws up in disgust.

Feelings... I can hardly repeat the word, even in my headspace. To me, it's a foreign concept, a disease I've never caught and don't plan to. *Feelings... for Juliana... my best friend's little—*

No, I block out the thought. *No, no, no.* I'm not going there, and never will. There's only one thing I want from her—from any attractive woman, for that matter. Sex. *S.E.X.* I repeat this familiar word in my mind instead, hoping to drown out the last one.

Once I'm successfully rewired and back to normal, I smirk. "Don't answer a question with a question." Elias shoots me a look, and I have to bite my lip from laughing. "Will you consider her game or not?" I ask again.

His answer is lackluster, but it's all we need.

"Fine."

SIXTEEN
HAYDEN

TEN HOURS.

Ten *fucking* hours.

That's how long Elias kept me chained to my cell—I mean desk—today. My precious Saturday *gone.* Sure, it's only nine o'clock and the night is still young, but my spine feels like it belongs to a centenarian. And I won't even start on how strained my eyes are.

I shuffle through the front door, my shoulders sagging low, as I dangle a plastic takeout bag in one hand and my keys in the other, aiming for my bedroom.

When my phone buzzes in my pocket, I don't hold back my groan. I can already picture the drunken photo sent to our boys' group chat or blasted across social media just fine without opening it. Judging by the time, they're probably at some bar scarfing down buffalo wings, shooting tequila, and getting familiar with members of the opposite sex, before they crawl to the next place.

Unfortunately, it's hard to bar hop crippled.

I trudge down a long hallway, mumbling curses under my

breath about the penthouse's size, trailing a hand across the wall for support. Juliana's nowhere to be found; there's not a peep to be heard, and darkness shrouds my surroundings, save for the city's faint gleam through the windows, the glow from the kitchen, and the sliver of light trickling out from beneath her bedroom door.

Intending to chow down on my sushi platter while cozied up in bed, I pass right by without a glance, until I notice something from the corner of my eye.

I quirk a brow at the piece of paper taped to the fridge. It doesn't take me more than three paces to recognize what it is —and who's to blame for its inception. Juliana really went to all the trouble, typed out our entire contract, printed it, then slapped it right in the center of my home???

A handwritten note reads in red ink at the bottom. *Thought you could use a little reminder* — smiley face. I stare at the two eyes and wide lips, taking them for what they really are.

A taunt. She's *taunting* me.

Why would I need a reminder? Of the rules my self-assigned nanny forced upon me? As if I could forget them, even if I tried. Which I'm not, seeing as my gaze trails down the rules, one by one, each more ludicrous and offensive than the last.

"No throwing parties..." I mumble to myself quietly, annoyance rising inside of me. "No social media posts... Sleep in separate beds... Remain romantically exclusive." My snicker rings across the empty kitchen. "Romance? What kinda guy does she take me for...?" I wonder, before all the humor dies out with the last rule, one I can't read aloud.

Practice sexual abstinence.

And right below is my own signature, now digitized for

all eternity, captured by a copying machine that I don't even own.

She just loves going the extra mile, doesn't she...

I do the mental math, counting the weeks from today to DreamScape, and grimace, as if faced with the judge's hammer. My sentencing? Two months.

Two.

Whole.

Months.

Without sex.

That's sixty days. *Sixty nights,* without doing the dirty deed. *Me,* the very definition of getting more ass than a toilet seat. I don't remember the last time I've been dry for so long. It goes against my lifestyle, my very nature. I'm not even sure if my brain will still be intact by the time the days are up, if I'll be the same Hayden Kingston.

What the hell did I sign up for?

PORN SUCKS.

Take it from someone who lost track of his own body count years ago, porn really, really sucks. Although, maybe that's my problem—having too much experience rocking the bed with too many women, as to acutely know when one is faking her own pleasure.

Like the blonde porn star on my phone, with the voluptuous fake tits and a schoolgirl skirt. Her moans are forced. Her tone about three notches past natural. The line between her eyebrows cinched way too tight. It's not her fault, either, seeing as Mr. Nine Inch Schlong And Anabolic Steroids is barreling into her at blazing speeds, hitting her cervix with the gentle care of a jackhammer, all after giving her zero attention.

No foreplay. No oral. No fingering. No butt-play, kisses on the neck, dirty talk, words of affirmation, licking, roleplay, flicking the bean, sensual massages... *Nothing.* He's the man who's afraid to eat pussy, yet dares ask for a blowjob, a sexual criminal without lube who places his own needs above hers. Which leaves the woman with only one choice, if she is to enjoy such a lousy experience—turning *herself* on.

Hence the fake moaning.

And yes, I acknowledge that this porn star is just doing her job; she's quite literally following a script, and porn isn't an accurate representation of real-life sex, but it sure does bleed into it. Bright lights in a staged living room with a straight-faced cameraman or not, she's still having to take every teensy-weensy ounce of her pleasure into her own hands.

As someone who's unashamedly starred in more than a few home videos, there's no bigger insult, and it's, in my professional opinion, the tell-tale difference between a playboy and a fuckboy.

Rule #7: A playboy never finishes before his sexual partners.

Just ask yourself. How could a fuckboy cater to such a rule, if the *oh-so mysterious and elusive* clitoris isn't even on his radar?

I'll give you a hint: he's not.

To conclude my monologue that no one asked for—yes, as surprising as it may be, I hate ninety-nine percent of porn, evident not only in my surprising values on women's sexuality but also its in-effectiveness on me. And by me, I mean the absence of my boner.

Rant over.

As Miss Blondie twists into a pretzel, I watch with about as much enthusiasm as I would if she were instead teaching trigonometry—fully clothed. I sigh, propping an arm behind my head. With empty takeout containers as my sole companions, my Alaskan king feels achingly barren. More nights than not, I have company or I'm slipping between someone else's sheets entirely. But never alone.

My lips flatline at the next ridiculous position, before I make to close the video. At this rate, I'm better off using my imagination, even if my fantasies defy my better judgment and inevitably circle back to Ju—

Ding.

A text banner drops from the top of my screen.

Olivia: *I'll show you mine, if you show me yours. ;)*

I suck in a breath and hold. *Now* that's *how you get my attention.*

My thumb hovers over the text, as I think back to the last time I was with Olivia. It's all a hazy blur of little talk and more action, if you know what I mean, aboard a private Gulfstream G650 on route to Miami six months back for a bachelor party. It was far from my first time joining the mile-high club, and it sure as hell wasn't hers, being that she's a flight attendant and it wasn't our first rodeo.

Olivia flies all across the world, working on different planes, some private, others commercial, and sometimes we just happen to be in the same area or aboard the same jet. We must've met on a flight... two years back? I don't know. But our conversations are always kept to a minimum. In fact, we probably haven't spoken more than ten words to each other, ever, save for occasional sexting.

Zero commitment, just how I like it.

Which is why, when I finally do click the message, the photo I'm met with comes as no shock.

My eyes trail from the only visible part of Olivia's face, her wicked smirk, down to the picture's focal point—her rack. A wet white T-shirt covers her unnaturally lifted breasts, leaving only so much for the imagination. Her nipples press taut against the thin fabric, just enough to make out their shape and color.

I don't hold back my groan.

Finally. Something to help tide me over.

My shirt's off in two seconds flat, leaving me in gray sweatpants with nothing underneath. I rip off the covers, bring the camera close to my face, and aim downward, revealing my body in all its glory.

And I *do* mean glory. I won't sugarcoat it. My physique is incredible. Plain and simple. This photo I'm about to take looks photoshopped, in more ways than one, and I'm not even showing my face. Just my deeply defined abs, gloriously sun-kissed skin, the magnificent city view as my backdrop inside a penthouse fit for a king, and most notably, my impressively large, perfectly proportioned, raging hard co—

...wait a minute.

I blink, noting the lack of activity *down there*. Squinting, I turn up my phone's brightness, zoom in and out in disbelief, even sway my head to the side, inspecting with my own two eyes, only to find a flat, underwhelming bump beneath my sweatpants.

That can't be right...

I bring up Olivia's photo again, confirming that my brain *does*, in fact, like what it sees. Once more, I study her breasts slowly, admiring their fullness and symmetry, wanting nothing more than to watch her peel off that pesky T-shirt.

When I'm practically foaming at the mouth like some horny teenager, I pull up my camera once more, grinning when I angle it—

Hey, what gives?

I bob my head to the left, then to the right, utterly flabbergasted at what's *not* going on in my pants.

Can this day get any worse?

I grumble, squeeze my eyes shut, and shove the dirtiest, most filthy memories of Olivia to the forefront of my brain. Ones where I'm taking her from behind inside luxurious bathrooms, forty-thousand feet high, bending her over the sink while her pencil skirt jumbles around her waist and panties pool at her feet. Her uniform's scarf coming quite handy in covering up all the marks I leave on her neck...

A low groan escapes me, as my hand sweeps down my core, delving beneath my waistband—

My eyes snap open.

I feel around, skin on skin. Dick, balls, everything. And by everything, I mean *nothing*. Nada. Zip. No erection, no rocket in my pocket, bone ranger, tent pole, saluting soldier, firm worm—whatever the fuck people call it *is just not there.*

My pulse spikes, beading sweat across my hairline. I'm twenty-four years old, built like a horse—an Arabian thoroughbred stud, specifically—with testosterone coursing through my veins, who's got a hot flight attendant on the phone, willing to show everything...

I should be like granite. Not a wet noodle.

Do I need to call a doctor or something?

Frustrated, I click back to her message.

I'll show you mine, if you show me yours. ;)

I stare at the text, hoping her intentions will re-solidify in my mind, but it doesn't take long before my brow tightens, all my focus shifting on the winky face. Then I'm gaping at the fridge all over again, at Juliana's little smiley face, the one she added just to taunt me. She had to of... Because maybe that's her exact motive—to be a huge, irresistible tease.

Wearing tight yoga pants, bumping into me at night, purposely feeding into my touch, choosing to sleep a few doors down, when she knows all I can think about is fucking her senseless.

Now she slaps our contract in my face, yet again, when she knows, deep down, that I'd much rather see my signature on a different contract altogether. One where she's obligated to share my bed each night, then she couldn't help but give in to my advances, her perfect body offered up for me to do with as I see fit.

My first demand would be simple. No pants. *Ever.* Not in the bedroom, kitchen, living room—nowhere in my penthouse. She'd strut around in nothing but a cropped T-shirt and a pair of panties... preferably the scanty kind... black and lacy... with a bowtie on the front, right below the diamond hanging off her belly button...

I grunt, low and guttural, as pleasure blooms down to my toes, a dark hunger ravaging in its wake, until I'm bucking my hips up into thin air, the friction against my sweatpants tantalizing, surely the furthest cry from thrusting into Ju—

My eyes, which apparently closed on their own, pry open, jolting my entire body into a state of alert. *Oh, don't tell me. Please, please, please...*

I look down.

Ahh, fuck!

Hard and raging with painful need, my erection bulges against my sweatpants, poking its domed head past the waistband. Arousal pumps through me, threading desire along my every waking thought, drowning out any ounce of shame I *should* feel. And it's all nearly too much to handle.

I grit my teeth, forcing my hips still, as I pull out my camera. This is all just a delayed reaction—yes, yes—after fantasizing about *Olivia*. Oh-liv-ee-a. The girl with the tits. Huuuugeeee tits. On my phone. No other girl, no, no, no. Especially not my best friend's little—

JUST TAKE THE FUCKING PICTURE.

Squirming, I readjust and slip my tip back into hiding, then snap a photo. Like clockwork, I test out a few more angles, but in a rush, I pick one before I go full photo-shoot mode. Hitting the send button, I soar down my contacts toward the letter *O*. But on the way, I pause... on letter J... on Juliana Brooks.

Don't do it.

My heart beats to a mischievous rhythm.

Do. Not. Do. It, I warn those intrusive thoughts.

Or what? they sneer back.

Or... Or...

My answer should be as easy as my next breath. There are a dozen reasons I shouldn't hit send. Maybe hundreds. But they're all trapped inside clouds of a brewing storm, now downpouring atop my head droplets filled with lust and possession, fueling a need to hear the girl who made me pledge my celibacy swear off hers. A desire so deep, I can't hear my own thoughts anymore—not even the intrusive ones. So, I do what's easiest...

I let them win.

~

AFTER FIFTEEN TORTUROUSLY-LONG minutes of complete radio silence, my erection is finally—mostly—gone, and so am I.

Out of my bedroom door.

I breeze down the hallway like a puff of smoke, hot and angry, yet quiet and undetectable.

Juliana thinks she can just ignore me? Leave me high and dry? What nerve she has. What gall. Every woman in Manhattan would beg for my attention—*begs,* for it—every time I step out my front door.

Exhaling sharply, I swing a left.

Has she gone downright mad? The picture is immaculate, with the perfect angle and perfect lighting and an even more perfect cock, the definition of a panty-dropper. If posted online, it would've had a going rate of at least five-hundred dollars, and I didn't even show feet.

Yet, her response is no response. I anticipated a lecture, a pounding on my door, an *ewwwww* text laced with denial, *something.*

I hang another left, aware I'm going in circles, until I actually turn down her hallway, spotting a light under her door. *So she IS awake.* Irritated, I make for her bedroom, meaning to pound on *her* door, only to hear the explanation she so obviously owes me.

Creeping farther into the dark hallway, I nearly trip over my own feet, catching the wall, a foot from her bathroom door. No light shines beneath it, but something else sure does...

Sounds.

Breathless sighs.

Sweet, delicious moans.

The first taste of my new addiction.

I press an ear to the door, listening intently. When I hear the evidence of her wetness, a sheer confirmation of what I already knew she was doing, my knees tremble, quaking with restraint. Blood rushes straight to my cock, painful and throbbing, before I do the only thing that'll keep me from kicking the damn door down.

Slip a hand beneath my waistband.

SEVENTEEN

JULIANA

I KEEP ASKING myself how I got here.

But all I have are piss-poor lies.

My pajama bottoms pool around my ankles as I lie in the empty bathtub, rubbing my clit in slow, slow circles. In defiance, I keep my eyes shut, ignoring the alluring photo on my phone, which sits on the lip of the free-standing tub. But it's as if Hayden's burned into my retinas, like a permanent tease in the back of my mind.

When the traitorous thoughts take over, I flick faster and faster, sway my hips harder, and soft moans breeze past my lips. I'm torn in two with an all-consuming pleasure, my every touch dripping away at my shame—

No.

I snap my eyes awake, clamping down on a moan as I cease my ministrations. An aching throb beats between my legs, begging for more, while I force any and all thoughts which start with an *H* and end with an *N* out of my headspace.

For the tenth time, I scan the bathroom, looking for a

distraction. *My* bathroom. Mine. A fact I'll surely never grow to accept, maybe because it's double the size of my old apartment, with floating, modern countertops, a shower fit for three people, and a wall of solid glass, overlooking a view I'd only see in my dreams.

The city lights stream in through the windows, faintly illuminating the marbled floors, walls, the evidence of my touch beneath my panties—and my phone. I whip my head away, after peeking for no more than a split second, but it's far too late.

Lust pours over me, branding my vision with rock-hard abs above a boner that's so large it has to be fake.

Or rather, that was my initial reaction.

There I was, minding my own business after a long day of work, getting ready for bed, pj's and all, brushing my teeth— then *boom.* A raunchy, dirty, *obviously fake* photo pops up on my phone. Just another spam bot on social media, I thought. Highly edited—no man's abs look *that* good, and that dick, even though shrouded in cloth, is clearly one only destined for porn. Again, probably edited. A scammer phishing for dangerous clicks.

That *is* what I thought. Truly.

Until I went to delete the message and saw it wasn't from social media or even a random number, but from someone I had saved in my contacts...

I squeeze my eyes shut once more, harder this time, mentally replaying the first porn scene that comes to mind, over and over. Or fantasies I've had about classmates. Anything at all, except the thoughts that led me here, which are embarrassing and unfathomable and polished with a thick coat of denial.

My most outlandish rationalization I've devised is that I'm

not actually in my body right now. Maybe I'm hypnotized. Or —okay, hear me out, I've watched enough Sci-Fi to know this *could* slip between the realms of possibility...

I've fallen victim to an intelligent host.

No, wait, really. I'm serious.

Someone—or *something*—has taken root in me. A life-form close to its animalistic origins, who's controlled by its primal urges, is using my body as some kinky outlet. The important bit being that it's NOT ME. Want to know why?

Because *that* complete absurdity is more believable than me *masturbating over my brother's best friend*. It would never happen. Not in a million years.

So, no. I have not, in fact, lost my mind. I'm just thinking of... someone else right now. Yeah.

Eyes fluttering, I sink a finger inside myself and stare out the window, letting my head rest and hair crane over the tub's ledge. I suck in my bottom lip, all but failing to quiet a whimper as I pump in and out.

If truth be told, I've only ever used one finger, but that doesn't stop me from imagining that I'm stretching around more. Another pair of fingers, entirely. Not belonging to *he who shall not be named,* but to Reid. A crush from college, who oftentimes, was the object of my fantasies, although I haven't thought of him in over a year.

But now's as good a time as ever.

Charging into an empty classroom on a dirty steed of distraction, Reid bends me over my desk roughly, lifts my skirt, and finds me drenched.

The city lights blur as my toes curl in the tub...

Reid hums behind my ear, full of praise, right as he delves between my panties, prying a moan from me—whether the desperate cry stays locked up in my fantasy or not, I'm not quite sure.

I buck against him, only to be put back into my place by his heavy arm sprawling across my backside, pinning me down. *Don't move,* he scolds, tugging my panties upwards, the movement plunging a wedgie between my slick folds, scraping delicious torture along my clit. Wearing a smirk, he watches me writhe and pant in a crazed heat, before he tugs harder, re-affirming his command.

"Fuck...." I groan, my voice escaping the fantasy...

In my mind, I obey. *That's it, keep still,* Reid purrs, as large hands peruse along my spine, then down the back of my thighs. Anticipation explodes within me when I catch him dropping to his knees, which has me squirming on a mewl.

A *whack* sounds against my ass. I inhale sharply, as a stinging sensation rolls across my body, trailed by a colossal surge of arousal. He sweeps my panties to the side, revealing my wetness, before two strong hands grip my ass cheeks, spreading them wide.

I grip the edge of the tub, bucking my hips against my finger, letting my moans ring true...

But inside my fantasy, I'm more patient. I roll my lips together, stilling myself once again, earning another hum of approval. But this time, the sound is *different,* in a way I can hardly explain. Deeper and huskier, yet... more controlled, as if my obedience comes as no surprise.

Warm breath tickles my pussy, before a voice growls...

That's my good girl.

I gasp, jolting in the tub, as those city lights sharpen back into focus. Frantic, I whip my head around in the darkness, but find no one.

That was Hayden's voice... in my fantasy...

A knot forms in my stomach as my gaze trails down my body, and I note the mess dribbling down my thighs and all over my hands. Withdrawing my finger from inside myself, I look out the windows again, shame burning my cheeks deep enough to see in the dark reflection.

Why can't he just get out of my head? I don't like him like that. Why would my brain replace Reid's voice with Hayden's, when I wasn't even fantasizing about him?

Because Reid would never be so demanding, those little devils whisper. My shoulders droop at their truth. *You only make him that way in your head. But Hayden would know just what to do with you, especially if he knew you were still a virgin...*

A shudder rattles through me, leaving my pussy feeling suddenly touch-starved. I shake my head, snatching my legs together, and focus on the city lights, as if they'll ease the torture.

Light flickers in the window's reflection with a buzzing noise, but I'm too stupid to realize what it's from, before I turn my head and find a new image on my phone. With an irritated huff, I look away, but the damage is already done. I give in, letting the picture hold my eyes hostage for far too long to be healthy.

No longer in bed and standing upright, mysterious dark-ness hides Hayden's surroundings, while the camera's flash reveals his body in all its mouthwatering perfection. Defined pecs and abdominal muscles take up the majority of my phone, while a strong chin peers through the top of the frame. Still clad in nothing but gray sweatpants, the fabric outlines his enormous length, which angles off to the side, pointing toward his hip, slipping beneath...

My interior walls clench around thin air at the sight of his bare tip peeking out of his waistband.

The photo's tagged with a message.

Hayden: *Oops, wrong number. ;)*

I groan, resisting the urge to touch myself, but unable to stop my thighs from rubbing together. So, he *did* mean to send that first pic. My teeth sink into my bottom lip as I hear his praise purr inside my head again.

"No, no, no," I whisper into the darkness, writhing against my agonizing need. Stubbornly, I exhale through my nostrils... in and out... in and out... until my heart rate drops and Hayden's fading away toward the outskirts of my consciousness—

Buzz, buzz.

I freeze, recognizing the sound instantly, seeing how my pulse spikes right along with it, directing my gaze like the yank of a tether. Another photo soars into our feed, same as before, but now his pants hang lower on his hips, revealing a bit more of *down there.*

Goddddd...

My nails dig into my palms.

Hayden: *Ignoring me, huh? Not smart.*

I can practically hear the disapproving *tsk tsk* of his tongue. Adrenaline rushes through my veins as I grapple for my phone with slippery fingers, shooting off a text at the speed of light.

Juliana: *Gross, quit it! I'm trying to sleep.*

But I'm too late—*buzz, buzz.*

My jaw goes limp, nearly smacking the ledge of the tub, upon seeing his sweatpants drooped even lower, revealing the full head of his cock.

The leash on my control finally snaps.

My hands dart back to where I want them—where I *need* them. I cry out, when my finger plunges through my entrance, straight to the knuckle, uncaring of how the tub may amplify my voice. My hips buck as fiery pleasure ripples through my middle, sliding me downward, farther and farther, until I'm flat on my back with my knees spread wide and ankles propped up on the ledge, granting me easy access.

Above my head, another buzz vibrates against the acrylic, but it's drowned out by the blood raging between my ears, and the fantasy burning a hole through my cranium.

But Reid doesn't stand a chance, not for two seconds. Him and the empty classroom, they *poof* from existence, dying on the wake of Hayden's deep chuckle. A shiver races from the top of my head to the tips of my toes, as my fantasy ebbs and sighs and transforms into something anew.

A place where Hayden has full control, where it's *his* lips plunging between my folds, and I'm no longer bent over a desk but pressed up against a wall of glass in the hallway outside my bedroom, just like the other day. But this time, he's on his knees while I'm completely bared to him, fully nude a hundred floors up, with my peaked nipples raking against the glass with each of his movements.

My back arches along the tub as I flick my clit with vigor, utterly devoid of shame...

But what's worse about this fantasy than the last, is although Hayden wraps his arms around my waist, locking me in place, he works me with patience. Like I'm his feast and this is his last meal, which he means to savor.

His tongue sweeps up my center with a groan, nearing my taint, then trails back down to my front, brushing my clit like the tease of a feather. Panting, I jerk back for more, but his arms squeeze tightly, holding me still. Satisfied, he laughs quietly, retracing back through my folds.

Over. And over. And over, again.

Until my moans echo throughout the bathroom, real life and fantasy fuse into one, and I'm mercilessly pumping into myself, in part hating how wet I am, how good *he* feels, while the other sings to his touch.

More, more, more—I need more!

I add another finger, not caring that it's my first time, crying out when I can only fit an inch, right as Hayden sucks my clit into his mouth. A scream lodges deep in my throat, escaping only as drowned-out whimpers, while he traps my sensitive bud between his teeth and flicks his tongue expertly.

My eyes cross in two, forming stars and the promises of regret, before a surge of ecstasy like I've never known tears right through me, swelling then crashing over a white fire. Desperate for more, I thrust harder, stretching myself in beat to every wave, every pulsation squeezing around my fingers, as a name so forbidden slips from my mouth.

Not once. Not twice. But—I don't even know how many times. I only know how it feels, and it feels right and liberating, like the morning sun, and warm and—

My euphoria fades, fleeting as it was captivating.

A-and—and...

I blink, squinting at my surroundings, at the shadow of remembrance stuck in my throat.

... *AND SO WRONG*, I finish my thought on a mental scream, as terrible, *life-ruining* embarrassment takes ahold of me.

Oh no oh no oh no oh no...

Wheezing, surely on the verge of hyperventilating, I readjust my panties, which might as well have been hosed down along with the rest of my nether regions, then yank up my pajama pants, trapping myself in an uncomfortable, soggy situation.

It's fine. Everything's fine.

I grab the ledge of the tub, pulling myself upright.

I'll just take a shower, then tiptoe back to my room. This penthouse is like a thousand square miles, and it's the dead of night. No one heard me, maybe not even God, and especially not the man belonging to the name I moaned out in the dark on a blinding orgasm all alone in my bathtub. Nope. Definitely not. Because this time, for once in my life, I'm in luck. I'm—

Like the looming of a deadly storm, my phone comes into view. Images and message notifications flood my lockscreen, but the most recent text is the only proof I need.

My worst nightmare has come true.

Hayden: *My name sounds so perfect on your lips, baby.*

Pure dread crumbles me to the floor, and suddenly, it's all but obvious why his pictures were in the dark, why he needed to use the flash. My eyes crawl to the door on the farside of the bathroom, which now feels hauntingly quiet. I wait for a sound, a creak of the floorboards, anything to signify a presence.

A minute later, I'm halfway convinced I'm imagining things, until goosebumps scurry across my skin. A taunting voice laughs behind the door, boasting with delight yet painfully strained.

"No need to be shy, Jules. Imagine how much fun we'd have if you let me in next time."

EIGHTEEN
JULIANA

I'VE BECOME A MOLE RAT.

Under the hood of my sweatshirt, my fingers dance along my keyboard, accompanied by the deafening silence streaming through a pair of headphones. With every light flipped off, save for my monitors, I sit in total darkness, surrounded by walls of drawn curtains, as if someone on the street or inside a neighboring skyscraper with a set of binoculars might see what marks my cheeks. What's been there for the past five days.

Shame.

All-consuming, inescapable shame.

Which no doubt swirls in my own eyes, too. Not that anyone's seen them, either, including myself. I've avoided mirrors altogether, including those at The Caffeine Cove. Yep, I even called out of my shifts this week, said I came down with the flu, when I know damn well I'm just avoiding any and all human interaction, since what happened.

Since what *he* heard.

An uncomfortable wave of nausea rolls through me,

prompting a debate of whether I should slither under my bed and never resurface. For a good fifteen-or-so years, at least. Tempting... very tempting, if it weren't for needing to eat.

My stomach growls, right on cue.

"Shhhh," I scold, typing a line of code.

Another rumble, louder this time. *You skipped breakfast,* it seems to say.

"We'll have a big lunch."

What is happening to me? Even a mole rat wouldn't talk to its own gut. This is a new low, Juliana.

A knot twists in response, squeezing a space that's achingly hollow. I grit my teeth, weathering the pain, and glance at the clock. Ten on the dot. I sigh, "Fine."

Clad in my finest attire—baggy sweatpants and an even baggier hoodie—I creep out the door, only to pick up the pace when I realize Hayden should've left for work an hour ago.

Sun blares through the windows like a glistening beacon, lighting up the kitchen in all its grandeur. Squinting, I speed by the marble island, stainless-steel appliances, and enter the walk-in pantry, which is, *again,* surely double the size of my old apartment. No shock there.

But there's no time to gawk.

I stand on my tippy toes, poking around in cupboards that are surprisingly well organized, searching for something quick and easy. A grab-and-go snack. Maybe a granola bar or cereal or—

"I'm not *that* late." Hayden's voice drifts from afar.

Shit.

I dash for the door, but he only grows louder. His tall frame turns into the kitchen, right before I switch off the pantry light, hide behind the door, and hope he doesn't notice that it's open.

"If Elias cares so much, I'll tell him to go take a hike—oh wait, he'd never leave the office."

My heart clammers against my ribs as I anticipate his entry, but when I hear the fridge open, I let loose a breath. Sneaking a peek around the door, I watch Hayden rummage through the fridge while holding a cellphone to his ear with his shoulder.

Surrounded by splendor only extreme riches can afford, he looks ready to get interviewed in some Architectural Digest video. Especially wearing that classic navy suit, which offsets the waves of his blond locks and molds to his body like a second skin.

Although, despite its tailored beauty, when he closes the fridge with something wrapped in aluminum in one hand, the other tugs at his collar, as if he's suffocated by the fabric.

"Exactly, you get it." He laughs at whatever the person on the other line said. "That's why I'm not stepping a foot into the office tomorrow. I don't care what he thinks. I'm not wasting another good Saturday, especially not one that's going to be in the nineties. He'd have to drag me by my ankles."

Unwrapping the aluminum on the center island, he reveals what appears to be a tuna melt. When he takes a bite, a chunk of tuna falls onto the foil, and I mumble a silent prayer that my stomach doesn't decide to get chatty.

"Mhmmm," he hums, chewing. "Well, he'd actually have to visit my apartment to do that. And you know how repulsed poor Elias is by large crowds, particularly ones with alcohol and fun."

Unease stirs within me. *Alcohol and fun? Here, tomorrow? Is he planning what I think he is...?*

"Oh, you know, bring the usual—Grey Goose, Dom

Pérignon, that fruity jungle juice shit Alex makes that blacks out half your night, a couple bottles of Don Julio, margarita mix, some Upper East Side girls..."

He laughs again as annoyance burns down my center. Whether my reaction stems from hearing him mention other girls, or because he basically confirmed my suspicions, is unclear. But I'm telling myself it's the latter.

Denial is one helluva drug.

I shake my head, listening to him spout off more details, which clearly breach our contract, until I'm blistering with anger, spewing steam from my ears.

"... yep, we'll be at it till sundown. Plenty of time for you and Sasha to get well acquainted, if you know what I mea—"

"You're not throwing a party here!" I storm out of the pantry, making it all but three steps before I freeze, snapping a hand to my lips.

Hayden's mouth hangs ajar, words failing him as he stares at me, eyes wide like saucers, until his lips curl into a wicked grin. "I'll call you back."

Uh, oh. Twisting on my heel, I beeline it straight toward my bedroom—

"Why not? This *is* my house."

I grind to a halt. *Why not...? WHY NOT?* I whip back around. "Uhh, maybe because it's in our *contract*," I spit, my finger slicing through air, toward the paper taped to the fridge.

"Contract? What contract...?" Mischief emerges in his eyes as he rubs his chin, effectively cranking the dial on my blood pressure. He looks behind him. "Ohhhh, yes. That thing."

"That thing has your name signed at the bottom, or did you forget?"

"Hmmmm. I do see that." He clucks his tongue.

"And what about rule number five? Do you see that?"

Both parties agree not to throw a party or use illegal substances in the shared residence, I recite in my head, just as I could all the other rules.

"I do. But I also see number one."

"What of it?"

He faces me, letting the sun strike his features, which are so beautiful they physically cause me pain. Mostly because I'm mentally replaying all the sounds he overheard the other night, wishing I could sell my soul just to rewind time or wipe his memories of the incident.

"Well, it says we have to act like a couple around my friends. Sorry to break it to you, baby, but my friends like to party."

"Bring me to a different one, then. It doesn't have to be here."

"I throw a party on the first Saturday of every month. Haven't skipped the tradition in two years. They'll suspect something's off if I don't."

I nibble on my lip, feeling as though I'm caught in quick-sand. "Jeremy might come over. We can't risk it."

His response is immediate. "He's out of town this weekend."

"No, he's..."

Wait a minute. I recall our conversation weeks prior, when he blabbered on about some tech conference he had just bought tickets for. I do the mental math, avoiding Hayden's cocky gaze. *Is that this weekend...?*

My face falls.

"Don't you worry that pretty head of yours." He takes a considerable step closer, then another, swiping a hand through his unruly locks, stealing my any hope of a rebuttal. "It's just a little gathering."

Little... gathering...

"Oh, and while we're on the topic of showing you off, I think it's time we get you some new clothes."

I perk up. "What's *that* supposed to mean?"

"It's just that, I usually date girls a little more..." He traces down my body, not bothering to hide his amused grin. "Showy."

Could he be any more rude?! I'm moments from tackling him to the ground or setting his rear end in flames, until I dare give *myself* a once-over.

"Don't get me wrong," he muses, "I'm all for the comfy look, but I don't think it's gonna fly tomorrow."

I ball my hands into fists, debating whether to send one flying at his perfect nose. "You think I'd wear *this* at a party? I may be a nerd, but I'm not socially inept." *Well, not entirely, anyway...*

His palms shoot out defensively. "Woah, woah. That's not what I meant—"

"And what's so wrong with my closet, huh?"

"Nothing. I'll admit, it could use a few more pieces but... I like the way you dress," he says, and I swear I detect nothing but honesty. My tension eases up, just a tad. "Unfortunately, though, the guests I invite to my parties, dollface, they're like bloodhounds, only their noses sniff out designer labels."

I bite my lip, fighting back a grin. *Dammit, Juliana, don't laugh! He's still using pet names, when you told him not to.*

He sinks a hand into his pocket, retrieving his wallet.

"I can buy my own clothes,"

"Not at these stores."

I cross my arms, denying the black card he offers me, even though I know he's right.

"Come on, Jules."

I turn my head, gazing out the windows.

"So, that's how it's gonna be, huh? Too proud to use my card."

"This isn't about pride," I scoff, but my tone lacks conviction, even to my own ears. *What else would it be about?*

"No?" he hums, taking another step, close enough now that his musky cologne frolics up my nostrils, clouding my judgment that's screaming at me to run back to my room. "Then I assume you're not too proud to discuss the other night."

My stomach drops. "Uh—Uhm... I don't know what you mean."

"You don't? Well, it happened four or five nights ago. I heard some interesting noises..."

Dreads wraps its tendrils around me, pinning my legs in place, and it takes every ounce of my effort not to vomit all over Hayden's polished Oxfords. *Please God, if you're listening, just smite me already.*

"Ew, I don't want to hear about your disgusting fantasies."

His brows tick upwards as he brushes his fingers down a strand of my hair, then twirls it around his pointer.

My toes curl in my slippers. "I-I mean... I think you're imagining things. Or had a weird dream."

"You're probably right. It *did* feel like one." He edges closer, forcing my neck to tilt back even more. "Want to know why?" When I can't utter a response, a low chuckle escapes him, and it's like I'm pressed up against that window all over again, a slave to my urges.

"Well, for starters..." His mouth is minty on the way down

to my ear, igniting heat between my thighs. "Usually, from my experience, filthy things don't slip out of such pretty lips."

I gasp, scrambling away from him. From there, it's all a blur. On a tidal wave of adrenaline, I snatch that damn black card from his grasp—to hell with pride—and scurry down the hall like a spooked cat, leaving his smirk in my dust.

"My PIN is seven-two-six-five!"

NINETEEN
JULIANA

"SO, JUST FOR THE RECORD..."

Mei cranes her neck back and back and back, tracing a pillar in the living room that stretches two-stories high, one of five in between the solid walls of glass. "When you said you were fake dating a rich boy, I didn't know you meant RICH rich. This is the nicest apartment I've ever been in, which is really saying something."

I chuckle awkwardly, picking at the side of my nail. "Uhh, yeah. I'm still getting used to it."

It's the first time we've seen each other since I spilled the deets regarding my odd predicament, explaining how Hayden swindled her into setting me up on a blind date, while having ulterior motives. And while she did take everything quite well—a little *too* well, if you ask me—it's still a little weird. But maybe fake relationships aren't that uncommon in upper society, which Mei certainly stems from.

Though, apparently not *this* sort of wealth.

With every step, her knee-high boots click against the

ground as she meanders alongside the glass, daring much closer than I would.

In awe, she gazes straight down, a near one-hundred-story drop, then flicks her attention across the huge space, inspecting the room, like she has all the others since arriving —with keen eyes.

"And the artwork is fantastic." She motions toward an accent wall, stopping before a gigantic canvas wrapped in an intricate gold frame.

I tilt my head right along with her, admiring this particular painting for perhaps the fifth time since moving in. Judging by the figures portrayed, the art piece is surely hundreds of years old, although I couldn't possibly name off the era. But I let it transport me there, anyway.

Sitting in a dimly lit grand hallway, women in elegant dresses sit upon fine upholstery, reading books and conversing with distinguished gentlemen, who sport top hats, fitted waistcoats, and linen shirts. Some even hold canes with white-gloved fingers. Lavishness and privilege is their backdrop, accented by oriental rugs, gilded mirrors, elaborate crystal chandeliers, and—

"This is definitely a Victorian piece." Mei pulls me from my fixation, answering my unspoken question. She points. "See this lady's outfit? That's a bustle dress, and the fan she's holding is made of palm leaves. And this gentleman..." she trails off, reciting facts with the fluency of a *Jeopardy* contestant.

"The artist's manipulation of medium is breathtaking, almost velvety, by their rich use of oil. It's just... wow," she sighs. "It's obviously an original, which must've cost Hayden millions. I could give a pretty accurate guess, but..." She tilts her head to the other side, nearing closer. "There's no signature. That's odd..." Her voice fades into a murmur, her mind swirling like some artistic Sherlock Holmes, riddled with mysteries and hypotheticals.

I tug on her sleeve. "If you think this painting is crazy, just wait for the rest of the tour. Some hallways may as well be inside a museum. A lot of them have an older feel, like this one, but"—I motion back to the living room, diverting her attention, lest we stare at this one the entire night—"I'd say the pieces do an impressive job at blending in with the modern space, but I'm no expert."

She hums in agreement, re-directing her artistic eye onto the contemporary chandeliers and wrap-around couch, the staircase winding up to another floor, and the massive fireplace, which earns a warm smile.

"My room didn't do your vase justice," I say, gesturing toward the mantel.

"No? I think it would look quite lovely beside your stripper pole."

I roll my eyes. "I told you, it's not mine."

"Mhmm, sure. Have you given it a spin yet?" *Oh my God, here we go.* I only shake my head. "Give Hayden a little show?"

"What? No!"

"Come on. I know you want to." I shove her shoulder, prying a laugh from her. "Okay, fine, maybe you don't. Although, maybe *he* could give you a show. I saw how hot he was at work—he really does his profile picture justice. But have you seen... more of him?"

I suck in a breath.

"You so have!" she squeals, and before I can even attempt denying, she interrupts, "How? Did you two..."

"No!" Oh, screw it, I can't flat-out lie. So, I'll... sprinkle in a little truth. "Well... We grew up together, remember? And his family had a pool, so... I could probably guess he still looks..."

"Uh, huh, uh, huh." She eggs me on like a small-town gossip, desperate for information.

"He's uhh... not ugly."

She props a hand atop her hip, over her high-waisted miniskirt. "Not. Ugly? Could you elaborate a little?"

"I mean..." Heat crawls up my neck, as I'm unable to meet her gaze. Maybe it's the intensity of her winged liner, or the fullness of her false lashes, but it's like she's staring right into my mind. "He's..." *Spit it out, spit it out.* I clear my throat, giving her a composed shrug. "He's fine."

Her grin grows large.

"What?"

She snickers. "Juliana, every girl knows that's code for *he's hot as fuck.*"

"N-no," I sputter. "I'm being—"

"Do you have a photo?"

Now my cheeks must *really* be two ripe tomatoes. *Is she psychic or something?*

Yes, I don't dare say. *Several, actually. Fully shirtless. Some show even more than that. All of which I've totally been meaning to delete. But it just... slipped my mind. Yeah. Funny how that happens. It's not like I've been staring at them for the past five days or anything.*

Because that would be weird.

"No, Mei, I don't have any shirtless pho—"

"Actually, wait." She winks, obviously aware I'm keeping secrets. "I want it to be a surprise when I come to the party tomorrow."

My eyes bulge, but then quickly shrink back to their normal size. I shouldn't be surprised. Despite her hectic schedule, Mei never misses a party. "I'd love for you to be there. I'll ask Hayden if it's okay."

"*Pfft.*" She waves a hand through the air, flashing her acrylic nails. "No need. I'll just show up."

I raise an eyebrow. Imagine possessing *that* level of confidence... "Are you sure? You won't know anyone, and I'm assuming I'll need to stay glued to Hayden's hip most of the night."

"Oh, I'm definitely coming. You summoned me for a makeover—which I've been waiting years for, by the way. I wouldn't miss seeing the results for anything."

I curse beneath my breath. *Does everyone have a problem with the way I dress?*

Grumbling a long line of protests, I glance down at myself, and for the second time in one morning, I think I look more out of place here than that Victorian painting on the wall. Except, even that finds a way to blend in because of its riches and elegance, while I'm like the sloppy pottery hidden in my room.

Maybe I could go for a little polishing...

"Don't make that face, Juliana. It'll be fun!"

My face scrunches more. "Trying on clothes after clothes after clooooothes, all day. Yeah, sounds like a hoot."

"Don't knock it till you try it."

"You know, I've always hated that phrase."

Her nose wrinkles, mirroring mine. "I kinda do, too. But it's true. I'm sure there's *something* you're looking forward to."

Mischief bubbles low in my gut, widening my lips into a feline grin. "Oh, there is one thing."

Her eyes narrow. "What's that?"

My hand sinks into my pocket, retrieving something cool

and metallic that I dangle in the air. "Hayden gave me his keys."

~

REMEMBER when I felt insulted by a dessert menu?

Well, the prices in these designer stores are so high, they don't just insult me and my lowly social class. They make me sick. And quite honestly, I think I *would* be sick, physically, all over these floors and clothing racks, if it wouldn't land me into a debt I couldn't afford for the rest of my life.

"How does it look?" Mei's cheery voice floats above the door of my changing stall. And by stall, I mean full-fledged beauty room, equipped with three full-length mirrors, a velvet chaise lounge, even an adjustable lighting dial.

Zipping up the back of the black mini dress, I approach the largest mirror barefoot, running a hand along the wool material now kissing my skin. Gold-tone buttons dot along the front, crossing thick stripes of white, before tapering off at the polo collar.

Honestly, it fits me like a glove, and I don't have any complaints, yet I still answer, "It looks fine."

"Fine?"

"Yeah, fine. Like—good. It looks good."

"That's what you said about the last five dresses."

She's not wrong. I'm a broken record at this point. I wouldn't say I'm lying, per se. They *do* look good. More than good, actually. Incredible. Until I check the price tags.

I fumble with the hem, already anticipating the number of digits, but it's no less shocking than the first time I flipped a tag over.

Three-thousand and seven hundred.

Dollars. Not cents.

Thought I'd clarify.

"Did you try on the pumps?"

"Not yet," I sigh, eyeing the bedazzled-pearl shoes lying on the lounge chair. The heels may only stand four inches tall, which is apparently short, according to Mei, but to someone like me, who exclusively lives in Converse or my house slippers, they may as well be the height of skyscrapers.

But I slip them on anyway, then mosey my way out of the stall on wobbly legs. Mei's brows tick skyward, cautious as they were the last time I walked out, as she gives me a look that says, *you're doing great, sweetie, but we'll practice later.*

Great. I'm a baby deer taking her first steps.

As if my adrenaline wasn't already high enough today. For a multitude of reasons.

First off, we nearly died on the way here. Twenty percent I'll admittedly accredit to my driving. There, I said it. But the other eighty percent lies beneath the hood of Hayden's sports car—if it can even be called that. Spaceship is more like. Or death trap. Yes, definitely death trap, seeing as a single strand of hair draped across the gas pedal sends the machine blazing into the triple digits.

It's short of a miracle we arrived on Fifth Avenue.

Which is a perfect segue for reason number two.

After Hayden left for work this morning, he texted me *Go buck wild,* then proceeded to list out each and every luxury store I was to buy from, all of which reside on Fifth Avenue and I can hardly pronounce. Again, it's the dessert menu, but taking a different form. Which would've been fine, if I could blend in, just like any other shopper, except Hayden must've called ahead or something, because the moment we stepped through the shiny gates of *Gucci,* the workers already knew me.

By name.

Well, more so by—

"Miss Brooks!" My personal shopper, Abby, all but drops my next round of clothes, gasping loud enough to turn the heads of others in the waiting room. "You look *stunning*. Oh my goodness, Carol—*Carol,*" she barks, waving her co-worker over. I catch Mei's eyes rolling to the back of her head. "Doesn't she look *dee-vine?!*"

"Ohhh, incredible, just incredible," she answers, shaking her head in awe, with dramatic hand motions and everything. You'd think I'm her daughter descending the steps before prom.

When they both disperse, moving on to grab my next round, I release a breath. "Jeez, I'm pretty sure she'd say the exact same thing if I came out in a trash bag."

"Definitely. You're just learning what power a black piece of metal grants a person." Mei smacks on her gum, blowing a large bubble, the act somehow rebellious in such a place. "But she's not wrong." She meets my stare. "You look amazing."

Warmth pools in my center, sweeping me into an unexpected wave of emotions, when I catch my reflection in a mirror across the room. The girl who stares back... I don't even recognize her. And yet... I feel *good.*

In reality, I may never be the girl who walks confidently into the party, without knowing a single soul there. Not even close. But maybe, just maybe... I could pretend.

"You're serious?" I whisper.

"Very. If this Hayden guy doesn't already want you as his real girlfriend, he sure as hell will tomorrow."

TWENTY
HAYDEN

WITH DORIS OUT of the office this morning, I've been left to my own devices. Naturally, I haven't done a damn thing. At this point, Elias and his telephone meltdowns are elevator music to my ears. I hum along to its beat.

Given that it's a weekday, so we're not the only souls in the building, I'm vaguely aware of the sideward glances coming from nearby cubicles. Employees peek past my tiny desk, toward my *boss's* office, exchanging whispers and concerned looks.

I guess he *is* on a rather impressive tirade, even for his standards, but his shouts quickly fade into the back of my consciousness.

Humming again, I throw in some toe taps and the occasional head bob, then my pencil is off to the races once more. Not filling out this balance-sheet-report-thingamabob-nonsense, but shading in the torso of the man I saw on my drive over here. The reason he caught my eye, you ask? He was wearing a three-piece, solid-brown suit.

Riding a unicycle.

I've always done that, drawn things or people who catch my attention. Nothing too crazy. Just some scribbles, here and there. If nothing was of note on a given day, I'll make up scenes in my head. Anything to pass the time.

With a bored yawn, I flick my wrist, outlining the shape of his curly hair, opting for a wide, lazy shading technique. Until I'm arching my back, drawing closer and closer, detailing each individual hair, then expanding outward, utilizing more of the document's real estate, invading lines of business jargon and financial numbers and—

"You never change, do you?"

My pencil jerks, slicing clean through his suit. Annoyance ticks my jaw, as the man who's always an overcast on my sunny day rounds my desk, looming right in front of me. I crane my head back, feeling like a child, but I don't show it on my face.

I smirk instead, plastering on a mask of innocence, loving when a vein flares across his forehead. "Whatever do you mean, Father?" He may control my trust fund, but I'll be damned if I let him think his coldness has any effect on me.

"Don't play dumb with me, boy." His arms fold across his suit-clad chest. "It's just like you're still in school. Scribbling little doodles, when you should be working. No wonder you never learn anything."

He snorts, shooting Doris a smile, who stands behind him, carrying a stack of paperwork. She returns a grin, yet to my surprise, when he shifts his gaze back to me, she offers me a look that I swear carries an undertone of sympathy.

When I stare past her frame, I catch half of the room snap their attention back to their work.

I'd attribute their prying eyes to the presence of their president and CEO, but it's more than that. Warren Kingston isn't *that* rare of a sighting, especially on this floor. Granted, I haven't actually seen him since starting my job over a week ago, but I'm sure that's because he's just doing what he does best—avoiding the pit stain of his family.

I digress.

Spotting a CEO outside the door of his Director of Finance? Not that remarkable. But you know what is? Seeing one chastise his lousy son, while his golden child wages fiscal warfare ten paces away. The employees here, they may eagerly run in the hamster wheel of capitalism, hungry for bonuses and promotions and recognition, but they'll take any chance they can get to watch a spoiled, good-for-nothing billionaire's son rot.

It's like Thanksgiving dinner to them, and I plan on cooking their eyes one hell of a feast, as long as it'll embarrass the man who brought me into this world, then hired others to raise me.

Standing to my full height, I clear my throat. "Well, aren't you—"

"I don't have time for your excuses." He breezes past my desk, aiming for my brother's office. "You're Doris's problem now," he says, before slamming the door shut.

I blink, as an aching silence spreads throughout the room. It takes a moment, but distant chatter soon picks up, unlike Doris's pitiful expression.

Don't worry, I want to tell her as I sit back down. *This isn't my first day under my brother's shadow.*

Returning to her desk, she stutters, for perhaps the first time in her life. "Uh-uhm... Could you update your father's time sheet? I have a lot of paperwork to catch up on."

"Sure." I pull up the program, thankful for the distraction. Something mindless and easy. Like purposely asking a question I've already voiced—"Remind me again, why we clock their hours? My brother and father aren't paid by the hour, obviously."

Instead of shooting me her usual glare, Doris plays along. "It's just a personal record us assistants keep, to help track of our bosses' whereabouts. It makes hunting them down easier, when they go radio silent."

"Ahh," I hum, scrolling through the now-familiar program. I've been tracking Elias's hours for the past week, so finding my father's timesheet is easy as—

Wait a minute.

I blink... then blink some more... then give Doris a look, who's engrossed in her paperwork. I even refresh the page— *three times*—because what I'm seeing *cannot* be right. "Uhhhh-hhh, Doris?"

"Yeah?"

"Why has my father only logged ten hours this week?"

She goes quiet for a moment.

I whip my gaze, finding her stare frozen and locked onto me, swimming with mysteries. *Did something happen? Why isn't she saying anything?* Cinching my brows, I look again, flicking through the prior weeks. Ten hours. Twelve hours. Nine, seventeen—even *three*. While my brother's working *eighty*, sometimes more.

He's got a pull-out sofa in there, for fuck's sake.

With each click, the answer becomes clearer and clearer, until I'm staring into Doris's mysteries once more, seeing right through to the truth.

He lets Elias do all the work.

A weight bears onto my chest, heavy and nauseating. Our father's supposed to be *teaching* him, working alongside him. Not using his prized pony like a sled dog. How long has this been going on? I want to ask, to pick Doris's brain until only air resides between her ears, but her lips are sealed too tight.

She may be an executive secretary to both of them, but she knows who reigns, who stuck me at this child's desk out of spite, and who it is that has the final say.

In everything.

NO MORE THAN twenty minutes later, my father's tearing back Elias's office door. "Well, you'll just have to buck up and get it done," his stern voice booms. "We all make sacrifices," are his ironic words of wisdom, before he storms past my desk without a glance, aiming for the elevators.

Bursting from her chair, Doris follows his lead.

Elias sighs from deep in his office.

"What was that about?"

He walks out, stoic as ever. "Oh, nothing."

"Didn't sound like nothing."

Leaning against the doorframe, he shrugs. "That's his weekly thing. Waltzes into my office, gives me a lesson, then goes along his way."

"He's got some poor teaching skills, if you ask me."

"Meh." He waves a hand through the air. "He's just stressed, from working himself to the bone, as usual."

I freeze up, as a colossal wave of urgency washes over me. If only my brother knew he was merely describing himself, least of all our father. Perhaps Warren Kingston used to fit such a description, but that's certainly no longer the case, not after the evidence I've seen.

With a pang of sadness, I watch Elias pull out his phone,

then bury his head in something that's surely work related. He needs to know. He *deserves* to know.

"I need to tell you something."

"Oh, yeah? What's that?" He doesn't meet my gaze, which is no surprise. Why would he? I've never said anything serious my whole life.

"I, uhh..." I loosen my collar, feeling suffocated. *Come on, just spit it out.* Expose our father, expose him as the asshole he's always been. "Uhm..."

But I can't.

Not when I can predict the chain of events that would follow, if I were to tell the truth. Elias would confront our father, who would easily connect the dots, straight back to me. What're the chances, Elias learns something so vital, after I've barely worked a week. It's too obvious of a coincidence.

Then he'd pull my trust fund for good.

Guilt shreds my heart in two, straight down the middle, when Elias finally lifts his head, and I stare into those glassy eyes. *He's still using...*

I clear my throat, using the guilt to my advantage. "I kind of... slacked off on that balance statement."

His lips thin. "Again? You've had since yesterday."

"I know. Sorry. I got... distracted with other work."

"Sure, you did." He shakes his head, pushing off the door frame. "Have it on my desk by the end of the day. Stay late, if you have to," he orders, then heads out the door, but before he passes my desk, my phone lights up, ringing loudly.

AMERICAN EXPRESS FRAUD DEPARTMENT, the caller I.D. warns in bold, which should send my heart plummeting. If it were any other day, it would. Instead, I bite back a smile.

That's my girl, I muse, before thinking better of it, my guilt long forgotten.

Elias raises an eyebrow. "Aren't you going to answer that?"

Wasn't planning on it, but then I'd have to explain why. Sighing, I pick up my phone, prompting Elias along his way.

A woman speaks from across the line. "Hello, this is the American Express Fraud Department. May I ask with whom I'm speaking?"

"Hayden Kingston."

"Mr. Kingston, we're calling about unusual spending activity on your Black Amex card." Urgency drips from her tone. Little does she know, it's just my fake girlfriend going on a mandatory spending spree. A certain hunger sparks within me as I imagine her swiping my card.

"How much?"

"Thirty thousand in the last two hours. At the department stores Gucci, Saks Fifth Avenue, and Dior."

My pulse spikes. *Did she listen to a word I said?* "Thank you. That's just my girlfriend. Please, reinstate the card," I say, before hanging up the phone and immediately dialing Juliana. Her sweet voice answers on the second ring.

"Hey, sorry, they said the card declined. I think I went overboar—"

"Are you shopping in the clearance sections? You should've spent one-hundred thousand by now, at least."

The line goes silent for several heartbeats. "What did you just say? I think I heard you wrong."

I pinch the bridge of my nose. "One. Hundred. Thousand, Juliana. Six digits, you should be there by now. What, did you decide to swing by the price club? You're not leaving Fifth Avenue until you've hit three hundred thousand."

"Three hundred—*what?* That's insane. I can't—"

"Yes, you can. And you will." Possession crackles along

my skin, bordering dangerously close to anger, when memories of her old apartment flash across my vision. "Every rack in that closet better be full, or I'm sending you back tomorrow."

"Have you completely lost your mind?" *Yes, what of it?* "We've got more bags than we can carry."

"What store are you at?"

"Uhhh... Louuu... Louuuie Voten..." she tries again, spreading a smile across my lips so wide my cheeks hurt. "Louis Vuitton." *There you go, baby.* "Why do you ask?"

I put her on speaker and zoom through my contacts. "Because I'm sending more personal shoppers. They'll carry your bags and bring them to the house for you."

More silence.

"Got that?"

"Yes," she whispers through the line, emotions caught in her throat.

"Oh, and Juliana?"

"Yeah?"

My gaze lands on my brother's office door. "Buy something business-y while you're at it."

TWENTY-ONE
JULIANA

SHOP TILL YOU DROP.

I've always found that to be a ridiculous expression, a gross exaggeration made by overly dramatic fashionistas. No one *actually* exerts that much energy while shopping, of all things, or wastes *that* much time at the mall. It just feels like they did.

Well, I'm officially here to set the record straight about all those rich housewives, living it up in The Hamptons...

They. Must. Be. CRIPPLED.

"Uuughhhh," Mei groans beside me on the couch.

Much like myself, compared to when we stepped into the first store, she looks positively wrecked. Her hair's a mess, her knee-high boots discarded on the floor, as she slouches over the armrest, wrapped in a black-and-gold *Versace* blanket, which cost a cool thirteen-hundred dollars. One of her several *thank-you* gifts from today.

"Tell me about it," I mumble, sinking farther down the couch. "My whole body aches."

Never in my life have I been poked and prodded to such

an extent, or been asked so many questions about a sense of style I don't possess. Thankfully, I had Mei as my cheerleader. But even still, I thought we'd never reach our goal of three-hundred thousand—a number I'm honestly numb to at this point—but we did. Just barely.

"Your feet must be fried."

Indeed, they are. My soles are tender, my calves burning with an aching tightness. I wiggle my toes inside my fuzzy slippers, finding little relief. "You have no idea—I got blisters on blisters."

She snorts, as another entourage of clothing racks rolls past us, aiming for my bedroom, pushed by men who look like they should be guarding the president. Dark suits, stern expressions, blacked-out sunglasses, the whole Secret Service wardrobe.

"Shall I call a masseuse, Miss Brooks?"

I nearly jump at the feminine voice behind me. A woman in a trendy two-piece suit rounds the couch, holding a clipboard. Sasha is her name, I think. I can't keep up.

I blink, swapping weird looks with Mei. *A masseuse? After shopping?* Where did Hayden find all these people? Is there some company rich people all know about, and just call up on the fly, whenever they need help wiping their asses?

"Uhh... that's alright."

"A cup of tea, perhaps? Or a hot meal. I could call in a private chef and—"

"We're fine with our waters. Thank you, though." I might sound blunt, but I can't bear another second of all this pampering and un-deserved doting... I'm at my wits end.

She smiles politely. "Of course, let me know if there's anything else I can assist you with. We should be done here shortly." With a curt nod, she disappears down the hallway.

"Whew." I release a breath, as does Mei.

"I'm pretty sure if you told her you wanted a kidney off the black market, she wouldn't bat an eye. She'd probably secure you express shipping."

Laughter spews from my lips, unable to contain itself. "Mei Nguyen, always speaking the first thing that enters her mind. Could you be any more morbid?"

"WOW..." Mei breathes next to my ear.

"I know..." I whisper back.

"That's really something."

"I know."

"Seriously, you might have the most pimped out closet this side of Central Park."

Admittedly, the closet was already stunning, even in its emptiness, but it's on a whole new level now, a transformation and attention to detail accomplished only by the hands of professionals.

Designer clothes drape off racks in a color-coded fashion, heels stand on pedestals as if they'll never set foot on pavement, and luxury bags peek from behind glass display cases under ambient lighting. Even freshly cut tulips lie across the center island, beside glass perfume bottles I don't recall buying.

Like a sail out of wind, I stand pencil-straight, stuck in the doorway, feeling as though one step, one *blink* too quick might wake me from this dreamland.

"You think so?" I ask, already knowing the truth.

"Definitely."

For a minute, I dare enter, letting the splendor sweep me

off my feet. In silent awe, I brush my fingertips across the silky fabrics and luxurious marble, all but wondering who I might become, if I slipped on a particular outfit. I even lean over the island and smell the tulips, basking in their freshness, until their scent turns up sour. Fleeting, like this made-up reality.

"It's only temporary," I tell Mei, watching her shoulders deflate. She gets it without further explanation—he'll likely return everything, once our arrangement is finished. This is all part of the façade.

"You can steal a few pieces—or more than a few." My lips upturn slightly. "It's not like Hayden would notice, especially since he's never here. Where is he, anyway?"

"He said he had to stay late at work."

Now, what he *does,* exactly, working under his father at Kingston Entertainment, I haven't the slightest clue. He's yet to bore me with the gritty details, mostly because I haven't asked. Hayden's not the only one who equates the corporate nine-to-five to prison. Or... he *used* to think that. Now, I'm not so sure.

"Until ten o'clock at night?"

I shrug. "It's not the first time."

"On a Friday," she adds.

An inkling of jealousy shoves its way into my heart, and I hate it when I realize she's right. There's no way the Hayden I've known my whole life is at work this late, and not picking up some gorgeous model at a bar. He's probably already driving back to her place.

"I'm not his real girlfriend."

Wrong answer! my common sense bellows. *How 'bout next time, go with a simple "I don't care."*

Mei folds her arms. "That may be true, but I'm not letting

my best friend date a liar. Even if it's fake."

I chuckle, hoping she doesn't hear my sadness. "I think you're a little too late."

"Maybe... Although, his lie *does* buy us some valuable time."

I arch a brow, noting the mischievous grin spreading along her lips. "For what, to play dress up?"

"No, silly... *Time to snoop.*"

"MEI... *MEI!*" I hiss anxiously, watching her fling back drawer after drawer inside Hayden's home office, only to find them empty. "We've looked long enough."

"Not quite."

She speeds out of the office, which I just now discovered in the last thirty minutes. Same with the poker lounge, another room with a stripper pole and red-leather couches, and a small library, all easy to overlook in the twenty-thousand-foot penthouse.

"I'm serious!"

I trail behind her, my sore calves burning with each step, as worry drips from my teeth. I'm a rule-follower, through and through. Always have been, always will be. And while I *do* live here, and have the right to go wherever I please, this feels wrong.

"He could be back any minute," I warn.

Mei swings a left, leaving my words in the dust. Clearly, none of our discoveries have scratched her detective itch.

"What are you even looking for?"

"I don't know, but there's something here. I can feel it."

What'd I say? She's turning into Sherlock Holmes.

Like a treasure hunter in search of hidden artifacts, Mei zooms up the winding staircase, down several corridors, through the gigantic ballroom, and halts beside a flappy door with a circular window. Similar to the one at our work, but much fancier.

"Where's this lead off to?" she asks.

"The service wing."

Curiosity sparks in her eyes, as she makes for the door—

"It's just as empty as the ballroom."

"You've been inside, then?"

"Well, no... But look through the window and you'll see."

When she bursts through the door, I roll my eyes. What follows is five minutes of searching through a—*big gasp*—totally barren kitchen. Empty cupboards, empty pantries, empty everything, even the extra storage rooms. So, as she makes her way down to the final door, which will surely be more of the same, I stop in my tracks.

"This is getting ridiculous, Mei. I've had enough snooping for one night. You and your psychic energy are wrong on this one."

"Just one last door!" she hollers.

I shake my head, swiveling on my heel. "Well, I'll be in the living room, after you see that I'm righ—"

A gasp rings down the hallway, lurching my heart, compelling me to turn back around, until I realize what she's doing... My lips thin. "Yeah, yeah, okay, Mei. You almost got me. I know there's nothing but dust in there."

When she doesn't respond, I sigh and whirl around, only to find her faced away from me, stuck in the doorway at the end of the hall, frozen, like a reflection of myself not long ago in my own closet. I cock my head suspiciously, marching toward her, positive I'm seconds from her *Aha! Gotcha.*

"What'd you find?" I ask, earning myself more silence, until I'm a foot from the doorframe, with anticipation coursing through my veins for reasons I can't explain, that I hear her voice. So breathless, I nearly miss it.

"Our missing artist."

What? Missing artist? I exhale sharply. Now she's speaking in riddles, thinking she's some—

Oh...

I switch on the brakes, my pace grinding to an abrupt stop, shoulder-to-shoulder with her, as a room like no other in this apartment comes into view.

Wowwww...

Colors... I've never seen so many colors...

"Our missing artist," I breathe.

Moonlight streams through an oval skylight, cascading onto the countless canvases below, scattered across the room. They stand atop wooden easels, lean up against the wall in stacks, and lie along the ground.

Unsure if Mei will ever break her hypnosis, after stumbling upon a modern-day Picasso's art studio, I motion my way inside, wary of my steps, as I inspect each painting, one by one, beneath the faint light.

Paint covers the entire canvas of some, with a glossy finish sealed over top, others are merely pencil sketches, while most lie somewhere in-between. Works in progress, clearly under the skill of an artistic savant, who seems to carry an appreciation for everyday life, for scenarios or people one may discover while walking the city streets.

Like dining in quaint restaurants, or exploring the grounds of Central Park. Until I reach the far wall, that is, where I discover a new collection that, even to my untrained eye, unmistakably shares a resemblance to the Victorian painting in the living room.

Could these really all be from Hayden?

I've never caught him drawing or participating in any art clubs during school, but why else would this studio exist...? It's clear that one artist is responsible for all this, as well as the majority of the paintings in the penthouse, given their similar styles.

Except, there's no way of knowing for sure, since none of the pieces are signed, not even the finished ones, just like the painting in the living room.

If Hayden is this talented, why wouldn't he sign his own —

My head whips to Mei, who is finally searching about, as the faintest of noises trickles into the studio. A door shutting, deep inside the penthouse. Our eyes connect, hers shimmering with wonder and mine shadowed with unease.

"Okay, act natural. We'll say we—"

"We?" she giggles, too loud for my liking. "Girl, please. You're the one who's gotta go put a straight face on for your *genius* of a fake boyfriend. As for me, the service wing's got an elevator. I'll just slip through that." She winks on her way out the door. "See you tomorrow, Cinderella."

I blink rapidly, utterly stunned. Why I am, exactly, I'm not so sure. I tell myself it's because she essentially just equated herself to my fairy godmother, who's sending me off to the ball with a whole new look, instead of the real reason.

The occurrence that's more shocking than me slipping on a pair of heels—though they're not glass, mind you—an event rarer than lightning striking in the exact two places, a chance phenomenon encroaching on the ledge not of improbability... but im*poss*ibility...

Someone thinks Hayden Kingston is a *genius.*

TWENTY-TWO

HAYDEN

WEAVING through the crowd of partygoers, I press my phone to one ear, struggling to hear Juliana's voice amidst the music thumping from the DJ booth next to the pool.

"I still don't understand why I have to arrive late to a party, when I live in the same house.

"HEY, MANNNNN."

A drunken slur sounds to my left, belonging to a fellow Sigma Alpha Epsilon alum, clad in board shorts, who I'm eighty percent positive is named James... or Ben, I don't know, but I hit him with the good-old Kingston charm either way, dabbing him up with a *long time no see,* then part ways on the pretense of needing to oversee some catering mishap.

"Hellooooooo?" my phone whines.

Oops. "What was that? You cut out."

"I said," Juliana snaps, causing me to bite down on a laugh, as I hand out a slew of fist bumps and head nods on my way back inside. "Why do I have to arrive late, when I live there?"

"First off, no one at this party is supposed to know that.

Only my family, once they learn of our ongoing relationship."
I hold the door open for a group of guests, earning a brush on
the shoulder from the girl in a black bikini, then try not to
overthink why it lacks the expected impact. "Second, I needed
time to plant a couple seeds about my new girl. Make sure
heads are turning, upon your arrival, you know?"

"Rigghhht..." There's no missing the worry in her tone, as
an elevator *dings* on her end of the line. *She must be on her way
up.* I quicken my pace toward the penthouse's private lobby.
"Also, did you mean to say new *girl*? Why not girl*friend?*"

Whew, now that's a dangerous question—or would be, if this
weren't a fake arrangement—like one massive bomb, waiting
to detonate right in my face if handled poorly. But in truth,
it's a multifaceted answer.

On the one end, there's...

Rule #8: A playboy keeps things casual and undefined.

So, why would I ever have a girlfriend?

On the flip side is the tactical answer pertaining to our
contract, which I'll entertain, for the benefit of both parties.

"We're dancing around a fine line here, Juliana. To my
family, yes, I'll introduce you as my girlfriend, but to my
friends, who've never heard me use such a word and my
name in the same sentence, you're just another plaything.
Public enough that, if my father were to ask around, he'd
discover you're in my same social circle, but not so serious
that people start gossiping—then Jeremy would hear. Basically, your name should only come up when someone asks."

"Wow, that is... that actually makes a lot of sense."

I smirk, passing through the kitchen. "Thank you, thank
you. I *am* a bit of a social mastermind."

"But there's still one thing I'm having a hard time
believing..."

"What's that?"

"How is Jeremy *not* going to find out? I know he's out of town this weekend, but I'm his *sister,* his only sibling. Won't people tell him they saw me with you?"

Andddd, 3D chess enters the ring, once again.

"Well, well, that's the beauty of this whole thing. You're his *younger* sister. Meaning... he may tell *me* about whatever's going on with you, because we grew up together, but no one else. To our friends, Jeremy might as well be an only child."

"Oh..."

The line goes silent, as her hurt rings between my ears, akin to nails on a chalkboard scratching along my heartstrings. "He's just protective over you, Jules, and for good reason. Our friends are—how do I word this, politely... not what you would call *long-term material.*"

Her snicker rings in my ear, lifting the heaviness inside me. "Did you just insult yourself?"

I enter the penthouse lobby, gaining the attention of a busty blonde, who looks vaguely familiar. We've likely hooked up before, and judging by the way she bites her lip while passing me by, tells me it could happen again. And I'd be open to it—actively seeking it out, actually—if I felt literally anything at all happening below the belt.

What the hell is wrong with me?

"I sure did. I'm the worst of us all," I purr, as I wait for the elevator, my words suddenly lacking conviction to my own ears. "Don't worry, baby. I'm self-aware."

An annoyed huff is her only response.

I smirk. Seems my pet names still get under her skin. Good. Flaunting her around will be easier than I thought. Whether or not she admits it to herself, she's *already* my little plaything, who responds so eagerly to my—

Ding.

T-to m-my...

Blood shoots straight to my cock.

Oh fuck...

I suck in a breath, battling a wave of faintness, like the aftershocks of a strong hit of nicotine.

Ohhhhh fucking hell...

Juliana steps off the elevator, and I'd swear on behalf of any religion, all I see is a goddess. Perhaps it's time for my conversion, for I've never felt so compelled to drop to my knees, only so I can repent for each and every one of my sins. Truly, in this moment, if a priest laid my hand atop some holy text, I'd tell him time has slowed to an aching crawl—and I couldn't be more grateful.

My gaze traces down her figure as I'm gripped by the most peculiar of sensations.

Nervousness.

As if, at any moment, she might turn and head right back down to the lobby, snuffing my party altogether. Because a girl who looks like *that*—she's got ten others to go to.

Flaring out at the end of its long sleeves and cutting off sinfully short at the thighs, a white, fishnet cover up drapes across her silhouette, but that doesn't mean it actually *covers up* a damn thing. Especially not the red bikini flashing beneath, sporting bottoms tied high on her hips and a triangle top that plunges low, low, low...

With every footfall of her heeled sandals, I'm drooling more and more as she bounces in all the right places. And when I spot the diamond shining inside her belly button, I nearly weep.

"Hey."

And her hair... *God,* it's perfect. Dark silky curls flow from her high-pony, bangs falling freely, framing her beautiful face, and—

"Hayden?"

My eyes snap to her green ones. Like some enchanted forest, they're impossible to look away from, as her flowery scent douses my senses.

I break from the mist. "Huh?"

"Umm..." Her teeth sink into her bottom lip distractingly. "You're still holding the phone to your ear."

I freeze, her words punching me square in the gut. *What is this, fucking amateur hour? Snap the hell out of it!* I slot my phone into my pocket quickly, clear my throat, and plaster on a look of cool indifference. Anything to get a grip on my long-lost dignity.

"You look... good."

But she's already wearing a wolfish grin.

Shit. And away it goes...

The upper hand.

At least, so I thought, until I intertwine my fingers with hers, and her confident gaze withers at the sight of the party, through the foyer windows. I squeeze her hand, dragging her attention back onto me—and the fear there, behind her stare, I wish I could squash it dead.

"Just stick with me," is all I say, even though I know the *real* reason she'll be okay.

I was wrong. So thoroughly wrong. I didn't need to tell a damn soul of her coming. She could show up all on her own. Early, late, on-time, whatever. Everyone would still wonder who she was, and worst of all, every man who's not blind would turn his head to look at her.

TWENTY-THREE
JULIANA

BEING on the arm of Hayden Kingston is the closest brush with stardom I'll ever experience. I don't know how much time has passed, it's all a blur, but the one thing I do know is suddenly the entire world wants to be my friend.

Hayden weaves us through a mob of rowdy party guests, all of whom glance our way at least once. "Oh my gosh, I love your heels!" a girl squeals from behind. I swivel my head, finding her trailing me like I'm Regina George. "Where'd you get them?" she asks over the blaring music.

I shoot her a smile, the forced one I've worn since my arrival. "Thanks, girl!"—*girl, really? Who are you, Mei?* —"They're from—"

Shit. Where are *they from?*

Uhhhhhh... Static buzzes through my brain.

"I'm sure you could guess, Emma." Hayden stops in the middle of the crowd, his hand sweeping down my backside, igniting sensations I'd rather not acknowledge—like the twinge of annoyance at him knowing her by name. "I'd only buy my girl Prada."

I arch an eyebrow, recalling his correctness.

"They were a gift, then?"

"Yes," I lie.

She smiles at me, but there's no missing the jealousy clouding her gaze, and I must be ten different shades of twisted from the satisfaction it brings me. When her eyes flick back to Hayden, I can practically make out the dollar signs in them as she bites her lip.

Before I'm able to contemplate my actions, I lean into his touch, placing a hand on his bare chest, between the flaps of his unbuttoned polo. I don't say anything, wouldn't know *what* to say in the first place, to mark him as my turf—*my FAKE turf*, I correct myself. *This is all part of our agreement. That's all.*

I peer up at him from beneath my lashes, noticing his smirk growing wider.

"My Juliana's spoiled rotten. Aren't you, baby?"

His deep tenor rolls across my skin, setting my cheeks ablaze. As for what's going on between my legs, well, I might as well jump in that infinite pool right now, lest I stand a chance of lying to myself later.

Giggling, I manage a shy, "Maybe."

In the reflection of his sunglasses, I watch Emma's nose crinkle. "Thanks for the invite," she says, before sauntering off.

I bite back a smug grin, although judging by the way Hayden cocks his head at me, I think he sees it, anyway. His lips part—surely on some snide remark—but I clear my throat before it surfaces, adding ample distance between us. When I bump into someone's damp backside, I apologize, even though I doubt they can hear me above the music.

"I thought you said today was a *small gathering*," I huff, air-quoting with my fingers.

"What do you mean? This is small."

My lips purse.

"It is." He gestures with the flick of his chin. "My rooftop terrace—coupled with the entertainment rooms—holds five-hundred guests comfortably. This isn't even half that."

With a scoff, I watch him take a long sip from his red Solo cup. "First off, I doubt that. Second, since when is a two-hundred-person party small?"

"It is in my world." He winks.

I roll my eyes, just as he takes off again. With a sharp inhale, I catch his shoulder, following close behind, before the crowd swallows me whole. "Where are we going now? Haven't you introduced me to enough people?"

Yes, my mind answers for him. *Yes, we most definitely have.*

From the moment I stepped through the elevator, he's pranced me around, introducing me to so many people that I doubt I'll remember a single name come tomorrow. Never have I lied to such an extent, dodging questions left and right regarding my family and how I came to know Hayden. So much so, that I'm surprised my tongue hasn't fallen off or my nose isn't the size of Big Ben, considering I fabricated at least twenty different stories.

Fortunately, there's a saving grace—the reason I've yet to crawl out of my own skin, managed to keep my social anxiety at bay in the most unlikely of environments, and haven't locked myself in my room by now.

Alcohol.

No, not me. I'm stone-cold sober. But everyone else? They're either so heavily intoxicated or high on who-knows-what, they won't possibly remember *anything* tomorrow, least of all the holes in my vague stories. Sure, *maybe* they'll recall my face or name later, but that's about it.

"Just a bit longer!" Hayden tugs me along.

"But my feet hurrrrt," I whine.

He stops by the edge of the pool, glancing down at my cramped feet. "You can take those off, you know. They're hot and all, but I wouldn't want you losing a toe."

"And risk stepping in garbage? I think not."

"Hey now, that's my party you're talking smack abou—" He sucks in a breath, noting the plastic cups and confetti at his feet, even a flip-flop or two. "Guess the cleaning crew hasn't made their rounds yet... Okay, yeah. There's a spot we can chill for a bit."

Thank God.

He retraces our steps back the way we came, flicking his head over his shoulder. "Do you really not want a drink? I mean, a *real* drink."

I flash him my plastic water bottle. "I'm good."

"Okaaayyy, whatever you say. I could have the catering staff whip you up something special—anything you want."

"It's fine, rea—"

Wait a minute. Actually...

He whirls around, hope sparking in his features, until his eyes meet mine through his dark glasses—then all that hope slowly dwindles. His shoulders sag, low and defeated. "Oh, no—Juliana, no."

"Hmmm." I tap my chin. "Something special, you say?"

"Nononono. Seriously? Pick something else. Literally, pick any other drink but that one."

I flash him a toothy smile.

Finally. It's about time this party got kicked into high gear.

～

GOSH, *we should've come up here a lot sooner.*

I sigh deeply, propping my bare feet atop the bamboo coffee table that matches the cabana, shielding us from the sun's setting rays, and sink into the couch. Wiggling my sore toes, I observe the party below. From the vantage point on our private balcony, the music is still loud but a bit more manageable, as I sip on my Shirley Temple.

Hayden pinches the bridge of his nose, as if I'm physically hurting him. "I can't even look at you right now."

I slurp louder, smiling when he groans.

"If someone asks, say it's a vodka cran."

"Who's gonna ask?" I gesture toward the empty seats. "Don't worry, *Hayden,* no one's here to see me cramp your style."

With a smirk, he drapes an arm across the backside of our couch, the movement flashing the grooves of his tan abs. For a split moment, his fingertips brush my shoulder, stirring a flock of butterflies in my gut. "You're right," he says, gazing down at the party below. "Guess I lucked ou—"

He sits up straight.

"What's wrong?"

"Sit on my lap," he answers quickly.

"What?"

"Hurry. Before they see."

"Before *who* sees?" I whip my head back and forth, searching the crowd, until I spot a group of eight or so—half girls, half guys—heading toward the balcony's private staircase. "I thought you said you needed a door code to get up here."

"You do, but they're Jeremy and I's close friends. I gave it to them."

I fold my arms. "That doesn't mean I have to be on your *lap.*"

"You really think they'd believe I took a girl up here, just to talk? All alone?"

My gaze ping-pongs back and forth, from Hayden's eyes widening like saucers, to the group below, who must've just made it to the party. In other words, they're not drunk yet. I gnaw on my lips, contemplating my other options that clearly don't exist, until they're at the foot of the stairs.

Fuck.

I shuffle to the other end of the couch, my heart lurching when Hayden picks me up by my waist and sets me onto his lap, a whirlwind of skin-on-skin that tousles both my hair and my brain. I fix my bangs, grappling for a sense of control, except when I do, I find myself not facing away from him but *toward,* completely straddling him.

"Uh-uhm..."

My breaths puff out on jagged waves as the warmth of his chest seeps into my palms, my knees digging into the couch cushions on either side of him. Adrenaline spikes through my brain at his presence, much too close to mine and mine much too close to his, and *God* does he smell good and—

He sweeps my hair off one shoulder, his voice hoarse when he says, "Close your eyes," as his capture mine, bluer than the pool below, than any ocean wave or mountain spring.

When I don't move a muscle, his hands trail down my spine, torturously slow, a shiver following their wake, before he grabs two fistfuls of my ass. By now, I can barely make out his words a second time, drowned out by the blood pounding in my ears.

"Close your eyes."

"But why—"

His lips latch onto my neck, right as I hear what I believe is a door click, but I'm not sure, not when I'm incapable of forming a single coherent thought.

I inhale sharply on contact, going rigid, as does he, until he kisses my skin lightly, cautiously, like the first taste of some delicate appetizer. And the groan that follows has my eyes fluttering shut and back arching into him, before he grips my nape, angles my head to his liking, and dives in for more.

A moan breezes past my lips, then another, when he works up the length of my skin, stopping at the crook between my neck and jawline. He suctions there, the noises from his lips resounding through the air, as he threads fingers thread through my hair, tugging at the root, focused on that one spot.

The attention is suffocating, so intense that I squirm in his grasp, panting like a wild thing, my cover-up riding up my waist as I sway my hips, my center sliding across something harder than granite.

"Mmmmm." His growl caresses my ear, full of hunger and untapped control, rippling a shudder through me. He bucks back against me, the movement spreading my legs farther and blooming pleasure out from my core.

Then my hands are in his hair, exploring its silkiness, while he suctions harder and harder, his teeth branding my delicate skin and tongue darting between his lips in tandem to soothe up the burn. Stifling another moan, I rock back and forth, building a sensation so sweet that—

A snicker breaks through our space, coupled with some juvenile *woos* and *ow-ows!*, enough to free me from my lust. Just barely.

"Ohhhh, man," a male voice teases. "Should we leave you to it, big dog?"

A possessive growl rumbles against me, this one nearly primal and tinged with anger, before Hayden's lips *pop* from my skin, releasing their suction. "No, come on in," he says, his voice like gravel.

And it isn't until he helps me back into the spot next to him, while giving his friends the shortest introduction of me possible, that shame burns my cheeks, shrinking me until I'm so, so small.

We didn't need to take it that far. What was I thinking? *Was* I even thinking? Now I'm sitting here, with a puddle in my bikini bottoms, throbbing between my legs, and a bruise forming on my neck, hardly able to look a single person in the eye, sitting around my *brother's* friends who—

I arch a brow. *Who don't give a flying fuck???*

Bros in polos or no shirts at all take their seats across the coffee table, and some right up next to us, while girls in scanty bikinis plop down on their laps. In a mere minute, they're taking bong rips, throwing back shots, setting up a game of beer pong, and filling the cabana with loud chatter.

I blink. Is it just me, or did they not just watch the intro to a live-action porno?

With my mouth ajar, I swing my head, finding Hayden staring down at me, smug as ever. But why? Why is he so pleased when his friends couldn't care less and I apparently have nothing to be ashamed of?

Wait. My shoulders droop. *If his friends don't give a crap... that would mean...*

He smirks, resting a hand on my thigh.

There's no reason to stop.

As I'm about to protest, his thumb begins tracing tiny circles along my skin, causing me to suck in my bottom lip. A shadow of satisfaction clouds his eyes, before he turns his head and starts up a conversation with the man to his right, which I can hardly hear.

Then I all but melt into the couch, not uttering a word to another soul, unbothered if *they* care or *I* care or anyone or anything. I just focus on his touch, which keeps a constant pace and steady pressure as it grazes down the inside of my thigh, but never close enough to where I want it.

The. Entire. Time.

For how long, I don't have the slightest idea. But by the time the group exits the balcony with bottles full of booze in their hands and a craving for the dance mob breaking out down below, only a sliver of the sun peeks above the horizon.

The door shuts, leaving us alone.

I don't move. I don't jerk back like always. I only sit, speechless, as the gears in my brain belonging to desire and common sense grind in a deadly duel. My gaze flicks up and down, between Hayden's wanting stare and his hand, still on my thigh.

"I'm... I'm going to..."

"Yeah?" He angles his head. "To what?"

"To get..." I swallow, grappling for my dignity. "To get a drink."

His eyebrow quirks, noting my Shirley Temple on the table, half full. But before he opens that tempting mouth and convinces me to stay, I'm already on my feet, heels in hand, rushing for the door.

~

I PICKED a bad day to wear my hair up.

Sitting on a barstool, sipping a glass of cold ice water, I brush my ponytail in front of my shoulder, hoping to conceal the hickey that's surely forming on my neck. Embarrassingly enough, it's my first time having one, and even though the sun has fully set behind the city skyline, I feel like I'm sporting one big flashing, slutty bull's eye.

What's worse, is I still feel him on my skin. His lips, his hands... even his voice resides in my mind, whispers between my ears. Tantalizing sounds I can't unhear that urge me to go crawling back to him and—

"Damn, girrrl!" a voice I know so well squeals over the music. "You look *incredible.*"

Shit, shit.

I banish the dirty thoughts from my brain, praying Mei won't read them on my face. "You already saw me today," I say, adjusting my hair once more. It's true, she did see me at her apartment all morning, when she slaved away at my makeup and hair, working a curling iron I'd certainly give myself third-degree burns with.

She steps up to the bar right beside me, and as she orders her drink from the bartender, I raise an eyebrow at her tall beachy heels and leopard-print bikini, her backside swallowing up the G-string. Dang, looks like I'm not the only one who got all done-up. Although, to someone like Mei, this might *actually* pass as a small gathering.

She smirks, giving me an up-down over the rim of her sunglasses. "That's true, but I didn't see all *this.* You put together such a cute outfit."

"Well, I have Pinterest to thank for that."

She shrugs as the bartender returns with her seltzer. "Thanks."

"Would you like another water, Miss?"

"Oh, no. I'm okay." I thank him before turning back to Mei, but as I do, my hair slips off my shoulder. My eyes widen, just a fraction while I brush it back into place. But when our gazes meet, hers twinkle with mischief.

"Seems like you've been having some fu—"

"So!" I interrupt, the surge of adrenaline amplifying my voice. "Did you just get here?!"

She bites down on a laugh, instead giving me a smile, one that says *we'll talk later.* "No, I've been here for a while. Just mingling—ran into a few people I know."

"Uh, huh. Uh, huh." I nod, nursing my water.

"I saw you a few times, actually."

Sweat nicks at my brow. She couldn't have seen... *what happened,* right?

"Only from afar, though—that's why I freaked out when I saw you up close. I hardly recognized you, especially without your glasses, but I assumed it was you earlier..." She lets her sentence fade, like bait on a hook, fishing for information as she takes a long sip, eyeing me over the top of the can.

Where is she going with this?!

When I don't bite, she twirls a strand of her hair between her fingers. "You and Hayden, you two seem a little... *touchy.*"

My stomach drops. I haven't a clue what she did or didn't see, but she saw enough. "Mei..." I put on a poker face. "Everything's fake, remember? It's just part of the agreement."

"Mhmmmm, sure, sure."

"I'm serious. I have zero feelings for him. *Zero.*"

Who are you trying to convince there, baby? I hear Hayden's voice inside my head, who shouldn't even be there in the first place!

"Okaaayyy, whatever you say. Well, do you want to know what I think?"

I roll my eyes. "No, but you're gonna tell me, anyway."

"Yep." She props an elbow atop the bar, scanning the terrace. Then points. "See that man?"

Sighing deeply, I play her little game, following the line of her gaze, searching and searching through the crowd, until—I gasp.

...until I find the man.

On the opposite side of the terrace, Hayden sits at the edge of the pool, his shins submerged in the water glowing off his shirtless chest in the night, as cigarette smoke puffs from his lips, billowing over his blond locks. His friends from earlier either sit or stand beside him, chatting and dancing to the beat, oblivious to his territorial demeanor.

As he stares right at me.

"I can't speak for you, Juliana, but that man right there." Mei flicks her chin, and for once, not an ounce of playfulness or teasing seeps through her tone when she says...

"He's not pretending."

TWENTY-FOUR

HAYDEN

Chain-smoking.

That's the only thing that's kept me from pounding on Juliana's door or kicking it down, when she inevitably doesn't answer.

Earlier, I lit my first cigarette in hopes of burning the taste of her off my tongue, but it didn't work. So, I lit another... then another... until I lost count. I'm at five, I think. Maybe six, but I still taste her minty breath, still *feel* her on my skin, her hair like the ghost of a shadow wrapped around my fingers, even as I soak in this in-ground hot tub.

Alone. The night sky my canopy, as the last of the cleaning crew take their leave, trash bags in hand. They made quick work as usual, picking up and scrubbing the patio, and finished at 3:30 a.m. on the dot, twenty minutes after the party ended. Another service will take care of pool sanitation tomorrow morning.

Nine times out of ten, I'm reluctant to see the party end, so I'll hop to another and power on till sunrise. Although, I'd much rather keep *my party* alive all night long, and I would, if it weren't for last time, when I opened my front door to a group of cops, who slapped a curfew in my face, citing some 'noise ordinance laws' nonsense.

Whatever. That's my response, usually. But not tonight. Tonight I'm...

Thankful for the peace and quiet.

And it *is* so very quiet, save for the hot tub jets rumbling against my back—and the soft creak of the terrace door opening. Rummaging through my cartridge for another cigarette, I don't look, assuming a crew member forgot something, until I spot a familiar red bikini from the corner of my eye.

My heart flutters as the last person I anticipated walks my way, barefoot, with a towel draped across her shoulders. Juliana's hair bundles atop her head in a messy bun, with her bangs falling around her face. Her makeup is gone, too, yet she's no less striking.

She stops at the opposite end of the hot tub, her toes hanging off the lip. "Mind if I join?"

I'm tempted to hit her with the good-old *if I ever say no to that question, feel free to lead me out to pasture,* but that's a little too morbid for her tastes and frankly too sour for my mood. So, I opt for a simple, "Go ahead," while lighting my next cigarette.

I take a long drag, hoping it'll lessen the blow when she removes her towel. Of course, it doesn't. She dips a toe in, making that *ow, too hot* face. What follows is a torturously long process of her easing in, with me trying not to ogle at the curves of her body.

Then, we sit in silence—not an awkward silence, but calm —for quite a long time, just aware of each other's presence. Occasionally, I sneak a glance her way, wondering when she'll berate me for earlier, for taking things too far like always, but instead, I find her overlooking the skyline with a peaceful expression.

That *is* what she came out here for, right? To tear me a new one. But I see no signs of her planning to, so I leave her be and shut my eyes. I lean back, letting the nicotine course through my brain, a numbing buzz that—

"Why didn't you tell me you were an artist?"

I snap to attention. *How does she...?*

A hint of guilt flashes across her features. "I found your studio." *Sorry,* her eyes seem to say.

"Oh. That's okay..." I shrug. "I don't know. *Artist* is a strong word. It's just a hobby."

More silence.

"Is that why you don't sign your name?" she asks hesitantly.

A knife twists in my gut. For a moment, I contemplate my response, then err on the side of truth. "A signature implies others will see it."

Her eyebrows pull inward. "But they're hanging all over your apartment. Some even have displays. Don't your friends comment on them?"

I laugh, cringing at the bitter sound. "Do you really think my friends are the artsy types? They don't notice stuff like that."

Her gaze lowers. She knows it's true. My friends, they're nothing but spoiled party rats. At least, that's what she must think—myself included in said group. Her head pops back up. "What about my brother? Does he know?"

"A little, yes. Although, I'm pretty sure he thinks I'm lying. I don't blame him. I'm not one to admit how much time I put into it, or take anyone into my studio. Painting helps me to... think. Or sometimes, *not* to think. To escape, essentially."

Why are you saying all this?

"But really, it's just a hobby," I add.

"Well, it shouldn't be."

Our eyes connect. Hers brim with confidence, and there's defiance there, too, a brewing challenge, if I dare question the statement, but before I do, she continues, "I don't know what you're working on with your father, but whatever it is, I think it's letting your talent go to waste."

Now *my* gaze drops. I wonder if she can sense the embarrassment rolling off me in thick waves. If only she knew the complete joke that I am during the day, the shadow outside my brother's office. And yet, I let her words swim in my brain, anyway...

She's just being nice. It's Juliana—that's what she does.

"Thanks." I force a smile. "That's sweet of you."

Her lips purse. "I'm being serious."

God, am I always such an easy read for her? I muse, ignoring the part of me that loves the idea.

"I know, you are."

When she scoffs, a thrill shoots through me. There's that defiance. Burn me alive, baby. "Okay, then, what if I told you Mei was also impressed? Like, *stopped dead in her tracks,* impressed, stuck staring up at your Victorian painting in the living room like some statue."

I blink. "Mei, your friend?"

"Yeah." She blinks faster.

Am I missing something here? "Umm... That's nice of her?"

"No, no. It wasn't out of niceness. Mei is a *fine art's* student. At Columbia. She's pursuing her master's right now, and even teaches a class there. She *breathes* this kind of stuff, and she noticed your talent straight away... She may have

even used the word genius, but don't let it go to your head,"
she mumbles, blooming a smirk on my lips.

Yet, her reassurance doesn't quell the discomfort stirring
inside me. I'm not quite sure how to handle such praise, especially from someone who's the polar opposite of all my
friends, who might actually know what they're talking
about...

"I think they're beautiful, if that counts for anything."

My breath catches. *It does. More than she knows.*

Perhaps she senses that, as I meet her gaze, not uttering a
word yet speaking volumes. Somewhere between the realms
of amazement, passion, and gratitude.

"Did you have a teacher?"

I break her stare, allowing myself to breathe again. "Yes, for
a short time, when I was young. My mother sent me to one...
The lessons stopped after my parents' divorce," I add, but
regret it immediately when I catch Juliana's expression falter.

Even though she's not her mother and would never be to
blame for her... *transgressions*... it's still an uncomfortable
topic.

In our adolescence, while Juliana's mother, Amber, was
our night-time nanny, she entertained an affair with my father
for several years, but what Juliana doesn't know—or, well,
she probably *does* know but isn't recognizing its importance—
is that Amber was just one of many for my father. A mere
speck in his vast portfolio of infidelity. Not to mention,
Amber was unmarried at the time.

And although their divorce probably *did* shape my
subconscious views on monogamy, it didn't affect my childhood *that* much. My mother, Sylvia, as much of the charis-
matic person that she is, she wasn't all that involved in my

brother and I's lives. What she lacked in the mothering department, she filled with nannies and babysitters and assistants and after-school activities like painting, all of which were reserved primarily for me, as my brother was too busy being mentored by my father from a startlingly young age.

While our mother was off...

I don't know, living life?

Socializing, traveling, gossiping at the country club, partying. The high life was her playground—and still is. Again, that doesn't make her a bad person, just... a distracted one, similar to that of how my father views me. Actually, he blatantly compares my mother and I's habits quite often, and did so even during my childhood, when I displayed signs of hyper-extroversion and a disinterest in school, stating Sylvia was the root cause.

Not because she was an absent mother—*nooo,* that couldn't possibly be the case—or, perhaps, *his* lack of interest in *me*. No. None of that is to blame for my innate desire to bring disgrace upon him. Rather, my genes. *Our* genes—my mother and me. We were born this way, and I was misfortunate enough to take after her and not him, who fucks anything that breathes or looks at him too long, all while wearing a wedding ring, then turns around and calls himself the mature head of the family and me a walking pit stain.

Like my art. Such a distraction. A lousy one, too.

My little doodles...

So yes, after the divorce, the classes stopped, for more reasons than just Amber or, by association, The Brooks family, who took me in at times growing up and who I love dearly. Amber included.

"We don't need to go into that, Juliana. You know how I feel, so please don't make that face."

She squirms, offering a simple nod, before she smirks. "Okay, now ask me a question."

"What?"

"I've been grilling you for the past ten minutes—it's only fair. Ask me something. Anything."

Anything.

Excitement rocks me at my core, but it quickly tapers off. I already know so much about Juliana, more so than almost anyone in her life. It's not often that your paths align with another's so closely, like the universe keeps stitching you back together, no matter if you've drifted apart.

Even after a five year-long gap, when I pushed her away and thought I'd never get her back...

I banish the memories, refusing to let them take hold. "Why don't you drink?" I ask the first question that pops into my head, genuinely curious.

She looks at me blankly.

"Alcohol," I clarify.

"Oh," she laughs. "I do sometimes, but not often."

"Any particular reason?"

A slight blush colors her cheeks. "I, uh... make bad decisions when I'm drunk."

My jaw clenches as thoughts of her with other men flood my mind, but I push them away and tease, "You, the most responsible person I know, making bad decisions? Those two don't belong in the same sentence. I don't buy it."

"It's true!" She giggles awkwardly, sparking my interest.

"Like what? Give me an example."

"Like, ummm..." She looks up at the sky, as if she'll find the answers between the clouds. "Oh! Like this."

I raise a brow, only for my heart to lurch into my throat when she hoists herself up, out of the water, and sits on the wooden planks surrounding the in-ground tub. Wet droplets slide down her body, so distractingly that I nearly miss where she's pointing.

At her belly button ring.

"So, that was a drunken decision?" I ask a bit too roughly, bringing a fist to my mouth, resisting the urge to bite into my flesh. *Don't stare, don't stare, don't stare...*

"Mhmm," she confirms, almost proudly. "Made a couple years back while I was still at university. Two tequila sunrises, I think they were. Yep, that did me in real good—I'm a lightweight, I admit. Then, while we were out exploring the city that night, we happened upon a piercing shop..."

"Mei tried to convince me not to, said I'd regret it the next morning when I sobered up. She was right. Plus, aside from keeping it clean, I was too afraid to touch it—and I certainly wouldn't let anyone else. But, as the days wore on, it grew on me more and more." She shrugs. "Now, here I am, still rockin' it."

...Oh, God. It's my turn to talk. How the hell do I respond to that?

Don't worry, Juliana, I think it's hot as fuck. In fact, me and the rest of the men in New York City, especially those who came to my party, are thankful for your drunkenness that night...?

No, no—ah, shit. That'd make it weird...

"Well..." I clear my throat, forcing my eyes to meet hers. "It sounds like it ended up being a good decision. So, why hold out today? It could've made the party more fun for you."

"You're not wrong, but I didn't want to..." Avoiding my gaze, she rolls her lips between her teeth as heat creeps up her chest.

My pulse jumps, knowing exactly where her mind is at, because mine's already there. *Been there,* since she left me in that cabana. "Didn't want to what?" I coo, hunger sparking within me when she presses a hand to her neck, right where my lips left their mark.

"To... to lose control," she whispers.

Control...

A single word—that's all it takes to snap the band holding back mine.

I rise to my feet, waist deep in the water, reveling when her eyes descend along my torso, then flick back up. "And why were you so worried about losing control, *Jules?*" I cock my head, inching closer, watching as a shiver courses through her.

"You know why," she says, so quietly I almost miss it.

"I want to hear you say it."

Wetting her lips, she lets her gaze fall.

Another step, and I'm encroaching her space, bumping against her knees. "Look at me," I purr, pinching her chin, lifting her to my stare, "and answer my question. Shall I rephrase it for you? *Who* is it that you were so worried you'd lose control around?"

When I pinch harder, a small sound escapes her. "...You."

Fuckkk. I grate my teeth, weathering the sudden tightness of my swim trunks. "And why is that?"

"B-because..." she stammers, her chest rising and falling. "Of what happened in the cabana."

I angle her chin, baring her neck to me. Even under the tub's soft glow, the bruise is glaring. Deep purple and round. What a shame the other side doesn't have another to match. Her pulse flutters when I brush a finger across it.

I smirk. "Wasn't that all just part of your act?"

"No—*yes*," she corrects with a huff, squirming under my attention. "I mean, I wanted..."

Her teeth sink into her bottom lip when I grab her by the nape, threading my fingers through her hair, just like before. "What did you want?" My heart pounds through my veins like liquid fire, anticipation wound intensely inside me as I await her words.

Her overdue confession.

"More," she breathes, so close to a moan. "I wanted more—"

She gasps as I grip tighter, the locks between my fingers pulled taut. I let my eyelids fall, before exhaling through my nose steadily. In and out... In and out... trying but failing to expel the thoughts flooding my brain, urging me to bend her right over the mahogany, over the edge of this tub, so she can scream my name for the skies to hear.

But I want to savor this.

I loosen my grip, trailing a touch down her arm. "Is that why you came out here—to pick up where we left off? Why you put on that bikini?"

She nods, the gesture so small it's hardly noticeable, as her thighs press together.

"Look at me," I say again. When she obeys, raising those doe-eyes up at me through her lashes, a thrill shocks my senses. "Did you slip this little bikini back on, so you could flaunt your tight ass and perfect tits around me?"

"...Yes." She swallows roughly.

A violent shudder tears through me as I contemplate dragging her to my bed, where she belongs, where she should've been since moving in. Instead, she's made me wait, teased me with her presence and longing glances, gave in to my touch, then sped off, and let me hear her in that bathroom, in the throes of her lust.

I don't care who her brother is or isn't, about our contract, or that ruining her will damn me straight to Hell...

I'm done waiting.

I slip a hand between her thighs, nudging them open. "Then show me."

TWENTY-FIVE
JULIANA

MY BODY IS A TWISTED INFERNO. A raging conduit of
lust. Hotter than the steam rising off the gorgeous man
before me and burning brighter than the satisfaction in his
eyes.

As for my mind, well, it slipped off the slope of sanity a
while ago, probably around the time the bruise on my neck
fully formed, or maybe while I was fantasizing about my
brother's best friend instead of sleeping. Now, look what I've
done. The place between my ears flows with carnal need,
void of thought or rationale, and yearns for one thing and one
thing only.

Hayden's touch.

I spread my legs, baring my center, watching as Hayden's
tongue sweeps across his bottom lip, beneath an expression
lined with restraint. Goosebumps rise along my skin, not
from the cool night air, but from the hands perusing down
my thighs, halting at my knees.

I gasp when Hayden shoves my legs wider. Stepping
closer through the water, he keeps them there with his body,

pressing my shins firmly into the hot tub walls, as he admires me on full display.

"God, you're fucking perfect," he praises, squeezing my thighs, his eyes swirling with hunger when he notes my nipples pebbling under my bikini. "Take them out."

I hesitate.

Our gazes lock, and for a moment, we just stare at each other in silence, his nose a hair's breadth from mine. Anticipation crackles between us like a live wire, deadly to the touch, forming a line that I may or may not cross.

I reach for my top, shivering when he murmurs, "That's my good girl," and spread the fabric apart, exposing myself. The instant his eyes flick downward, his shoulders droop, his whole body releasing tension on a sigh. At first, I'm unsure if he likes what he sees, until he lets out a low curse.

"You could have me on my knees with those, Juliana."

I bite down on a jittery smile. "Could I?"

"Yes, and more..." He trails a hand straight down my middle, grazing my belly button ring ever-so softly, stopping above my bikini bottoms. "With this."

I inhale sharply as he tugs the fabric upwards, giving me a slight front wedgie, the motion a reminder of just how slick I am underneath. He smirks at that and tugs again, rougher this time, forcing a whimper out of me, then another when he sweeps farther down.

"Every man wanted you tonight."

I'm about to protest, to tell him he's crazy for thinking that, but a yelp escapes instead. He presses a thumb to my clit over the fabric, the sensation almost too intense to bear.

"N-no, they didn't," I manage to get out, as he presses firmer, my legs shaking, splashing in the water.

"They did." He eases up, then begins my delicious torture

—rubbing tiny, steady circles over my sensitive bud, as if he has all night. I suck in my bottom lip, pleasure bursting along my nerve endings.

"They would've done anything, said anything to you, to see what lies under *this*, to have you wrapped around them all night." Jealousy swims beneath his tone, but he keeps a constant, teasing pace, rendering it impossible for me to argue. "But they didn't try, only stared at your tempting body from afar, because they knew you'd warm *my* bed tonight. Isn't that right, Jules?"

"Yes—*yes!*" I moan, embarrassment hot on my cheeks as I sway against his finger, craving more friction.

His dark chuckle breezes over my skin, before he leans closer, spreading me wider and constricting my movements. "So needy." He *tsks* with his tongue, watching me writhe. "When I haven't even truly touched you yet."

I grunt in frustration when he withdraws his touch, leaving me wanting, only to go utterly still as he grazes down the edge of the fabric, near my opening. He waits a moment, looking into my eyes, as if I might stop him. When I don't, he brushes it aside, exposing my flesh.

"Fuckkkk," he groans roughly, his knuckles whitening along the edge of the tub. "Are you always this wet for me?"

Yes. "Sometimes."

"So, I'm fucking a liar tonight, am I?"

"No!" I cry out as his fingers descend upon my bare clit, rubbing harshly.

"Don't lie to me," he growls, flashing a devilish grin when I grind against his hand, doubling over into his chest. He grabs me by the hair, tugging my neck back to look up at him. "Just a greedy little liar, aren't you? Prancing around my apartment in those tight yoga pants that show off your ass, when your pussy's soaking wet underneath, huh? Does that sound about right?"

Fuckkk! I take his punishment, my mouth open on a silent scream. When I nod vigorously, he laughs.

"That's what I thought." He drops to an abysmal pace, and it's just as brutal. My legs tremble involuntarily, riding out the come-down, but I find no solace as he works me over, smirking when he hears my pleading mewls. "What else are you hiding, hmm?"

Doing away with my dignity, I whine, "Nothing."

"Nothing?" he repeats, staring down at me. His jaw locks, an idea seemingly popping into his head, which transforms his entire demeanor. Dark shadows swirl across his eyes, so vivid I swear I can make out the possession in them like a living, dangerous thing.

"Who else has seen you like this?"

My lips part. *Is he asking what I think he is?*

"N-no one," I stammer.

"I'm not going to tell you again, Juliana. *Do. Not.* Lie to me." He pushes against my clit, holding firm, until I'm whimpering for mercy—

"Okay! One..." I grit my teeth. "There's one guy who's seen."

He goes rigid...

Powerful breath flares through his nostrils, tainting his features with jealousy. "Just one?" he manages to get out.

"Yes," I say, but it sounds more like a plea, as his ministrations grow more purposeful.

"His name?"

What? Why in the world does he need to kn—

His eyebrows lift, a silent warning.

"Jonah! His name was Jonah."

"Last name?"

Good grief!

"I-I don't remember," I admit, which seems to please him.

"So, this *Jonah*," he spits, like his name's got a bad taste. "He was your first?"

Oh, no.

Shame burns my cheeks. "Not exactly..." Hayden's stare only intensifies, and I know he won't accept a vague answer. *Could this get any more embarrassing?* "We, uh... met at a frat party, fooled around, but umm, never really went... *all the way.*"

Suddenly, the pressure relents.

Hayden stills like a statue. "Wait, are you saying—"

"I'm a virgin," I finish for him, ripping the bandage clean off, only to watch his expression move through a myriad of stages.

Starting with disbelief.

Pushing off the wall, he leaves me barren and exposed, questioning every decision which led me here. He mutters to himself, things like, "That can't be right... there's no way, I thought..." which quickly divulges into shock—"I know you're... but I didn't think..."—until he arrives at a state I'm not sure what to make of.

Swiveling around, he marches back my way, powering through the water and making my stomach flip in anticipation. His muscles flex under the moonlight, rippling with each step, and his devilish smirk grows wider and wider. "Fuckkkkk," he grunts, more to himself than me. "You really shouldn't have told me that."

"Why?" Expecting his judgment or some snide remark, I reach for my bra to cover myself up, but he snatches my chin before I can.

"Because, sweet, *innocent* Jules..." He tilts my chin, angling my neck to him like earlier, except now it's the opposite side. "I get to be the one who corrupts you." His lips latch onto my neck, and a free hand simultaneously falls upon my clit, flicking brutally.

"*Oh!*" I cry out, reaching for his biceps, my nails digging into his skin. Shivers race up my spine, one after the other, as he laps me up with his tongue, moaning a guttural sound, sucking hard, harder than the first time with a greater intention of leaving a mark.

"Fuckfuckfuckfuck..." I grind against his hand, whimpering when his fingers thread through my hair, exploring their depths, then pull taut and guide me to the ground.

Lying flat, coldness seeps into my backside, but it's quickly forgotten as Hayden hoists himself out of the tub, drapes his body over mine, and entangles our limbs, water trickling off his skin like a warm blanket.

Wet suction resonates out into the night air, while he works up the column of my throat, painting a trail of saliva. Until he stops and focuses on that one spot at the crook of my jaw, sucking and biting, then darting his tongue out to soothe the burn, all while grinding his leg into my sex.

Desperate, I buck against him, coating his thigh with my slickness, squirming beneath his weight in a crazed heat.

"Fuck, baby," he groans, his lips *popping* from my skin, leaving behind a thumping soreness as he retreats to the water.

"What're you doing?" I pant, my sex throbbing with need.

"Making sure you forget his name."

Jonah?

My mouth opens, but no sound comes out, only a squeal when strong arms wrap around my thighs, then yank me to the edge of the tub. I look down, past the grooves of my body, and find him at the end, staring back at me, his mouth inches from my pussy.

I gasp, holding in that gulp of air, because all I see are my fantasies flashing before my eyes, the ones where Hayden buries his face between my thighs.

Oh, fuck, oh, fuck, oh —

His breath tickles against my flesh. "Are you drunk?"

I quirk a brow. *What an oddly timed question.*

"No, of course not."

"Good." He sinks a finger past my entrance, pinning me down by my waist when I buckle at the intrusion. "Then you won't be able to explain away this bad decision, will you?"

Fire rages down my middle, making coherent thoughts nearly impossible, as I stretch around his finger, allowing more in, little by little, its size longer and thicker than I'm accustomed.

Explain away? Why would I —

Then it hits me.

This—what we're doing right now—isn't the bad decision he's referring to.

He is.

Hayden Kingston, Manhattan's most notorious heartthrob, a self-proclaimed playboy, who collects broken hearts like they're diamonds for his Rolex or trophies to stomp beneath his patent leather loafers. In his eyes, love is a game, which makes falling for him the worst decision of them all.

But I'm *not* developing feelings—I can't be.

I won't allow it.

"It's only lust," I say without wavering, injecting confidence into my tone, even though it doesn't quite resonate down to my bones. "There's nothing more between us."

His finger stops abruptly, halfway inside of me.

A mysterious shadow flickers across Hayden's features, something that looks an awful lot like hurt. And my goodness, could I not devise a more unbecoming expression for him, like a wilted flower in a storm that, for reasons I can't explain, almost convinces me to retract my statement. Except, in the blink of an eye, I wonder if I really *did* imagine it all as he stares back at me, wearing his usual haughty smirk.

"Right?" I ask, anyway.

He snorts. "Who do you think you're talking to?"

His finger curls upward, hitting a spot that has me arching my back and rolling my eyes up into the sky, until it retracts, forcing a moan from my lips. My insides clench around air at the sound of his deep baritone as he curses, inspecting his finger glistening under the starry lights.

"So fucking *wet.*"

I whine, squirming against his hold.

"And needy, too." He brushes my clit, chuckling at my frustrated grunt. "Put your feet up on the ledge. I want your knees in the air... Yes, just like that. Now spread them... wider... wider... That's it." I suck in my bottom lip when he slips his finger back in.

"You just love doing what you're told, don't you?"

I nod, words beyond me, as my inner walls clamp around his retreat, savoring the sweet burn.

"*Fuckkk,*" he growls, raising hairs along my arms. "Such a tight little thing."

A string of whimpers fumbles from my lips on his return, pushing farther than before.

"Shhhh, be my good girl and take it." He brushes a hand down my inner thigh, soothing away the last bit of pain, until he curls his finger higher, homing in on that one spot.

I bite my lip, tears stinging the corners of my eyes at the newfound pleasure radiating through me. As his pace increases, I moan loudly, swaying back against him to the beat of his rhythm.

"Right there, baby?"

"Yes, yes!"

"God, your tits are so fucking perfect. I love watching them bounce for me... Pinch your nipples." A breath shoots from my lungs when he thrusts hard, all the way in for the first time, his skin smacking against mine in quick repetitions. *"Pinch them."*

I wail into the wind, grabbing hold of my breasts as I slide along the mahogany, then pinch, squeezing harder and harder as he drives home. Relentless, he captures my gaze like a possessive animal, hungry to watch me come undone.

And I do.

Writhing and kicking and moaning things that're foreign to my own ears, my eyes cross in two, as his palm slaps against my clit on every thrust. *Smack, smack, smack, smack,* he finger-fucks me, building that wave inside of me higher and higher, like a light slicing through my center.

Shock pummels my senses, realizing what I'm about to do. Something I've never achieved around anyone else, let alone from another's touch. My eyes widen like saucers, meeting Hayden's smoldering gaze, all remnants of my pride and dignity or whatever the hell I used to care about long gone, as I gasp, "I-I'm going—I'm going to—"

But my words are cut short, shoved right back down my throat, as Hayden does the most wicked, most evil thing he's ever done in his twenty-four years of existence. *He rips his finger out of me,* killing my orgasm at its peak.

Oh. My. Fucking. God.

Anger explodes brighter than any flame as I meet his mischievous stare. Releasing my nipples, I fling my hands forward, ready to tear that smirk right off his li—

He snatches my wrists midair, bundling them in his tight grasp.

Pins them to the ground.

Wait, what is he—

Then *shoves* his face into my pussy.

I cry at the top of my lungs, as he buries himself into me like a starved man, like someone who doesn't want to come up for air, before he sucks my clit into his mouth, and proceeds to blow my every fantasy to the moon. His tongue works at blazing speeds, flicking between his teeth, raising that wave inside of me ten-fold, until it comes crashing over my head, like a screaming fire in my ears.

Then *I'm* screaming—actually. Thrashing and panting, riding out every last sensation, each interior clench around emptiness a burning wish, a desire above all else that I was wrapped around Hayden's cock.

"Fuuuuckkkkk," I moan, low from my gut, grinding against his mouth, savoring my slow come-down. He groans back, sticking out his flattened tongue for me to use, while he watches through those thick lashes, brimming with satisfaction.

When my heart rate plateaus, I release a breath, halting my movements as tension eases from my muscles and—

Hayden sweeps his tongue clean through my middle, causing me to jolt backward as a sting sears through my sex, a mix of pleasure and pain. "W-wait, I'm really sensitiv—"

I suck in a sharp breath as he laps up my center again. "Ohh, are you? But you taste so sweet."

Knowing what's coming next, I mewl, struggling with all

my efforts as his biceps loop around my thighs, dragging me closer.

"Hold still for me." He sweeps through me once more, torturously slow, a deep moan reverberating against my sex as he tightens his grip. "Just one more taste." Another round, and I'm buckling against him, this time with a little more pleasure. "Such a good girl, so wet for me." *Again...* "That's it, give me easy access." *Again...* "Oh, you're taking it so well." *And again...* "One more, baby, won't you let me?—*Mmmmmm, fuck.*"

I thrash and thrash, to no avail, until I'm totally spent, whimpering for mercy.

His eyelids fall.

"Your"—*lick*—"cum"—*lick*—"is"—*lick*—"so"—*lick*—"addicting"—*lick...*

I don't know how much time passes, and judging by the surprised look on Hayden's face when he finally *does* come up for air, he doesn't know either. Then I'm left throbbing and panting and sweating like a mess, as if I never came in the first place and need him all over again.

Releasing his hold, he smirks, wipes his mouth with the back of his hand, and hoists himself out of the water, pointing his gaze toward the terrace exit. Sensing dismissal, I make to pull up my bikini bottoms, which are completely soaked, as for everything else below my waist.

"Not yet." He stops me. "I'm going to get you a towel.

His eyes flick to mine, already on the ground.

"A better one," he clarifies. "For cleaning up."

I sit up, feeling rejected. "That's okay. If that's all I can... um... I'll just go rinse off in the shower."

He snickers.

"What's so funny?" My eyes narrow defensively.

"Oh, nothing. Just the fact that you think I'm anywhere near finished with you."

A shudder ripples through me.

"Whether this is all just lust or not..." His gaze crawls across my body, spiking my arousal. "You can scratch that little bit about sleeping separately off our contract. From this point forward, while you're still living under my roof, you're *mine*. My little plaything, remember? Who's expected to warm my bed, so I can keep her up all. Night. Long."

My jaw falls slack, but I have no time to process as he whips around, aiming for the door. "Stay put. I'll be right back," are his departing words.

I blink, watching him stride across the terrace, waiting for some type of post-nut clarity moment, for the inevitable regret and shame... but it never comes. Although, something else does, something wildly unexpected—and a little crazy???

A giggle.

Very, *very* quietly, I laugh, covering my mouth with a hand, like the birds might hear me a hundred stories high and gossip to their friends. A grin spreads along my lips, wide and proud, as a sort of euphoria overtakes me. Whether endorphins are to blame, or deep-rooted feelings wrapped in a thick encasing of denial, I don't really care.

I just know that I'm happy in this moment, and that the rest of the night will only bring me further—

Ring, ring, ring... a phone sings from the opposite side of the hot tub, lighting up in the darkness. I whip my head, catching a shirtless backside entering the penthouse. "Oh, Hayden, I think"—the door swings shut—"...someone's trying to call you..." I mutter.

Oh, well. I wait out the rings, until all is quiet. *They'll just leave a voicemail and he'll call them ba*—

RING, RING, RING...

I purse my lips, the sound blaring through the peaceful terrace once again, until it stops, only to start up a *third* time.

Adrenaline jolts me to my feet.

Maybe it's something urgent.

Pattering my damp feet across the mahogany, I creep closer... only for my heart to sink further and further... until it's oh-so obvious that I should turn back around, that I shouldn't subject myself to a closeup view of what's most certainly a pair of *tits* waiting on a video call.

I crouch low, tears pricking my eyes—ones that shouldn't even be there, but they are anyway. Through blurry vision, I watch those unnaturally large breasts jiggle about, their pierced nipples twisting by bright red nails, all below a name at the top of the screen. A name already in the phone's contacts, beside a message containing winky faces and other suggestive emojis.

Olivia: *Let's finish what we started the other night.*

TWENTY-SIX
JULIANA

STOP FUCKING CRYING!

Urgency crashes into me. Adrenaline and anger and a sadness I'm too weak to admit, as I race down the hallway aimlessly. I swipe a hand across my cheek, flustered when I wipe away tears I already knew were there. But I discard of the evidence, anyway, swiping the mess on my soaked bikini bottoms, feeling a sense of betrayal—

You asked for it, whispers that little devil on my shoulder, who is happy beyond measure, as if he shot the angel off the other. So, so very smug that I'm in such a predicament, having stooped to levels so low, that when I burst through my bathroom door, I hardly recognize the reflection staring back at me in the mirror.

Another sob wrenches my ribcage, but I swallow it back down violently, *stubbornly,* as if I can wish the feelings away or ignore them completely. Maybe rewind the last hour or two of my life, if I just... *breathe...* in and out... *good, good, like that...* in and out... in and—

Sounds like you're reliving it all. In and out? Just like he used his finger to—

SHUT UP! I scream back, my expression in the mirror contorting into that of a deranged murderer. Red eyes, flared nostrils, chest heaving... In response, all I hear is its high-pitched cackle, echoing inside my mind. Overpowering and victorious, like I handed my insecurities a megaphone. *Dammit, am I going crazy?*

My emotions resurface once more.

Inhale... exhale... inhale... ex—

"Juliana!"

No, no, no, go away, go away, go away...

Inhaleexhaleinhaleexhale—

"Juliana, please!"

When his voice cracks, another sob escapes me, turning my next breath into frantic gasps for air.

What a great actor he is. No, seriously. He's had plenty of time to practice. That sound of brokenness, of desperation. It's all fake. Well-rehearsed, pre-planned, probably after he hung up with that girl, whoever she is. Maybe he even joked around with her, said he just bagged a helpless romantic— a.k.a. a moron, who thought she could play the role of the promiscuous girl, the cool girl, the DTF girl, and come out unscathed.

Then I'm sure he told those tits to wait up for him. Why? Because he's gotta come grovel, to ensure there's a next time. Well, there won't be, but unfortunately for the moron, the damage is already done.

Boohoo, poor, poor Juliana, taunts that little devil. *Such a victim, as if you weren't the one who joined him in that hot tub after slipping this little red bikini back on. News flash. You're the one playing games, sweetie. Games with yourself.*

It's true. I really must be, but I didn't anticipate how I'd feel afterward. The... *contentment.* The joy. Truly unexpected. How is it possible that shame didn't overwhelm me? *That's* what I expected, regardless of the phone incident—wallowing in regret from the act alone. Not crying from deep-seated jealousy or the fact he messes around with other women.

Nonetheless, here I am.

Wanted to get fucked.

Instead, got fucked in the head.

When I hear steps bounding outside, growing louder, another warm tear slips down my cheek. I dash for the bathroom door. My pulse spikes in rhythm to his frantic puffs of breath, until he's seconds from my discovery. "Julianaaaa, please, just come outside and let me—"

The rest of his lie is cut short by me, slamming the door on its hinges, then twisting the lock. His gasp rings from the other side, before he calls my name again, his hand fumbling with the doorknob until—

BANG, BANG, BANG, the knob wiggles some more, followed by a desperate chorus of pleas. And *fuck,* does he sound sincere, but I entertain none of it as his attempts at trickery fade into the blackness of my mind.

Staring at my reflection, I keep a level head—I really do—until I begin peeling off my bikini. Then the tears flow.

I'm never going to forget what happened, am I? When a man promises to ruin you, is this what he means? Sentencing you to a lifelong cycle of forever comparing your sexual encounters to him, to this one night, knowing none will ever live up to it?

I ponder the idea, almost in horror, as I free my hair from its tie and meander to the shower. A shower so luxurious, it could fit four people easily, and yet, as some of that banging pierces through my mental fog, I find myself wishing I was back in my cruddy apartment.

Turning the handle, water cascades from the waterfall shower head, drowning out the sounds from afar, and coating the room with thick steam.

After what happened, I don't know why my instincts led me here. Sure, I need to clean myself off, lest I sleep like some miserable, shameful mess, but... as I step inside, letting the heat roll down my cheeks, I wonder if they just wanted to blur the distinction between tears and water.

Just as calmness settles over me, those little devils multiply in numbers, their ranks forming a choir I can't escape as they whisper unsettling things between my ears...

Oh, Juliana, when will you ever learn...?

Guess your skin isn't as thick as you thought...

Now you're just another one of his conquests...

What were you expecting...?

You let him steal a piece of you, again...

Again...

Again...

Again...

The word resonates in my mind, replaying on a vicious feedback loop, in tandem with the water beating against my scalp. I let my eyelids fall, watching as those tiny droplets morph into something else. A memory from a different time. Five years ago, to be exact.

Confetti.

"YEAHHHHHH!!!" Jeremy pounds his fists on the table, rattling our fancy silverware. *"Woo, woo, woo, w—"*

"Shhh!" I hiss below my breath, embarrassment painting my cheeks brighter than a fire engine as little pieces of paper rain over

my head, sticking to my clothes and dotting along my acceptance letter to Yale University. "Not so loud!"

"Sorry, Sis." He sounds like a broken record as he retrieves yet another confetti popper from his pocket, ready for the next letter.

"Oh my god, how many of those did you bring?"

"Fourteen. One for every school you applied to."

I shake my head, hiding a smile. "Thanks, Jer. You seriously thought I'd get accepted by all of them?"

"Of course, Miss Valedictorian." He nods proudly, as if he wasn't one himself.

Hiding a smile, I sweep the colorful mess into a neat pile beside our appetizers, then add the letter to one of two stacks—the yesses and the nos. So far, the acceptances are in the lead, with UCLA, Northwestern, Brown, and now Yale, standing taller than the rejections—Stanford and Amherst College.

Sure, the nos hurt, but I wasn't expecting a clean sweep, not after applying to such competitive schools. Still, I'm grateful Jeremy is here for moral support.

Just one year ago, I listened as he recited his Valedictorian speech in front of his entire graduating class, one year ahead of mine—a task I'm petrified to face in the coming months. Then, at the end of that summer, he flew off to Princeton University to study Electrical Engineering. I can vividly recall watching him open his admission letters, one by one, in our living room with our whole family around.

I didn't want that kind of pressure, but I also couldn't handle this alone, so I asked the person who could best relate for support. Luckily, Jeremy's spring break lined up with mine, so he was already visiting home. Although... if I'd known who he was going to invite, I would've reconsidered.

As if I summoned his presence, a man approaches our table. All

I need to see are the designer sweatpants and Gucci slides from the corner of my eye to know it's Hayden.

"Shitttt. You're alive." My brother devolves into his macho alter-ego as the two exchange some weird bro handshake.

Hayden takes a seat to my right, across from Jeremy, and removes his sunglasses, revealing a pair of icy-blue eyes I can't hold for more than two seconds. With a groan, he squints at the light, swiping a hand through his disheveled locks.

"Sorry I'm late," he mumbles groggily, to no one in particular.

Jeremy snorts. "No worries. I didn't think you'd be able to crawl out of bed after last night."

"Spring break is wild, isn't it? Well, not as wild as the parties our frat is throwing this week, I'm sure. I'm flying back tonight, so I don't miss another one, which means..." Hayden smirks, reaching for a menu. "I gotta get some breakfast in me."

Breakfast? *I tap my phone.* But it's four in the afternoon...

Oh, who am I kidding? Hayden's always been a night owl. Or a vampire. Actually, yeah. With looks like those, definitely a vampire —Edward Cullen and Chris Hemsworth's love child, no doubt.

I sneak another peek at Hayden as he gazes down at his menu. Except, that peek quickly morphs into a stare, sweeping across his sharp jawline, sloping down the bridge of his straight nose, and delving between those silky blond lo—

"Okay, what's up next?"

I jolt at the sound of Jeremy's voice.

Dammit, Juliana, quit staring! *I scold myself, whipping my gaze elsewhere.*

Not for my brother's sake, who wouldn't notice me staring if I'd pulled out a pair of binoculars. Me, having a crush... on a boy... those two things just don't mix in his brain. He's like an overprotective dad with selective eyesight, who still thinks I'm eight years old.

So, no. This whole not staring at my brother's best friend thing — it's something I've been working on. Or trying to work on, more like. Since... I don't even know how long.

Maybe since middle school, when I finally admitted to myself that I had a crush but was too shy to do anything about it. Or perhaps freshman year, when I quickly realized how different I was from Hayden's type, judging by the cheer squad — half of whom he either dated at one point or fooled around with. The intimate details of which I could never escape, not when he visited my brother so often and the wall between our bedrooms is as thin as paper.

To Hayden, I'm like a subtle draft breezing through the room, inconspicuous and overlooked. Just a geeky girl in glasses he grew up alongside. Which is why he's more interested in food than my admission letters.

Still, his presence doesn't make this any easier.

As I pick the next letter, I clear my throat, catching the sole attention of Jeremy. "This one's from U Penn."

"Ohhhhh, maybe you're destined to be a Quaker."

"We'll see, we'll see..." I tear open the envelope, shaking my head when Jeremy starts drum rolling on the table. On the outside, I may appear nonchalant with each letter, but inside, I'm anything but. My stomach's like a bowl of spaghetti dumped into a KitchenAid on high speeds. That is, until I read the first word:

Congratulations!

I release a breath. "I got in."

POP! Confetti blasts across the table, showering me in praise once more, as our silverware rattles like there's an earthquake, water spilling over the rims of our glasses. "WOOOOOOOO — OW-OW-OW!!!!"

"Oh my god, shush!" I shield my face behind a menu, feeling the gazes of those sitting at nearby tables burning right through the paper. "You're gonna get us kicked out!"

Jeremy's laughter bellows through the air, causing Hayden to cringe at its volume. "Oh, we would've been by now, if Hayden's dad didn't own the place."

My jaw goes slack. I look over at Hayden, whose head still buries between a menu, boredom plain on his features. A subtle smirk is his only confirmation.

I shouldn't be surprised. Sometimes, it seems as if Warren Kingston owns half of Manhattan. It's no wonder the staff didn't bat an eye at Hayden's sweatpants. Being the son of a billionaire— it comes with many perks, I've learned throughout the years.

Releasing a steady breath, I select the next letter, sighing as Jeremy digs into his pocket. A pang of disappointment strikes me when Hayden flips to another page.

*Jeremy leans over the table eagerly. "Which school is it?" he asks, exactly how an impatient kid pesters his parents with the classic—*are we there yet, are we there yet?!

"This one's for Princeton."

Hayden's gaze flicks over the top of his menu, so subtly I almost miss it, before it darts back down. His jaw ticks, and I swear I catch something I've never seen flicker across his features...

Nervousness.

No, no. That can't be right. My eyes are just seeing what they want. That's all.

I shake my head, before my thoughts spiral out of control, take a deep breath—and just rip the damn thing open.

Silence.

"...what is it? What does it say?"

I release a quick breath. "They accepted me."

Noise erupts from our table as Jeremy somehow outdoes all his previous outbursts. The confetti, the woo-woos, *the table pounding, all of it and then some, until his commotion dies down, and the strangest thing happens.*

I meet Hayden's stare, who's looking directly at me. Like actually *looking at me, as if I exist in his world, a minor blip on his radar. "Congratulations." His voice is calm, his expression cool, yet it's enough to stir butterflies in my stomach.*

"Thank you," I say shyly.

The rest of the applications carry on like before. Jeremy is overly eager, while Hayden remains a quiet shadow, who's more interested in his menu, his food, and our waitress. As I open each remaining decision, I'm met with a roar of celebration or Jeremy's words of encouragement. You'll get the next one, *he says, before I move onto the next.*

All in all, most schools accept me, which you'd think would ease some of my tension—if it weren't for the letter I saved for last. Nerves ripple through me, revealing a slight tremor as I grab it.

Jeremy rests a hand on my shoulder. "Whatever happens, it's going to be fine."

"I know," I whisper, my tone unconvincing in my own ears.

Hayden lifts an eyebrow, acknowledging us for the first time in ten minutes. "What's so special about this one?"

"It's her top choice."

Hayden freezes, his hand halting midway through wiping a napkin across his lips. His eyes narrow, speaking with food still in his mouth. "I thought Princeton was."

My stomach flip-flops, so violently I miss the worry dripping from his tone, as I swipe a thumb across the letters on the envelope's front. "Columbia has a better Video Game Design program."

When he doesn't respond, I look up, finding him scarfing down his food again, without a care in the world about what lies inside this envelope. A twinge of disappointment strikes me, but it doesn't stand a chance against the sickness that overcomes me when I stare down the letter.

"Remember, whatever happens, it's meant to be."

I breathe deeply through my nose. He's right. I know he's right. There's no changing the outcome. The rest is up to fate. So, I surrender to it, and with two words, I reshape the trajectory of my future.

"I'm in!"

~

MOM LOOPS *her arms around my middle, hugging me tightly. "I know I've said it twenty times by now, but I'm so proud of you, sweetheart."*

Emotions catch in my throat as I hug her back, but I manage to keep them in check. "Thanks, Mom," I say, my voice hardly audible over the music blaring through the hallway from the living room.

"Sorry again about the ruckus. I promise we'll be just as rowdy next week when we throw you a celebration party."

I snort. "I doubt Grandma and Grandpa and the rest of the family can outdo Jeremy and his high school friends."

"I don't knooowww, you'd be surprised," she teases with a chuckle, stepping back. "Well, I'm off to bed, sweetie. Get some rest —if you can."

"Night, Mom."

I watch her walk down our narrow hallway and disappear around a corner, before heading into the bathroom I share with Jeremy, flip on the shower, and crank my speaker to full volume.

Mom's right. It's going to be impossible to fall asleep. Not because of my brother's party, but because of the excitement flooding my veins, like a shot of dopamine straight to my cranium.

But I'll try, nonetheless.

Steam billows from the bathroom on my exit. Wrapped in a fuzzy bathrobe, with my damp hair draping behind my shoulders, I hum the beat of my last song on the short trip to my bedroom. When

I shut my door, the thumping music softens, just a tad, before I twist around and—

I gasp as my heart nearly catapults from my chest.

My computer chair swivels around toward me, revealing Hayden in his usual attire. Navy chinos, shiny yacht shoes, a short-sleeved pressed polo that shows off his tan arms. He's straight off the front page of a fashion catalog, the spitting image of cocky Manhattan royalty.

Here. In my bedroom.

With shadows churning in his blue eyes.

"H-Hayden? Are you o—"

"So..." His gaze peruses across my tiny room, for perhaps the first time—and maybe the last. "You're just going to leave, then?" His words slur slightly.

"Umm..." I pick at the side of my nail, unsure of what to do with myself. "Aren't you supposed to be on a plane to—"

"Answer me, Jules." I roll my lips, like always, when he calls me by that nickname. No one ever does, and even if they did, it wouldn't sound like that. *"You're going to Columbia, not Princeton?"*

I shift uncomfortably, stuck by the door as water drips off my hair and splashes against my heels. Why does he sound so upset? *"Yes, I am. Is that a problem?"*

"Is that a problem, is that a problem," he mutters to himself, shooting to his feet, standing to his impressive height. "Yes, that's a problem. Have you not thought it through?"

"What???" I blink. "Of course, I have," I scoff. "Would you like me to list off all the reasons?"

"Yeah, yeah." He steps toward me, nostrils flaring. "Go right ahead."

What the hell's gotten into him? Who does he think he is? Like I need his approval to attend some university?

"Fine," I snap, and it only darkens those shadows. *"Where do I start —hmmm..."* I tap my chin. *"Oh, let's start there. Reason number one, which I already stated. Columbia has a great Game Design program..."*

His lips flatten as he creeps closer.

"... Reason number two. It's only a short drive away, which is quite ironic, isn't it? With you saying I'm *the one leaving and all, while you and Jeremy are off in New Jersey..."*

Tilting his head, he steps again, this time closing a considerable distance, causing my stomach to somersault.

"... N-number three..." I avoid his intense gaze, soldiering on. *"They offer a great financial package..."*

His presence crowds me against the door, my heart racing at a million miles per minute, muted by the music on the other side. If my brother knew I was in here, alone with Hayden, in nothing but a bathrobe... he'd raise hell.

"There are also many research opportunitie—"

"How about the part where I won't be able to look after you there?"

My lips part on a gasp...

"Huh? Have you thought of that?" Minty breath clouds my brain, mixed with alcohol and subtle traces of tobacco, slurring his words even more. *"You're just gonna go off and—who knows?—join a sorority, party on Greek Row in some tight dress, where any arrogant prick can get his hands on you..."*

Again, nothing comes out, rendering me speechless, stunned beyond measure. Because... if I'm not trapped in dreamland right now... I'd say he sounds...

Jealous.

And I mean... really jealous.

"Y-you're just drunk," I manage to say.

"Very perceptive of you, Jules." He chuckles a warm sound,

racing a shudder through me and dousing my senses with another wave of alcohol. "You're right. I am drunk. Not hammered, but just enough to call off my flight, stumble my way in here, and say things I really shouldn't."

Hope sparks within me, but I quickly squash it. "Sure, but you don't mean anything you're saying."

"No? Drunk words are sober thoughts."

My brow arches quizzically.

"You see? This is why you need me—for guidance."

"You're not making any sense."

He sighs. "Truth is, Jules. I already knew the answer before coming. That you'll go where you want to go, do as you want to do. It's in your nature. Which means... I'm only here for selfish reasons."

I freeze as he pinches one of my damp locks, trailing a touch down its length. When he reaches the end, I stammer, "What're you trying to say?"

He leans in closer, invading my space, pressing my backside more firmly against the door. Resting his forearm somewhere above my head, he stares down from his tall height, right in my eyes, straight through to my soul. For a moment, I think he's not going to say anything, that he's finally sobered up and realized his mistake, until he murmurs...

"That you're mine, no matter where you go."

Mine...

A single word from his lips, and I'm floating on air.

Goosebumps ripple across my skin, and warmth radiates outwards from my chest, like sunlight breaking through clouds, past years of tiptoeing, feeling invisible, and questioning if I was enough —not just for Hayden, but for anyone.

"I... I am?" I croak, tears stinging my eyes.

"Yes, you always have been." He brushes the side of my cheek. *"But in case you forget..."*

His hand sinks into his pocket, emerging with a gold chain wound around his fingers. An oval locket dangles at the end, adorned with a unique, intricate pattern that catches my eye fleetingly, before he loops it around my neck. His skin brushes against mine, sending a new wave of sensations as he secures the clamp into place.

On his retreat, he pauses, his lips only an inch away, so close I can feel his breath puffing from him on choppy waves. His eyes flicker between mine, left and right and back again, just as mine dart between his, until they trail low, down to my mouth, and pause, burning with fire, yet stifled with hesitation...

I wet my lips —

And his come crashing onto mine, claiming their first touch —

I wretch the memory from my mind, killing it there.

Draping my towel over the ledge of the tub, I walk across the steamy bathroom, naked, amidst the silence seeping through the other side of the door. Like the penthouse is fast asleep.

Alone, at last.

Approaching the sink, I avoid my reflection, as I crouch down and pull back the lowest drawer, revealing a gold chain. Intricate shapes etch into its oval locket, forming unique flowers and other dainty designs. It's beautiful, really, a reminder of my magical first kiss. After that night, I never took it off, not once.

Until I saw an actress wearing it three weeks later. Hand-in-hand with Hayden Kingston, son of billionaire Warren Kingston, plastered across the front page of a celebrity gossip site.

I was an idiot then for not throwing the necklace away. Guess I'm an even bigger one now.

I slam the drawer shut.

It's like those little devils said. Hayden deserves more credit. Maybe he's a genius, after all. A master of hearts, who excels at precisely one thing.

Stealing little pieces.

TWENTY-SEVEN
HAYDEN

OLIVIA MEANS NOTHING TO ME. I deleted her from my contacts. I never answered that video call. And if our paths ever cross again, whether forty thousand feet in the sky or here on the ground, I won't give her a second glance. That's what I would tell Juliana...

If she ever speaks to me again.

I've endured nine days of radio silence. Nine whole days of locking herself in her room and ignoring my knocks, the papers I've slipped under her door, my text messages, phone calls, voicemails, even emails. Hell, I'm two days shy of sending a carrier pigeon. Anything to convince her to just *talk* with me or look me in the eye or not dash from the kitchen the second I enter.

But the thing is... even if I got her to listen to me, what would I say after all that? Demand why she cares so much? I'm not even ready to answer that question. She said it herself —there's nothing more between us. And it's me we're talking about here, so... why is this all such a big deal? And why am I *willingly* ghosting Olivia and every other girl who's hitting me up like normal?

I mean, seriously, ever since Juliana moved into my apartment, I've let my number one, number two, three, four, and five just float into the wind, without even intentionally playing hard to get. It's like my instincts are revolting on themselves, screaming one big *fuck you* to...

Rule #9: A playboy maintains multiple dating prospects at all times.

So, yes, if I want to avoid self-destruction, these are all incredibly urgent questions...

That I sweep to the furthest corners of my mind.

"Her presentation starts in five minutes." To my left, Elias checks his watch, leaning back in his chair that's positioned at the head of the conference room table. "If she's late, I'll have to give her spot to one of the others waiting outside."

"She'll be here."

I think.

If it weren't for her ghosting me, I'd have no doubts. This is her end of the fake dating arrangement—gaining an audience with the man who chooses Kingston Entertainment's sponsors for this year's DreamScape. And as of right now, mostly, that's Elias, who will listen to all the presentations for the Indie Creator Showcase today. But, when I texted her a couple days back about the presentation, she never replied.

"Here." A notebook smacks on the table in front of me, along with a pen. "You'll be in charge of my presentation notes."

I blink. *Pen and paper? What're we, in the stone ages?*

"Is there something wrong with that?" he asks when I remain silent.

Besides having to do my brother's bitch work, oh nothing.

"Uhh, yeah. What about a laptop?"

His smirk tells me it's intentional. "You can type them up later."

Asshole.

"Why the long face, Hayden?" He snorts. "Worried your little *lady friend* will think differently of you? Come on now. I doubt it'll make her forget your last name. Besides, no one would blink twice seeing an assistant taking notes."

I wet my lips. "Right."

"Wait..." A smile grows along his lips, sparking annoyance inside me. "No—*no,* don't tell me."

I roll my eyes, anticipating his next words.

"She doesn't know you're my assistant?" He sucks in a breath, trying to stifle a laugh, only for it to come bursting out. "Oh, man, this is going to be fun, but... what is it she thinks you do here...?"

That I'm under Dad's wing, I don't say.

"No, wait." He holds out a hand before I sell him some nonsense. "Don't tell me. I don't want to know. That'll make it even better."

I exhale sharply, mumbling a string of curses.

Elias checks his watch again. "Two minutes."

My knuckles thrum along the table as I search for her through the solid glass surrounding the meeting room. Cubicles dominate the floor's massive space, with employees shuffling about. Some walk past the rows of chairs along the farside wall, occupied by the hopeful game devs, mostly men. But no Juliana.

Sweat pricks at my temple. *She wouldn't miss this, would she? All she does is work on that game.*

As time wanes on, doubt creeps in, and I wonder if I'll return home to her things all packed up. Maybe she came to her senses and decided I'm not worth the hassle, that she's better off moving back to that shoebox she calls an apartmen—

My heart constricts.

Carrying a laptop, a woman in a plaid skirt swings around a blind corner. A matching blazer drapes off her shoulders, cutting off at the waistline over a dark blouse. Her block heels eat up the carpet in confident strides, swaying her slicked-back ponytail. She's one hundred and ten percent corporate, with an academia edge—and turning the heads of every man in the room, some blissfully unaware she's their competition.

"There she is," I breathe.

Elias traces the line of my gaze, squinting at the end. "Hold on... isn't that Jeremy Brooks's sister?"

"Yep," I say, cringing at how proud I sound.

He watches her approach, shock marking his features. "What the hell's a girl like that doing messing around with you?"

My jaw slackens. Wow. Okay, then. Obviously, I'm not at all surprised he recognized her, but... I didn't expect his reaction to be *that* brutal.

"No offense," he adds.

"Gee, none taken." Irritation flares inside me as his head tilts, still focused on her.

"Is it just me, or does she seem pissed at you?"

Fuck, why is he always so perceptive? For a guy who never leaves his office, he sure can read people.

I meet her gaze through her glasses, its intensity sending shivers down my spine. "Oh, uhh... we're just going through a rough patch, is all. We're off and on, remember?"

"Right, right, like that girl's laid-back about anything in her life."

Goddamnit, does he have to sound so intrigued?

The glass door glides open, and in strides undoubtedly the prettiest girl in the office. I can't help but stare, especially since it's my first time getting a good look at Juliana since what transpired over a week ago. Conference room or not, all I see is the hot tub's ambient glow on her features, her mouth gaping on a lust-filled moa—

I burst to my feet, mirroring Elias, as he buckles his suit jacket.

Juliana plasters on a polite smile, one apparently reserved only for my brother, as her gaze swings to him, bypassing me with a flicker of annoyance.

He clears his throat, accepting her handshake.

"Mr. Kingston." She nods, a bit shyly, earning a hearty chuckle.

"Juliana, I know it's been quite some time—years, if I recall correctly—but please, Mr. Kingston is my father. To you, I'm just Elias."

When she giggles, I'm tempted to yack all over his shiny Oxfords, particularly as she breezes past me without a glance, aiming for the podium at the end of the long table.

I sit back down awkwardly, catching Elias's smirk.

Great, this is gonna be a total blast.

With swift precision, she connects her clunky laptop to the projector, boots up a myriad of programs, half of which are cluttered with code and indescribable things, before the first slide of her presentation fills the screen. She even fiddles with the dials on the side of the podium, drawing the electric blinds across the floor-to-ceiling windows, shading us from the sun.

After a deep breath, she looks to Elias.

"Whenever you're ready."

IF I DIDN'T KNOW any better, I'd assume Juliana doesn't have a shy bone in her body.

Her voice booms through the conference room, radiating confidence in both her tone and posture. Throughout her extensive explanations of her game's backend, including server management, code, network architecture, data integration, most of which I nearly blacked out for, she hasn't stumbled once.

Whether she's drawing strength from her obvious passion over her indie game, or from her resentment toward me, I'm not sure. Although, I'm leaning toward the latter.

For only the second time in the past fifteen minutes, our eyes connect. A fire burns behind hers with promises of murder, before they swing back to Elias, who rests his chin on a fist, captivated by every word that leaves her lips.

I grind my teeth, looking down at my notes, which are— *wow, would you look at that?*—half-assed and hardly legible, even to my own eyes.

With a sigh, I return my attention to the vertical, mobile gameplay captured on the screen.

Cosmic Kitty Defense, that name will never cease to amuse me. I've heard a bit about it from Jeremy and Juliana, but I've never actually *seen* the game. And at first glance, from someone who's never touched a controller and thinks whoever does is a raging nerd...

It looks kinda fun.

My pulse spikes, watching the pixelated aliens encroach

toward the farm in the center of the screen, filled with adorable, helpless kittens. Which are... surprisingly detailed. Same with the grassy textures. I arch an eyebrow, watching the blades sway against some invisible wind.

"This is Mabel." Juliana points at the sole human character in the game, a grandma holding a pitchfork. "Controlled by the player, she's tasked with protecting her farm. Initially, she can only perform melee attacks for defense, but as the waves of aliens increase, so do her powers. She'll gain new weapons, all of which adhere to the game's theme, right down to their names, like the paw-some plasma cannon, purr-fect laser pointer, catnip cluster bomb, et cetera. And, from the game's latest update, the kitty litter sand trap—as you'll see here."

Juliana gestures in perfect sync with the video, as the player zooms through their inventory, selects a gray icon, and taps on a cluster of aliens. In response, Mabel treks to the nearest side of the farm on surprisingly quick feet, sticking close to her kitties, then hurls a projectile to the exact location, bursting a cluster of sand beneath their feet, effectively slowing their movements.

My teeth sink into my bottom lip. *Good grief, does she pitch for the Yankees? Quite the cannon arm, Mabel has there.*

Another minute rolls by of demonstrating other abilities, each with their own unique set of graphics and defensive strategies, until the gameplay stops and a new screen pops up, asking the player if they'd like to proceed to the next level. Instead, Juliana swings back to her slideshow.

"Advertising," she reads off the bold title, then abandons the bullet points for her memory. "I advertise on social media platforms and a few search engines, targeting users who are interested in tower defense games and real-time strategy,

redirecting them to download CKD on their specific operating system's app store."

She clicks the little remote in her hand, flipping onto the
next slide.

"Newsletter. These go out to my biggest fans, keeping
them in the loop about new features or bug fixes. It's all pretty
straightforward. As of this week, I have twenty-five hundred
sign-ups." A touch of pride breaks through her tone, and
unexpectedly, I feel it too, as she angles the remote to the
screen and—

A finger taps on my notebook. "Write that down," Elias
says, much too loud for my liking. When Juliana pauses,
offering a strange look, he smirks.

Dick.

The rest of her presentation follows the same suit,
touching on other avenues of finding players, like reaching
out to niche communities and posting on gaming threads. In
addition to hosting other advertisements on her game, which
serves as her main source of revenue, aside from players
buying the game outright.

All in all, when she clicks to the final slide with a simple
"Thank you," I'm impressed. Stunned, actually. Not only by
her presentation skills, but her creative imagination, technical
knowledge, business prowess, and the hard work she clearly
puts into the game. And going off of Elias's thunderous
applause, he is too.

"Wow. Thank you, Juliana." He stands, checking his watch.
"We've exceeded the presentation's time limit, so we don't
have time to chat. However, rest assured, Hayden took notes."

"Sorry about that, I didn't notice the time," she chuckles, a
bit anxiously, as she watches him head toward the door,
presumably to let in the next candidate.

"No worries. Really, it was a pleasure."

"So... you liked it, then?" Hope gleams in her eyes, only to fade as he sighs, his hand clutching the door handle.

"Look... it's a cute game, and I'm genuinely impressed by the effort you've poured into it. I have no doubt it'll succeed —*in its niche category.* But... based on our market research, we're looking for something a bit more mainstream, like a First-Person Shooter, for example, or a racing game... It's just... I'm having a hard time believing this game will appeal to a wide audience." He offers her an apologetic glance. "I wish you the best of luck, though," he says on the way out the door.

Deafening silence suffocates the room as I watch Juliana's heart crumble into little pieces at her feet. In turn, a chunk rips off mine when she turns her head from me, collecting her emotions, then grabs her things in a hurry.

"Juliana..."

Laptop in hand, she rushes past me, eyeing the ground.

"His word isn't the end-all, be-all."

She stops halfway out the door, and although she doesn't say a word, I can feel the question burning through her mind. One I hate the answer to, even more than she does.

"My father's is."

Her shoulders sag, only to perk back up when I murmur, "I think your game is amazing, if that counts for anything."

TWENTY-EIGHT
JULIANA

NOTHING TOPS A THIN-CRUST MARGHERITA PIZZA, especially not one from Vinny's Corner.

Nestled in the heart of downtown Brooklyn, Vinny's just screams homey vibes, right down to its warm cherry-oak walls, traditional ceiling fans, overhead Tiffany lamps, red-and-white checkered tablecloths, and dozens of family photos hanging from the walls.

Family owned since 1935, the business shows no signs of slowing down. Luckily, we beat the lunch rush and snagged a booth.

"Good Lord, Jeremy, slow down. You're going to choke." Mom shakes her head, watching him scarf down a huge slice of an extra-large meat lovers' pizza, which he ordered all for himself. I swear, we haven't had our food for longer than five minutes, and his pizza's almost gone.

"Sorry," he mumbles through a mouthful of food, prompting more head shakes as he finishes the crust and immediately swipes another slice. "I'm starving. I just got done working out."

I snicker, glancing at his sweaty gym clothes. "Yeah, no need to explain. We can smell you just fine."

A grin marks his lips, but they have no time for a retort—only chewing. And that's precisely what they do for the next two minutes straight, until not a single slice remains. Not that I'm surprised. It's a known fact Jeremy was born with an extra stomach. He's like a vacuum, or a human garbage disposal.

I gesture toward his tray. "Don't let those crumbs go to waste."

His gaze drifts to Mom and I's pizza,

"Oh, nonono. Not a chance." I nudge our tray away from him. "You're the one with the big Silicon Avenue tech job. I think you can manage buying yourself another round."

Sinking into the booth, he groans, "No way. I'm tapped out," and pats his stomach, as if bloated, when I know there's nothing but rock-hard abs underneath that would remain intact, whether he ate an entire second pizza or not. Just another Jeremy Brooks fun fact—he's an athletic freak. Guess those genes skipped a sibling.

Mom laughs at our typical banter, then looks at Jeremy. "So, besides your day-to-day with work and such, how's my son? Have you been hanging out with your friends—Kyle, Jonah, and all them?"

He nods. "Yep. The same crowd, as always. Although Hayden's been a bit dodgy these past few weeks."

Oh, no.

I squirm in my chair, praying to the heavens my face isn't redder than our marinara sauce. I thought for one day, just one lunch, I could expel Hayden from my mind. It's one thing, secretly fake dating your brother's best friend, but it's a whole other ball game to be staring him right in the face, after semi-doing the dirty deed on a penthouse terrace not even two weeks ago.

No wonder Hayden's been ghosting him.

Mom swipes a napkin across her lips, swallowing down her food. "Huh, weird. That's so unlike him. Maybe he's—"

"He's sick," I spit out, but regret it the instant both their gazes lock onto me

Jeremy arches a brow. "How do you know that?"

Dammit, dammit—what the hell was I thinking?!

"Oh, uhh..." I clear my throat, trailing my eyes across the wall of photos, as if the Vinny family might lend me a hand. "I mean, he's *probably* sick, would be my best guess. You know, there's a terrible flu going around."

Flu season, in the summer? those little devils cackle in my ear. *Are you trying to blow your cover?*

"You're probably right. I think one of my co-workers just had that." I let loose a breath when Jeremy shrugs, only to suck it right back in when I catch Mom giving me a smirk, her eyes glistening with secrets.

"Anyhoo." I laugh, cringing when it sounds forced, then quickly change the subject before Mom asks any questions. "How was that Vegas tech conference? I haven't gotten to hear about it yet."

His eyes light up. *Bingo.*

"It was awesome. Even better than last year's conference. I met tons of people in the industry, from all over the world, some who also work on Silicon Avenue, so that was cool. Listened to all the panels and guest speakers. They saved Innovex's new microchip unveiling for last—that was huge. I didn't think they could top their Nano-x's processing speeds, but they did. That company's releasing chips like hot cakes. *Oh,* and there was this new..."

I smile, listening to his rambles. His passion emanates every new story, and I wonder if this is how I sound to other people while explaining my own job. Not the coffee shop barista position, but the one I've poured my heart and soul into since freshman year of college.

It's... refreshing, hearing it from the other end. Although I'm a programmer in the tech industry, that's as far as I'm able to relate to Jeremy's job, aside from the very basic sense of physics I had to learn for my game. He may be a programmer, too, but he's skilled in much lower-level, more archaic languages that look like alien script even to my own eyes.

So, as much as I'm able, I ask him technical questions, genuinely curious of his insights, all while Mom's smile grows bigger and bigger in my peripheral, bursting with pride.

When our conversation dies out, she turns her attention onto me. "What about you, sweetheart? How's work been?"

Grimacing, I gulp down my Orange Fanta, for once wishing it was spiked with alcohol. "Oh, you know, the usual. Some lady dumped her latte on the floor yesterday—intentionally. Made a whole scene, saying I got her order wrong, which I didn't."

Mom's nose wrinkles in disgust. "What did your manager do about that?"

"Meghan?" I don't hold back my sour laugh. "Nothing, of course, besides making *me* apologize, give her a free latte, and mop up the floors."

"She's just useless, isn't she?"

"Uh, huh... Mei, on the other hand, she would've put that woman on a gurney, had I not held her back. She's like a Pitbull."

Mom snickers. "I had a friend like that once, growing up. They're good to keep close. Much better than being stuck with a lazy, grade A-hole boss, because *boy*, have I sure had those, too... Anyways"—she leans forward, curiosity shining beneath her stare—"tell me about your *real* work. How've sales been? Have you noticed an increase since the new feature?"

I'll never get over hearing my Mom talk about video games—well, just about mine. She sure as hell hasn't ever spoken about any others, let alone *played* another in her life. She's as far from techie as a person can be, which always has me wondering how she ended up with the likes of an electrical engineer and an indie game dev for children.

Go figure.

I'm about to answer honestly, that sales *have* improved since the feature launched, not by a ton, but a steady increase. In essence, I'm chuggin' along. That is, until Elias's little remark weasels its way into my head and torches all my hopes to ash.

I'm having a hard time believing this game will appeal to a wide audience...

His words stab right through my heart, just as they did after my presentation. Yet, another thing I tried to keep from today's lunch, but his doubts about my game haven't left my mind since, so why would they disappear now? Life's never that convenient.

It's not like he's my first-ever critic, either. I've had plenty. Friends I thought were friends, random internet trolls, genuine enthusiasts who just simply didn't like the game. Then there's myself, possibly my own worst enemy, at times —shout out to imposter syndrome.

All of that, I can live with, can shake off those doubts and move onto the next day, just fine. But Elias... there's something different about his remark.

First off, he's not someone who's poking fun, teasing, being spiteful, or *trying* to get under my skin. He's speaking the truth from a business standpoint. That's just who he is.

Secondly—and this is the real punch to the gut—he isn't criticizing the actual content of my game, like the graphics, the efficiency of my code, the server speeds, the user interface design, or anything I can actually improve on. No, he's doubting the entire *genre*. That cutesy, tower defense mobile games can't hold up in a wide market, and wouldn't prove appealing to the DreamScape audience. A theory that, if true...

Is one tough pill to swallow.

I wish I could confide in my mom about it, without inevitably spiraling into uncomfortable topics that would only be exacerbated with Jeremy sitting across the table. So, as a last resort, I fudge the truth.

I sigh, plastering on a worried expression that proves a bit too easy to fake. "Things are kinda stagnant, which feels a lot like a downhill slide, especially after such a big feature."

"Oh, no. I'm sorry to hear that, sweetie..." Her shoulders sag, clearly not what she was expecting, but she bounces back quickly, like she always does. "I wouldn't look too into it. It's just summer, is all. People are out enjoying the weather. They'll be back inside, playing games, once things get colder."

Wow. I force a nod. That's... something I haven't thought much about. If I wasn't lying, I'd take that insight to heart. "You're probably right," I say.

"Everything happens in due time." Stretching her arm across the table, she places a hand over mine, seeping comfort into me that I genuinely feel, despite keeping secrets. "Your father and I couldn't be more proud of you."

"I know."

"And..." she hesitates, as a darkness I rarely see flickers across her gaze, filled with sorrow but also strength. I know her next words before she speaks them—as I'm sure Jeremy does, too. "And I know Daniel would be too, if he were here to see it."

Silence grows between the three of us. My eyes connect with Jeremy's, his swirling with shadows.

Like my brother, I never quite know how to feel whenever Mom brings up our biological father. It's not like I met the man, and Jeremy could pretty much say the same thing, since he passed away when he was only a one-year-old, while I was still in the womb.

Daniel Lawrence was his name. A car crash is what killed him, Mom said, on his way to a job site. He worked as a carpenter and married our mother, who was his high school sweetheart, when they were both twenty-two. But to Jeremy and I... that's all he really is. A name and a story. A good man we never truly knew, who left this earth in a tragic way.

We lucked out, in a horrible, twisted kind of way, that our mother is by far the most deserving of the *Supermom* title. She really did it all, filled that gap so well that we didn't even know we had one.

She went to Jeremy's football try-outs, danced with me at the father-daughter dances, chaperoned our class field trips, and even managed to be the loudest cheerleader at our science fairs, all while teaching second grade at our private K-12 school, Riverside Prep on the Upper East Side. Unlike our classmates, the sons and daughters of senators, celebrities and CEOs, Jeremy and I would've never been able to attend, if it weren't for her active participation in the school affairs, granting us free tuition.

Truly, truly, truly, she did it all, and then some.

Years later, she met Raymond "Ray" Brooks, who was a substitute teacher for her class. The two got together when I was nine and Jeremy was ten, then married several years later, after Mom asked for *our* approval of him. It was an easy choice. We'd already started calling him Dad, as he naturally stepped into the role of our father figure. It wasn't long before we willingly took his last name. To this day, I still remember him breaking down in tears when we said yes.

Today, our dad teaches ninth grade geometry at a local public school, and our mom is still a second grade teacher at Riverside Prep. It's not the norm, having dual teachers for parents, but it does come with a few privileges. Yes, we had to learn the importance of staying frugal, but we also utilized their knowledge of the school system, which undoubtedly aided us throughout our studies and while applying to colleges.

I know Jeremy wouldn't put it any differently, including his appreciation for our mom and her enduring strength, which is why those shadows quickly lift from his gaze as he places a hand on her shoulder. He doesn't say anything, yet a glassy film waters over Mom's eyes as if he did.

I bat away my own emotions. "I know, Mom. I know he'd be proud of me. And he'd be just as proud of you."

She squeezes my hand, hers revealing a slight tremor. *Thank you,* she mouths, blinking those tears away.

～

FOR THE REST of our lunch, those lingering doubts found their exit from my headspace, without me even realizing their absence. Although, something else slips through the door those thoughts left wide open. A memory, one that brings me warmth, even when I've tried so desperately to hate the man who repeated the beautiful words I once said to him, back to me.

I think your game is amazing, if that counts for anything...

And what does this man get in return, for days on end? A cold shoulder. Except... even with all my efforts, that coldness thaws, piece by piece, as his words sing their soft melody. Is it enough to put a stop to my silent treatment later today? Probably not. But...

Come tomorrow, I'll have no choice but to talk with Hayden.

And more.

TWENTY-NINE
JULIANA

FOR BILLIONAIRES AND THEIR FAMILIES, The Kentucky
Derby is like a short jaunt to a local lake.

A little getaway that's not too far of a drive, but instead of
packing up a minivan or Tahoe and hitting the road, assistants and flight crews warm up their private jets. Then *poof*, in
a short couple of hours, they're touching down at Bowman
Field and strolling into Churchill Downs within minutes.

At least, that's been my experience so far.

A day of unprecedented firsts for me, and I feel they're
just beginning.

My first time flying private, which is... very weird, to put
it simply. Glamorous. But weird. Not only did we skip TSA,
bag check, and the long lines you'd experience at a normal
airport, our chauffeur drove onto the track and right up to the
plane. A Gulfstream G700, Hayden called it, nicknamed his
Passion Pegasus. Putting that eye-roll-worthy name aside, it's
his jet. As in, his alone, like the Kingston family wouldn't be
caught dead sharing a single plane.

Then there were the amenities. Most notably, the crew of

flight attendants who served us—the only two passengers on board—full-blown, hot breakfast. I'm talkin' sausage, hash browns, pancakes, orange juice in champagne flutes, eggs, the whole shebang. Guess billionaires are too good for that crackers and trail mix crap they serve while flying commercial.

And then... *Hmmmmm...*

I swear, there was something else—

Oh, yeah. How could I forget?

About this boulder on my head.

I groan, scratching my scalp beneath my humongous hat. Pink, feathery, with an excessively broad brim, it looks like a flamingo landed on my head.

"Quit fidgeting." Hayden tugs on my arm, leading us through a crowded hallway inside the historic racing complex. "It's not gonna fall off."

I know that, I don't say. *How could it? What, with the twenty bobby pins digging into my scalp, securing the frilly monstrosity into place.*

Instead, I just nod.

This morning, I devised a plan to survive today—speak to my fake boyfriend, only when necessary. I'm still cross with him, obviously, for reasons that shouldn't even matter. Nonetheless, here I am, on the arm of perhaps the most eligible bachelor in Churchill Downs, pursing my lips in stubborn silence.

"Still not talking, huh?"

Hayden weaves us around a flock of boldly dressed women, who each crane their necks at him, their eyes sparkling with appreciation beneath those giant hats, before flickering down to me. And burn with jealousy.

Not that I blame them, of course. I'm sure they can smell

his trust fund oozing from the seams of his all-white suit. And even I know, in the throes of my resentment, that Hayden's disgustingly attractive, more so than usual. Like, *painful* to look at, when the sun hits him just right, which makes this whole silence thing that much harder.

"Okaaayyy." He opens a door to another hallway, holding it for me. "After you," he hums, close enough to my ear that butterflies flutter deep in my belly.

Dammit, does he have to be such a gentleman? I make the mistake of meeting his gaze, only to be struck with another barrage of feelings I can't ignore, before passing through the doorway. "Thank y—"

I suck in a breath, but it's too late.

His laugh bellows behind me, the deep baritone warming my cheeks. "So, flattery is your soft spot, huh?" He offers me his arm, which I'm obliged to take. When I do, he tugs me closer than necessary and whispers in my ear. "Shall I attend to your every need, then, *Jules?*"

I grit my teeth as a shudder ripples through me.

"Ensure you don't have to worry about a thing? Handle any inconveniences or change of plans. Pull back your chair. Fetch you drinks. Flaunt you around on my arm—oh, would you look at that? Guess that's just natural."

He swings a left, entering a corridor with an old-fashioned ambiance, and I swear the crowd naturally parts for us—*for him.* As we move through them, their eyes seem to drift onto us, like flowers pointing to light, while he murmurs, "And shower you in compliments...?"

Oh, no. Stay strong, Juliana, stay strong.

"Like how breathtaking you are in this dress?"

My lips roll between my teeth as I feel the weight of his

stare. He rubs his chin with his free hand, as if he's mentally digging into some gentleman's arsenal, a playbook of sorts.

"That you're the epitome of grace and style?"

I whip my gaze onto him, my eyes narrowing. *Is he...?*

"Your elegance—*truly* captivating."

Oh, he's definitely—

"And such a *splendid* conversationalist."

My jaw drops, and before I can think better of it, my hand goes flying, aiming for his—

He snatches my wrist from midair, inches from his suit-clad chest. With a smirk, he tugs me close—*too* close. His minty breath basks my senses, forcing me to crane my head up to look at him.

He feigns a gasp. "My goodness, were you about to *hit* me, Miss Brooks?" His eyes bulge. "Why, that's not very ladylike of you at all. You'd think I brought a wild animal as my—"

A laugh bursts from my mouth, but I quickly stifle it, pressing my lips together tightly as if my life depends on their silence.

His lips twitch—

The rest comes spilling out, light and airy, like fizz bubbling over a glass rim. And his eyes. They're crystal-blue water, like waves lapping up a shore in delight, and *God* does my heart ache as they soften, as his hold on me loosens.

Fine. When I can't flee from the room, maybe I'm no match for his charm. There's no shame in that—what girl is?

"Come on," he whispers, tugging me along.

"Wait, isn't seating that way?" I point as we pass beneath an overhanging sign.

At the sound of my voice, he smiles wide, flashing me a row of his porcelain teeth. "Yes, but there's something we need to do first."

~

I SHAKE MY HEAD. "I should've known."

He sparkles with mischief. "Yes, you really should have." Flicking his chin, he gestures to the flatscreen mounted high above the *Wagering Counter,* displaying the names and trainers of all twenty horses in the race.

Gambling. He took me here to gamble.

"Pick one."

"What? I don't know the first thing about horse racing."

"Come onnnnn." He nudges me. "I know who I'm picking."

"Oh, yeah? And who's that."

"Hayzeus, of course. He's got the best odds. Some even think he'll win the Triple Crown."

"Boringgggg, what about an underdog—or, I mean... under-*horse?"* Our eyes connect as his entire body deflates like I pricked him with a sewing needle. "Sorry, sorry. Untimely dad joke. Uhh..." I search through the horse names, neglecting the odds written right beside them.

"Stirrup Trouble, Horsen' Around..." I mutter to myself, my eyebrows lifting higher and higher with every name. "Mane Attraction, Luminous, Baby Got Back, Practical Choice —" I snicker, locking gazes once more, before I whip back to the television. "Uhhhhh... Canterbelle. Yep, Canterbelle is going to be our winner."

Hayden sighs. *Finally,* his eyes tell mine.

He makes for a waging booth, eyeing the—

I bump into his backside as he comes to a sudden stop.

"Wait a minute." He squints up at the television. "Canterbelle? He's got *terrible* odds."

I round to Hayden's front, so he can see my hand shooting to my hip. "So? I said I wanted an underdog."

"Yeah, but... Juliana, you picked the underdog *of* the underdogs. His odds are *seventy-to-one*. Don't you know what—"

"Of course, I know what that means." I resist an eye roll. "If Canterbelle comes in first place, I'll win my bet times seventy."

"Okay, then you *do* realize how astronomically unlikely it is for him to win. Experts base these odds off previous races and the horses' bloodlines, you know. They're accurate for a reason. If you wanted an underdog, you could've at least gone with Mane Attraction at thirty-to-one odds. You know, something a bit more plausible than an alien spacecraft landing on the track partway through the race."

I suppress a laugh, not because of his theatrics, but expecting the reaction my next words will surely provoke. "You think I looked at the odds?"

He deflates, yet again, but worse than he did from my dad joke. Like a whoopee cushion, void of air and humor. "What did you say...?"

I blink. *Yeah? I said what I said.*

"Well, what in the world did you base your bet on, then?"

"Their names." *Duh.*

His face falls, so, so very far, and it takes all my strength not to combust into a fit of laughter. You'd think I took his favorite toy away.

"Well, let's go place our bets!" I breeze past him cheerily, smiling even brighter when his groan sounds behind me. Approaching the only open waging booth, I unhook my purse's latch and—

"Don't even think about it." Hayden beats me to the counter.

I arch an eyebrow. "Huh?"

He gestures to my bag. "Money. You don't need any when you're with me. In fact, I'd prefer it if you left all your cards at home."

I stagger backward, just a step, my jaw hanging low on its hinges. I try to respond, except I just... *can't.* All that escapes me are inaudible noises. Sure, he's lent me his Black Amex once before, but that was because I needed new clothes *for our arrangement.* No other reason, right...? Then why is he acting the same way now? I can easily pay for my bet, which has nothing to do with our arrangement, anyway.

"Okay..." I breathe, as the feminist inside of me rattles in its newfound cage. Little does it know, I can hardly hear anything. I'm too busy mulling over a single word.

Home.

And the fact that, when it left his lips, my initial thoughts weren't of my apartment.

But *his.*

A possessive fire blazes behind his eyes as I feel him reading mine. "Good." He grins, swiveling on his heels to face the teller, sinking a hand into his pocket. "We'll do five thousand on Hayzeus and Canterbelle."

WHAT?!?!

I rush up beside him and hiss, *"What are you doing?! I wouldn't have bet on Can—"*

"Here, baby." He offers me his wallet. "Be a doll and count out my cash for yourself, will you?"

Cash?!

I freeze momentarily, meaning to argue some more, if it weren't for the teller's gaze. I snatch his wallet. Who has ten-thousand dollars cash just lying around in their wallet? Is he some drug dealer? He must've meant hundred, not thousand. There's not even enough room for—

My heart drops when I flip it open, revealing a considerable stack. Hesitantly, I comb through it, finding each bill to be a thousand dollars. There must be at least thirty, all showing considerable signs of use. They don't even print these anymore, and there's only a set amount in circulation. How did he get his hands on so many?

Gaping, I sense Hayden's presence near, his hand settling at the small of my back.

"Be sure to count out loud."

My toes curl at his voice's rough timbre, only for my teeth to bite into my lower lip at the sound of his satisfied hum as I pull the entire stack from the clip. Pinching the first bill, I try not to dwell on how many hours at the coffee shop it represents, before snagging it from the stack.

"One thousand." I pull another. "Two thousand, three thousand..."

His touch sweeps up my spine and back down, trailing goosebumps.

"Four thousand," I force out. "Five thousand, six thousand, seven thousand..."

"That's it."

I swallow roughly, my mouth drying beneath his unwavering gaze, as satisfaction fills up the air around him, stealing the oxygen from my lungs. "Eight thousand..."

"Louder," he murmurs.

"Nine thousand..."

Heat floods between my thighs when he hums, again, and right as *ten* leaves my lips, his brush against my ear. "Such a good girl, bleeding my wallet dry. Do you want more, baby?"

Shock pummels through me with a sharp inhale. I meet his eyes, mine flicking between them, searching. *He's serious.* I could take the rest of what's in here, and he wouldn't think twice. In fact, he *wants* me to. Something so far from necessary, in the eyes of our contract, that it has my head spinning.

I snap his wallet shut, and quickly pass over the money, gaining the teller's attention, who made herself quite busy with whatever's oh-so urgent on her computer. Embarrassment marks my cheeks, but only a mild blush. I'm too preoccupied, focusing on the hand still pressed against the small of my back.

With a polite smile, the teller slides over two vouchers, then zips along to another booth. I hold my breath, aware of Hayden's intoxicating nearness as I grab the vouchers and...

Don't move a muscle?

On any other day, I'd take this as a perfect moment to dash off, to shake the emotions that're wound deep inside me while devising excuses for their existence. But... not today. I turn to Hayden, staying close in his presence, as if he's a warm fire on a windy night, and hand him his voucher.

I crane my head—and there's that softness again.

I'm taken aback at the smile he beams down at me. He doesn't speak a word. No snide remark. No sultry innuendo. No humor. Just... a smile filled with something I grasp instantly. Maybe because it's reflected in his eyes, too.

Longing.

And for perhaps not the first time, but the first time it's been strong enough not to deny or diminish or cover up with the wrongs of our past...

I feel it, too.

The attraction.

"We don't want to miss the race." He offers me his arm, and taking it is like second nature.

HAYDEN GUIDES us down a hallway that's noticeably emptier than it was ten minutes ago, pressing a phone to his ear. "Yes, Dad, we're on our way up now."

Nerves bundle in my gut as we turn a blind corner, every step like a countdown toward not just a figure from my past, but one who holds my future in his hands.

Warren Kingston.

"Save us two seats... No, not for—no, Dad, I told you, I brought my girlfriend."

I stifle a smirk. *Girlfriend.* That's new to his vocabulary— but also novel to my ears, which could be to blame for why my smile is growing.

"Yes, Dad," Hayden sighs, riddled with annoyance. "You heard me, right. I said girlfri—"

Warren's voice elevates, breaking through the line, just enough for me to hear. "Enough lies, boy. Don't bring one of your *whores* around the family..."

Shit. They may be working together, but it seems their father-son relationship is still in the dumps.

Hayden tenses against me. *"I said she's my —"*

He stops us abruptly in front of a corridor as he drags the phone from his ear. "He hung up on me," Hayden says, his forced chuckle hinting at his lack of concern. Maybe he assumes I didn't hear Warren's remark. Honestly, I wish I hadn't, but it's not like that would make what's coming any easier.

"Ummm..." I tug on his sleeve, pointing back to where we came. "I think we passed it again."

"That's cute, Jules. You think we're general admission?"

"I thought that's all there was. Where are we going, then?"

He gestures to the sign above. "Take a guess."

Eyebrow cocked, I search through the names and arrows, until I pause at the top.

Billionaires' Row.

THIRTY

JULIANA

I HAVEN'T SEEN Warren Kingston since my brother's graduation six years ago.

In preparation for today, I looked him up online, thinking it might soften the blow. I found the usual stuff. CEO and founder of Kingston Entertainment. Fifty-nine years old. Two sons, Elias and Hayden Kingston, from his first marriage to Sylvia Kingston—now Sylvia Van Doren. Since his divorce, over a decade ago, Warren has remarried several times. Four, maybe five times—I don't remember. As of last year, his new wife's name is Clara, who has a six-year-old son of her own, although I didn't care to dig much deeper than that.

But... even with all my research, the escalator ride up to the fourth floor feels like an eternity. My heart palpitates in anticipation. Nothing like rekindling with your mom's ex-lover, who's also your *fake boyfriend's dad,* to put your mind at ease.

Just riveting.

As we step off the escalator, Hayden casually intertwines

his fingers with mine. I'm about to question it until I remember. *Oh right, now we really gotta act the part.*

We round a corner, and my anxiety picks back up. Sensing my worry, Hayden brushes a thumb along the backside of my hand. Butterflies swarm within me at the touch, especially when I realize this is the first time we've held hands—only for embarrassment to quickly follow.

Getting jittery over some boy holding my hand. What am I, twelve years old?

"It's going to be fine," he says.

I whip my head, finding his expression strained. Why does he sound like he's reassuring himself? But there's no time to question it as we turn another corner and behold an astonishing view.

"Woah," I breathe out, as we descend a short block of steps, entering onto a secluded balcony overlooking the track. "I didn't know we were *this* high up. You can see everything."

Hayden hums beside me, pointing. "There's the starting gate, where they'll load in the horses." He motions to the right, toward a giant white pole in the center of the near-side track. "And there's the finish line... and the winner's circle over there..."

He trails on, until a man wearing a uniform approaches us. "May I take your coat, sir?"

"No, I'll keep it for now, thank you."

He nods respectfully, before disappearing down the balcony, hugging the railing. I raise an eyebrow, watching him go as he enters a small, secluded area, partially obscured from our view at this angle. Rows of occupied seats populate the space that's noticeably less cramped than the bleachers below, with servers gracefully balancing trays of cocktails and hors d'oeuvres on their white-gloved fingertips.

My palms grow clammy.

Billionaires' Row.

Hayden tugs me along, and slowly but surely, our vantage point expands, revealing more filled seats farther down, near the railing. As we descend a flight of stairs, passing row after row, we earn smiles and even a few waves, all of which Hayden returns. My confidence surges.

Maybe Warren won't recognize me, I think. *It's been so many years, he probably forgot about my existence. Then I can say my name's... Emily or... Becka—yeah, definitely Becka. He'll go for that, right? And Hayden can just play along.*

Hayden stops us at the bottommost step, before the row in front of the railing. Seated right by the stairs, clad in a striped, finely pressed suit with a full head of peppery gray hair, is Warren, who I recognize immediately.

Fear slithers its way into my headspace, but I squash it dead, plastering on a pleasant expression, while the following two seconds wane on like *hours.* Warren turns his head casually, meeting my knees at his eye-level, before a scowl marks his lips, his thoughts plain as day.

Don't bring one of your whores around the family...

I check my temper as his gaze travels higher up my body, and that frown grows more grotesque. That is, until he reaches my face. Upon seeing my lips, his own part on a silent gasp, and when his eyes meet mine, they burn with surprise, as if I'm a ghost who's revealed herself after slapping him on the cheek.

For a moment, he just stares, pupils blown wide.

It's scary, really, how much they all look alike. Hayden. Elias. And Warren here. Blue eyes. Strong features. With unmistakable bravado. Aged, yet so similar, except he doesn't radiate an ounce of Hayden's infectious charisma—until all that disgust slicks off him like rain, replaced by a warm smile.

"Juliana." He stands, rising to his impressive height, about two inches shy of Hayden's. "What a surprise. Hayden didn't tell me you were coming. It's so lovely to see you."

Wow. A breath escapes me. I don't know what kind of reaction I was expecting, but it wasn't a welcoming one. Feeling a sense of comfort, I return his smile. "And you too, Mr. Kingston."

At the sound of his name, something flashes in his eyes, something I can't quite explain, except that it's cold and kills the light in them as they flicker down to my hand intertwined with Hayden's. In a flash, they dart back up and that something vanishes so quickly, I wonder if I imagined the whole thing.

"It seems I approve of Hayden's date, for a change." Warren shoots his son a playful wink, then spreads his arms toward me for a hug. "Bring it here."

You're just paranoid, those little devils whisper, talking sense for a change as I unclasp from Hayden's touch. *Just seeing things you think you should.*

I motion forward...

I mean, look at him. He clearly cares about who Hayden dates and has even taken him under his wing at work.

Letting his arms loop around me, in a gentle embrace...

Judging a man for his past, when he seems to have chang—

Lips brush against my ear. "You look just like your mother."

Those little devils SCREAM in my headspace.

RUN, RUN, RUNNN!! they wail on my shoulder, louder than the angels crying on the other, their choir catching fire at their feet.

But I don't move a muscle—*I can't.* I only stand, frozen, utterly rigid, on his retreat, discovering a revolting smirk dancing across his lips. Then it, too, vanishes, fast like lightning. Dripping with disdain as his gaze drags over to Hayden.

"As usual, your lateness prevented us from saving your seat."

Hayden tenses at my side. "The race doesn't start for ten minutes."

I blink, hardly registering their conversation.

When he doesn't reply, Hayden scoffs. "What about that one, right there?"

Managing a breath, I break from my stupor, and trail a gaze down the line of chairs. Indeed, there's an empty seat right next to Warren's. One more over sits a red-haired young boy, and next to him, I catch the eyes of a woman with similar hair, presumably in her thirties. Instantly, I know it's Clara, who boasts a smirk, shamelessly eavesdropping on their conversation.

"That seat's for Elias," Warren answers.

"But he doesn't watch from up here. He never has." My heart sinks at the twinge of sadness leaking into Hayden's tone, despite his stoic demeanor.

"He might this year."

Clara bites her lip, stifling a laugh, brushing a hand down her son's designer suit, who, I'd wager, is sitting where Hayden usually does. It would be so easy for her to sit him on her lap and free up the space. Under the weight of her stare once again, I feel her scrutiny, as though she views me as inferior, deserving of the bleachers below.

"Although..." Warren muses. "I'm sure Elias wouldn't

appreciate knowing he made a lady stand. Juliana can have his spot."

Clara's expression cracks in half.

"W-what?" I falter. All the hairs on my body stand on end when I find Warren motioning to the empty seat right beside his.

"It'll give us time to catch up." He smiles, innocently.

The choir belts out another blood-curdling scream.

No, no, no, no—

Hayden loops his arm through mine, towing me up the stairs with an annoyed huff. "We'll manage."

BY THE GRACE of some miracle, a mere two minutes before the start of the race, a couple offered us their seats, one row behind Warren's and on the opposite end of the balcony. Apparently, Billionaires' Row has a lounge they preferred to watch from.

How very lucky for us—and generous of them.

I'm not sure if I'm thankful, though.

My eyes slither over to Warren, who's still beside a vacant chair. It's like he crawled out of my nightmares.

You look just like your mother...

I dart my focus back to the track—*where it should be*—and watch handlers guide each horse into the gate, securing them in their respective nooks. Jockeys sport white pants and flashy striped or polka dot uniforms, mounted on saddles with bold numbers.

Sixty seconds.

Stay focused now. Don't. Look. Don't...

Dammit. My eyes act on their own accord, swiveling to steal another peek at—

I inhale sharply, catching Warren's gaze. His body angles down the line of the track, so he's not overtly turning his head, but... there's no mistake. He's looking right at me. I snap my gaze straight ahead, cursing myself that I didn't do it sooner, as the heat of his attention burns through my skin.

"Did you see Hayzeus?" An arm drapes across the back of my chair. The moment it does, as if I got a death wish, I look again, so fast my brain hardly registers.

Whew. I'm safe.

"Jules?"

"Huh?" I glance up, finding Hayden encroaching on my space. When his knee brushes against mine, my cheeks warm for a whole different reason.

I much prefer his attention.

"I asked if you saw Hayzeus. Or did your hat get in the way?" He flicks its brim, the motion disturbing the bobby pins, in turn tugging on my scalp.

"Hey!" I swat him on the shoulder, earning a big smile I'll probably see in my dreams tonight. "Yes, I saw him." *I think.*

"What a specimen, am I right? He's got this in the bag. Sorry to say, but your little Canterbelle doesn't stand a chance."

I roll my eyes. "You should root for Canterbelle, too. It's *your* money on both of them."

His playful expression falters. "No, that's your money on your horse."

"Hayden, come on—"

"I mean it. If Canterbelle wins, you get the payout. So, it's your money."

My lips part, my mind turning up blank. "Are you joking?"

His brow furrows, as if offended. "Of course not, baby. Why would I be?"

I can't hide my smile, feeling a flutter in my chest, strong enough to overlook what he called me.

Settling back in his chair, he props an ankle atop his knee, an arm still draped across my chair, wearing a look of... *pride?* Absentmindedly, his fingertips brush across my bare shoulder. "Besides"—he strokes some more, making it hard to think —"this is all for fun. We didn't bet much."

"Ha. Ha. Now you're just messing with me."

"Hmm?"

"How is ten thousand dollars not that much? Come on, Hayden. No need to prove anything. I know you're rich and all, but no one thinks that's a fun-sized bet."

He snickers.

"What's so funny?"

"These seats were thirty grand."

What?!

"A piece."

WHAT?!

A deep chuckle escapes him. "God, you're cute."

My head spins. *Oh my—*

BANG!

I whip my head toward the noise, just in time to catch the horses blazing out of their gates. *"And they're off!"* the announcer blares through the speakers. My heart lurches in rhythm to their hooves, kicking up dirt as they battle for the inner rail.

I search through their ranks, realizing I don't have a clue who is who. "Uhh..."

"You little fibber," Hayden murmurs. "You didn't see Hayzeus, did you?"

My teeth sink into my lower lip, earning a *tsk, tsk, tsk* from his tongue.

"Canterbelle is number fourteen. Riiiiight—there." He points. "Ohhh, he's in the middle of the pack. Not bad, not bad. Nothing like my number two, though, in red. Right th—"

I look over, finding him aghast, then follow the line of his gaze. Number two...? "Uh, oh. Seems the first pick isn't doing so hot. Is he... *behind Canterbelle?*" I watch in disbelief, as they sprint down the near stretch, approaching the first bend.

"No, no, no, that can't be right."

"Wait..." I gasp.

"It's Canterbelle, surging through the pack!"

"Oh my god!" I smack Hayden's arm as he buries his face into his palms, riddled with shame, watching through the slits of his fingers.

As they round the second and final bend, my chest heaves wildly. Canterbelle is *right there* in the lead, neck and neck, with another horse.

"It's Canterbelle and Practical Choice, on the home stretch, pulling ahead! Four lengths... Five lengths... Six! They're stride for stride, arriving into the final furlong! Ohhh, it's coming down to the wire. Who's it gonna be?! Oh my goodness, it's a photo finish!!!"

The crowd roars as they cross the tall white post, at the exact same time. Bright camera flashes light up the finish line in rapid succession, capturing the spectacular moment. Calamity rocks the floors below, shaking the foundations of Churchill Downs. Cheers pour through the air, as thousands of spectators leap to their feet.

Hayden and I, we're no exception.

Actually, we're the most rambunctious pair on the entire balcony. Amidst high society who clap politely and exchange courteous nods, we laugh in each other's arms, jumping and *wooing* and squealing like little kids, forgetting all the rules that bind us, blurring the lines between reality and the terms of our contract, until they're as indistinguishable as the trampled finish line below.

All while, the world awaits a picture-perfect decision...

THIRTY-ONE

HAYDEN

MONEY LOOKS GOOD ON EVERYONE.

Juliana, though? She's in a league of her own.

I suppress a groan as she leans over the lounge's balcony, neglecting the fact that it's four stories high, and watches the winner's circle through a small pair of binoculars. Her dress is spectacular—a solid shade of lilac, stopping just above her knees. It's classy yet strapless, and cinches tightly around her figure.

I don't care how much it cost me.

She needs ten more.

"That's a lot of flowers." She leans farther, spiking my adrenaline.

I glance toward the winner's circle. She's not wrong, though there aren't any more than usual this year. Primarily roses. Hedges curve around the circle, forming a horseshoe shape that contains a flock of photographers snapping photos of the horse prancing around, as if it knows its accomplishment. A blanket of roses drapes across its backside, behind the jockey holding an enormous bouquet, mounted atop a saddle labeled with the number eight. Not two, as I had hoped.

"I should've guessed," I grumble.

"It *was* the practical choice." She laughs, her body convulsing against the railing.

Another wave of fear jolts me, prompting me to loop my arm around her waist. "That's enough." She gasps quietly, as I pull her from the ledge.

A giggle escapes her when she meets my eye. "Now, Hayden. I would've never assumed you had a fear of heights."

My lips press firmly. *I don't, but it seems with you, I do.* "You never know. These railings have seen better days." I shrug, appraising them, before holding back a grimace. They're wrought iron and appear freshly polished.

She hums, like I have *chicken* written across my forehead.

I clear my throat. "I guess I'll have to adopt your genius betting strategy next year. Just pick based on the names."

"That does seem *practical.*"

I cringe. *Oh my god, she's relentless.*

She busts up laughing, the pleasant sound floating across the open air. When she peers through the binoculars again, this time at a safe distance that my heart can handle, I lock eyes with my father over her shoulder... and there's no missing the disdain in them.

He didn't appreciate our celebration at the end of the race. Said we made a spectacle of ourselves—no, wait. Correction. That *I* made a spectacle, and that it reflected poorly on our family. Nothing new there. I could blink the wrong way, and he'd have something to say about it. I've always known that, from a young age.

So... why am I getting worked up, just holding his stare? I can usually brush him off easily, but right now, as every second drags on, the more I'm tempted to go over there and smack that look off his face. Our connection doesn't last long, though, broken when he swings his focus back to his wife, Clara.

Wife. I nearly laugh.

I'll never understand why he insists on marriage, when he can't hold one down for longer than three years. I'd pity Clara, if she wasn't just in it for the money—and I can confidently say that, without having spoken to her for longer than ten minutes. Sure, sometimes, true love can exist despite thirty-year age gaps, but... come on. It's *him,* of all people. And Clara, I just know her type. Stuck up. Power hungry, in her own unique way. Although, besides her upgraded lifestyle, I'm unsure what's in it for her, long term, since she's well aware of his marriage history and signed an iron-clad prenup.

And I mean, *extra iron clad.* God forbid another Sylvia comes along and rakes in half my father's money. After the divorce settlement, he nearly died from a stroke outside the courthouse—that's no exaggeration. Warren Kingston would choose money and power over the air he breathes, every single time.

Which is why his marriages don't last long. He gets bored. Tempted by another brush with power, or a different woman, entirely—contrary to that of his loyal appearance.

I study him closely, as he meanders about the balcony. Flaunting his wife on one arm, he introduces her to everyone he comes across with a proud smile, including her son, Sebastian, who holds his hand.

I look away as inevitable envy flares within me.

I hate him for making me jealous of a six-year-old boy, for the explanations springing into my mind... It's all an act. He's appeasing her, slipping on a fake mask while favoring her son, just to get between her legs tonight—and tomorrow night, and so on, for a year or two. He doesn't actually care about her or that boy. That *innocent, blameless* child, who deserves a real, loving father figure in his life.

I loathe every one of these thoughts. Not because I know they're true and are more certain than the sun rising tomorrow morning. But because somewhere deep down inside of me, in a place mangled and charred and unrecognizable, there's a part that *wants* them to be true.

I'd wonder if he was purposefully provoking my jealousy, but that would imply he actually cared enough about me to do so.

"Oh my gosh! Are those the owners?!" Juliana's voice reels me back to reality. She snickers. "They're wearing cowboy hats with suits on."

I smirk. When I said she was cute, I meant it. "Those are the trainers, most likely. A lot of horse owners are just regular people looking for investments."

"You mean *rich* people."

"Sure, yeah, same thing. Most of them are here, in this lounge—or watched from our section."

She swivels around, shaking her head. "Hayden, Hayden, Hayden... Only you would call thirty-grand derby tickets a regular-person thing. Most people aren't billionaires, you know."

"Hey, now. I know we're in *Billionaires' Row* and all, but not everyone here reaches that status. Actually, I'd say most are just millionaires."

"*Just* millionaires?" she scoffs.

As a trail of grumbles breezes past her lips, I bite mine to keep from laughing. Nevertheless, I can't help but add, "Or they're celebrities. Well, a lot of them are both, but... You get what I'm saying."

"What??? I haven't seen any... well... I guess I've been focused on the race." Her eyes sweep across the balcony, and sure enough, in no time at all, they pause, narrowing. "Wait... is that...?"

I trace the line of her gaze, finding an eccentric-looking man at the end. "Ahh, yes, it is."

"Holy shit."

I grin—she rarely cusses.

"I-I just listened to his new album last week."

"Oh, yeah? I did, too, along with the rest of the country."

"Wow..."

I appraise her in all her astonishment, loving every bit of it. In fact, I'd like to see some more. "You wanna meet him?"

"What?! No!" Her eyes widen like a startled deer, nerves bursting about her.

"Are you sureeeee?"

"No, no!" She huffs and puffs. "I'm good, right here."

"Okaaayyy. Tell me if you change your mind."

Not another minute passes, and she's gaping at yet another person. "Oh my... don't tell me..."

"Mhmm," I confirm. "That's her."

"No way... I *love* her movies! And that show—the one that just came out. I'm blanking on the name..." She snaps her fingers. "Ahh, whatever. But she's *amazing* in it, and..."

She trails off, explaining some drama series I know nothing about, before she spots *another* celebrity, which sprouts a whole other tangent. Even so, I soak up each of her words—I mean, *actually listen*. Not sighing and nodding, thinking about something else, as I would with any other girl. And the longer she rambles, I start to realize something. Well, *admit* is more accurate, because it's always been there...

There's something between us.

Beyond physical attraction.

And it's mutual.

I feel it. She feels it.

Although, she's probably still in denial, as I have been, for obvious reasons. We're polar opposites. Jeremy's her brother. My promiscuous nature... Honestly, I think we could work those things out. I could change. I *am* changing, as a result of being around her, even if a part of me opposes the transformation. It's just a fact.

But there's also another fact.

"You deserve someone better," I whisper.

Her rambles stop abruptly. For a moment, she wears the same expression—happy, carefree, as if she didn't hear me at all. Until her smile falters, and I know she did. I wait, feeling sick, as I anticipate her *what?* or *why would you say that?* or perhaps the classic *what do you mean?* The feigned innocence she loves to play, myself included.

It never comes.

She only stares, holding my gaze with a strong, almost defiant grip.

"Don't go any further down this road. Not with someone like me."

"And why not?"

I nearly stumble backwards. I knew it. I knew it, down to my core, but hearing her *not* deny it... "I'm not good for you, Jule—" My throat burns. *"Juliana."*

That's right. Juliana. No more Jules. Don't make this any harder on her than necessary.

Hurt flickers across her features, before it's squashed by fire. She huffs. "How very vague of you, Hayden. Is this about... what happened in the hot tub? I know we said it was just physical, but if you're more interested in Olivia, you can just say tha—"

"I don't *give a fuck* about Olivia."

Her eyes bulge, and *fuck* can I not unsee the satisfaction in them, and the way her lips twitch at the corners... Sweet Juliana, she wants me all for herself, a possessive liking we share in common—something I'll never be able to shake, unlike her beloved nickname.

You're going to have to. For her sake.

"So... This is about the necklace..."

Shame thunders through me, powerful and inescapable. I snap my attention away from those captivating emerald eyes, but find no solace. Five years, and I'm still haunted. There's a reason I never bring it up, never *think* about what happened. Now is no exception.

She drops to a whisper. "Look... I thought about it and —"

I whip back toward her. *"No."*

Goddamnit, no. She will *not* forgive me for that. My breaths come out choppy as I pace before her, not caring if I draw attention. I thread a shaky hand through my hair, tempted to yank the locks from my scalp.

"That's not it," I say, and it's no lie.

She tracks my movements, gnarled in confusion, before she snatches my shoulder. "Then what is?!"

I look down at her, straight on. *Christ,* she's so beautiful. So perfect, I don't even know how to act around her. Unconsciously, my body gravitates toward hers, until I'm basking in her aura at an inappropriate distance, wishing more than anything that I had the guts to humiliate myself, to scream from the rooftop of Churchill Downs that...

I'M A FUCKING LIAR!

A worthless. Good for nothing. Liar.

And Juliana deserves better.

Sure, she had a little crush on me in high school and maybe it's rekindled this past month, but unlike me, she's changed, grown, worked on herself over the years, has accomplishments that should reflect in her partner. A man who wouldn't *lie about working under his father,* thereby reaping benefits he never earned, essentially dangling the promises of a respectable match under her nose, someone who can talk business, has a promising future, can impress her friends and family.

Someone like my brother.

He really is my carbon copy, physically, except he comes with all those shiny accolades. Maybe the two of them should give it a try. I saw the way he looked at Juliana in the office, the intrigue that simmered in his eyes. Even better, he's in an open relationship, an engagement that's strictly business, so he's free to entertain Juliana all he wants. Invite her to his office at any hour. He's there all night, working hard, anyway, so no one would question it. Well, not until they heard the dubious sounds oozing from those thin walls, while he's got her bent over his—

I jerk away violently, surprising her.

"Hayden?"

"I-I'm... I'm gonna..."

I book it across the balcony, aiming for the French doors into the lounge. She calls after me, but my strides are too long for her high heels. I'm blinded, consumed by a fury of my own making, with one destination in mind.

~

THE MEN'S RESTROOM.

Maybe not the most glamorous choice, but it has surprisingly low foot traffic, and it's the only place I could guarantee Juliana wouldn't go looking for me. And she hasn't, for the ten minutes that I've sat here, fully clothed, sitting on a closed toilet lid. Enclosed by the four walls of my stall, I'm alone with my thoughts.

I got the reins on my anger, finally, but...

Juliana must think I've lost my mind. I more-or-less confessed my feelings for her, told her to stay clear of me without providing a solid explanation, then ran off. I completely ditched her, *my date,* in a place where she knows next to no one and—

I hear the bathroom door swing open, along with a familiar voice.

"...if he doesn't like my offer, he can go pound fucking sand. Tell him that, verbatim."

Through the crack in my door, I catch Elias's suit-clad frame march by the stalls, pressing a phone to his ear.

"Yeah, yeah, that's another problem. Just have the files on my desk as soon as possible..."

He retraces his steps, pacing, zooming by again.

"No, it can't wait until Monday... Well, why don't you use that little Econ degree Harvard handed you and answer that for yourself, huh...? Exactly. The Stock Exchange is closed on weekends, so we need to hit this now while market volatility is low."

I hold back a sigh. Of course, he's working. I shouldn't be surprised, given that he never sat down in his derby seat, and I doubt he was actually watching from somewhere else, but... did he really need to come in *here* for his phone call?

He swings by again, pinching the bridge of his nose. "No. It needs to be done sooner than that. Call in another analyst. An intern or two, if you must... Yeah, well, capitalism doesn't sleep, just because it's their Saturday. This is what they signed up for... Yes, I'll make it there in time. I'll notify the crew to prepare the jet for departure."

My heart sinks, listening to the strain in his voice. Guilt eats at me for having been upset with my brother, even if it all *was* just in my head and I hadn't spoken a word to him. What's all that stress good for, if he never has a single day off?

"You have three hours, max. That's when I'll touch down in New York."

When his pacing stops abruptly, I angle my head, peering through the slit, until I spot him standing in front of the row of sinks, looking at himself in the mirror. His face doesn't really seem to show *any* emotion, despite his stressful tone. He's just... staring, blankly.

Heavy pressure weighs down my chest. I don't know why, exactly. It's not like he's having a mental breakdown from a problem that's surely not far from what he handles on a daily basis. However... when he sinks a hand into his pants pocket, I instantly pinpoint the reasoning for my concern and predict exactly what I'm about to see before it actually comes into view.

A small plastic baggy, filled with snowy powder.

I blink away an onset of tears, refusing their coming, yet I'm unable to look away as he prepares the line with his credit card. Right there, on the bathroom counter.

"Tell Katie to order in cappuccinos with extra shots, and some food from that Thai place around the block. My usual."

Tossing down his card, he gives himself another look in the mirror. This time, I see the dread there. In his eyes, whirling like a dark vortex. He sighs. "It's gonna be a long night. Goodbye." *Click.*

Silence envelops him, reaching the walls and every corner of the bathroom, so eerie I wonder if he can hear my shallow breaths as he stares down at that white line.

Stop him, a little voice whispers.

From snorting coke? He's a Kingston. He despises being told what to do. Perhaps I could brush the substance from the table? Steal his drugs? His pockets are endless, in both cash and connections. He'd have his next fix before he's airborne.

Save him.

Save...

Tears well, yet again. I know too much. I've seen our father's work logs, the *proof* that he abuses Elias, after training him his whole life as a prized pony, then turns around and secretly chains him up like an ox to pull a heavy carriage while the other hitches a ride up top. It's sickening. Exploitative—of his own son.

Elias won't listen to me, I tell that voice.

Try anyway. You're his brother. Who else will?

Certainly not Mom. She isn't around enough to notice, never was, and we don't have any other siblings.

He's alone... Truly, alone in this.

Time crawls as Elias leans over, pressing a finger to one nostril and angling the other.

Save him!

But I'm frozen. Struck by horror and drowning in guilt, watching him inch closer.

SAVE HIM!

I bolt for the door, only to freeze once again at the sharp

sound of his inhale. I'm too late, useless, staring as the stall door swings on its hinges, unveiling the full scene.

Elias stumbles back. "Ughhhh," he groans, squeezing his eyes shut. "Fuck..." He sniffs again, pinching his nostrils, until his eyes open.

And meet mine in the mirror.

I knew what to expect, but it's no less shocking. The redness in them, the veins crawling across the whiteness... it's brighter than the distinct shade of blue we share. As the high sets in, his pupils dilate, and hazy clouds roll over like a glassy film.

His jaw clenches. "Were you listening that whole time?"

I don't respond. I *can't*.

He swivels around, flaunting his Armani suit. "You got something you'd like to say?"

Yes—DAD IS USING YOU!!!

But the truth lodges in my throat, caught between guilt and the fear of his reaction.

"Ohhhhh, I get it. You just want to stand there and judge, huh?" He encircles me, his steps unsteady, but his gaze piercing. "Seeing that you eavesdropped on my conversation, you damn well know *some of us* have responsibilities to uphold. So what, if I need a little help? Everyone does it. Who the fuck are you to judge me? Are you some saint, all of a sudden? You don't have the right, and you definitely don't have the experience to understand what it's like to be in my shoes. The things I've accomplished for our family's company."

"At what cost?"

"At what cost—at what cost...?" he grumbles, pacing aimlessly, cursing up a storm. "That's how you cope, isn't it? Oh, poor Elias. He's just soooo miserable. Did you ever stop and think, for one minute, that I could want this life? That I *want* Kingston Entertainment, the titles, the corporate life-style, everything. Well, I do. It makes me feel—"

"OOF." He slams into a corner of the wall, buckling at his knees. I rush over to help, but I'm met with his outstretched hand. "Don't touch me."

"You need help, Elias."

"Spare me." He dusts off his sleeve, turning to leave.

Tell him, tell him, tell him.

"Wait!"

He doesn't.

"Dad's overworking you!"

He grips the door handle as a sarcastic laugh rips through him. "You don't say."

"No. I mean, you work *more* than him. A lot more."

He freezes. For a moment, he's just silent.

Thank God. Maybe I'll get through to him, after all.

In a flash, he whirls around and bounds toward me, his lips coming an inch from my ear. *"YOU'RE JUST JEALOUS!"*

I jerk away, cupping my ear, knocking into a stall. I can hardly hear his next words as a violent ringing blares through my senses.

"You always have been. Need to invent fucking lies to help you sleep at night." He paces, faster than before, clutching his chest as he wheezes, emotions caught in his throat, enough that I wonder if somewhere, deep in his consciousness, he senses that I'm right. "You're jealous Dad picks me over you, that he sees something in me. Now you're just trying to get between him and I—the good thing we've always had going..."

I grapple for the stall door, nearly sliding on the tile as it swings on its hinges.

"Pathetic," he spits.

"Elias..." I groan, meeting his eyes.

He hesitates, a flicker of regret crossing his expression. Rolling his lips, I can almost make out their apology—or perhaps that's just wishful thinking. With a curse, he aims for the door.

Guess I'll never know.

THIRTY-TWO
HAYDEN

MY HEAD IS A FUCKING MESS.

I can't unsee the bewildered expression Juliana's been wearing since I left that bathroom—which is a whole other problem. She hasn't spoken a word to me, not on our drive to the airport or since takeoff, a half hour ago.

I sneak a glance her way.

She lounges on the couch that hugs the plane's right side, her heels discarded on the floor. Twirling a strand of hair between her fingers, she stares out the window, lost in thought. I sigh, returning to my own window, sinking into a plush recliner on the opposite side of the plane.

And that's how it goes, for a while. I steal a glance, hoping to catch her eye, but don't, then return to my window to contemplate the last three hours of my life. Rinse and repeat. Until she gets up, moves to the side of the couch nearest me, and breaks that silence.

"It's because I'm different, isn't it?"

I inhale sharply, but she holds up a hand, halting my protest.

"That's why you couldn't give me a straight answer—instead said I deserved better, to soften the blow. I'm not a billionaire or a millionaire or some celebrity, like everyone else in our section..." Her shoulders slouch, spiking urgency in me to counter her harsh self-assessment. "I didn't belong."

"That's not true."

She gives me a *yeah right* look, to which I raise an eyebrow.

"Even Clara knew it."

"Fuck Clara," I say—and mean it. "You were the most beautiful woman there."

Fuck subtlety, too, apparently.

She looks away. Even though I catch the blush staining her cheeks, it does little to lift her frown. I make my way over, sitting right beside her, speaking to the backside of her head. "You think I belonged?"

She snaps back around. "What kind of question is that?"

"A serious one."

"You're stupidly rich, *Hayden,*" she huffs. "One of the wealthiest men in New York. Of course, you did."

"Are you so sure?" Now I'm the one who can't meet her gaze. "I was given everything I have."

A pang of sadness strikes me as the jet's hum fills the space between us. I wouldn't know how to respond, either.

"And your brother wasn't? You're just describing generational wealth."

He was given more, actually, I don't say. Rather, "He's got something to show for it. He used that privilege to better himself, while I've never worked a real day in my life."

Her forehead creases. "Huh?"

There it is.

The true reason she deserves someone better. I swallow,

contemplating the best way to deliver the blow, but it turns out I don't need to as I watch those wrinkles fade, realization dawning on her features.

"You're not under your father's wing, are you...?"

I laugh bitterly. "What do you think?"

"But why were you taking notes that day? During my presentation? It looked like you worked at Kingston Entertainment."

"I do. Beneath my brother, as an assistant. I was taking notes for *him*. It's supposed to be an internship, but really, it's just a means to humiliate me. I sit right outside Elias's door, where everyone can see. All I'm assigned is scut work, no opportunities to actually grow or learn anything. And you know what? I don't blame them. I don't *want* to work, knowing I'd just screw it up. I'm not like Elias. I'm just a waste of—"

I fight back a sting of tears, but *fuck*, they come, anyway. Whipping my attention elsewhere, I suck in a jagged breath, feeling their warmth slide down my cheeks.

Pathetic... Elias's words ring true.

"Don't say that—*Hayden.*"

Tender hands cup my jaw, reeling me back into focus. I'm met with the hugest, most concerned green eyes. As I blink away another warm stream of tears, shame shudders through me, but she's holding me hostage, coupled with the soft thumb pads sweeping along my jaw, catching those tears.

Juliana whispers, "Don't ever think such a thing."

"Even if I didn't, I still haven't earned a damn thing. Not my trust fund. My apartment. Now my public humiliation, a reminder of just how useless I am to the family. Truly, my father's given me everything in my life. He controls me. It's just the truth."

I blink furiously, my gaze drifting from hers once more. I should've never opened my mouth today. Now, look where it's gotten me. Trudging up trauma no one wants to hear about, least of all Juliana, who's had to fight for her accomplishments. She's just being nice. Saying the right thing. She doesn't actually—

Her touch grows in strength, her nails nicking my skin as she whips me forward. *"Look at me,"* she says—and I do. What I see, though... I feel it in my soul. Gone are those doe eyes, crushed by defiant fury, so potent it shouldn't belong to someone so gentle, except...

It's my same old Jules.

"Look at me, Hayden," she repeats, my name pleasing on her tongue. "Look at me, and answer one question. Can you do that?"

I nod, the movement an untraceable whisper, because, despite her faith in me, no words could change my circumstances, the privileged lot I've blown away. The control I lack, seized by the heartless man who passed me his genes and great fortunes, but revels in reminding me of my astronomical failures and meritless existence and lack of—

"Did Warren Kingston give you your talent?"

Every. Fucking. Ounce. Of air. Seeps from my lungs.

"W-what...?"

Despite her startlingly calm demeanor, Juliana's nails dig deeper, low at my nape, commanding my attention. "It's a yes or no question. Did your father give you your talent?"

"I-I..."

His words flood my headspace, drenched in poison.

You never change, do you...?

Don't play dumb with me, boy...

It's like you're still in school...

Scribbling little doodles, when you should be working...
No wonder you never learn anything...
"No..." I breathe out. "He didn't."
Little doodles little doodles little doodles...
My. Little. DOODLES.

I gasp audibly, choking on my own saliva. That's why! Why he never acknowledged my artistic talent—like my teachers had in my youth. Why he diminished their praises, belittled and cast aside the one single thing that set me apart, and still does. Because—

"Then he can never take it away from you."

I wrench free from her grasp, eyes blown wide, my tears long forgotten by ways of understanding. All these years, I've been so blind, conditioned to loathe myself. I should've known, should've seen through my father's deceit. And yet...

Juliana did.

"How...?" I ask, and of course, she understands my question.

"Ohhh, Hayden. Don't you know?" There's a slight humor to her tone, yet her eyes still gleam with seriousness. "Something strange happens when insecure people see someone happy in their uniqueness. They catch a glimpse of something they themselves want, but are too fearful to take their own steps toward it. So instead, every now and then, they'll knock you down a peg or two, in hopes that one day you'll be miserable, right alongside them."

Holy shit.

Stunned isn't really the right word, yet I soak in hers. Each one of them, unsure of how to conjure up a response, but I think my expression does the job just fine. Mouth ajar on a fixed gaze, I'm consumed by a profound amazement of the woman before me.

Who just called *Warren Kingston* insecure.

"Or... What the hell do I know?" She winks at me. "I just program a *little game* all day."

Wow... Did she scoop inside my brain? I guess I overlooked the part where I invited a mind reader into my apartment, who I apparently share more in common with than I've ever thought. And her passion... the determination she had to set me straight and rid me of my sorrows...

Shame consumes me. "After the way I treated you all those years ago, I don't deserve your kindness."

"Maybe not," she admits. "But... after what happened on the terrace, I saw how my silence hurt you. As a friend, I should've talked to you. Sure, I had the right to be upset about the necklace thing, but..." Her voice wobbles, effectively scraping a shard of ice down my throat, before she steadies herself. "We *were* quite young. I don't blame you, for not knowing how you felt about me. I know you said I deserve better, but I'm sure that's how you feel now about—"

There she goes again. About to forget me.

"No," I interject. "My feelings were as real as they are now."

Her breath hitches, emotions rolling through her stare, as her body gravitates toward me, closer and closer, before she jerks back to center. "You don't need to sugarcoat it, Hayden. What happened, happened. Perhaps you lost interest or—"

"No. Just... no. Stop right there."

Her shoulders slouch in confusion.

I huff a sigh. Five years, and the mistake still haunts me. There's a reason I never speak of it, let alone *think* of the ways I must've hurt her. Sometimes, though, I dream about it, of how she must've found out. On a tabloid or some gossip site.

I look away, hoping to make it easier.

"Everything I said to you that night, in your room... it was true. I don't care if we were young, I knew how I felt. Didn't want to, honestly, but there was no denying it, once I found out you weren't coming to Princeton. I was angry—so, so angry—and couldn't bear the thought of all the *pricks* who'd throw themselves onto you. So, I thought I'd give them something to look at. Maybe then, they'd realize you were off limits. Or that you'd remember me, from time to time."

"Is that why you gave the same necklace to that actress? Ensure everyone in Hollywood knew she was taken?"

I cringe, her sour tone delivering a stinging blow. Looking her in the eye, I say, "I'm sorry," and mean it, deeply, even though I know it'll do little good, especially since I took advantage, knowing she was inexperienced, and stole her first kiss, needing that claim on her.

"I was dumb. *Insecure.* Something I'd never dealt with before, not when it came to girls. When I left, I was convinced you'd forget about me, no matter what. So... I convinced myself that I didn't care, that *I'd* forget about you before you did me. I moved onto new flings—models, influencers, fucking anybody—flew through the dating scene like I was speed running Monopoly, and kept doing so, until you came back into my life. I even gave that *stupid* actress—I don't even remember her name—the exact same necklace, hoping I'd feel the same way about her, about any other girl, but I just couldn't. *And I still can't."*

A glossy film coats Juliana's eyes, but she blinks rapidly, fighting off the emotions. I don't blame her for hesitating. Why would she trust a word that passes my lips? She pushes anyway, and even though she stares straight down into her lap, she asks on a mere whisper, "What are you saying, Hayden?"

I pinch her chin, lift until she meets my gaze, and reveal those doe eyes I know so well. *God.* She's so beautiful. I keep saying it, but... how is she this breathtaking? How could any man not help but fall for her?

I lean in, encroaching on her space, my heart clenching when her eyes flick back and forth between mine.

"That I treated you as if you were just another conquest, when I should've treated you like you were *everything.*"

She melts into my touch, drawing closer, so near that her cherry scent wafts through my nostrils, bathing my senses in all things *her,* and deterring even the simplest thoughts. Her eyes flutter down to my lips, and mine hers. Soft and supple, they part on a jagged, minty breath—a tantalizing preview of the second taste I've craved for five years.

"What about my brother?" she manages to ask.

I barely hear her question over the blood pounding in my ears. What about Jeremy? Oh yes, he'll kill me, no doubt, but I'll die a happy man, if only I seize another shot at the other night. Except... I realize something, in her nearness, in the wake of all that's been said.

I don't want to ruin Juliana. *I want to cherish her.*

If she wants to take it slow, we'll take it slow.

If she wants more, I'll drop to my knees in worship.

Anything and everything can be hers.

As long as it's from me.

Which poses quite the problem, you see, for these feelings insult the most cardinal rule of them all...

Rule #10: A playboy never falls in love.

"Fuck it."

I crash my lips to hers, my eyes fluttering shut. On contact, I pry the most deliciously *addicting* whimper from her —as if she's yearned for this exact moment for just as long as I have. The sound rumbles against my skin, and it's all I can manage to keep still, to only cup her jaw lightly.

Letting her decide how far to take this.

Our lips resound on her withdrawal. Short and sweet, exactly what I expected. Not much different than our first kiss. She's probably just testing the waters. She's a virgin, anyway—

Before I can take a full breath, she crashes back for more, her tongue bruising my lips in a blinding kiss that splits my mind in two. I groan as her fingers thread through my hair and her tongue darts past my lips, wanting nothing more than to see her writhing beneath me.

But still, I hold the reins on my control. Meeting her, stroke for stroke, savoring her sweet taste, trying not to think about where she tastes even better. Indeed, I banish those sinful thoughts, as I'm unsure of how far her intentions go...

That is, until a hand presses between the lapels of my suit, flat against my chest, and pushes me to lounge back into the couch. With her lips still on mine and my eyes still shut in darkness, her body cranes over me with the movement, farther and farther, until I feel the full weight of her on my lap.

As she straddles me.

THIRTY-THREE
JULIANA

HAYDEN'S HOLDING HIMSELF BACK. I know he is. And maybe that's a good thing, but... I want to witness all that restraint crumble.

My knees sink into the leather on either side of him, jumbling the hem of my dress higher up my waist, exposing my panties—not that he can see them with his eyes closed. Above the jet's hum, our kiss resounds into the air, sucking and lapping one another as I trail both hands down the backside of his neck, dragging my nails through his hair.

He groans softly.

Not enough.

Growing bold, I nibble his bottom lip, tugging until it plops back into place.

A growl rumbles against my skin.

I open my eyes, just a tad, catching his knuckles whitening along the edge of the couch cushion. But *still*, he doesn't touch me. I bite harder, repeating the motion with more aggression.

"Fuckkk, Jules."

Oh, God, his voice... deep, gravelly, guttural, everything a girl could ever want, and it only hikes my arousal higher, enough that I'm veering off course, trailing my lips across his jawline, dropping down to his—

I freeze as doubt creeps into me. *Is it weird for a girl to kiss a guy's neck?* Not wanting to find out if it is, I'm about to venture back, until his head falls back on a curse. Confidence surges through me, but I hold back, just in case, giving him a peck, then another, a tiny bit lower.

He shudders.

I bite down on a fiendish smile. "You like that?" *Kiss.*

A grunt is his only reply.

I sneak another peek, catching him clutching the cushion. *Why won't he touch me?* I wonder, even though I know the answer.

"Is it just me, or are you a little stiff?"

Kiss, kiss, kiss...

He grits his teeth. "I have... to be... gentle with you."

"Do you?"

"Juliana..." he warns.

A part of me trembles at his seriousness, understands that I may just be in over my head, that I shouldn't want it any other way for my first time. But the other part of me... it quickly takes over, needing to see him come undone, to unravel because he *can't* control himself when it comes to me.

I latch onto his throat, moaning louder than necessary. His response is immediate as he shuffles beneath my weight, rocking my body along with him, his pulse fluttering under my tongue as I lap up his sensitive skin. Mimicking as he once did me, I work down the column of his throat, then back up, leaving a trail of saliva in my wake.

He groans, drawing out the sound, but not as loud as

when I latch onto that spot at the crook of his neck and jawline, sucking greedily.

"That's right, baby. Mark me as yours."

"Mhmmmm."

I home in that one spot, nicking him with my teeth, then licking the burn before sucking some more. Shivers explode across my body, as fingers brush up the backside of my thighs, but it's not enough. I need them gripping my skin, pinning me on my back, having their way with me.

I need *more.*

Sinking lower, my middle comes in contact with hardened steel, through layers of fabric. Boxers, slacks, and my panties, which provide the sweetest friction as I grind up his length, brutally slow. Slipping back down, my tongue syncs with the tempo of my hips.

Another warning. "Julian—"

My lips *plop* from his skin, releasing their suction, before they're brushing against his ear, bellowing out the most high-pitched, porno-worthy moan they can muster. As I sway a little faster, I go for his other ear to—

I gasp as two hands smack against my ass cheeks, stinging on contact, before grabbing generous fistfuls. "You're a little faker, huh? Just trying to get me riled up—let's see what that gets you, shall we?"

He bucks against me, grinding his bulge through my center, prying a yelp from my lungs. I suck in my bottom lip as he sways again, faster and faster, gripping my ass and lifting my weight, working me along his shaft in tandem with his pace, until I'm whimpering with pleasure.

"Ohh, does that feel good on your clit?"

"Yes, yessssss." I grind back against him desperately, keeping his pace.

He lets out a low curse. "I can hear how wet you are."

With a moan, I arch my back, bringing new sensations.

He chuckles darkly. "Good girl, louder. I want my crew to hear how soaked you're getting."

"Fuckkkk." I grip his shoulders, rocking until I'm squeezing my eyes shut, panting like a wild thing. "I want..."

Hayden grabs me by my nape, his fingers threading through my locks as he forces me to look down at him. "What do you want, Jules?"

"Your cock," I whine.

"Such a filthy mouth. Say that again."

"I..." Heat simmers across my skin, under the intensity of his stare. "I want your cock, Hayden."

His lips twitch. "Where?"

"In my..." I hesitate. He wants to hear me say the obvious answer—but I got something better. *"In my mouth."*

Eyes bulging, his movements halt abruptly. "Have you ever...?"

I shake my head, feeling my cheeks flush.

He clamps down on his lip as hunger flashes across his features, but he restrains himself, remaining still. "Are you sure?"

"You did for me."

Tsk, tsk, tsk. "Wrong answer, Jules. My only concern is *your* pleasure. Not mine."

Now it's my turn to smile. "I want to," I say honestly. "But... there's something else."

He pinches my chin. "And what's that?"

I clear my throat, suddenly wishing I hadn't pushed. "I want to give you head, but..." *God, this is so embarrassing.*

"Tell me," he coos.

"I want to be *told* to."

His grip tightens, as a shiver visibly racks through him. "So, that's how you want it, then—rough? You think you can handle that?"

I roll my lips between my teeth, suddenly aware of just how big he is beneath me, and I haven't even seen all of him. I don't need to. I'm probably in way over my head, but I *want* to be able to handle it.

He grins wickedly at my silence, and his next words would no doubt have me weak in the knees, if I were standing. "You want me to break you in, baby?"

My eyes fall by their own accord, as my inner walls clench around air, but he doesn't accept that, apparently, as I earn my clit a stern thrusting, blasting pleasure through me and snapping my eyes open.

"Hmm?" He coils a hand to the front of my neck, the shadow of a necklace, applying light pressure. "You want me to stretch you out? Have that tight pussy wrapped perfectly around my cock before we land?"

Fuck...

"Yes or no?" He adds more pressure, delight flickering in his stare.

I wet my lips. "Yes."

A rumble sounds from deep in his chest. "Then get on your knees."

Yes! I—

Pain reverberates outwards from my left buttocks, in response to the *whack* sounding in the air. *"Now*—I'm not going to tell you again."

Every hair on my body raises on end, peaked with excitement, as I scramble off his lap, rush to my feet, and—

"Take your dress off, too."

I obey with haste, earning a hum full of praise, followed by a vicious curse once the fabric pools around my ankles.

"Dirty *fucking* girl." Widening his stance, his eyes flicker to the ground, where my knees quickly drop. In a flash, he's tossing his jacket across the couch and unbuttoning his shirt. "Matching bra and panties? What were your intentions for tonight, hmm?"

"N-nothing," I stammer.

Heat stains my skin when he cups my jaw, lifting my head to look at him—and good lord, what a magnificent sight he is. Lounged comfortably with an arm draped across the backside of the couch, Hayden flexes his abs, glistening in all his tan glory. An impressive outline bulges in his tight pants, angled off to the side, leaving little mystery about what's coming my way. And his chin... it's held up high as he peers down at me, the embodiment of wealthy arrogance.

"Nothing? What about that sweet pussy—is it shaved, too?"

My lips part, the answer lodged in my throat.

He burns with satisfaction. "Unbuckle my belt, Jules."

I nearly whimper when he brushes a thumb across my lips, before he drapes that arm along the couch, too. Hands free. His lips curve in a devilish smirk as he watches. Nerves and anticipation thunder beneath my skin as I fumble with his belt. When I unhook the clasp, granting access to his zipper, I hesitate, glancing his way.

"Look at you, waiting for permission. Such a quick learner."

My toes curl at the praise.

"Have at me, baby. I'm all yours."

Say no more.

I practically yank off his zipper, but when I'm presented

with his light gray boxers, and the delicious outline underneath, I slow down... and trace a single finger up its length. Instantly, Hayden's legs quiver, along with the flexing of his abs, all while his mouth hangs ajar on a silent *O*.

As I tread back down, I don't hide my smirk, because I truly, *truly* think I might've found myself an addiction.

Adding more pressure, and the rest of my fingers, I sweep across his length, exploring, enjoying his every grunt and sharp inhale, especially when I focus on his tip—yes, he *really* likes that.

"Are you sensitive here?" I purr, stroking lazily, forming a fist around the fabric.

He grits his teeth, his legs trembling violently. "Yes, you wicked thing. You could have me howling."

My smile widens. Okay, maybe I like that a little too much. I ease up, whooshing a breath from him, only for him to suck it right back in, as I slip a finger beneath the band of his boxers.

Maybe he's nervous, I think. *This* is *the first time I'll see him, barring the bathroom incident.*

I meet his stare, learning just how wrong I am. He's brimming with confidence, every part of him, and when I pull down his boxers, I understand why.

He springs free, before falling and smacking against his skin with a dense *thud*. My insides clench at the sight, my mouth watering at what's surely, by conventional standards, the perfect cock—far surpassing anything I've seen in porn.

Long and thick, his length lies across abs so defined they look photoshopped, the focal point of a sinful *V* converging from his hips. Two distinct veins crawl up his underside, nearly reaching his domed tip that grazes the lower crescent of his bellybutton.

He's huge. So, outrageously massive that my sex throbs, despite me wondering how the hell he's going to fit.

"Don't worry, baby. I know just what to do with you," a deep voice says, reading my mind, snapping me from my trance—Shit, was I drooling? My eyes roam across steel abs, but when they meet Hayden's, I quake with shock.

A dominant, fiery lust burns behind them, and a smug grin tugs at his lips, his arms still draped across the backside of the couch, as he enjoys the view. Me. Clad in nothing but a bra and panties. On my knees at his feet. His gaze flickers to his manhood, then back. A silent command, one I obey immediately.

Scooting closer, I size up the beast, nervous tension crackling inside me. Here I was, worried about how he's going to fit *in* me, when I don't even know if he'll fit in my *mouth*. So, I start with a simple touch, scraping a nail down his shaft, feeling the weight of his cocky stare, not really expecting much of a reactio—

His legs quiver at my sides.

I stop and look up, finding his mouth parted.

Using an additional finger, I scrape some more, watching as he grits his teeth, all but pooling satisfaction in my center. For another minute, I tease him, loving every grunt and hiss that passes his lips, until they stop completely when I grip him at the base.

Whatever remained of his composure slips right off his features—his posture straightens, his hands shoot to the edge of the couch cushion. Standing him to attention, my pulse spikes, not quite knowing how to proceed into such unfamiliar territory. Hesitantly, I lick his tip where its ridge meets the underside of his shaft, exactly where he was sensitive before.

Hayden's entire body shudders beneath me.

I pause, smirking. *Oh, this is going to be fun.*

I try again, slower this time.

He hisses through clenched teeth, legs trembling violently. "You just love playing with it, don't you?" he manages out.

Yes.

Lick...

Lick...

Lick...

A groan escapes him, and it's like a shot of dopamine straight into my brain. The seductive sound replays in my mind, heightening my arousal, urging me to lap him from the base all the way up his length, before swirling my tongue around his tip.

"Fuckkkk." His head falls, resting on the backside of the couch. Around and around, I circle him, keeping a torturously slow pace, until he's whimpering the most delicious noise, rocking his hips in a steady rhythm. "Look at me—look at me... *yessss...*"

He curses viciously when I slurp him into my mouth, just an inch, but it's enough to earn an involuntary thrust. His cock glides down my tongue, prying my lips wide, hardly able to compensate for his girth. Fighting back a sting of tears, I suck hard on his withdraw, moaning around him.

"Fucking hell, Jules." He inhales sharply, his jaw hanging low while he watches me bob up and down. "Goddddd... are you sure this is your first time?" he asks, and there's no mistaking his jealousy.

I *pop* him out. "You're my first," I say sweetly, seeing his gaze smolder with possession.

I drive my head back down, earning another curse, but I'm only able to make it a few inches before my throat spasms, and a loose lock sticks to my gloss. He grins at that, gathering my hair in one hand, wrapping it around his fist, his other clutching the seat in controlled restraint.

But that's the problem. *His control.*

It should be blown to bits, my hair ripping at the seams. Instead, he's fastened a leash on himself for my sake. And I've had enough.

Gripping his base tight, I work him up and down, increasing my pace suddenly. I lock my eyes with his, never veering from their sight as I pinch my eyebrows, sporting the poutiest, most desperate look I can muster, hoping I match my only reference—porn. When shock flashes across his expression, I know I hit my mark.

"Juliana..."

I taunt him with a little giggle.

The hand gripping my hair tightens, pulling at the roots, as the other whips to his mouth, forming a fist. "I know what you're doing," he grits out when I take him a little deeper.

I moan, sending vibrations that have him biting into his flesh.

"You sure you want that, for your first time?"

I bat my lashes innocently.

Shadows emerge from his features. "You're very tight down there," he cautions.

Don't care—*Blink, blink, blink.*

"Fuck..." He pulls his fist from his mouth, revealing a row of teeth marks. "Look at you, begging to be taken rough. So perfect. On your knees, worshipping my cock." Heat floods between my thighs, throbbing painfully at his praise. "Hollow those cheeks, baby." I suction harder, whining as I do. "Yes, just like that..."

His eyes roll back, only to burst open the instant my

fingertips begin exploring his inner thighs. At first, I'm unsure of where I'm headed, or what I'm even doing, just lazily stroking as I bob my head, keeping eye contact without using my hands, until I feel him quiver as I traverse too close to his balls.

His stare widens with surprise, but quickly darkens with promises of repercussions. I'd shoot him a wicked grin, if my mouth wasn't preoccupied. Hopefully, he can decipher the mischief in my eyes.

I inch closer to that forbidden spot.

"Careful," he warns.

A hiss sings through his teeth, when I brush his delicate flesh with the pad of my thumb. Easing up my head movements, I focus on my new discovery. Gently sweeping the opposite direction, I explore the surprisingly smooth texture as it tightens to my touch, all while Hayden practically melts into the couch, his eyes glossing with a hazy film and lips moaning throaty sounds that would make the devil blush. Surely, he's in utter bliss.

Until I scrape a nail across his soft skin.

Every muscle, every fiber in his being stills.

"What did I tell you, Juliana?"

An excited shiver bolts down my spine when I meet his stare. It's poised for punishment, and mine answers with a challenge. He lifts an arrogant eyebrow—

Scrape, scrape, scrape, I scratch his balls, bobbing the tip of his cock past my lips repeatedly, the motion bouncing my breasts.

A small sound escapes him, and *shit...* the look on his face... something in him cracks, like a splinter down everything he knows. The fingers in my hair, the ones clenching the couch cushion, even his *voice*—they all tremble. At long last, I witness a man well past his breaking point.

Hot breath puffs his cheeks. "Last... warning..."

With another giggle, I bounce higher, driven wildly by lust as I abandon the scraping and instead tug on his—

"That's it."

THIRTY-FOUR
JULIANA

HAYDEN BOLTS TO HIS FEET, nearly causing me to fall on my ass, but I catch myself and race to my feet—

I grunt as he shoves me back down by my shoulders, forcing me to my knees once again, scraping my skin against the carpet lining the jet's interior. Stepping closer, his cock smacks against my lips, knocking the wind from me. I turn away on reflex, despite it stirring the embers of my arousal.

A hand clutches my nape, applying pressure that's sure to leave a mark, angling my head straight up. Through rows of washboard abs, all flexing between his silky long-sleeve left casually open, I meet Hayden's gaze.

And it sets me ablaze.

"You want to be broken in rough, huh? That's what you want? For me to *use* your holes however I please? Well then, how about you start by opening up that mouth you love to tease me with."

My lips part—only a hair. It's all I can muster, my mind turning up blank under the intensity of his stare, one that says I was born to be at his feet. Radiating superiority, there's no question who owns this Gulfstream.

"Do as you're told."

Fuck, he's so calm.

I do my bidding, holding his gaze, desire shining back at me as my inner walls clench around emptiness, aching with need.

"You can do better than that."

On a struggled mewl, I open my mouth wider, unhinging my jaw until I hear crinkling sounds.

"Good girl, as wide as you can go... That's it."

Threading fingers through my hair, he grabs me on either side of my head and positions it to his liking, keeping me there in an iron grip. I whimper, waiting for his entrance, the tip of his cock brushing my lips, teasing, bumping my chin with no regard.

"Why don't you bat those pretty lashes up at me? I want a good look before I make a mess of them."

I instantly obey. A string of desperate sounds escapes me, singing a sweet melody to Hayden's ego. He just smirks down at me, amusement marking his features when I whine, my jaw growing sore.

"So impatient." He *tsks*. "You want my cock, Jules?"

I nod vigorously—or try to, my efforts proving futile against his hold.

"Then stick out your tongue."

Overcome with lust, I propel my tongue ou—

I choke but fail to produce a sound, as Hayden buries his cock into my mouth with ruthless force, crashing into the back of my throat.

"FUCKKKK."

His fingers thread deeper, tugging every hair taut along

my scalp while he holds me in position, stuffing me as full as possible. Tears sting my eyes, and my throat convulses, just when a shudder ripples through him, so violently I think he might topple into me, before he yanks himself out.

I gasp, air whooshing into my burning lungs. Grappling for something—his legs, the couch, anything—I pant, almost in a state of delirium. That is, until I spot the long string of saliva drawn from my lips to Hayden's tip, the sight dripping lust like molten fire through my veins. Suddenly, it severs in two, coating my chin in spit. Feeling a blush, I bring the back of my hand up, meaning to wipe it off—

"Don't." Looking up, my heart palpitates when I meet Hayden's eyes. "Leave it there." I roll my lips, to which he raises an eyebrow, arrogant as ever. "Did I say I was finished?"

Stifling a moan, I unlock my jaw and slide my tongue out, earning another brutal thrust. Again, Hayden holds me there, burying himself all the way, this time earning an involuntary cough that coats his length in saliva, mingled with his loud groan resounding over the jet's hum.

He tears himself out on a gravelly curse, noting how that trail of spit draws another line, thicker than before. When it breaks in half, coating me in even more saliva, satisfaction emerges from Hayden's stare, before he plunges himself back in, allowing less time for recovery.

"*Fucking hell,*" he growls, wrenching back out just to immediately stuff me full again. Blinking furiously through the sting, my insides spasm along his length, as I suppress a cough.

"Relax, your throat, baby." Pulling out, he plunges back in, holding longer. "There you go," he praises, impaling me again... "Look up at me—yessss, my perfect girl." And again...

"Don't you close those pretty eyes. I want to see them water."
And again... "You're making such a mess, Juliana," he scolds,
filling me all the way. "So greedy, taking me to the base."

Thrust, thrust, thrust, he fucks my mouth, until he's blazing
into me with savage force, keeping a brutal tempo, and I'm
slurping him down, moaning and sucking around him,
ringing sloshing sounds in the air.

I hold his gaze through the savory burn, recognizing the
lust in his eyes as it's surely mirrored in my own, rising
higher and higher with his every grunt, with every droplet
dribbling from my chin and splashing on my breasts, until
I'm beaming him the most toothy smile I can manage, shame-
less in my newfound ecstasy. So consumed, I couldn't care
less if the whole crew hears us or sees us or passes us right
down the aisle—and he hasn't even *touched* me down
there yet.

But, no matter, my pussy throbs for attention, impossible
to ignore, thoroughly soaking my panties in my slick need.
Sliding a hand down my torso, I slip a finger beneath
the top—

Hayden halts his movements, right before he's about to
thrust back in, and snatches my wrist, yanking me to my feet.
I bump into his bare chest and backpedal as he crowds me,
his steps meeting mine with intoxicating nearness.

"Not before I have my fun," he murmurs into my ear.

I clutch his biceps for stability, my palms slipping along
his shirt's silky fabric. "What do you—"

My back collides into a wall, right as his hand descends
upon my clit, slipping beneath my panties. I cry out when he
rubs harshly, pushing off the wall only to knock into his chest,
trapped between two immobile forces.

He curses loudly, resting a hand on the wall above me for

support, while the other works me up and down. "You're *drenched*, Jules." With a grin, he watches me combust. "All this for me?"

My body writhes in my confinement, bumping into his chest then the wall and back again, pleasure scattering from the apex of my thighs, my eyes rolling to the back of my head.

"Look at me, baby."

Panting with fervent desire, I flutter my eyes ope—

Before I can even meet his stare, he plunges not one, but *two* fingers past my folds, and much to my surprise, I manage to take them all the way to the knuckles. Fire rips through me, mostly pleasure but also pain, as my inner walls clench tightly, stretching to compensate. Tilting his head, pumping fast, Hayden drinks in my reaction, wearing a triumphant smile.

"Look how worked up you got, just by sucking my cock. Your pussy's already begging for more." His fingers curl upwards, homing in on a spot that has me doubling into him. "Does that feel good?" He chuckles, already knowing the answer.

"Yessss," I whine and grind back against him.

"And what about this?" He adjusts his angle, working me vertically while simultaneously pushing in and out, his palm rubbing my clit as he buries deeper, the powerful sensation bursting like stars all around me.

Legs trembling, I whip a hand over my mouth, muffling a moan, abandoning my bravado about not caring who sees— we're *right* next to where the flight attendants sit, separated only by a door.

Hayden catches my glance, his glinting with amusement. "Awww, look at you, using your inside voice. How polite," he taunts. "That won't last long."

I shoot him a look, eyes narrowing, but I can only hold it for a split second, before he yanks the front of my bra down, spilling my breasts over the fabric, exposing my peaked nipples. Rumbling with hunger, he barrels into me, knocking my back against the wall, and suctions one between his teeth.

"Fuck!" I gasp, darting to cover my mouth.

He growls at that, pleased, flicking his tongue against my sensitive bud, sucking and toying with it, biting and tugging until it pops back to center, before he switches to the other with a groan.

I whimper as he drives into me still, crumbling at the attention, like putty against the wall—only to tense up when his ministrations grow stronger, more purposeful, steering me toward a blinding light that has me shaking, struggling to stay upright.

He groans again, meeting my eyes through his thick lashes, brimming with satisfaction, hiking me further up the wave of ecstasy, until I—

"I'm going to—"

I suck in a breath, anticipating him to deny my arrival like he did in the hot tub, except this time, his fingers stay right where they are. In fact, they thrust harder, keeping a punishing pace as he drops to his knees before me and splits my whole world in half.

I cry out on my release, loud enough that surely even the pilot hears, just when Hayden buries his face between my thighs, lapping and sucking my clit. Squeezing my eyes shut, I grip his hair instinctually, threading my digits through the silky locks, earning a drawn-out groan. The vibration tickles my sensitive flesh, urging me to grind against him shamelessly, riding out the waves while my interior walls clench around him.

When I'm all spent, quivering against him, he withdraws fingers drenched in my wetness, and immediately sinks them into his mouth, looking up at me. My lips part, my mind turning up utterly blank, as I can only stare while he sucks off the juices, his blue eyes brightening in an insatiable frenzy.

Popping them from his lips, his gaze swivels to my pussy.

"Hayden..." I whine, pinching my thighs, only worsening the throb at its apex.

"Just another taste, baby." He trails a touch up my legs. "Don't you want to be my good girl?"

When he palms my stomach, pressing me flat against the wall, I whimper, baring my thighs for him, earning another round of praise. He spreads my puffy lips and hisses below his breath, "So wet," before swiping a tongue through my center, searing brutal pleasure when he reaches my clit.

"Fuckkk," he grunts. "Your pussy is so sweet, Jules."

A chorus of mewls fumbles from my mouth, when he makes another pass. And *God*, does he look positively sinful. Bare from the waist down, with a collared button-up draped off his shoulders, his hair tousled in the sexiest way, and strong abs that ripple to each of his movements, above a glorious erection that's still raging.

I flush when he catches me staring at it.

"You think you're ready for me, hmm?"

"Yes," I say, despite the waver in my tone, nibbling my lip.

He smirks. "No, you're not ready yet." I grit my teeth when he licks once more, shaking with pleasure, needing him all over again. "Not until you take three fingers."

My eyes bulge. *"Three?"*

"You have a lot more opening up to do, baby, if you want me to fit."

Wetting my lips, I glance past him again, the mere sight of

his cock making me salivate, quickening the thrumming between my legs. "What if... What if I want to stretch around... something else?"

Our eyes lock, his smoldering with lust.

"You're sure about that?"

Maybe.

"Yes." I nod, squirming as his breath tickles my clit.

"You're gonna have to be a bit more convincing." He licks through me, slower this time, causing my fingers to bury through his hair, tugging his locks on a moan.

"Yesssss." I pant, as he laps up my clit lazily, focusing there. Rocking against him, blood pounding in my ears, I whine, "Yes, Hayden, pleaseeee," and sigh when he eases up his pressure.

Rising to his impressive height, his lips shine with my wetness before he wipes it on the back of his hand and slinks his long-sleeve to the ground. He flicks his chin, gesturing to the couch. "Show me how you want it."

Excitement sends my feet in a hurry, until I'm at the foot of the couch, near the armrest that Hayden's suit jacket drapes off of, and freeze...

How do *I want it?*

I run through all the positions I've seen in porn, most of which I don't even know the names to. Missionary, doggy, and cowgirl. That's it. I roll my teeth, unsure of how to decipher between the three in terms of pleasure or approaching your first time. So, I just rely on instinct.

Feeling the weight of Hayden's stare on my back, I peel off my panties, revealing my soaked center, pooling them around my ankles. I unhook my bra, too, not making much of a show, before lying on the couch, flat on my back with my head by the armrest, spreading my legs with my hair sprawled across the leather.

But...

The moment I look down at myself, I'm struck by a wave of insecurity. Not because of my looks. Rather, from my choice of position... There's no doubt, I picked the simplest one. He's probably disappointed over it and not at all surprised.

Sighing, I swing my head toward him, toward someone who has so much experience and probably thinks I'm boring or too—

My breath catches.

About five-or-so paces away, Hayden just stands there. He's fully nude in only his dress socks—but that's not new and can't be to blame for the way my heart palpitates in an erratic rhythm. No... it's the way he gawks at me, the look on his face...

It's of pure, unequivocal *devastation*.

"Hayden?"

He doesn't budge.

I glance down at myself, for a moment contemplating if there's something stuck on me, or maybe I'm lying weird. Did I forget to shave my legs, and he's just now noticing? Nope. They're silky smooth. And my toenails, they check out, too. Their paint is all shiny and without chips, for once. Then what is it?

My brow furrows as I return my attention to—

"Hayden?" I breathe again, finding him a foot from the couch, peering down at me with that same expression. Without a word, his gaze roams down my body, then swings back up, his eyes softening when they reach my face, staying there for several shaky breaths.

I'm about to prod him a third time, until...

"You're fucking breathtaking, Juliana."

I suck in a breath as a tingling warmth spreads all around me, setting my cheeks aflame. Searching his gaze, I find only sincerity, which catches emotions deep in my throat, stealing my words. Not that I have time for a response, anyway.

In a flash, he drapes his body across my center, sinking me farther into the couch, and crashes his mouth to mine. His tongue darts between my lips, stealing a breathless moan that he answers with his own, the throaty baritone racing goose-bumps along my arms.

Lost in his essence, I touch him—his hair, his cheeks, his strong chest, sweeping my fingertips wherever feels right. He groans at that, exploring my mouth deeper, tasting minty, our tongues meeting stroke for stroke.

He prods my knee. "Lock your..." *Kiss.* "Ankles..." *Kiss.* "Around me..." *Kiss.*

I hardly register his words, too consumed by our connec-tion, but do as I'm told, wrapping my legs around him without opening my eyes, only for them to snap open when he bucks his hips. I moan into his mouth when he slides his shaft up my center, rubbing my clit and coating his underside in my wetness. On his return, I rock against him, greedy for the sensations he brings.

I peer down, through the slight opening between our bodies, and watch as he sways again. *Fuck,* he's so big. There's no way I'll be able to take it all. I squirm against him, slipping along his length, the thought only driving my arousal higher.

"I want it, Hayden," I whine, feeling impossibly empty.

His lips twitch. "I can tell, baby. Listen to how wet you are." He sways faster, back and forth, ringing the sound of my slickness around us, mixing with the whimpers that fumble from my lips. "That's it, so needy for my cock. You want me to stretch you wide, Jules? Have you screaming for the whole crew to hear?"

"YES!" I grind against him, only for him to unlock my legs and pin my knees into the sofa, baring me to him. Panting from the sudden lack of skin-on-skin, I watch Hayden move with quick efficiency.

Reaching over my head, rummaging through his suit jacket, he retrieves something gold and square, which I quickly realize is a condom. *Magnum XL* prints across the foil packaging, right above *For Her Pleasure.* He tears it open with his teeth, shooting me a wink. My insides squirm. Could he be any hotter? In two seconds flat, the rubber cinches around his base, and his mouth is back to giving mine all its attention.

Nervous air floats about me when I feel his tip prod my opening, but I focus on his lips, his taste, until I'm begging for his entrance—

All the oxygen expels from my lungs, stolen by the immense pressure stretching my opening wide, wider than ever before, my mouth forming an *O* with the absence of any and all sound. But not Hayden—he grunts loudly, panting and shaking profusely, his brow lined with restraint.

Looking down at me, he trembles as he clutches the armrest. "So... *tight...*" he exhales, surprise plain on his features, while I can only meet his stare and put on a brave face, not letting the pain show. That is, until he withdraws to his tip, and an inkling of pleasure drips into my veins, and grows on his next entrance, chipping away at the sting.

"Fuckkkkk," he growls in my ear and pushes my knees down, driving in a little farther. I cry out on the intrusion, clutching his biceps as my insides stretch to compensate, clenching around him in response. "You feel..." His entire body quivers, sweat nicking his hairline. "Incredible..."

Confidence surges within me when the pain fully subsides. "Are you all the way in?"

He grins wickedly.

Uh, oh.

"Baby, I'm not even halfway."

Oh, shi—

His lips brush mine in a blinding kiss, his scent blasting through my senses, and he drives in deeper. I writhe against him, my wail muffling into his mouth.

"Shhhh, you can take me." He withdraws slowly, swelling newfound pleasure, before it vanishes as he sheaths back inside, opening me even more. "Such a good girl, stretching around my cock."

I whimper at the praise, which only drives him faster, inching farther and farther, until the pain dissipates completely and his hips smack against mine for the first time, stuffing me so full I wonder if he'll come out my throat.

"Fuckkkk, Haydennnnn."

Something carnal flashes in his eyes, his grip bruising my thighs, pinning me beneath his weight. "That's right, say my name." He bottoms out, holding it there, watching me writhe against him to no use, before withdrawing and driving to the hilt again.

Over... and over... and over...

"Please, Hayden," I mewl. "Pleaseeee..."

He smiles. "Please, what?"

Thrust. Hold... *Thrust.* Hold... *Thrust.* Hold...

"Fuck me... *fuck me!*" I scream, and it's enough to sever the final strand holding back his control.

Pushing off his elbows, hoisting himself upright, he

wrenches out of me and immediately looks down at himself, grinning savagely. Confused, I follow the line of his stare, discovering the evidence of my lost virginity smeared in subtle red streaks along his condom.

But I can't gawk for long, before he grabs my hips roughly, flips me around until my stomach sinks into the cushion, and crashes his cock back into me.

My cry pierces through the air, then another, and another, as he shows me no mercy and blazes into me at full force, his hips clapping my ass with punishing resolve.

"Is this what you wanted, huh? To get fucked senseless?"

"Yes—*Fuck, yessss, Hayden!*"

He grips my hair, shoving my cheek into the couch, and brings his lips to my ear. "Such a perfect girl. Louder, baby. Scream for me."

My eyes roll to the back of my head as I bellow at the top of my lungs, rendering my throat raw while he barrels into me, grunting on every entrance. I clench back against him, hungry for more, losing track of time or where I am as I climb that mountain of ecstasy, burning like a white fire.

His hold tightens, pulling my hairs taut against my scalp as he fucks me harder. "Come for me, Juliana. Come on my cock."

At his command, I topple over the ledge, writhing against him and whimpering through my release. My grip tightens along his shaft with intense strength, heightening each sensation.

A cocky laugh sounds in my ear, proud and victorious. "That's right. You know who owns this pussy, don't you—"

Hayden inhales sharply on a gasp, his body shuddering against mine. "Oh, my—*Ohhhh, fuckkkkk.*"

He topples over, whimpering a sound I know is my life's

undoing, as he comes right alongside me, bucking his hips desperately. His arms shake on either side of my head while he hisses and curses up a storm, until all his weight crashes onto me.

Breathless, he pants in tandem to my rapid heart rate, releasing his hold on my hair. When he unsheathes himself, I let out a quiet moan, meeting his eyes an inch from mine, finding them blown wide with shock, something I'm sure is reflected straight back at him.

And for a while, we just lie there, basking in each other's presence, until the fasten seatbelt sign illuminates, and a flustered flight attendant informs us of our descent.

THIRTY-FIVE

HAYDEN

I'M RUINED.

Yes. Me. After what transpired last week in my jet, *I'm* the ruined one...

I clack on my keyboard, without a clue as to what I'm typing or what I'm working on or, honestly, where I even am. And how could I possibly know these things, when all I see, hear, and *smell* is Juliana?

At first, it just started out as replaying what happened on that jet, over and over and over again, which soon evolved into fantasies. New positions, new locations, new sounds I could hear from her. And then?

We started executing them.

She's insatiable, ripping our contract off the fridge—whatever the hell that means—while sleeping in my bed, demanding more from me. And you know what? *I'm* the one being run ragged. Me. Not her. How's that even possible? That hasn't been the case with a woman—or women, plural—since... I don't know, forever? Since the dawn of mankind, when my genes were first introduced into the pool?

I mean, that's what I do: fuck. But now?

I hardly sleep any more, seeing as I'm too busy bending her over a new surface, every morning and night, while simultaneously thanking the heavens for her appetite. I think she's determined to fuck on each countertop, sofa, accent chair, bench, ottoman, even the loungers on the rooftop terrace.

Luckily, my penthouse is twenty-thousand square feet and fully furnished.

Humming along to the beat of a song I can't put a name to, I *clickety-clack* some more, entering numbers into what I *think* is a spreadsheet. I squint, leaning forward until I'm two inches from the monitor. Grids... cells... dreadful decimal points... Yeah, this is definitely a spreadsheet. Although, the numbers don't make any sense. Why do some have letters in them...?

Oh, well.

Clickety, clickety, clack, and they fade away, morphing into something *much* more interesting. A scene of the most delicious kind, that I most definitely plan to reenact tonight. It starts off as a sound. A whisper, really. Mewls and whimpers, from those pouty lips I so crave, until it grows in vigor and volume, into wails and desperate moans, begging for release.

Before I'm blessed with an image.

Juliana's hair loops tightly around my fist, her face angled straight to the sky, as I relish the way her mouth stretches wide in ecstasy while I take her from behind. Pinned against the floor-to-ceiling windows in my main living room, neglecting all the furniture, her breasts slip along the glass in tandem to my thrusts. Hips clapping against her bare ass, I drive to the hilt without mercy, the sound amplifying in the large space, mingling with her cries of—

A hand waves in front of my vision—a real hand.

I jerk back, snapping to attention. With every blink, the monitor in front of me sharpens, revealing a long line of gibberish clogging up a single cell. I release my pointer off the *A* key, killing the endless string of them.

Oh my god. I'm in the office. Thank fuck no one saw tha—

"Ahem."

Shit. I forgot about the hand.

As my gaze creeps upward, I mentally tally who could've caught me zoning-out, before confronting the worst possible scenario.

Great. That's just great.

My father only sighs—the anthem of disappointment. Rounding to the front of my desk, I watch as his eyes crawl across my paperwork, covered in *doodles*. I wait, folding my arms across my chest, anticipating his deprecating remark.

Except, it never comes.

Clad in his signature gray suit, he relaxes on the balls of his heels. "I spoke with Elias yesterday."

My heart clenches.

Maybe Elias blabbed about our fight. Conveniently leaving out the cocaine part, of course. While opening up about his struggles with work is wholly out of character for my dearest brother, it's not impossible. Although, it's much more likely that he spun the tale, painting me as an aggressor —meanwhile, my ears sustained some damage. Perhaps he's trying to get me fired, growing tired of seeing me outside his sparkling office.

I *would* lean toward this theory, but... even though we haven't spoken a word to each other in the past week, we lock gazes, every so often, on his way to and from his office. And his eyes, they swirl with... *something*. Shame? Anger—

directed at me or himself? I'm not sure, but I do know one thing.

They're red, cloudy, and glassy as ever.

And I worry broaching the subject again will only make things worse.

Meeting my father's stare, sweat beads on my hairline. "What'd you two talk about?"

"He presented me with his top picks for DreamScape."

Air whooshes from my lungs, only for adrenaline to surge through my veins. DreamScape is next week. If I'd had heard about his decision a month ago, I would've rolled my eyes and scoffed that she cared so much about a silly game. But now... Now I find myself *fearing* for Juliana's sake—a profound, gut-wrenching fear—for the decision I know could change the trajectory of her future.

Absentmindedly, I twirl a pen between my fingers, failing to calm my nerves. "Oh, yeah? How'd that go?"

"Why didn't you tell me Juliana's game was up for consideration? Granted, I didn't know she was a game dev, myself, but you must've. She *is* your girlfriend." He smiles, and it appears surprisingly genuine.

"Oh, uh..." I scratch the back of my neck. "I wanted your decision to be impartial."

"Hmmm, that's clever of you."

My brain does a double take. *Did he just compliment me?*

My reaction must be written all over my face because he gives me a knowing look, then pulls a chair over, sits in front of my desk, and releases another sigh. Not one I'm used to hearing. Just... a plain old sigh, seemingly not even directed at me.

"It must be strange for you," he says, avoiding my gaze, "with all that went down between me and Amber. Now here you are, dating her daughter. I know you two grew up together and all, but still... it must've been difficult, coming to the race and putting on a straight face, especially for Juliana."

I blink, tempted to look behind me. *Is anyone else hearing this?*

"Look"—he meets my stare head-on—"I know we rarely see eye-to-eye about anything, least of all who you're dating, but... she's good for you—and I mean that."

My breath hitches—wait, no. That's not possible, when I'm not even breathing. As always when my father is near, my defenses rise high, but the longer I study him, replaying the sincerity in his tone in my mind, they gradually lower, inch by inch. His words hang heavy in the air as I struggle to find my own, until a lump forms in my throat, and I say the only ones that make sense.

"She is."

Silence spreads between us, in the wake of perhaps the first understanding we've ever shared. Although this was the whole intention of our fake dating agreement, part of me still believed I'd never gain a sliver of my father's approval, even with her at my side. And I hate to say that...

It feels good.

In light of the conversation I had with Juliana, I still planned to stay at this dull job, despite how much I'd love to leave. The harsh reality is, he has total control over my trust fund, and I can't risk the consequences of quitting, at least until my public image is no longer on his radar. But this... this right here... maybe it's a good sign of what lies ahead for us.

"She'll need to record some clips of gameplay, so we can have someone from the tech department put together a trailer for the showcase."

My jaw drops. *Jeez, I almost forgot.* "Are you saying she made the cut?"

"Yes."

Excitement crackles through me, whether she was Elias's top choice or not, she apparently was my father's, who truly has the final say. "Wow!" I exclaim, a bit too loudly. "She's going to be so happy."

He chuckles at my outburst as he reaches into his pocket, fishing out something metallic and slender.

A flash drive, really? God, he's so old school. I hold back a snicker, watching him slide the device across my desk.

"Have it back to me by tomorrow, if possible." He stands up to leave, but before he goes, he glances at my drawings, and for the second time, the strangest thing happens.

He doesn't say a word.

THIRTY-SIX
JULIANA

SO, what, I tore our contract off the fridge? I couldn't stand the sight of it anymore. Sure, it probably gave Hayden a world of mixed signals, but it doesn't make us *real* boyfriend and girlfriend. Although...

It doesn't necessarily make us *not*.

Either way, all I know is this past week, with every day that comes and goes, the latter is starting to sound more appealing. So, yes. I threw away our contract—and may have shredded it into itty-bitty pieces beforehand—even though my exact motives are still in question.

Besides, it's pointless now, anyway. I haven't heard a peep since my presentation. I'd say my chances of being picked as Kingston Entertainment's sponsor are next to zero.

I won't lie, I'm quite distraught over it, maybe more so than the last few years of applying, just from the fact that I had a one-on-one audience and still didn't land a feature, but that's not the reason I've hardly worked on my game this week.

Let's just say, as of late, I've been a tad... *distracted.*

Perhaps one might say a teensy bit... *busy.*

With my mind... *elsewhere.*

I won't get into the nitty-gritty. In fact, I can't. Not without wasting my precious lunch break for the third day in a row. Which is why, this morning, after finishing up with *that which can't be discussed,* I promised myself I'd use the time today to work on fixing a bug.

It's a weird one, and I'm lucky a player was kind enough to message me about it, otherwise I probably would've never discovered it during my own testing. The error triggers only under very, very unlikely circumstances. Mabel has to be in the exact spot at the exact time, when deploying a kitty litter sand trap, for her to throw it in the complete opposite direction.

While that may sound bad, with this bug in particular, detection is harder than actually fixing it, which is why I should be even more ashamed that I've pushed it off this long.

So far, I've managed to stay focused and am already halfway done. However, it's proving quite difficult to tackle the other half with the way Mei eyes me from across the table.

"Got something on your mind?" I ask, even though I already know what her mischievous look is about.

"Huh? Who, me?"

I deadpan.

"Oh, nothing." She twirls a dark lock between her fingers, stifling a smile. "You've just been glowing."

Rolling my lips, I return to my work, trying to avoid thinking of anything that'd veer me off course. "You know why," I say, hoping she'll leave it at that.

Of course, she doesn't.

"I know, you know, I know."

My eyes bulge, earning a giggle from her.

"I just like hearing about it, is all."

I feel a blush creeping onto my cheeks, which ignites into a blazing heat as she continues.

"Just the little things. You know, like how you lost your V-card and joined the mile-high club at the same time—I mean, who does that? With a billionaire's son, no less? Aboard a private plane, after attending a derby as his fake girlfriend..."

Mei's voice fades into the background of my mind. I ensure to nod and hum every now and then, lest I seem too interested—which is her cue to start grilling me with questions. I've gotten pretty good at walking this fine line with her, and can gauge precisely where she is in the story just by reading her facial expressions. Maybe because I've heard it nonstop, incessantly on repeat, since I confessed everything to her earlier this week.

It took me two days before I caved, and when I told her, you'd think I won the Nobel Prize, not lost my virginity. *That's* how excited she was. From then on, it's been question after question, gushing and gushing, as she offers me bedroom advice while simultaneously asking about mine.

I nod some more, her enthusiasm temporarily pulling me from focus.

"...and the way he *looked* at you during his party." She sighs, all dramatic and dreamy, resting her chin on a fist. "I just knew right away how he felt about y—"

A sound of disgust emanates from behind me, one that's instantly recognizable before she even rounds my chair. Meghan swings into view, arms crossed, as always. "And here I was, thinking you finally gave up on that useless game."

Annoyance rakes up my back. "Sorry to disappoint," I mumble, avoiding her intense gaze.

"What was that?"

"Nothing." *Bitch.*

From the corner of my eye, I catch Mei's hand motions behind Meghan, and I just know she's flipping her the bird, even in the midst of customers. I clamp down on a laugh, only for all that humor to dry up with Meghan's next words.

"That's what I thought." *Seriously, what a grade-A bitch.* "I'm gonna need you to work an extra shift next week."

I hesitate, fingers stalling on my keyboard. "What day?"

"Friday."

Dammit. "Ohh, uhh, sorry, I can't do that day."

"I wasn't asking." *More hand gestures from Mei.*

I squirm in my chair, trying to ignore the uncomfortable sensation worming its way through my insides. I'd rather stab my own toe than argue with my boss, but here I am. "Uhmmm, I seriously can't. I have plans."

"Do you now? And what is it that's so important?"

"I'm going to a gaming convention."

Her face falls, before her lips curl in revulsion. "What?"

"You know, where you can play games still in beta, meet developers and cosplayers, enter tournaments, watch new trailers. This convention is *the big one*—as many enthusiasts know it as—called DreamScape. It's actually held in west Manhattan and is put on every year by—"

"Oh, no." She holds up a hand, her mouth pressing into a tight line. "Please, don't explain." A laugh spews from her lips, but she quickly stifles it, only for another to sneak through, then another, until the whole dam breaks loose.

As always, I keep my eyes downcast to my laptop, waiting for the storm to pass. Usually, I'm quite numb to Meghan's taunts, which are a bi-weekly occurrence and almost like some managerial ritual for her at this point, but today... Today, there's an unmistakable sting.

It's obvious why. Even though I've attended DreamScape for the past six years, this is the closest I've come to tasting victory. No matter, I'll still watch the Indie Creator Showcase with genuine excitement, like always, but this year will be a little more sour.

Meghan composes herself, though a few giggles linger. "So, you'll work next Friday, then?"

Sadness trickles inside me as I avoid Mei's pitiful stare. Who am I kidding? I'll save myself some pain by not attending. "Yeah, I'll be here."

"Good, good." Meghan turns to leave, but pivots one more time, unable to help herself. She encroaches on my space, lowering her voice to just above a whisper. "I'm only trying to help you, Juliana. You know that, right? With all that work ethic, you could do something worthwhile, instead of wasting time on something so juvenile, a game *clearly* no one's interested in..."

I push her out of my mind, observing her lips chatter away as she savors every word. Except, the longer she rambles, the more someone else's words snake into my heart. Elias's. His doubts, weaved with my obvious feature rejection, year after year, replay in my head. Over... and over... and over again, until I'm sinking my teeth into my bottom lip, clamping down on my wobbly chin.

Ching... Ching... Ching...

Maybe I *should* just quit, close my laptop while I still have a shred of dignity left.

Something tugs on my sleeve...

I still have my degree. I could start applying for corporate tech jobs. At this rate, I'd make more money.

Ching! Ching! Ching!

Although, that may prove difficult with a hole in my resume.

Another tug, more aggressive this time.

I'd have to erase all evidence of my indie background. Companies don't value candidates with entrepreneurial roots.

CHINGCHINGCHINGCHING—

"JULIANA!"

I wrench from my trance at the sound of Mei's bark. "Huh?" I look around.

"Look—look!" She holds up a phone.

Meghan groans. "Would you silence that nuisance? It's giving me and the rest of the customers a migraine."

I squint, realizing it's mine. Banners pop up on the lock screen, one after another, overlapping so quickly I can hardly read them. Until it hits me—and I'm weightless. I sink back into my chair, tears welling in my eyes.

And listen.

CHA-CHING!

CHA-CHING!

CHA-CHING!

CHA-CHING...

"Hellooooo, yoo-hoo." Meghan comes up behind me, lowering her head just above my shoulder, squinting just as I did. "What're you waiting for?!" she booms in my ear. "Turn it off. What even are all those?"

"Orders," I whisper.

She goes. Fucking. Silent.

Until…

"That can't be right—*give me that.*" She snatches my phone from Mei's grasp, clacking on the screen frantically. "See?" She huffs when it goes silent. "It's just a glitch." She taps some more. "Now there are only chat messages. No orders. *Oops... Shit,*" she curses beneath her breath. "One had a link. Wait, what the—"

A feminine voice blares through the phone's speakers. "NO, MABEL, NO!!"

I snap to attention, my posture straightening like a steel pole. *Is that...? No... It can't be—*

"MY KITTY!" Laughter erupts from the device. "Ha! Gotcha. Sorry, alien boy, my tom cat's not coming aboard your spacecraft."

IT IS HER.

Oh my god, oh my god, oh my god.

I bolt from my chair, sending it toppling behind me, without a care in the world if the ruckus draws attention or not. Invading Meghan's space, my heart clammers as I witness the last person I'd expect on this *entire planet* playing my game.

"No way..." I breathe.

Sporting a glittery tube top, sweatpants, and a pink head-set, a girl with flaming red hair lounges across the armrests of a matching-pink gamer chair, burying her head into her phone. She takes up about a fourth of the screen, but the rest of it... is *my* game.

Cosmic Kitty Defense.

I blink, praying to literally anyone who might listen to not wake me from this dream, as I watch her deploy sand traps and zap aliens with a laser pointer.

"Yuck, look at that hair." Meghan's face scrunches up like a raisin, only for her hands to reveal a slight tremble, shaking the phone when she notes the chat box zooming with activity on the left side. "Who is that?"

"PixiePlays."

She whips her fiery gaze onto me. "Pixie-what-now?"

I don't hold back my snicker, catching eyes with Mei, who's just eating this up. Gosh, for a girl who's only two years older than us, Meghan really is slow with this stuff. "PixiePlays. That's her gamer tag. She's a live streamer, who plays video games."

Meghan goes totally blank, like a lightbulb that's lost its charge, until there's a flicker. "You mean, this footage, it's happening right now?"

"Mhmm."

She scoffs over Pixie's contagious commentating. "Who in their right mind would watch someone *else* play a video game? Nobody does that."

"Uhhhh..." I tap on the screen. "Fifteen thousand people do."

"WHAT?!"

Mei busts up laughing—literally slapping her knee, tears pricking her eyes, as Meghan taps on the phone mercilessly, angling it this way and that.

Seriously, how is this girl in her twenties? I think, watching as she grows more frustrated, fiddling with the device like it's a jigsaw puzzle. During which, I catch countless order banners dropping from the top of the screen, one after another at impossible speeds, each reinforcing my confidence.

And it's then that I realize something, recalling the conversation I had with Hayden, the one about people and their insecurities. I meant what I said, every single word—*for him.* Yet, how can I so confidently pass him on such advice, then turn around and not act on it for my own sake? Sure, I've dealt with naysayers, from time to time. With grace, even.

But it seems I've let one slip.

I snatch my phone out of Meghan's hands, roughly.

"What the hell?" she barks, swiveling on her heel, pinning me with a stare that, ninety-nine times out of a hundred, would have me apologizing.

This is the one percent.

I breeze past her to gather my things—my lunch, my laptop—and stow them all away in my backpack.

"Where do you think you're going? Your shift doesn't end for another two hours."

Zipping up my bag, I ignore her, not even offering her a glance. I assume she's folding her arms—her obnoxious toe tapping will come next.

"Hello???" I glance down at her feet. *There it is.*

I release the knot at the neck of my apron, disregarding her completely. "You'll have to find someone else for that shift next Friday."

"And what the hell gives you the nerve to talk to me like that? Again, I wasn't asking. Just so we're clear, you're *my* employee."

"Not anymore." I slink my bag over my shoulder, letting my apron fall to the ground, and look Meghan square in the eyes.

It's time to take my dream full time.

"I quit."

She stumbles back, only a step. For a moment, she just stands, frozen like a statue, her face blistering redder than a tomato, void of oxygen. Until she breathes steadily, feigning composure. "Fine. You think I care?" She lifts her chin proudly. "If you want to lose your job over a stupid convention, be my guest. It doesn't affect me one bit. I'll just have Mei cover that shi—"

"FINALLY!" Another apron zooms across my vision, rocketing into Meghan's chest like a high-speed ballistic. She

grunts when it strikes her, prompting her to stumble back even more, nearly falling on her butt.

"I quit, too!" Mei announces to the entire coffee shop, looping her arm in mine, laughing like a maniac as she ushers me toward the exit. The scene whips heads, triggers gasps, and even causes a lady to trip on her feet, spilling her latte all over the floor.

Meghan's expression sinks deep into despair, especially upon hearing Mei's parting words.

"Uh, oh, Meghan. Guess you'll have to mop that up!"

I STARE at the flash drive in my hand.

Sitting at my computer, amid the city's skyline at night, my room's never felt so quiet. Hayden told me the good news an hour ago. I should be yelling from the rooftop, jumping for joy—*I was,* at first. I still am happy, but now I'm also confused. Torn in two.

I glance at my monitor, which displays the email I've been praying years for.

CONGRATULATIONS, *Juliana!*

WE ARE THRILLED *to inform you that your mobile game, Cosmic Kitty Defense, has been chosen to be featured in our Indie Creator Showcase at this year's DreamScape, New York City's premier gaming convention! Your game impressed us with both its exceptional creativity and engaging gameplay, and we truly believe it would stand out at the event, alongside other talented indie* creators. *Please, confirm your acceptance so we can move forward and gather the necessary information from you.*

BEST REGARDS,
The DreamScape Team

THEY OBVIOUSLY SAW PixiePlay's stream and how fast my game's been moving up the app store charts. So, again. I *am* happy, so beyond thankful for the publicity my game saw today, the sales, for Kingston Entertain's offer and now DreamScape's. All of it.

But now I have a choice to make.

Kingston Entertainment or DreamScape.

It should be simple, one would think. Bypass Kingston Entertainment and go on my own—I'll land the feature either way. Then maybe I'd squash that doubt in my head, the one that says I only made it this far because of Hayden.

But the truth is, *I didn't.* This email proves it. I landed the feature all on my own, fair and square.

So, now I'm at a crossroads, one dependent only on my pride, really. Part of me wants the glory, wants to see *only* my name next to my game. However, there's another factor that I can't ignore.

Having Kingston Entertainment as my sponsor shows credibility, establishes market trust. A way to really put my name out there, behind a mega-corporation that's establishing their roots to become a titan in the gaming world. That's a huge deal. Any indie dev would kill to be in my position.

So, I do what any of them would do...

Plug in the flash drive.

THIRTY-SEVEN

JULIANA

I'M IN PARADISE.

Surrounded by gaming panels, Q&A sessions, booths offering VR experiences, meet-and-greet opportunities, tournaments, and so much more than my nerdy brain can comprehend, the sheer size of DreamScape amazes me every year, without fail. An ambient shade of blue glows throughout the convention center, its air crackling with enthusiasm and anticipation.

There's just something so exhilarating about being amongst like-minded individuals, who all share my love and passion for gaming. I'd stay forever if I could, but I'll settle for exploring wonderland until its doors close at 9 p.m. A solid ten hours, then rinse and repeat for two more days.

Fortunately, the Indie Creator Showcase is on day one. Otherwise, I'd be forced to battle my nerves for the entire convention. I'm excited, obviously, but I think my anxiety is pulling ahead by a slim margin.

"Sooo..." I nudge Jeremy's arm. "How are you liking the convention so far?"

His head whips this way and that, just as it has for the last two hours. I bite down on a laugh, eyeing his outfit. Sporting athletic shorts and a cut-off tank, Jeremy looks like he's ready to hit the gym—nothing new there—or perhaps gobble up one of the scrawny attendees who pass him by and offer curious glances.

On the outside, you'd never guess Jeremy has an electrical engineering degree, which makes it all that much more surprising he's never played video games, given that his classmates undoubtedly did. I chalk it up to his social circle growing up.

"Well, I gotta say, it's a lot to take in, but I'm enjoying myself."

"What's been your favorite part?"

Taking the lead, I weave us through a throng of people, spotting anime graphic tees, hats adorned with recognizable gaming logos, and various other nerdy accessories. There's a wide array of attendees. Some rock casual attire like hoodies or sweatpants, others take the convention very seriously, wearing things you'd never see on the streets, even in a place like New York City.

Jeremy points out such an individual, a girl in a skin-tight pink-and-blue jumpsuit. She struts by with a headset snug around her ears, flaunting the girly blaster in her hand, shooting Jeremy a wink. His steps stutter, before he whirls around in a one-eighty.

Oh boy.

"The outfits," he sighs, letting her go. "Definitely the outfits... who was that? She has to be famous."

I snicker. "Maybe. She's obviously a cosplayer."

Jeremy quirks a brow.

"It's where people dress up as characters from video games. Sometimes anime or movies, too."

"Who was she supposed to be, then?"

"D.Va from Overwatch," I answer instantly. "She's a very popular cosplay choice. Along with..." I scan around the room, knowing I'm bound to see others. *"Oh,"* I gasp, pointing. "There's a really good Peach—you know, from Mario Kart?"

"Uhhh..."

Oh my god, who doesn't know Mario Kart?

I try again, gesturing to a man working a concession booth, handing out hotdogs in a solid-yellow pants and hoodie combo, complete with cute ears jutting out from his head. "Pikachu? From Pokémon first gen?"

He squints. "Ohhh... Yeah, yeah," he agrees, like he has absolutely no idea what I'm talking about.

Holy shit, I don't understand. Did my brother not have a childhood?

After several more attempts with no luck, Jeremy shrieks in my ear, slapping my shoulder with one hand while pointing with the other. "Oh, oh! I know that one! That's uh... uhhh... come on, come on..." He snaps his fingers, cursing beneath his breath. *"Zelda!* That's Zelda!"

Relief pours over me as I trace the line of his gesture. Thank God, my brother knows at least one video game. Maybe he's not completely hopeless after a—

I reach the end, at what I find has all that hope deflating from me. A boy, around ten years old or so, waits in line beside his parent for a game demo, carrying a foam sword and shield, draped in a green tunic. Not a whimsical dress like I expected.

"Jeremy..." I pinch the bridge of my nose. "That's not Zelda."

"Huh?" He double takes. "No, that's definitely Zelda."

I shake my head. "Zelda is the *princess*. That's Link, the boy who saves her."

He blinks. "What?"

"Oh my—never mind!" I storm through the crowd, unsure of where I'm taking us with grumbles hot on my breath, leaving Jeremy's laughter in my wake.

And that's how it goes for a few hours. Strolling around with Jeremy, showing him all the best attractions and experiences DreamScape has to offer, all while answering every one of his noobie questions. We both have a blast, waiting for the clock to tick down to the indie showcase, until it's too close to delay what I've been dreading any longer.

Seated across from Jeremy at the food court, I set my chicken wrap down on our table, sighing quietly. *Here goes nothing.*

"So, uh..." Nerves prick along my skin—as if today wasn't scary enough. "There was something else I wanted to tell you about my feature."

"Hmm? What's that?" Jeremy asks through his mouthful of food, grease from his double-patty cheeseburger slipping down his wrist.

My heart thunders, enough to wobble my speech. "My feature is sponsored by a corporation."

His eyes bulge. "Really?! Holy crap, Juliana, why didn't you tell me sooner? That's amazing! Which company?"

I clear my throat, forcing my eyes to meet his. "Kingston Entertainment."

The air hangs between us...

He just sits there, smiling wide, while that grease races

toward his elbow, only for his expression to falter, like a crack splintering across a mirror. "You mean... like... *Kingston* Entertainment?"

He thinks he heard me wrong? Oh, no. This could get worse than I thought. "Uh, huh." I nod, wincing when his burger goes down with a hefty *thud,* and I can almost make out the gears churning in his brain by his forehead wrinkles alone.

"Like... *Hayden's dad's company?"*

I nod again, my heart somersaulting into my throat.

"I mean..." He grabs his napkin, a little too rough for my liking. "Congratulations, Sis, but... I'm just curious"—he scratches the back of his head, caution swirling behind his stare—"how did you go about landing that? Did they have tryouts or something?"

Tryouts. Oh, Lord help me. I'd laugh, if any part of this situation was the least bit funny.

"They did, kinda... And I *did* present my game, but umm..." I swallow, breaking our gaze. "Hayden and I, we've been..." Come on, Juliana, out with it. Just do it. *"Hanging out."*

Jeremy straightens. His lips part. And those eyes, they're stuck in some sort of trance, hazing over enough that I question if he even sees me.

Okay... he's not screaming... Maybe this won't turn disastrous, after all? Except... Okay, he's *still* not blinking. "Jer?" I wave a hand. "Jer—"

"What. Do you mean. Hanging. Out?" he clips, and—oh no, is he *shaking?* I narrow in on his hands, watching them tremble and clench into fists.

"U-uhmm... j-just, uhhh..." Fuck. What can I even say? The truth must be written all over my face, every dirty little detail.

Redness creeps up his neck, roaming over veins that flare with anger. "Have you two..." He looks away, smacking his lips, before whipping his gaze back onto me. "Has he...?"

Touched you? my mind finishes his question, prompting an onslaught of unwelcome images. I push them away and speak as calmly as humanly possible, holding out my hands toward him. "Okay, Jer—"

He bolts from his chair, sending it crashing behind him. *"That motherFUCKER."*

Even though none of his anger is directed at me, I stand on shaky knees. "Jeremy—"

He laughs a brutal sound, running a hand across his jaw. "So, that's why he's been avoiding me?" he asks, but doesn't, lost in his own thoughts. "He's too busy *preying* on my little sister?" Another chuckle escapes him, and it's straight from a serial killer's mouth.

"Won't you just listen—"

"Where is he?" he asks, void of emotion.

Adrenaline spikes through me.

"Juliana. Where. Is. He?"

"I-I don't—"

His fingers tremble violently as he swipes them through his hair, flicking his eyes through the crowd, searching for his target. He bounds in a random direction. "When I get my *fucking* hands on him—"

"Jeremy, please." I catch him by the shoulder, unable to stop the wobble in my voice. Only then, does he look down at me, his gaze softening. "Without Hayden, I wouldn't have landed a feature," I lie, sprinkling in a bit of truth. "He's the only one who vouched for my game. If it weren't for him, I wouldn't have gotten considered for their sponsorship."

Anticipation winds tightly inside my chest as I watch Jeremy gnaw on his lip.

"I mean it." I shake him.

"I know you do. But it isn't you I don't trust around Hayden—I don't trust him with *you.*"

I can't help the smile that creeps onto my lips, or the wall of emotions catching in my throat. I squeeze his shoulder, easing a teensy bit of that tension. Oh, Jeremy. My big brother. No longer my defender on the playground, but my loyal Doberman, who's ready to send a billionaire's son to the ER.

"Please, Jer. Today's already stressful enough."

The rest of his rage slinks off his back like running water. "I know it is... I'll let him off the hook—*for now.*"

THIRTY-EIGHT
JULIANA

I HOLD OUT MY ARM, letting the security guard inspect my wristband. With a *hmph,* she props open the backstage door, waving for my entrance.

Turns out, Kingston Entertainment can—*literally*—open some doors that the developers in the Indie Creator Showcase don't have access to. Luckily, Elias snagged me a backstage pass and gave his own to Hayden, stating he was too swamped with work to attend. According to Hayden, that's a running theme with his brother, and I believe him.

What a bummer, though. That guy would've looked even more out of place than Jeremy. Well, I guess Hayden does too, but he at least attempted to blend in, swapping his polos and chinos for a pair of ripped jeans and a basic T-shirt. Although, let's be real...

There's no blending in with a face like that.

I know it. The security guard who hardly checked his wristband knows it. Even that backstage worker with the headset on, sneaking glances over her clipboard—she knows it. I'd be jealous, but... who can blame her?

Okay, maybe I'm a little jealous.

Matching my stride, Hayden intertwines his warm fingers with mine, as if he picked my emotions out of thin air—or just read my facial expressions. He squeezes, erupting all sorts of butterflies in my stomach.

This handholding thing, it started last week, and it's only becoming more frequent—and natural. At first, only he would initiate. In the kitchen. After sex, sometimes during. Then I started to. While watching movies in the living room or sunbathing on the terrace. I think I understand what it all means, and I *would* bring up such a conversation, if it weren't for the doubt lingering inside me that believes someone like Hayden doesn't do labels—or monogamy, for that matter— whether he confessed feelings for me or not.

So, I guess I'm just riding this flirtatious dynamic while I can.

"Does Jeremy know about us?"

"Uhh..." My mind turns up blank. "No," I lie. *Now's not the time.* "Why do you ask?"

"No reason. Just that when I ran into him on the way to meet you, he seemed a little... *off.*" I suck in a breath, thankful when it doesn't draw his attention. "He acted fine, I guess, but there was something in his eyes—I don't know. I'm probably just paranoid. Not to mention, I've been dodging him for weeks, for obvious reasons, so I'm sure it has to do with that."

"Yeah." I pale. "I bet it's that."

As we venture farther and farther backstage, I'm careful not to trip over the sea of wires scurrying across the floor, connected to audio booths and makeshift tables littered with technical equipment. Alongside my anxiety, sounds from the main stage grow louder with every step of our approach. The music, the announcers on stage, and the roaring crowd all reverberate through the floor and echo in the open space, until we stand beside the stage's massive golden curtain, nearly deafened by such proximity.

At our vantage point, we have a partial view of the crowd and a perfect one of the main event screen, which is bigger than any movie theater screen this side of the Hudson and currently plays a first-look trailer for a certain first-person shooter. Although it releases in a couple months and is extremely hyped-up by the community, it's not my type of game, so instead, I observe the crowd, searching for familiar faces.

After a good minute, I give up, but according to Jeremy's texts, Mom and Dad made it and can't stop gushing about me to everyone seated around them. Even *Mei* is in attendance— oh, who am I kidding? She makes time for anything. I'm thankful, nonetheless.

Other than Jeremy, I didn't have time to speak with any of them because they all arrived later than us, specifically after I learned of our backstage access, something I wouldn't pass up in a million years. Nothing to fret about, though. I'll visit them after the indie showcase, which is in...

I sink a hand into my pocket, retrieving my phone.

Ten minutes.

Taking a deep breath, I exhale through my nose steadily, but find little comfort. At least my feature isn't going first— that would be a lot of pressure. My slot is number three, which I took as a sign of luck. Good things happen in threes, right?

I just hope whoever put the video together knew what they were doing. Hayden mentioned that the flash drive's gameplay footage would be handed off to someone in the tech department. Given the vast number of employees at Kingston Entertainment, I'm sure they found someone capable.

So, why am I still nervous?

There's probably no getting around it. I've only waited five years for this moment.

I shudder when soft lips brush against the hollow of my ear. "It's going to be fine," Hayden says, over the current trailer's intense music, sweeping a thumb across my hand in soothing, side-to-side motions. As I meet his stare, he smiles. "More than fine, actually. It'll be perfect."

Standing on my tippy toes, I stretch for his ear, meaning to thank him. Except, when my lips reach their mark and his arms instinctually loop around my middle, I *still* can't help myself. "You mean *purrrrr*-fect."

His body tenses against mine.

"What's wrong?" I ask, feigning ignorance, clamping down hard on a laugh when I feel him stiff as a board, only for a snicker to come bursting out a moment later.

I squeal as his arms tighten, locking me in a death grip. He pulls me close—so close, I blush at the thought of all the event workers around us—the motion burying my face into his chest, before he cranes low to my ear. *"Juliana Brooks,"* he warns, earning another wave of giggles. I squirm against his hold, before they spill out of his mouth, too.

When he releases me, I pat down my hair, furiously, and—

My breath hitches.

With his head tilted slightly and a soft smile resting on his lips, Hayden gazes at me. Not at my body or my hair or exploring the planes of my face. Just my eyes, so unwavering that I can't veer from his, held captive by an electric, strange warmth blossoming at my core, like peering into a tranquil lake that whispers secrets just below the surface.

"What is it?" I breathe out, amid a quiet moment between trailers.

"Nothing."

"You sure? You look like you want to ask something."

His smile widens. "It can wait until after the showcase."

Not only does that feeling not dissipate for the next longest five minutes of my life, but it seems to have curbed my anxiety, with the help of Hayden's reassuring hand-squeezing, all the way until the final second.

The lights dim across the convention center, casting a mauve glow over the audience, as an announcer strides across the stage, illuminated by a spotlight. My eyes roam over the massive crowd, spiking my pulse and prompting more squeezes. Hayden and I share one final glance, before the announcer lifts the microphone to her lips.

"Wow, wasn't that something?" her voice booms. "Let's give another round of applause for all the amazing trailers we've seen tonight, huh? Give it up!" She claps, high in the air, winning enthusiasm from the audience, who erupts with whistles and cheers.

When the commotion dies down, she struts in our direction, working the stage. "Thank you, thank you. For all our DreamScape veterans, I'm sure you know what's up next, don't you?" As the crowd sparks up again, she nods, swiveling back in the opposite direction, her heels eating up center stage as her blonde ponytail bobbles. "That's right, it's time for DreamScape's Indie Creator Showcase!"

My soul momentarily leaps from my body at the hollers that follow—louder than any applause earned before. A proud smile spreads across my lips.

"But!" She pauses, letting silence stretch out. "Ohhhh, I got you there, didn't I? Before we dive into appreciation for our most beloved indie devs, we have one more surprise up our sleeves—or should I say, one last loot drop..." She waits again, allowing laughter to spread across the space.

I roll my lips at Hayden's drawn-out groan.

The announcer chuckles into the mic, beaming a radiant smile. "Yes, we're all about surprises here. So, now. Tell me, gamers. Are you prepared for one. Last. Trailer?"—*gasps, including mine*—"Uhhh huh, you heard that right. Get ready to be blown away by the unveiling of a never-before-seen mobile game. Here's a DreamScape-exclusive preview—let's take a look."

Darkness descends upon the convention center, enough that I can't see the announcer walking our way, until the clicking of her heels grows louder and louder. On her passing, she offers a friendly smirk, as the sounds of beachy waves lap over the audience, providing a calming backdrop for the trailer's voiceover.

"Ever dreamt of escaping to paradise...?"

On the cry of a seagull's call, color fades into the screen, revealing a bird's-eye view of a charming remote island, its sandy shores and swaying palm trees slowly drawing nearer.

"Welcome to Coral Island. Here the sun always shines, the waves dance endlessly, and locals greet you with open arms." The music stops abruptly, mimicking a record scratching. *"Well, they would—if it weren't for their claws."*

Fun, upbeat music takes over, blending the harmonies of a marimba with the cheerful strumming of a ukulele. Our vantage point snaps to the ground, providing a first-person view of walking past the palm tree line and onto the sand, which crawls with cute, animated crabs. In flocks of three to four, they dance for the audience, snapping their claws to the beat.

I smile at their unnaturally large eyes, thankful for the distraction. Call me childish, but *this* is my kinda game.

Soft lips tickle my ear, causing a shiver. "I think this one's already got you hooked."

I stand back on my tippy toes. "What can I say? I'm an easy sell."

Hayden snickers, twisting me around and tugging me close. The heat from his body seeps into my back, like a comforting blanket, before he loops his arms around my center. Sinking into him, I let my head fall on his shoulder, catching his toothy grin, as the music intensifies.

"But their peaceful haven is about to face its greatest challenge yet..."

Off the shore, a fleet of wooden ships appear on the horizon, rocking against the current while their crossbone flags flap in the wind.

The screen goes black.

And bold text fades in, emerging from the darkness.

A KINGSTON ENTERTAINMENT PRODUCTION

My brow furrows. *That's odd. I didn't know they...* I twist in Hayden's arms, discovering him just as intrigued, only for my entire world to stop spinning once I turn back around.

PIRATE ISLAND DEFENSE

No...

"Arrrghh!"

No no no—

Gameplay flashes on the screen, and the mere sight of it rises bile in my throat, stirs my stomach with a sickness I've never known, so turbulent I don't register how stiff Hayden's grown behind me, or the hands that wrap around my biceps, holding me upright from faintness. I blink, my breaths puffing out choppy as I fight to stay lucid.

"Play as Mak, Coral Island's newest human inhabitant," that cursed voice booms, as an exact carbon copy of my mobile game with altered graphics blasts across the screen, earning *oooo*'s and *ahhhh*'s from the crowd, their eyes shimmering with delight.

Strong hands give me a shake.

"Juliana?" a man calls.

The voice sounds vaguely familiar, but far off. I hardly hear him. Not because of the speakers, but the blood pounding in my ears that drops my ankles in quicksand and submerges my head under rough waters—like the sea thrashing against the hull of the pirate ships sailing toward a cute, animated island positioned in the center of the screen.

Right where my farm would be.

And the boats... they populate around the perimeter, with the same frequency as my aliens.

"Protect your friends from notorious crab-nappers..."

Mak traces around the island's perimeter, this way and that, weaving between crabs and poking pirates who reach the shoreline with his spear.

Another shake, rougher this time.

"Juliana?!" a scream echoes through the water, swallowed up by the crashing waves.

"Level up, gain new skills, and blast those pesky pirates off the shore with gadgets like the seashell barrage cannon..."

No, no, no...

I watch the revamped animation, a bundle of seashells exploding from the barrel of a turret cannon, except the mechanics are identical to my paw-some plasma cannon. An idea that took months to conceive and weeks to program.

"Or slow their movements the instant their feet touch the sand with the crab claw sand trap."

NONONONO—

This can't be happening. I'm dreaming, I'm dreaming, I'm dreaming. WAKE UP ALREADY. Strip me of this nightmare —because that *is* what's happening. This isn't real life. How could it be? How else could something like this happen? How—

A face flings into my field of vision, an inch from my nose. A man...? Blond. Attractive. Blue eyes that blow wide with urgency. His lips are moving, sputtering fast, uttering words drowning in despair and deafened by adrenaline, until they burst through the surface, breathing life into a man I know better than anyone.

A man I thought I trusted.

"YOU HAVE TO BELIEVE ME. I DIDN'T—"

Every venomous word that slithers from his tongue plunges back below the surface, spiraling like torpedoes straight to my heart, reflecting to the sharpened precipice of my mind that only sees one thing...

Hayden handing me that flash drive.

I bolt from his vicinity. From that wretched screen. From EVERYTHING, and book it through backstage, heaving for breath as my chest contracts and tears well in my eyes. But I swallow them down, too proud to let them show, when he's calling my name behind me, hot on my tail while I weave between startled workers, running aimlessly, until I spot the exit.

How could I be so *stupid?* Hayden played me for a fool— fucked with my head, then fucked me, then *fucked my entire career.* No one's going to believe me, a little indie dev, against a mega-corporation. With what money could I face them in court? Contend with their army of lawyers? They'd swallow this up, bribe the media to spin it in their direction—that *I* stole the game from *them.*

It doesn't matter if I'm ranking on the charts or that Pixie-Plays livestreamed my game, Hayden and his dad—who he's probably been conspiring with since barging back into my life —they know this and did it, anyway. Hayden even gave me the flash drive on the *exact same day* I went viral, which was surely loaded with hidden malware, all rigged to dupe Cosmic Kitty Defense's programming without my knowledge before it got handed off to that *tech department guy.*

"Juliana, wait!"

Fuck! I nearly trip over a wire, bursting through the door on a scream. "LEAVE ME ALONE!"

A tear finally skates down my cheek. I swipe it away, whipping my head to find the security lady holding Hayden at the door, presumably to protect me. He argues with her, watching as I burst through a wall of attendees, letting the crowd swallow me whole. I weave between them and knock into shoulders, while my adrenaline spikes too high to bother with apologies.

I don't know, I don't know, I don't know, my conscience cries in a frantic feedback loop. I don't know what Hayden did or didn't do. All I know is I don't trust him, and I can't bear to look at him or be near him—or witness Jeremy pummel him into an early grave right here at DreamScape if their paths should cross.

And same goes for my family, who's undoubtedly searching for me with broken hearts. I can't bear their sorrow or their optimistic schemes of retribution, not when we're ants against a serpentine giant. I want a quiet space, where I can gather my thoughts and mourn without fear of Hayden finding me.

So, I let my instincts guide me the rest of the way.

To Mei's apartment.

THIRTY-NINE
HAYDEN

I'VE TURNED New York City on its head.

For three miserable days, I've torn through the penthouse, searching for Juliana. Staked outside her parents' and Jeremy's apartment complexes, knowing better than to knock on their doors, unless I'm fiending for a black eye. Or worse.

After no such luck, I grilled that Meghan character at The Caffeine Cove for information, even though Juliana told me she quit last week. I've even started waltzing into places she never frequents. Certain restaurants on the complete opposite side of the city, gyms, boutiques, grocery stores, wandering aimlessly like some heartbroken zombie on speed, as if I'm just going to happen upon her at the Westside Market.

But of course, I haven't, and she won't return any of my calls or respond to any number of my exhaustingly long text messages. She's camped out at her best friend's apartment. I just know it. Problem is, I don't know the first thing about Mei, least of all where she lives. I debated hiring a private investigator, if it weren't for the inevitable questions they'd ask.

So, I'm pivoting to the next most productive course of action...

Blowing off steam.

Ding.

I burst through the elevator door, slipping through the narrow gap when it's just wide enough for my frame, nearly sidelining a patiently waiting man in a suit. Molten rage seers through my veins as I zoom along the perimeter of a sea of cubicles, earning weird looks I couldn't care less about.

Out of my peripheral, Doris's head pops up. "And where in the world have you been...? Hey, where do you think you're..."

A couple more turns, and I'm met with a wall of offices, all surrounded by glass. Like exemplary figureheads in fish-bowls for the employees in cubicles, executives, and other higher-ups peacefully clack on their keyboards or talk on the phone, secluded behind oak doors adorned with impressive plaques. I make note of each one as I storm by.

Chief Legal Officer.

Managing Director.

Chief Technology Officer.

Senior Vice President.

Executive Vice President.

CEO & Founder—

Oh, would you look at that? He's actually in today. With Elias, too? Gosh, how could I be so lucky? Hopefully, I don't disrupt their meeting. Nothing's worse than a family feud.

I throw open the door. *"WHAT THE FUCK HAPPENED?"*

The door slams from behind, trapping me in the silent fishbowl with two corporate sharks. One who sits behind the massive oak desk, the city skyline his backdrop. The other twists around in his seat across the table, eyeing me.

Elias frowns. "Jesus, Hayden. You look like shit."

I do. Baggy eyes, no doubt. Greasy hair. And I can't recall what I'm wearing—probably the first thing my fingers grazed from off the floor after getting two hours of sleep.

I look past his shoulder, to the man wearing a smug smile. The parasite I call father. "I said, I'm here for some *fucking* answers."

He chuckles—actually *chuckles,* as Elias's brows cinch in confusion. "Can't this wait, Son? We're in the middle of something."

"Did you really just call me that?"

He grins, like he knew it would tick me off.

I'm sure he's reliving his little acting session last week, when he pretended to give two shits about me and my personal life and resisted those jabs he so desperately wanted to fling at the sight of my drawings, or the quality of my work. Here, at his own company, hovering over the tiny desk *he* put me behind.

My fist flexes at my side, yearning for his jaw.

"What's going on?" Elias bounces his gaze between us.

"Oh, you don't know? Well, how could you, right? When you're always locked up in your office—"

"Enough with the theatrics," Warren cuts in.

"Fine. Go ahead and tell him yourself. Tell him how you *stole Juliana's game,* then unveiled it to DreamScape as a Kingston production."

Elias straightens, disbelief marking his features as he looks to our father. "Is that true?"

"Yes," he answers instantly, not a hint of remorse in his eyes. "Oh, don't give me that look. I did what was necessary. If Kingston Entertainment is to become the next titan of the gaming world, then sponsoring games isn't enough, and you know that."

Elias is silent for a moment, bouncing his knee nervously. "Yeah, but—"

"But nothing." Warren shoots from his chair, rounding his table in a flash, only to stare down his heir, whose face angles toward his lap like a scolded child. "I didn't sire you to act so *weak,* to pity a girl of such inferior birth, whose only purpose is to serve—"

"You're sick!" I shake with fury, my vision bleeding with a red haze.

His eyes dance with delight at my outburst. "Careful now." They flick over my shoulder, signaling that I must've drawn attention. "You'll risk sounding like you have actual feelings for this girl."

"That's just it, huh? You couldn't stomach seeing me happy at the derby. Why you made *me* give her the flash drive. You just needed to soil the first good thing that's happened to me, didn't you?"

Now his predatory steps amble toward me. Sinking his hands into his pants pockets, he stops a hair too close to seem natural, just by a hair, though, ensuring that I'll take notice, but the spectators outside won't. Same goes for his smug aura, which oozes from his pores like smog, sagging the bookcases lining the room's partition walls.

With a sigh, he speaks softly, as if extending me sympathy. "Hayden, Hayden, Hayden... don't fool yourself. You would've soiled it all on your own."

My teeth clench, so hard I fear they might crack, and it takes every ounce of strength I have in me not to tackle him with the whole office watching. I can feel the weight of their stares on my backside, brimming with anticipation, like fuel for my impulsivity.

"How can—"

"And even on the off chance you didn't fuck it up," he interrupts with a sneer, "she wasn't going to stay with you. Girls like that—who are *beneath* our kind of wealth—they're all the same. Fun for a time, until their insecurities catch up with them. It's inevitable."

I break from his vicinity, pacing down the wall of books, passing Elias's bewildered stare. *"Do you even fucking hear yourself, sometimes?!"* I pivot, discovering the mob of employees, all of whom I'm sure can make out my muffled shouts through the glass. "God, I can't wait to watch her sue your ass. She's been working on that game for *five years.* You think no one will notice what you did?"

A laugh spews from his lips, enough that he topples over slightly, tears pricking his eyes. The sound only heightens my anger. "Oh! You're too funny! You think she could take us on in court? Battle the entire Kingston legal department? Are you delusional, Hayden, or just that dense? You might not like what happened—not approve of what *I did for this family*—but you don't have to. What's done is done. Her and her family, they're *nothing* in the light of ours. Do you understand that?"

No, I don't say, pacing harder, the treads of my shoes shaving down the carpet, likely to catch flame if he keeps talking.

But he does, on and on, comparing our two families in the most offensive, disgusting way, as if he regards Juliana's family as livestock. And it's in the throes of his monologue that I decide, at the end of it, I'm ending *him*—by revealing his work logs. Hell, I'll print a stack off in the copying room, flaunt it off to our lovely crowd here, maybe decorate their cubicles with the evidence.

That *is* my plan, until I hear the next words slip from his lips.

"I should thank you." He steps in front of my path, causing me to halt and stare directly into his icy-blue eyes, our proximity almost nose-to-nose. "You did such a great job, getting her all warmed up to you."

Something inside me snaps.

Something that tells me his humiliation can wait.

That really... he needs a broken nose first.

As time slows to a crawl, I cock my arm back for a punch, not a care in the world if an employee has their phone recording and the footage ends up plastered all over gossip sites by tomorrow morning—in fact, I hope it does. I'm counting on it. Driven by rage, I throw all my weight into—

Rough hands grab my shoulders, yanking me back like I'm weightless. I writhe against the hold, as my arms lock behind me, before my cheek slams into the bookshelf. "Get off me!" I bark at the security guards, my exhales hissing through my teeth, charged with pent-up energy.

The sounds of metal against metal fill the air, cutting through the silence. Not a single employee utters a word through the now-propped-open office door. They only stare curiously at their CEO, who crosses his arms over his chest, facing his troublemaking son.

"No need to cuff him. He'll walk it off."

FORTY

JULIANA

SO, I gave that whole wallowing in self-pity thing a fair shot... It didn't work. Luckily, I've found something else.

Hip-hop blasts through the speakers lined on the walls, rattling my brain, infusing my veins with energy.

Who knew so many people could cram into a single frat house basement? Amid disco lasers and glow-in-the-dark T-shirts and body paint, I throw up my arms, dancing shoulder-to-shoulder with complete strangers—except Mei, who's effortlessly cool, puffing a joint pinched between her two fingers, swaying her hips to the beat while sipping from a red Solo cup in her other hand.

I already finished my drink—my *third* drink.

Turns out, Mei doesn't have to finesse anyone to get into Columbia's notoriously exclusive frat parties—even as a pair of single girls. She doesn't text ahead, bring a pack of drinks or a plus-one who's still part of Greek life, nothing. As an infamous alum, she just shows up on any given doorstep, purses those red-painted lips, and the fraternity door atten-dant clad in a collared shirt, tailored chinos, and daddy's money grants us swift entrance. In fact, those doormen, they even recognized her. Every. Single. One of them, and this is our third party on Greek Row tonight—or maybe our fourth? I don't know. Time is irrelevant, like my problems.

Thanks to my new friend.

Alcohol.

Who I flirted with earlier tonight, but rekindled a flaming love-affair with on our entrance to this basement, when we went straight to the bar—AKA, a fold-out table in the corner, next to the makeshift DJ booth operated by the guy in *sunglasses* sucking on a vape like it's an oxygen tank. On the table, our drink choices were simple, housed in clear plastic jugs labeled with glowing pink Sharpie. *Vodka* or *Tequila.* Even with the pineapple and cranberry mixers nearby, those sounded intimidating, so I sided with option three. *Jungle Juice.*

Wrong. Choice.

Or, the *right* choice—question mark?

I bang my head, writhing between bodies as the juice goes straight to my brain. Sweat slicks off my brow, as a new song thumps a quicker tempo, my Converse crunching atop the sticky floor with every stuttered step. Through the smoky haze, I catch Mei's eyes and laugh for no good reason, causing her to do the same.

"I gotta pee!" I announce over the bass, shaking the room.

Her lips brush my ear. "You won't like the line."

Soon enough, I discover just how right she is.

"Uuughhhh," I groan, earning her smile as I shift from foot to foot, doing the potty dance. Never before has ten minutes felt so much like ten hours, and we're only halfway to the uni-sex, single-toilet bathroom, crammed at the end of a skinny hallway clouded with cigarette smoke.

"I told you not to break the seal so early in the night."

I blink. "What the heck's that?"

"I already told—well." She snickers, giving me a funny look. "You probably forgot. It's when you go to the bathroom for the first time after drinking. Then, you'll be running to pee all night long."

My face scrunches, as I sway and bump into the wall. "Ish that even true? Soun's like a bunsh of hogwash."

Mei's eyes bulge.

"Wha'? Whassat look for?"

"Oh, nothing," she says sweetly. "You're just hammered, is all."

"Huh? Noooo, I'm noooot—" I stumble backwards, knocking into someone behind me. "Ssssorry, so sorry!" They laugh it off, their eyes hazy with who-knows-what. Mei's giggles fill the air, alongside my own. In no time at all, we're hunched over, hands on the wall for support, laughing hysterically for no apparent reason.

"Stop—*STOP!* You're gonna make me PISS MYSELF!"

"Ahh!" She smacks the wall, her labored breath coming out in wheezing snorts. "That's... so... funny. I can't fucking... breath!"

Through my teary eyes, I inspect the line. Shit! We're still five people out. What the hell are people doing in there? Having sex? Oh my god, oh my god, I need to distract myself right now. Think or something else. Or I'm gonna—

Ring, ring, ring... A buzz vibrates in my jeans pocket.

Perfect timing!

I whip out my phone, squinting at the caller I.D. The letters blur into one, then duplicate into three, swaying uncontrollably.

"Oh, no." Mei hovers over my phone. "You don't want to —"

Click. "Hellooo?"

"Juliana! Oh my—thank God. I've been looking all over for you. Juliana, I'm—"

A smile blooms across my lips at his voice. "Oh, heyyyyyy there, Haydennnn." From my peripheral, I catch Mei pinching the bridge of her nose, squeezing her eyes tightly.

What's her deal?

"Uhmmm, are you...?"

I giggle. "Am I what?"

"Drunk."

A laugh spills out of me. "Whaaattt, noooo! Well..." I twirl a strand of hair, biting my lip. "Maybe a li'l bit. I'm waitin' in line to pee." I suck in a breath. *Why did I tell him that?! So stupid! Oh, whatever.*

A little snort comes through the line, but Hayden's amusement is short-lived. "What frat are you at, Jules?"

My brow furrows. Why does he sound so serious? And— wait, hold up. "Heyyy, how do you know I'm at a frat party?"

"Because they all play the same shitty music."

Yet another giggle escapes me. "Wow, thaaasss pretty schmart of you."

"Oh, yeah? I'm sure you really mean that. Now, fess up," he coos in a flirtatious tone. "Tell me which frat you're at."

I sink my teeth into my lower lip as an inexplicable tingling sensation tightens in my belly. "I dunnooo..." I answer honestly. "I could ask M—Heeeyyy, wait a minnit. I'm 'sposed to be mad at you."

Silence spreads through the line until, "You can be mad at me at home, where I know you're safe."

Home.

My anger resurfaces, raging through my drunken state, as we inch closer to the bathroom, with only one guy ahead of us. Hayden thinks he can call that penthouse my *home,* after what he did to me? There's a reason I came here tonight. *To forget about him.*

"Juliana—"

"You can shhtop righ' there." I jut my hand out, as if he can see it. "I'm not tellin' you where I am, ssssho quit ashkin'. Don' wanna be 'round you."

Oh, no. I gasp in a moment of mental clarity. Is that what I really sound like? I look to Mei, who props a hand on my shoulder and purses her lips at me in a way that says, *yeah, you really do, and you're not even supposed to be talking to him.*

Shit. She's right.

I unclench and clench my fist repeatedly, nostrils flaring as I push thoughts of the indie showcase from my head—and blink away the sadness that accompanies the memory, enduring the unwelcome mental clarity it brings. Breathing deep, I focus on my speech. "I don't. Want to. See. You."

More silence. "Juliana," I ignore the wobble in his voice, that feigned concern. He's just trying to lure me back into his web. "I know you don't want to talk about it, but if you would just—"

In a flash, I bring the butt of the phone to my lips, an inch from the microphone. *"I said. I don't. Want. To see you."* There. That should do it. I hold the speaker to my ear, only to hear more of his nonsense. With a deep sigh, I prepare for another round, bringing the microphone back to my li—

"YO, BRO, TAKE THE HINT. SHE'S JUST NOT THAT INTO YOU."

I stumble back a step, bumping into Mei, stunned as the guy at the line's front retreats from the phone and shoots me a wink. "You're welcome," he says, then saunters toward the now-vacant bathroom.

Stunned, I lift the phone to my ear. "Um..."

"Who was that?"

A shiver runs down my spine at Hayden's icy jealousy. When I don't respond, his tone turns deathly calm. "I'm not going to ask you again, Juliana. If you don't tell me where you are, I'll—"

Click.

I swivel around to Mei. "Good riddance."

She shakes her head. "Girl, you're gonna regret that tomorrow."

"Answering his call? Yeah, you're probably right," I admit, suddenly feeling too sober. "Whatever. Let's just keep the party going. I need another round."

Her eyes twinkle with delight. "Now you're speaking my language."

ONE MORE CUP of jungle juice did the trick—or was it two? Who knows, but I feel *electric* as I let the music take ahold of me. Its beat pulses through my body, shocking my veins with erratic energy, while the disco lights seep through my closed eyelids, intensifying every sensation.

As the night wears on, the basement only grows more crowded, time waning, slipping away with promises of dancing forever. Until something bumps my shoulder, causing my eyes to open to a flock of four-or-so guys darting toward the stairs.

"Come on, come on!" they shout, patting each other's backs, earning more followers. Locking with Mei's gaze, it's obvious she's curious, too. So, she follows them upstairs with me in tow, stumbling with each step. "Did you see?" I overhear a girl talking with her friend but don't catch the rest.

"Is thishhh normal?" I ask Mei, leaning on a wall for support, watching as a group rushes toward the front door. "Do ya kno' what'sh goin' on?"

A fraternity brother passing by answers for her. "Some guy pulled up in a crazy car."

I roll my eyes. All this fuss over a car?

"Let's go look!" Mei tugs my arm, dragging me through the foyer, so aggressively I trip on the way out the front door. Stumbling across the porch, I grasp a pillar protruding from the white railing before I nearly fall flat on my ass, barely registering Mei's breathless words.

"Oh my god..."

Swaying with disoriented vision, I dust off my hands, staring at the teak planks beneath my feet.

"It's straight out of a movie..."

What's she going off about?

"Huh?" I look up.

For all the blood to drain from my face.

Just there, parked along the sidewalk, is the sleekest, meanest yet most *beautiful* car I—or any of the gawking college students scattered across the lawn—have ever seen with my two eyes.

Sleek and impossibly low to the pavement, metallic blue streaks across the length, mingling with glossy white paint that reflects off an overhanging streetlamp like shimmering diamonds. Boasting a distinctive grille, its headlights pierce through the night, illuminating those who circle the coupe and snap photos, leaving ample room for the mysterious man leaning against the passenger side, who folds his arms across his chest.

And stares right at me.

Fire rages behind Hayden's crystal-blue eyes, projecting heat that simmers down my middle. A challenge brews in them when I don't budge, and only burns brighter as he opens the passenger side door, unveiling the car's all-white interior, bathed in a gentle glow. He holds it open, his gaze unwavering in the still air, so quiet I hear faint whispers.

"Is that a Bugatti Veyron...?"

"Who is that guy...?"

"Do you know him...?"

"I think I've seen him somewhere..."

Curse the butterflies buzzing in my stomach—I'm not moving. I don't care how frantically they flap, when those on the lawn follow the line of his stare and land on me, their lips parting on gasps as they bounce between us.

How did he find me, anyway? Sure, he knew I was at a frat party, and it probably wasn't hard for him at which school, but... there are over a dozen parties on Columbia's Greek Row tonight. Did he really go barging into all of them, one by one? His intense demeanor alone says yes.

Mimicking his attitude, I cross my arms at him, hoping he can see how pissed off I—

"Whoooopsie!" Without my support pillar, I stumble backwards and grapple for the railing, just barely catching it. I steady myself upright, only to watch Hayden stomp through the yard, my vision splitting him in two.

Adrenaline spikes through my center, lurching me toward the front door. As well as they can manage, my steps quicken in a hurry, meaning to sprint all the way down that spiraling staircase so I can disappear on the dance floor.

Closer, closer, come on. Almost there—

An arm juts out in front of me, smacking a hand against the doorframe. I bump into an immovable force, grasping something firm and warm beneath silky fabric.

"You either walk, or I'm carrying you."

Flaring with drunken rage, I jerk away at the sound of Hayden's voice, whipping my head up to meet his shadowy gaze. Oh, he's dead serious—but so am I. "Are sh'you outta your mind? I tol'ya what I said on the phone. You can't jus'—"

"I'm not asking permission, Jules. You're coming home with me, or I'll end up killing the man who lures you to his."

My jaw drops to the ground, right as I hear Mei squeal behind me. Why isn't she doing anything?! I gape, words beyond my capabilities. He's all talk. Rolls up, causes a big scene. Now he's just lying—it's what he does best, it seems. He wouldn't actually—

"Option two, it is."

"Wha'? Wai', wha' are you—"

I gasp as my world flips on its head—along with my *actual* head. Bent at his shoulder, my hair sprawls downward, tracing the planes of his back, bouncing with his every step.

"Hey!" I bark. *"Put me doooown!"*

In response, his hold around my thighs tightens, my only solace being that I sided on jeans instead of a dress. He'd have me flashing every person on this lawn, all of whom watch with amusement—or envy.

I lift my head, spitting the strands of hair stuck to my mouth, just to find Mei with her hands covering hers, eyes blown wide with shock.

"Mei?! MEI! Don't jus' shhtand there!"

FORTY-ONE
JULIANA

BY SOME MIRACLE, I didn't throw up last night.

Not during the insufferably quiet car ride—although the thought of emptying my guts all over his pearly-white interior *was* quite tempting. But alas, I held it back, even in the penthouse's private elevator and the kitchen, when Hayden force fed me bread while badgering about drinking water. And, by the looks of it, my bed made it out okay, too.

All alone in my room, I squint at the morning sun streaming in through the windows. I hate to admit it, but I *missed* this bed—but not as much as I miss Hayden's. I scoff with no one to hear, before quickly convincing myself it's because of the Egyptian cotton sheets. They *were* properly hyped-up.

I don't remember everything that happened last night, but I can recall the important bits, including some choice words I said to Hayden. All an accumulation of built-up rage from the past five days that spilled over. And the worst part of it all? He just sat there and listened, letting me get everything out, letting my voice boom through the penthouse like a vicious onslaught, while he nursed my drunkenness.

It makes hating him that much harder.

But my trust is shattered, like irreparable glass.

Sitting up in bed, I wince at the dull ache throbbing in my temple. It should be worse, I know. I scan the room, discovering things that palpitate my twisted heart.

A tall glass of water on my nightstand beside a bottle of Advil. I take two. A bucket on the ground by my side of the bed, presumably for throw up. It's empty. A long pillow laid across where my back was while asleep—this one chokes me up the most.

He followed the cardinal rule of drinking: when someone's on the verge of blacking out, lay them on their side and position a pillow along their back to prevent choking if they vomit in their sleep.

I shouldn't be surprised. Hayden *is* a professional at this whole partying thing, which is why, even while having taken such a precaution, there's still a large imprint atop the comforter on the opposite side of the bed. He must've laid there once I fell asleep after screaming him out of my room.

That, I remember, and wish I had forgotten.

Remorse shivers through me, doubling in intensity when I spot the most thoughtful of all his gestures, resting on the bench at the foot of the bed.

Breakfast.

My stomach growls at the sight—and what a sight it really is. Meticulously plated on a wooden tray meant for bed, bacon, sausage, hash browns, and a glass of orange juice complement the main dish. An omelet. Stuffed with chopped peppers and seasoned with parsley flakes, the eggy, cheesy goodness is not only cooked but folded so perfectly, I know it was Hayden's doing.

What a surprise it was, learning a billionaire's son—who no doubt splurges on Michelin-star meals—is an impressive cook himself. Hayden prepares most of his own meals and intentionally cooks in moderate amounts, leaving little to no leftovers.

I had the pleasure of tasting his first dish two weeks ago, a few nights after the derby. Steak, lobster risotto, and roasted Brussels sprouts out on the terrace as the sun dipped below the horizon—

No. Stop that. Am I a masochist all of a sudden?

Pushing the memory away, I crawl across the sheets before settling back under them, positioning the tray over my lap on its two legs. Cutting a wedge off the omelet, I groan on my first bite, then stifle the sound, stubbornly. Then do it all over again with the next taste. I would've never thought it possible to *chew* defiantly, but I do, until only crumbs remain.

I stare at them, then at the imprint on the bed and the Advil on my nightstand, effectively flaring the guilt in me. I heave a sigh. Drunk and taken against my will or not, I should apologize for last night. I was quite an unpleasant abductee.

After a quick shower, I patter my bare feet out of my room, pass through the kitchen and attached dining room, all while trying not to think about how accustomed I've become to the penthouse, until I end up outside Hayden's door.

Nerves trickle through me—only to dissipate when I open the door and find the grand bedroom empty. Same with his bathroom, as well as the main living room and the terrace. For ten minutes or so, I search and search throughout the penthouse, flinging open doors—*gosh, there are a lot of them*—just for the rooms to turn up empty.

And with every knob I twist, something strange yet still predictable happens...

I grow angrier.

Why am *I* the one on the hunt for *him?* Why am I even looking for him? So what if he nursed me back to health for one night? He *conspired* with his father to ruin. My. Life. And last night, sure, I went off the handles, but he could've at least said the word *sorry.* For anything.

Perhaps he knew you didn't want to hear it, a little angel suggests.

I flick her off my shoulder, at the exact moment my irritation proves clarifying. I know where he is. Why didn't I think of it sooner? I breeze through the penthouse, letting muscle memory do the work, while my brain's too busy conjuring up the next nasty thing I'll say when I find him.

It brews and it brews, some hateful concoction on my journey through the main living room, up the floating staircase, through the ballroom and into the server's wing, until I'm bounding like a lethal tempest down the hallway.

Toward his studio.

I should just leave and not make things any worse, but the retribution is too tempting. Even an *ounce* of it. That's all I can afford, really—hurling atrocities his way, so maybe he'll know just a fraction of what it felt like standing by that stage, at the summit of all you've worked for, only to witness your future slip between your fingers like sand.

Hastening my steps, the studio door draws near, until I graze that final knob and instantly whip it back, as the past month replays in my mind like a dreadful slideshow. A chain-reaction of events, beginning with Hayden's disgruntled signature across a meaningless contract, culminating on that fateful day he handed me a flash drive, beaming a smile, despite knowing the device would incinerate my world to ashes and—

The door swings open, ever-so slowly on its hinges, and what I see stops my heart completely.

In the middle of the studio, perched on a colossal easel amid a sea of canvases, rests a half-completed portrait of a woman. Frozen in the doorway, I squint in disbelief, because... gosh, that can't be right. That woman... she sure looks like *me*.

I approach on languid steps, unblinking, as I hold my breath and admire the canvas that towers over all the others around it. Where vibrant paint doesn't shine, pencil lightly sketches the rest of the masterpiece, immortalizing a moment in time left in the past.

His pool party.

A lump forms in my throat. *Has he been working on this for that long?*

It appears so. The delicacy of those strokes, bringing my appearance that day to life, sparing no detail—that doesn't happen overnight. He really didn't miss anything. It's like he snapped a photo of me with his mind for reference.

The fishnet cover-up, flaring at the sleeves, drapes over my body with its meticulous square cutouts, all atop my *exact* red bikini, down to the little ties dangling off my hips. The curious thing, though, for a man like Hayden? He opted for an almost blurred effect, softly obscuring my midriff, as if not wanting to draw attention away from what appears to be the painting's focal point—*my face.*

And *God,* it's so detailed. Although only half complete and split vertically down the center, it's like staring into a mirror that day. Wispy bangs. Hoop earrings. Hair looped through an elastic, positioned high on my head. He even remembered my lip shade and how I swapped my glasses for contacts.

Wow...

Enchanted by wonder, I inch closer, daring to brush a finger against my eye and its distinct shade of green, half expecting to feel the silkiness of my lashes instead of dried paint.

I cover my lips and stare, hands trembling and knees locking me into place, as my emotions catch the wind in my throat. Why would he...? A sad shudder rattles me to the bone at the thought of how very wrong I've been about Dream-Scape and the hell I've put Hayden through. All I've done is point blame his way. If he really is the monster my mind's deemed him to be these past days, then why would this be here?

"It's for your birthday."

Whirling around, I find Hayden leaning against the door-frame, appraising me with a soft expression—just like last night. Unable to suppress my emotions, I sniffle a wet sound and clear my throat, doing little for its rawness.

"My birthday isn't for five months."

He pushes off the doorframe, closing the distance between us on leisure steps. "I'm taking my time with it."

I look up at the skylight, blinking furiously. "Why...? Why would you...?" I falter, already knowing the truth before he speaks.

He pinches my chin gently, tilting it up until I meet his gaze, causing a tear to spill over and skate down my cheek, another slipping in its wake as he murmurs, "Because I love you, Juliana."

Drawing in a quivering breath, my eyes flick between his, basking in their proximity, as those three beautiful words recite in my mind, each rendition bringing more tears. *Get it together.* I sniffle, definitely looking like a blubbering wreck.

Cupping my jaw, he catches a tear with his thumb. "Gosh, Jules, I didn't mean to bring on the waterworks. Who knew I had such emotional depth?"

I bite my lip on a wide, toothy smile, a giggle clattering through me. That's the best part about Hayden. He always knows how to make everything better.

He swipes more tears, until the well is all dried up. Nerves jitter within me as I gaze up at him, speechless, a response right on the tip of my tongue, like an anxious jumper on a diving board, because... barring family, no one's ever told me they loved me before and I've never uttered the words myself.

But of course, his mind's in tune with mine.

"You don't have to say it back. I'll be here either way."

But that's just it. *I'd* be here either way. Before Dream-Scape, I knew that after our arrangement ended, someway, somehow, my heart would wander back here, to this very penthouse, standing outside his bedroom door, longing to be inside. Not on account of these past few months, but because of the past fifteen years.

Looking into his oceany depths, I gently brush a hair off his brow, as if I know I'll be doing it for a lifetime. "How could I not say it back...? Hayden, I've loved you since we were children."

He stumbles back, just a step, eyes bulging like I physically struck him. "Y-you... You have?" he croaks.

"Yes," I whisper, hearing my soul sing. "I've known since that day we drove from your family's estate for the last time, and I prayed I would see you again."

His palms cup my cheeks, applying just enough pressure to make them tingle. "Oh, Juliana..." He blinks, rapidly, looking to the sky, higher than I did moments ago. "That's just... that's—" In a flash, he pulls me into a hug, his arms wrapping securely around my neck.

My cheek squishes into his strong chest for a second, then two, three... until his body shakes against mine, trembling with emotions, igniting mine all over again, but for different reasons. Guilt.

"I'm sorry." His shirt fabric muffles my voice before he eases up. I catch his gaze staring down at me. "I'm so sorry." My chin wobbles. "I shouldn't have..."

"I know—*shhhh.*" He brushes my hair, soothing my worry. "I know, baby."

I blush, despite everything. "I shouldn't have jumped to conclusions after what happened. I could've at least given you the benefit of the doubt and let you explain. And last night..." I choke up, shame taking its hold on me. "I was *awful.*"

He shrugs—actually *shrugs.* "You could say you were passionate."

"I'm serious."

"Oh, I know you are, and I can't wait to imagine alllll the ways you'll make it up to me." My lips part as a shiver bolts up my spine, causing him to chuckle. "But really, Juliana, you didn't call me anything worse than I've heard before. I knew what I was signing up for when I pulled up to that party last night. You were drunker than a skunk."

My nose scrunches. "Bet I smelled like one, too."

When he doesn't respond, I whack him on the arm playfully.

"Owwwww," he drawls, clutching his bicep like I slugged him with a bat, jaw dropping in shock. "You just love roughing me up, don't you? First, you light my ass up with that vicious tongue, now you're going after my good looks? The audacity..."

I hardly touched him!

"Ohh my—" I roll my eyes to the back of my head, my hand absentmindedly winding up for another—

"See!" He jerks away, pointing.

I gasp and snatch my hand back, watching as a huge smile spreads across his lips. When he laughs, I can't help but join, which only encourages him more, until our laughter bellows through the studio, echoing to the farthest reaches of the penthouse. Gradually, our hysterics soften, leaving only lingering chuckles that slowly fade into silence—a comfortable silence.

Until my reality trickles back in.

I look at my feet. "Your father acted alone, didn't he...? Tricked you into slipping me that flash drive..."

"Yes."

Fuck. I clench my fists.

"Then there really is no hope. My game's lost."

He lifts my chin, anguish swarming his features. "Don't say that."

"Why?" I cringe at how broken I sound. "It's the truth. What hope is there for me, against someone like him? With his type of power and connections? Not to mention, I can't contend with whatever team of lawyers work for your family's company."

When doubt flickers in his otherwise strong gaze, I know *team* wasn't the right choice of word. *Army* is more fitting.

Tugging me closer than ever, he sighs softly, bringing his warm lips to my temple. "Don't worry, baby. I'll make this right."

FORTY-TWO

JULIANA

"SLOW DOWN, Jeremy. Your father won't be happy if he comes home and discovers there's no casserole left."

His spoon clatters against his plate. "Sorry, Mom."

I snicker. Leave it up to Jeremy to eat three portions on his own—his appetite's even worse than during high school. Although, some things have stayed the same since those years, most notably our childhood apartment.

As notorious penny pinchers, nothing goes to waste and nothing gets replaced, unless absolutely necessary. Take the oriental rug beneath our feet, for example. I don't remember a time when it wasn't in our cozy apartment. Or this dining table the three of us sit at. There's no doubt in my mind Mom and Dad will pass it down as inheritance. To their credit, it still looks brand new, as with most of the other furniture and decor.

Obviously, going from Hayden's penthouse to my childhood apartment is quite the shell shock, but there's no mistaking the homey solace I feel here, especially when digging into my favorite comfort dish, chicken and zucchini casserole. Strictly cooked by my mom, who always claims it's the simplest recipe in her repertoire.

What can I say? I'm a simple girl.

I take another bite, savoring the mozzarella's tangy richness, while simultaneously witnessing Jeremy's appetite roar back to life. Hunched over, he shovels spoonfuls past his lips like he's plowing snow. Honestly, the sight is a bit jarring for my eyes, which strangely makes me smirk, because that means it has to be downright agonizing for Mom—

My smile falters.

At the head of the table, Mom gazes off into space, her expression laden with worry.

"Mom?"

"Huh?" She snaps out of it, and the look disappears. "Oh, sorry, sweetie. I'm just tired, is all." Picking up her spoon, she smiles at me—and it couldn't seem more forced.

Guess I'm not the only one having trouble ignoring the enormous elephant in the room.

DreamScape.

Since the horrible event, it's been a week. Five days of wallowing in self-pity and ignoring Hayden, followed by two days of making love with him. And I do mean *love*. The word keeps slipping off my tongue, maybe more than his—before, during, after, at random times of the day, as if we're trying to see who's gonna get spooked and run first. Or... maybe it's the other reason.

Forgetting what happened.

Sure, we should devise a plan of action, but I told him I needed a breather. Call it unproductive coping but... obsessively worrying over the same problem day after day after day, it gets exhausting. I was exhausted—*still* am, apparently, seeing how the first words from my mouth when I strutted through my parents' door were *"I don't want to talk about it."*

So, the elephant remains...

I did, however, blab to my mom about Hayden. I mean, she's not dumb. She could easily put two-and-two together, once we finally *do* talk about what happened and I inform her Kingston Entertainment was meant to—*just*—sponsor my game. So, even with Jeremy here with a sore wound over the truth of me and his best friend, I came clean to her the instant we sat down at the table, prepared to weather her onslaught of questions.

But they never came. Turns out, she suspected us all along, even hit me with the whole *"oh, honey, I've seen how you've looked at him your whole life."* Which made Jeremy turn green in the face and me doubt the validity of such a state-ment. That is, until I remembered that look she gave me at Vinny's Corner. She knew. Moms always do, don't they?

I appraise her again, frowning. "Mom, you haven't touched your food. Are you sure you're—"

Her head bobs up suddenly, swaying her locks, the auburn hue more pronounced than the hint in Jeremy's and my own hair. "Warren is behind what happened, right?"

Oh, no. I really thought I could delay this conversation. "Umm—"

"I mean, it was *his* company that *stole* your game, so of course it was him." When I remain silent, she pushes, "Am I right?"

"Yes."

Despite her assumption, she sinks back into her chair, shadows darkening along her pretty face. "If I'd known you were competing for his company's feature, I could've warned you. Warren Kingston corrupts everything he touches."

I squirm in my chair at the sound of his name on her tongue. It sounds wrong, like metal scraping metal, maybe because she hasn't spoken his name in years. Over a decade, since that night we sped off into the night, after she pepper sprayed him over a camcorder. I remember the events of that night clearly.

Sure, at such a young age, I couldn't grasp what I'd seen, but as I got older, I slowly realized I watched my own mother have sex with one of New York City's wealthiest men —a memory I actively shove to the furthest depths of my mind. Including the fact that she was his nighttime nanny *and* his mistress for several years. She wasn't seeing anyone romantically at the time, that I know of, but Warren was married.

The whole thing's never made sense to me. According to my mom, she's only ever had two boyfriends in her life, both of whom she married. Monogamy is obviously important to her, so... why?

Throughout our adolescence, that was the original elephant in this apartment, until it grew too old and died. I have no doubt she told Dad—she tells him everything—but Jeremy and me? We never spoke of it, hardly to each other, even. I never dared to ask that burning question, not once, growing up.

And I won't now.

"He's awful," I agree simply, leaving her the option to drop the subject.

"No, Juliana..." She pauses, earning the attention of both her children, as she gnaws on her lips in a way that tells me I should brace myself. "Warren's so much worse than just a serial womanizer."

For a split second, I catch Jeremy's stare. Suddenly, guilt

sparks within me. Whatever she's about to say, it's for my sake. "Mom, you don't have to—"

"Yes." She lurches forward, only to settle back down, lowering her voice. "Yes, I do. I hoped I'd never have to dredge up the past, but... it's time you two know the truth."

Jeremy goes rigid, as do I.

The discomfort written all over her face is palpable as she heaves a sigh. "I just want you two to know, I only kept this from you, because I never wanted to make you feel guilty. That whatever I did, it was *my* choice. Not yours."

From my peripheral, Jeremy's Adam's apple bobbles, and when Mom starts thrumming her knuckles atop the table, I get a queasy feeling in my belly. The anticipation, it's too much. Way, way too much, so I blurt, "Is this about the camcorder? I-I mean..." I rake a hand across the back of my neck, regretting my impulsiveness. "Seems like the obvious guess to me. It's the last time we saw him."

"It is." She lowers her gaze. "I knew you'd understand what you saw when you grew up. But that's about it. I entertained an affair with a married man. Nothing more, nothing less. But..."

At her silence, Jeremy leans over the table, burying his face into his palms, his voice muffling against his fingers as he watches through their slits. "Just tell us, Mom. It's okay."

"Let's just say, that video... it proved how..." She clears her throat, nodding to herself. "Nonconsensual it was."

Jeremy's bolts from his chair, sending it skipping from the table harshly.

"No—no." She holds out her hands. *Calm down,* they tell the six-foot-four, two-hundred-and-fifty-pound gym rat, whose face is redder than blood. "He didn't force himself on me, but... he did..." As she swallows, something in her eyes disassociates from her next words. "He blackmailed me."

My hands shoot to my lips, mirroring Jeremy's reaction. He faces away, though, toward the kitchen, stuck standing like a statue, leaving all the questions up to me.

"How?" is the only one I can muster.

She looks elsewhere, too—as it all comes spilling out.

"Warren started taking notice of me early in my teaching career, not too long after Daniel's passing. He'd send flower deliveries to my classroom, sometimes bring a bouquet himself during my lunch break. It was flattering at first, but I wasn't into older men, specifically ones with a wife. He took the rejection quite well, it seemed. Then, a year later, after Hayden's first day in my class, he offered me a nighttime nanny position. It felt a little strange, given how I knew he pursued other women while being married, but..."

On her pause, Jeremy creeps back to his chair, not bothering to pull it back up to the table, as he listens, folding his hands in his lap. When I look, his knuckles are white, trembling with composure.

"I needed the money. Sure, I didn't have to pay my children's private school tuition, but making ends meet was hard enough on a single income. Plus, I could watch you two at the same time, so I took the job. Not long after that, he started pursuing me again. Subtly groping me—in ways he brushed off as accidental. Flirtatious remarks. Invasive questions. Gifts. It kept getting worse, despite refusing his advancements, to the point where the money wasn't worth it anymore. When I told him to find a new nanny—that's when we had a serious problem."

Every hair on my arms raises. *This can't be good...*

"He told me I'd remain his nighttime nanny, for however

longed it pleased him. That I was to stop resisting him, or else..."

Finally, she drags her eyes back to center, flicking them between us with a harrowing look she tries so desperately to mask. But it's ghastly, haunted by shadows, as if the memory itself yanks her back to the past by her ankles, nails scratching and splintering along the floorboards.

I give her a subtle nod. *It's okay.*

"Or else he'd get you two kicked out of school."

Bile rises in my throat. *IT'S NOT OKAY, IT'S NOT OKAY, IT'S—*

Jeremy springs to his feet, nearly tripping over his chair, sprinting toward the kitchen, before hurling into the sink violently. As he dispenses the rest of his dinner, wave after wave, I only stare into Mom's eyes, fighting the tears in mine.

If what she's saying is true—*which it is.* I saw it with my own two eyes—that means Warren blackmailed our mother into having *sex* with him, or else her children couldn't attend private school. She could never afford the tuition without the scholarships, and Warren was on the school board. Riverside Prep's richest parent and most *generous* donor, the whole school knew.

He'd have our lockers cleaned out the very next day.

A groan signifies the end of Jeremy's sickness, before he comes clomping back to his seat. It's hard to look at him. I've never seen him so distraught, and I'm sure he'd say the same about me. As for our mother—the real *victim* of this story—by the way she angles her chin high, letting the truth ring clear, it tells me she doesn't think Warren deserves my tears.

So, I don't let them fall.

"Mom..." I kill the wobble in my voice—or try to. "That's..." *Fuck.* What does someone say to that? Now I understand why she was concerned about our guilt. Their affair lasted for two whole years. How did she withstand that? Another wave of bile hits me when I know the answer.

For her children's futures.

"I'm so sorry," I say, feeling useless.

"Don't be. Now, you listen here—both of you." She pushes Jeremy's shoulder, earning his attention. "I made my choice. I did what I did, and there's no reason either of you should feel any shame. *He's* the monster and to blame for all that happened."

"I know, but... it feels like he won."

"Did he?" Mom smirks. There's that defiance. "I made a point of moving on with my life, while he stayed the same man he's always been. And the best part, his sons went to Riverside, so he *had* to watch as I left him in the past."

That manages a smile from me, but damn, it's a crooked one.

Jeremy wakes from his daze, huffing a loud sound laced with anger. "I don't understand. Why would Warren pull the stunt that he did with Juliana, if he knows you have that incriminating tape?"

Mom scoffs, answering immediately. "I'll tell you why. It's simple, really. Warren's not all that hard to figure out, once you're under his talons. He underestimates women intellectually, and views them as inferior—probably stems from the relationship he saw from his parents. I'm sure he thinks I lost the evidence after all these years, or maybe I'm so dumb I threw it out. On top of that, Juliana, if he knew you were working with Hayden, he'd count on you blaming him for everything. Meaning, when you eventually turned to me for help, I wouldn't consider using the tape. It's dirt on Warren, not Hayden, after all."

I blink.

Then blink some more.

Swiveling my gaze onto Jeremy, I find him doing the same. What the hell's going on? Did I miss the story of when she obtained her psychology degree? Did our mother—*who teaches second graders*—walk straight from an episode of *Criminal Minds?*

If she didn't just roast Warren enough, Mom torches another blow, charring him around the edges. "It all links back to his arrogance, which makes him sloppy—and stupid."

Holy shit.

"U-uhm," I stammer, catching Mom's expression light up with delight. "So, uhh... what do you think is our best course of action?" *Miss Detective.*

"We march him straight to court."

My stomach drops.

Oh, no. I was worried she'd say that.

Noting my skepticism, she continues, "We might pull it off with this kind of evidence. Hire a lawyer and—"

"Oh—oh!" Jeremy smacks the table. *"I know just the one!"*

I arch a brow. "You do?"

"Yeah. At the Vegas conference, I met this guy—kind of an intimidating fellow, if you ask me, but I digress. Guess he works with security systems, has some side projects he wouldn't answer literally any questions about. Just vague answers. Probably works as some military contractor, I bet, his tongue tied by some insanely high security clearances..."

My eyes bulge. *Get to the point!*

"Sorry, sorry! Anyway. He's from New York and told me his wife's a lawyer on Silicon Avenue. Her name is Lauren Astor."

I stew on it... "Nope. Doesn't ring any bells."

"Worth a shot. I've heard the name once or twice. Pretty sure she's a data privacy lawyer."

"*Hmph.* Well, she sounds exactly like what we need, but how are we gonna afford that?"

His lips flatten, so thin I can't help but laugh. "Your new boyfriend is a billionaire. I think you can manage."

"Technically, he's not my—"Oh, please, who am I trying to convince? "Warren controls Hayden's entire trust. You really think he'd allow that money to go toward his opposition?"

"Shit, I didn't think of that..." He scratches his head. "Well, I'll still reach out. Maybe we can work something out, I don't know..."

My heart sinks, running low on faith. And my mind... it's running low on options.

Reaching across the table, Mom's hand finds mine, and I worry I feel too little of its warmth. "We'll come up with something."

FORTY-THREE
HAYDEN

MY PLAN IS SIMPLE.

Barge into my father's office, demand he publicly confess to stealing Juliana's game, or else I'll ensure his piss-poor work logs become the business of the entire office.

He can scream and shout all he likes, threaten my trust fund—hell, he can make the call to his bank and pull the plug right in front of me. I don't care. I may have let his actions slide while Juliana enjoyed some mental rest days, but I'm not standing by and watching her suffer for one more second at the expense of the piece of shit who calls himself my father.

Warren is a plague, whose time has come to rot.

I bank a left, choosing a different route to his office than last time to avoid Doris, who would gladly rip me a new one for ditching work for a week straight. Surprisingly, HR tried calling several times and left stern voicemails about me playing hooky, despite the scene I made in my father's office. Maybe Doris tipped them off, demanding my return, only so she can throw scut work on my desk. If only she knew the truth. Perhaps she will, maybe even in a few short hours.

Breaking through the maze of cubicles, I behold the wall of glass, housing executives and other higher ups, all clacking away on their keyboards like last time. Except... I squint, heaving a sigh. What a shock. My father's not in his office.

Wearing a frown, I retrace my steps and come out the opposite end of the maze, only to meander down another hallway, en route to the elevators.

Dammit, dammit...

I planned to confront him at work, where he can see first-hand what's at stake for him, witness all who would stare him right in the face through his office windows, if he foolishly decides not to comply. Given his absence, I'll settle with plan B—knocking on his front door. It'll have to do. I'm not waiting any long—

I skid to a halt as a soft sound floats into my ear, so faint I nearly miss it. I listen intently, realizing it's a woman. She seems sad... *really* sad. Cupping an ear, I creep toward the whimpering noise until I find myself outside the breakroom, its door cracked, just barely enough for me to peer inside. Listening to that heartbreaking sound, uneasiness churns in me, enough that I dare a peek.

Only to immediately regret that I had.

"Please... you won..." Juliana sobs into her hands.

Across from her, my father sneers in satisfaction.

"Please... I'll do anything..."

My heart tears in two, eyes filling with tears, but my feet... they're encased in fortified cement as I stare out to sea, gripped by the sight of a tsunami barreling to shore.

"Anything?" he muses, encircling her, and I can't unsee the way his eyes trail down the length of her body, evoking my revulsion.

Eyes wide and frantic, she tracks his movements, hardly

able to hold his gaze. "Yes—*anything!* I mean it. I'll do anything if you just add my name to the developers' credits. I won't tell anyone what you did."

He stops before her, much too close for comfort. "Ohhh, and why would that matter? No one would believe a word out of that pretty mouth of yours."

"I-I..."

A scream lodges in my throat, listening to her stutter, pointing her gaze to her feet, while he runs a hand down her arm.

"T-there have b-been rumors."

Pinching her chin, he lifts her to eye level. "Have there, now?"

"There have."

He chuckles, craning her neck farther back, inching even closer. "I'm listening."

"Online... there's been talk online. On gaming forms." A snicker escapes him, but she pushes ahead. "One of my followers was at DreamScape and recognized the similarities between the games."

He yawns dramatically. "I'm just *quivering* with fear," he taunts, flashing a wide smile.

"He posted about it—and it's been getting reposted."

Silence descends over the breakroom. Just for a split second—but enough to reveal my father's interest, although Juliana may not notice.

"How cute. You think that's what concerns me, hmm? A little internet gossip from a handful of your *fans?"*

Another sob rattles through her, then thunders through my bones. *Fuck! Move, dammit!* I tell my legs, earning no response, as if my mind-to-muscle connection is severed by despair.

"Please..." she blubbers a wet sound, tears gliding down her cheeks. "I'll do *anything*," she repeats, pleading. "I'll pose as someone else and deny their claims. Start up new rumors as a distraction. Tell my followers it's just one huge coincidence. Even confess to your board, tell them it was *me* who stole the concept—that the pirate game's been in development longer..."

His head tilts curiously.

Chest heaving on struggled breaths, she powers on. "Just add me to the developers' credits, that's all I ask. I've worked on this game for years, and you've squashed its chances of success. I don't have the resources to compete with yours."

I'm going to be sick, I think, when he catches a strand of her hair, twisting it between his fingers. Juliana shies away, squirming, only for his grip to tighten, reeling her chin back into place.

"Look at me," he murmurs, his voice barely audible to me. "That's it... You're just like your mom. Think you can get anything you want by spreading your legs."

Nonononono...

"W-what?"

"Don't play coy, Juliana. It's just us here, no one else." His voice turns rough as he sweeps a thumb along her jaw. "I saw the way you looked at me at the derby."

Her mouth slackens. *"Wha—"*

"Don't try denying it." His eyes roam down her figure once again. "Why else would you wear such a low shirt when coming to beg for my mercy, hmm?" he taunts, despite her shirt being perfectly modest.

He *tsks* at her silence, brushing a hand across her arm as a blush creeps up her neck—and the sight of that red stain... it's twisted. Appalling. And kills a part of my soul. I don't know if she actually feels an attraction toward my *father*, or if grief has rendered her one last option. Frankly, in this moment, I don't care.

I just need to save her.

Adrenaline surges through me when he leans closer than ever, traveling a hand down the small of her back, his gaze fixated on her ass.

Please, please, please, please, I beg for that cement to crumble.

As he retreats, I swear I catch her cringing, before she masks the look with fright.

Come on, come on! A crack splits down my bondage.

He grabs her by the nape, forcing her to look at him.

FUCK, MOVE! Another splinter.

"Care to know how to get what you want? You can start by unbuttoning your blouse, then I'll *think* about adding your name."

Like the snap of a band, I break free. Blinded by rage and fury and promises of familial murder, I reach for the door handle, meaning to tear it back on its—

I gasp when he whips around. "But that can wait," he says, bounding for the door. "I have a board meeting in ten minutes. Conference Room A. You'll come and make your little confession, then we'll find a quiet place, and you can show me how much you want it."

Before I can gauge her reaction, I sprint down the hallway with the intention of coming back and turn a corner, right as the door creaks open. Warren's humiliation can wait, even just for ten minutes, because right now, there's a more pressing matter...

Juliana needs me.

FORTY-FOUR

JULIANA

I CAN'T LOOK Hayden in the eye.

I couldn't when he came into the breakroom after Warren left, offering sympathy I probably didn't deserve. And I definitely can't now as I enter the crowded conference room.

Donning an air of authority, each and every board member sitting around the long oak table drags their attention onto me. Their eyes are calm like water, yet sharper than a scalpel, capable of deciphering my every emotion, while theirs stow away in their briefcases. As one of only three women in the room, and perhaps the sole blot of color among a sea of charcoal suits, I'm a minnow in shark territory.

And they know it.

At the head of the table, Warren rises to his feet upon my entrance, prompting his corporate foot soldiers to do the same. Hayden is amongst their ranks, seated next to Elias with pen and paper, ready to take his notes, reminiscent of when I presented my game in this exact room.

My stomach twists into a knot when Warren gestures to me. "Gentlemen, I'd like you to meet Miss Juliana Brooks."

Almost in unison, the entire room nods in my direction, offering reserved smiles, and I wonder if they were programmed that way. With the exception of Hayden, who looks moments from fainting. I make the mistake of catching his eye, only for a split second, but enough to see the anguish in them. In the breakroom, I told him not to interfere, to let me do what I have to do.

Warren notices our connection, his smirk growing even more crooked. "Miss Brooks has an *announcement* for us. It won't take long." Taking his seat, he nods toward the podium, prompting the entire room to follow suit.

The walk to the front feels like an eternity, every step like trudging through wet sand that threatens to snap my heels in half, sending me crashing to the floor with everyone watching. However embarrassing, I'd choose such a fate over enduring my current circumstances.

Stepping behind the podium, I sweep a hand along the polished oak, finding familiar comfort, until fear grips me once more when I turn back around. I clench my fists, steadying their shakiness, while I peer down the long table, under the weighted stares of at least twenty corporate bigwigs.

Their silence is crippling, maybe worse than Warren's smug expression that burns brighter as I stutter, "I-I... I have a-an announcement for..."

I pick the sides of my nail, feeling fire rage on my cheeks and my heart thump a thousand beats per minute, stealing my words by lodging them down my throat. Taking a few breaths, allowing more agonizing silence to spread across the room, I try again.

"I'm... h-here t-to..."

Hayden covers his mouth, pity and absolute horror

shining in his eyes, a stark contrast to the pure delight dancing in his father's. Warren bites down on a laugh and says, "You'll have to excuse her nerves. She's a bit on the shy side."

Amusement scatters down the table. Subdued chuckles. Whispered comments.

Even from here, I catch Warren eyeing my breasts, unabashed by the gravel in his tone as he asks, "Aren't you, Juliana?"

I swallow. *He's unchecked with power.*

"...Yes," I breathe.

"Go on." He wets his lips, voice booming down the table, filling every corner of the room, unlike mine, which is a soft whisper in comparison.

"Th-this is... rather difficult for me... so, yes, please... excuse my nerves." I stare down at the podium, unable to shake Warren from my peripheral, who rests his chin atop folded fingers, his satisfied sneer widening with my every word. "I've come t-to... tell the truth about something that's rather embarrassing."

I lift my gaze, roaming it down the line of unfamiliar faces, until I reach one dear to my soul, letting it linger for far longer than I should. Leaned back into his seat, chin wobbling in torment, Hayden wears his heart on the sleeves of his Armani suit, except it's mangled and mutilated, his cheeks dampened by the sorrow streaming from his tear ducts. He composes himself, not drawing any attention, but just barely.

Choking down a sob myself, I move along the line to Elias, the only one in the room whose face reveals second-hand embarrassment, visibly affected by my nervousness.

Then there's the two-headed viper at the head of the table, the CEO at the forefront of America's entertainment industry, who's wrought egregious evil into this world. Used people for his own pleasure. Corrupted families, including his own, even turned that wickedness onto his offspring, one of which he appraises with repulsive joy, reveling at the sight of his tears.

Warren Kingston.

There's no telling how many lives he's destroyed. Which is why, when he swivels those ice-cold eyes onto mine once more, I hold his gaze like a bull facing down a matador.

He grins back, waving that red cape.

I stand firm in the ring, unyielding, resilient, patient...

"We're all listening," Warren taunts.

Shifting on my feet, exhaling on wary breath, everything about me embodies that helpless girl Warren loves to prey upon—everything but my eyes—as I sink a hand into my pocket, quiet and undetected.

"E-everyone here d-deserves to know... the truth..."

Warren leans over the table eagerly, devoid of any soul.

"And th-the truth... i-is..."

My fingers curl around cool metal, retreating with stealth as I watch his grin expand into a cruel smile, growing wider and wider, until—

I slot the truth into place.

"I've played you for a fool."

Warren's expression falters, lips parting on some retort he hasn't the time to voice before—

"MOAN LOUDER OR YOUR KIDS WON'T BE STAYING AT THAT SCHOOL MOAN LOUDER OR YOUR KIDS WON'T BE STAYING AT THAT SCHOOL MOAN LOUDER OR..."

Fiddling along the side of the podium, I twist a dial beside the USB I plugged in, blaring Warren's unmistakable voice

even louder through the conference room's speakers. And
damn, they sure got some powerful ones installed.

Glass walls rattle around us, board members cover their
ears and lurch to their feet. Outside, employees wander from
the restraints of their cubicles, furrowing eyebrows and whispering to one another, all while Warren Kingston, seated at
the undisputed helm of his empire, withers as the bull overtakes him.

His eldest son gapes his way, while the youngest laughs
uncontrollably, teetering on the verge of utter hysteria,
blending joyous tears with fake ones, as I...

I revel amongst the chaos.

As it turns out, I'm an incredible actress—and so is
Hayden. After Mom slipped me a snippet of her camcorder
video last night, I listened to it on repeat until I was numb,
lest I give the man who abused my mother any of my real
tears.

Then, I stayed the night at Mei's, said I needed a girls'
night, ensuring Hayden wouldn't try to talk me out of my
plan. If he learned of such a video, he'd fear for my safety
when confronting his father, but I was—and still am—beyond
caring, blinded by a thirst for vengeance. The next morning, I
marched myself into the office and put on a grand show,
baiting Warren into granting me an audience with his board
of directors.

None of which Hayden was supposed to see. No, I cannot
emphasize enough how much I *seriously* wish he hadn't. Now
I'll be mortified about it for the rest of my life, despite never
having been so tempted to knee a man in the groin or vomit
on him as I was during my entire time with Warren.

But the reality is... Hayden *did* see everything. When he
barged into that breakroom, all concerned for my safety and

completely sidelining the fact he had just watched what appeared to be me *selling my body to his father* for trivial accolades, I had to let him in on my plan.

I gave him two choices. Either refrain from joining the meeting, or attend and give a performance.

He sided with witnessing his father's downfall.

Warren bursts to his feet, laden with rage. Bounding toward me, his mouth curves into a vicious frown, spitting words I can't hear over the speakers until he's steps away.

"Turn it off. *Turn it off. Turn it off! TURN IT OFF!*"

He cranes over the front of the podium, eyes murderous and bloodshot and piercing right into mine, his head red like a rocket about to launch off his neck. Even *still*, I can hardly hear him. I just smile brazenly, more than happy to suffer a couple years' worth of hearing damage for this moment, which only proves to deepen his wrinkles and bleach his knuckles a starch white as they clutch the podium's edge.

An inaudible laugh escapes me, watching him search about frantically, his exhales seething through clenched teeth, puffing out his cheeks. He makes for a wall outlet and strips the cord connected to the podium, plunging the conference room into a dreadfully painful silence.

Well, maybe only for himself.

Uncovering their ears, each board member stands like a mannequin in a shop window, not voicing a word. It's so quiet, one could hear a pen drop. In fact, I think I *do*. Somewhere outside, amid the impressive flock of employees huddled around the glass, peering into the fishbowl. Not even *their* lips move, plunging this entire company into a stunned limbo.

Perhaps, there's no reason to gossip. Everyone heard what they heard.

Warren Kingston. Their CEO and Founder.

Blackmailing an innocent woman.

"You little *bitch*. You better wipe that smile off your—"

"Ahh!" Across the room, Hayden doubles over in laughter, smacking the table. He stands beside Elias, who stares out into space and is the only person in the entire room sitting.

Warren whirls around. "Ohhhh, I bet you enjoyed that, didn't you?"

"You're right. I did." Hayden swipes at a tear, amidst his lingering chuckles. "I wish we'd caught it all on tape."

"Well, this is obviously a jab at my reputation," he says, not to Hayden but to his board, puffing his chest out, chin pointed high. "I have nothing to hide. The audio clip is clearly fake."

"Would you like me to play the full video?" I threaten, praying he'll say no. The audio was scarring enough.

Warren pauses, offering me a skeptical look, to which I raise an eyebrow. *Try me.* Straightening his tie, he ushers about the room, a politician campaigning for support.

"And what might that prove? Let me shed some light on the situation for all of you. This young woman—my youngest son's girlfriend—socially engineered her way to the top, gaining an audience with my board, just so she can humiliate me for her own gain. I have no doubt, the minute I adjourn this meeting, she'll be vying for a hefty check. Only then, she will admit to the video's false nature."

I shake my head, watching as he digs himself into a deeper hole. He rounds the table, addressing the other row of members, enunciating his words with the flick of his wrists.

"You see, in this day and age, artificial intelligence knows no bounds. Its capabilities surpass mere text and image generation, stretching into the troubling realms of video manipulation, taking the form of Deepfakes. Yes, I'm sure you've heard, anyone who possesses a speck of technical knowledge and a knack for evil can architect slanderous falsehoods by manipulating voices, even faces—"

"What about the woman in the video?" I interrupt, smirking when his back goes rigid. He swings around, composed, yet, even from across the room, I can still feel the heat of his lethal glare.

"What about her?"

Eyes slot onto me, suddenly flinging me onto center stage of a presidential debate—behind a podium, no less, with an audience fixed behind the confines of a glass wall, who I'm half-convinced deserves a bureaucratic wave. Instead, I square off my shoulders and address the members of the board, as they settle back into their seats, one after the other.

"It's true. Deepfakes are no secret and can prove dangerous in the wrong hands. Public figures—such as Warren, here—are the most likely victims of the crime, largely due to the vast amount of video footage available online, which provides ample data for A.I. learning algorithms..."

From the corner of my eye, I watch Warren's face sink deeper into despair with my every word. Poor guy, going toe-to-toe with me over such a subject. Over any technological topic, for that matter. Above the slump of his drooping shoulders, I catch Hayden's features glowing with pride as I continue.

"But the question still stands—what of the woman in the video? I can assure you, she's no household name and has lived a relatively simple life. There's no online data set on her, which would make fabricating her presence into the video all that more difficult. Furthermore, this woman could personally verify the authenticity of the footage, proving Warren's involvement."

All eyes drift onto Warren, including those behind the glass, awaiting his rebuttal. Although, he appears too dazed to make an attempt. Lips parted. Unblinking. Pale like a ghost. I mean, I don't blame him—even I surprised myself there.

"W-well..." He clears his throat, fumbling for control. "I don't see her here in this room, do you? Unless you're accusing my vice chairwoman or assistant treasurer of—"

"She's in the lobby." I hold up my phone, then bury my head, swiping past the lock screen. "Shall I call her up?" Met with no answer, I tap some more, humming. "Remind me, what floor are we on? Eighty-six?"

I wait... and wait...

"THIS IS AN OUTRAGE!"

There it is.

Huffing and puffing, Warren storms around the room, aimlessly, left and right, back and forth, directing the attention of the crowd outside like a drunken conductor.

"YOU THINK YOU'RE SO CLEVER, HUH?!" he screams to no one in particular, sweat dripping off his brow. *"WELL, GUESS WHAT? THIS BOARD ONLY CARES ABOUT MONEY! YOU THINK THEY GIVE TWO SHITS WHETHER OR NOT I FUCKED MY KID'S SLUTTY TEACHER?! I COULD'VE LINED HER UP WITH HER WHORE FRIENDS AND FUCKED EVERY ONE OF THEM, MARRIED OR NOT, AND THESE ASSHOLES WOULD STILL BE RIGHT HERE THE NEXT MORNING..."*

There's no describing the looks on the board members' faces, including Elias's, as they witness their CEO lose his mind. Except, the longer I study their expressions, the more I recognize shame. So microscopic, I nearly miss it. Perhaps, there's truth to Warren's words—we're in a den riddled with money-hungry honchos.

So, when I catch Hayden's gaze a second time and find it even smugger than before, I simply nod, prompting him to pull out his phone and start tapping away. Enacting phase two. Made possible by the delicious little secret he unveiled in the breakroom that'll make this even sweeter...

"THEY STAGED A COO! THEY..."

Ding. Ding. Ding...

A few board members look to their pockets.

"BOTH OF THEM! SLIMY, ENTITLED BRATS, AFTER MONEY THEY DIDN'T EARN..."

Ding. Ding. Ding...

Hushed whispers skate across the room as they share and point to their phones...

"SUCH A FUCKING EMBARRASSMENT ON THIS FAMILY! UNDESERVING OF SUCH A STRONG LINEAGE! A WASTE OF PRIVILEGED POTENTIAL! A GLARING PIT STAIN ON OUR—"

He halts abruptly, the last of his rambles echoing between the glass, mingled with the growing urgency in the air. The board members shake their heads to one another, hiss beneath their breaths, gesturing to their CEO, until a woman clad in a pristine, ebony two-piece suit bursts to her feet—

Right as Elias peers over his phone at Hayden, both exchanging a look that lingers. Relief outpours from the youngest, while the eldest swims in his pool of understanding, yet surfacing from a pained regret. The sight is something I can't begin to comprehend but will never forget, as it's telling of the most heartfelt of discoveries...

Hayden cares more about his brother than the demise of his father.

The board woman scoffs at Warren. "I thought the whole reason you aren't in your office much is because you oversee movie sets."

He hesitates, before arching a brow. "Yes, that is—"

"He told *me* he was delegating foreign rights," another says.

Warren doubles down, shaking his head. "What are you all looking a—"

"Your work logs." Hayden's voice rakes up his father's spine, to which he can't help but twist the knife. "I sent them to every person on your board—including lower management, which may be why we're amassing quite an audience."

Lips curling with disgust, Warren flicks his gaze toward the glass, only to slither it back to his youngest son. He rounds the table on deliberate steps, until he stares right down at Hayden, arms crossed.

"I don't clock my hours," he challenges.

Hayden smiles up at him. "Oh, but your assistants do."

Warren's expression fractures like glass.

Rising to his feet, reaching heights surpassing Warren, Hayden looks *down* at his father, an inch from his nose, seeping all the air from his lunges—and the room.

"How ironic that you sat me at that tiny desk yourself, assigning me a station that would later prove to be your downfall. I was surprised, too, to discover all the power personal assistants possess. Every email address in the company at my disposal, and every executive's work logs." Hayden snickers in his face. "One click, and I sent the proof you throw all your work onto Elias, your own son, to everyone in the room."

More whispers.

"What do you do all day, hmm?"

Amid the hushed accusations, a little sound escapes Warren.

"Want to know what I think?" He *pokes* him in the chest. "I think you're off doing nothing productive. I rarely smell a whiff of alcohol on you, so you're not an alcoholic. Your eyes don't scream substance abuse, which leaves only one answer." He throws a quick glance down the line of chairs. "Spoiler alert. It's the obvious one."

Fists clenching at his sides, Warren grits out. "And what's that?"

Hayden bites down on a laugh, eyes twinkling with delight. "That you're off being a manwhore." Like scorching steam, blood rises up onto Warren's features, popping veins and flaring his nostrils, when Hayden nears even closer. "Takes one to know one, huh?"

Combusting in a fit of rage, Warren shoves Hayden back into his chair, storming past Elias, who's finally woken up, like an angry funnel cloud, forming far off in the horizon. His father's at a safe distance—for now.

"I AM YOUR CEO!" Warren thrashes his arms through the air, gesturing to his entire board, hair disheveled and surely falling out before our very eyes. *"YOU ABIDE BY MY RULES, WHETHER YOU LIKE THEM OR NOT! I OWN OVER FIFTY PERCENT OF THIS COMPANY'S SHARES! THERE'S NO DETHRONING ME, EVEN IF YOU WANTED TO..."*

I sigh, tuning into his tantrum, but not before executing a crucial step in the third and final phase of my glorious plan.

Send a single text to my mother.

Juliana: *We're ready for her.*

Leaning onto the podium, I close my eyes, listening as Warren throws himself into further hysteria, shaking the glass behind me. I listen and listen, humming along to its beat, until my eyes open by some outside force.

A presence.

Judging by how the board members veer their gazes, I'm not the only one who senses it. Every person in this room stops and stares, anticipating *something* as the crowd of employees parts in two.

That is, everyone but Warren, until...

Even he turns his attention, just as the crowd breaks, revealing a woman of auburn hair and unrivaled authority, who has Warren sinking into a chair that's not even at the head of the table.

Briefcase in hand, Lauren Astor struts through the crowd, flaunting her designer pantsuit with every step, and it's like the world stops breathing, until those perfectly manicured fingernails grace the door handle.

Our family's lawyer, whom I met last night and aided in devising such a plan. Although a bit intimidating at first, Lauren is like all the little angels on my shoulders fused into one person. A compassionate soul who, after hearing my family's story, agreed to take our case on Pro Bono, despite her obscenely high retainer as a senior partner at Astor Associates that specializes in data privacy.

The door seals behind her, caging Warren in with a predator. As she nears him, he shies away, until he's craning his head up at her.

"Do you know who I am?"

"Yes," he says dryly. "I think everyone in this room does. So, get on with it. Why are you here, Lauren? Silicon Avenue must be dreadfully boring as of late, and all the drama surrounding your family must've blown over, for you to waste your time on sexual misconduct allegations with flimsy grounds."

As if he were scum stuck on her stiletto, her gaze descends upon him, while somehow managing to tilt her chin upwards, proudly. A signature move, no doubt.

"We'll see how flimsy a jury thinks that video is, after I call you to the stands." All the color drains from his face. "That's right, this matter will be settled in court. On behalf of the Brooks' family, you are hereby served, for your crimes against Amber Brooks and also her daughter, Juliana—or did you think your egregious copyright infringement on the gaming world's largest stage would go unnoticed?"

"Fine!" He bursts from his chair. *"Serve me,* then. Represent that bitch *and* her daughter." His vicious gaze swings over to me, but it's short-lived, as his aimless stomping picks back up. He breezes past Lauren, who catches my gaze with a wink. *"That's why you came all this way, huh?! Serve me some fucking papers that I'll just hand to my team of lawyers—"*

"No."

He stops in a random spot, chest heaving.

"Your lawyers have already received the papers. I'm here —in this room—for an entirely different reason. Of a more... personal courtesy, if you will."

"Fucking lawyers, always speaking in riddles. What personal courtesy?"

"Aiding in a transition of power."

Several board members perk up.

Warren hesitates... "What the hell do you mean by that?"

She only smiles, her teeth blinding between her red lipstick. "Exactly what you think."

The room stills, awaiting Warren's implosion, except... his

roar never comes. Only a snicker. Quiet and harmless sounding, like a comedian winning over his chuckle. And then another. Until they're pouring out of him like waves, tears stinging his eyes, as he pounds the table, doubling over the oaken slab in laughter.

"WHEW! Which university handed you that law degree, again? I think you may want to consider getting a refund. Sorry to break it to you, sweetie, but I own over fifty percent shares. Which means—let me put it plainly for you—there's no voting me out as CEO, no matter how much they despise me."

Lauren waits out his laughter, unimpressed. "Thank you for that enlightening summary, but you forgot one slim detail."

"Sure, sure. And what's that?" he drawls, actually *rolling his eyes* in a board meeting.

"The board has the power to relinquish your duties as CEO, if they elect a Kingston heir, with an eighty percent majority vote. In this case, one of your two sons."

One by one, eyes slide down the table, to the near-identical brothers seated at one another's side. Hayden smiles, proudly—not back their way.

But at Elias.

Warren follows their gazes. "No, no... that's not true."

Lauren only shakes her head, chuckling.

"Tell them," he warns.

"Tell them what?" she sing-songs. "The truth? Let me recap. The board may initiate a vote at any ti—"

"DON'T FUCKING LIE!" He storms toward her, not slowing his pace, intending to intimidate her, only to grind to a halt an inch before colliding with her as she stands her ground. "You have no bases to—"

"Actually, I do." She throws her briefcase on the table. Unclasping the hooks, she slaps down a hefty packet on the table. "Check the board's bylaws yourself. Section fifty-two, article six. In fact, why don't you all?" More packets slide across the oak, one landing between Hayden and Elias.

Grumbling up a storm, Warren tears through the packet, only for his shoulders to crumble... then harden back to their regular steel in seconds. "This is a fucking lie," he seethes, as the packets get passed around. "A fabricated, false document aimed to—"

Hayden bolts to his feet, sending his chair soaring behind him. "All in favor of electing Elias as CEO, please rise!"

Gasps ring out, not just in the conference room, but from behind the glass. For a moment, none dare to move, earning a wicked grin from Warren. "That's right. You're all so righteous until your profits are at stake. No one wants to take the risk on an untested young—"

A member rises, the woman in the ebony suit. Her gaze is defiant.

Warren scoffs. "I've always known you've hated me, Gloria. Well, guess what? No one ever sides with your proposals, and they won't start now—"

Another member stands. A man who avoids his stare completely.

"That's just great, Bill—"

And another. Then another. So quickly Warren doesn't have time for a snarky comment. One after the other, members rise to their feet confidently, earning *cheers* from outside the glass, as Elias just sits there, stunned, crumbling into his seat with the most sincere look on his face, staring down the long line of members.

All standing unanimous.

Mind blown, still standing behind the safety of my podium, I watch as the glass rattles amid the roaring crowd, prying snickers from those inside the conference room. Employees jump for joy, laughing and slapping their hands against the glass. You'd think it's New Year's Eve or something.

Warren must not be one for parties, because the sight absolutely blows a fuse with him, to a level I didn't know he could reach at this point. His face is impossibly red. Hair sticking straight up like a mad scientist. And his feet clomp hard enough to puncture right through the carpet as he bellows at the top of his lungs, throwing the biggest of all hissy fits.

All while I get the most comical view, from my vantage point. I watch it all, see it all coming, almost in slow motion.

The unhinged tirade. Tearing the paper packets, flinging them into the air. Spitting gut-wrenching words at *both* of his sons. And the security team splitting through the crowd, bursting through the door, before *tackling* Warren.

"Get off me!" He writhes against the ground, his stomach spilling below his collared shirt, rising more with his every movement. *"GET OFF ME!"*

"Stop resisting," they order calmly, repeating several times, to no avail, before slamming his cheek into the ground, bundling his wrists behind his back.

Slowly—*oh-so very slowly*—Elias rounds the table, taking his seat at the head, right above the whole scene.

"Tell them to get off me!" Warren screeches, looking up at his son, when metal against metal clinks through the air.

The guards pause and look to the man seated on the throne, waiting for orders...

Elias leans back, crosses his feet at the ankles, the soles of his feet two inches from Warren's face. He struggles angrily, as his son utters the first command of his reign.

"Cuff him."

Squeals erupt from outside, and they only rage on, combusting into hysterical fits, as the guards cuff and haul Warren to his feet, dragging him until he abandons his defiance and uses his legs. On their way out the door, Elias stands, giving one last command...

"He's never to set foot in our lobby, ever again."

When our room explodes in their own form of celebration, I bound toward Hayden's contagious laughter, entranced by its call, until...

Outside grows mysteriously quiet.

Curious, I swivel on my heels, only to discover a scene that has me rushing out the door, pushing through the path in the crowd, and arriving at the end...

My mother stares Warren down.

Donning her usual getup—jeans and a colorful blouse— Amber looks at Warren, as if he's *nothing*. She wears no smile. Offers no smug expression. In return, he meets her gaze unwillingly, every muscle tense with the horrid realization of who's to blame for the loss of his throne, his titles, *his power*.

For perhaps the first time in his life, Warren has nothing to say.

But Amber does.

"I warned you not to mess with my family."

FORTY-FIVE

HAYDEN

YESTERDAY WAS A FEVER DREAM.

After the crowd dispersed and our father was far from the premises, Elias went into a state of shock. His new position hadn't sunk in yet, but that didn't stop his board from swiftly taking over. They provided him counsel. Scheduled meetings with department heads. And whatever other boring things coincide with becoming America's largest entertainment corporation's new CEO at the ripe age of twenty-eight.

I didn't stay to watch it all, and instead went to lunch with Juliana, Amber, and their lawyer, Lauren, the latter of whom footed the entire bill, thanking us for the "most entertaining ten minutes of her career." She even bought us a round of drinks, ones we literally *toasted* to my father's ruin on the grounds that it was just the beginning.

It was toxic, and I loved it.

In fact, as I stroll through the cubicles for perhaps the last time, I realize the entire office would've loved the toast, too, and have maybe already clinked their own glasses.

There's no mistaking the upbeat presence in the office. Not

just on this floor, but in the lobby, the elevators, and undoubtedly across all one hundred and five floors. Employees smile brighter. Hang over their cubicles, chatting. Some even share doughnuts and other sweet treats.

I know gossip travels fast in an office setting, but this is on a whole new level. I have no doubt videos of my father's dramatic exit are spreading through this company like wildfire, because yesterday, the crowd of spectators did more than just watch security drag my father from the conference room. They wore radiant smiles, whipped out their phones, and recorded the scene all the way down to the lobby.

Their enthusiasm toward his ousting proves my father's cruelty stretched beyond just our family and makes me wonder what other atrocities he inflicted. I may never know what he did to garner such a reputation with his staff, but judging from his transgressions against Amber, I don't want to find out.

In the breakroom, when Juliana told me the hell my father put Amber through... it was another nail in coffin, split right through the final one already there. I couldn't watch from the sidelines when he met his reckoning. I had to be in that board meeting. Not just for my own gratification, but Juliana's.

Warren deserved every light we shined on him. Amber's audio snippet. His pitiful work logs. His poor understanding of his company's bylaws. The board turning on him, elevating Elias to power. All of it.

For so long, he had me believing Amber, the woman who practically raised me, willingly entertained his affair for years. During and after my parents' divorce, I fought the urge to blame her by reminding myself Amber was just one of many affairs for my father, while simultaneously seeking her love, a substitute for my own mother's absence.

More often than not, the task proved challenging, at best, which means... learning the truth must've been absolutely heart wrenching for Juliana and Jeremy, who were just as clueless as I was.

Too bad Jeremy was swamped with work and couldn't join the celebratory lunch yesterday. Juliana was glowing with a sense of justice, something her brother would've shared had he been there. Although, perhaps his absence was fortunate—or intentional.

Aside from sending the occasional text, outlining in grave detail each and every thing that'll happen to me if I hurt his little sister, Jeremy hasn't spoken to me much. Yesterday would've been his first time seeing us together, since finding out about our feelings toward each other. Even though nothing is official—*yet*—the lunch could've still turned ugly. Whether we're in a public setting or not, there's no predicting how Jeremy will act, when the time inevitably comes.

Amber, on the other hand... Despite my tendency to cause trouble as a child, I must've done *something* right in her eyes, because not only did she welcome my affection toward her daughter, she didn't even seem surprised.

Trust me, I'm still counting my blessings.

Near the top of that list is what I'm doing today—breaking my corporate handcuffs. Sure, I've only worn them for a couple of months, but they hurt my wrists.

As I approach my workstation, I anticipate Doris's verbal slashing, only for my shoulders to droop lower and lower with every silent step, until I'm looming over my tiny desk, finding hers empty. Elias's office is dark, too, a sight rarer than a deserted Central Park on a sunny Saturday.

I sigh, slapping my moving tub down on my desk, feeling stupid the second I do. Why did I bring a box? I can't have over three items in these drawers. A sketch book and a pouch stuffed with graphite pencils, charcoal sticks and a straight-edge. Other than that... maybe a name tag, but I'll just leave that behind for—

Like an army closing in from the distance, a subtle rumble vibrates through the floor, growing heavier, alongside the sounds of synchronized steps. I whip my head, as others in the room do the same, before a fleet of suits rounds a corner, trailing one man.

Elias.

Bursting with pride, I watch my brother delegate the group with his chin pointed high. His lips move on some silent command, directing a minion away from the flock, bustling in a hurry, just as another joins and awaits orders. I inhale sharply when I spot Doris keeping pace at his side, clipboard in hand, as always.

Gosh, when did I get so attached?

As they draw near, oblivious of my existence, my brother's voice elevates in strength.

"... the quarterly performance overview must extend to the accounting department and heavily focus on middle management." A woman bolts from the group, disappearing through the cubicles. "Regarding the marketing department, our recent decline in sales among younger demographics calls for a bottom-up approach. Inform the director to expand upon their internship program and to prioritize recruiting talent with fresh perspectives." Another runner takes off. "And as for—"

Catching my eye, Elias stops abruptly, causing his corporate entourage to halt in unison—okay, kinda creepy. "Head over to Conference A and start the presentations without me."

And just like that, they're off, marching like little green army men, except for Doris.

"Take notes in my absence," he instructs her, approaching my desk with a serious expression. "I'll be there shortly."

But Doris doesn't budge, her gaze flicking to me then wandering toward the group and back again. She thrums her nails over her clipboard, before scampering over.

"Mr. Kingston?"

"Yes?" He turns at the foot of my desk.

"Shall I push Marco's supply-chain presentation to last? I presume he has some questions he'd prefer you answer directly."

Elias hums. "Yes, go ahead."

"Perfect." As she turns to leave, she hesitates, side-glancing at me once more, noticing the box on my desk. "I see you're moving on."

Nerves bundle within me. I've never quit a job—never even *had* one before. What do I say? Farewell? It was a pleasure? Honestly, it wasn't. Doris isn't to blame, but it's the truth. This isn't the place for me, even if I had a shiny office like Elias, so I can't really thank her for all her valuable lessons. I was a terrible assistant and certainly a dreadful partner to work alongside.

So, I don't sugarcoat any lies. "I am," I say, offering a genuine smile, despite anticipating her snarky comment, possibly along the lines of *good riddance*. Except... nothing of the sort comes. In fact, she returns the smile—something I didn't know her lips could do.

"Well... best wishes for your next chapter." She nods, before trailing after the group.

Elias blinks, stunned.

"What's that look for?"

"I, uhh... I'm just surprised, is all. You got Doris all teary-eyed over leaving."

I snort. "Yeah, right. I said two words to her. Plus, she wouldn't have even come over, if it weren't for her question."

"Maybe, but I can't recall a time when she said goodbye to *any* of her junior assistants on their last day. Not even one girl who worked under her for two years."

"Seriously?"

"Mhmm."

"God, she's just ruthless, isn't she?"

"Yep. But that's the kind of person I need under me to do this job. Or..." He winces. "My new job," he corrects. *"And* my old job. I couldn't do either without Doris."

"How does it feel being the big dog, huh?" I nudge him. "One day in, and I'd say you're already up to speed."

When he shrugs, I nudge him harder, giving his shoulder a shove. A Kingston being modest? Not possible. "Come onnnnn. You know it's true. Walking in here, you looked straight out of a movie."

A smile creeps across his lips. "Okay, fine. Maybe being CEO is going to my head, even more than being Director of Finance did."

We both glance at his old office, shrouded in darkness. When I shift my focus, I find him wearing a serious expression again. "So..." I lower my voice. "You took Dad's office, then?"

"Temporarily. I'm having this one remodeled."

I raise an eyebrow. "Really? What for? I can't imagine anything was out of date."

He shifts on his feet, surely debating his words, until he sighs. "Look, Hayden... I came to say I'm sorry for the derby —for everything." Surprise knocks the wind from my lungs when I catch the remorse in his eyes as he continues. "These past few months, I shouldn't have treated you how I did. I know you were only trying to help me."

As he looks away, his rare sniffles prompt forgiveness from me. "Elias, it's okay, I know—"

"No." I'm met with his hand. "It's not okay."

Oh, Elias. Stubborn, as always. I walk into his field of vision, holding back emotions when I see his teary eyes. "You're my brother. Of course, I forgive you." A shudder rattles through him, enough that I pull him in for a hug. He stiffens on contact, his arms loose at his sides. "Come on, Elias. It's a hug. Ever given one before? It's a two-way thing."

His wet chuckle sounds in my ear, followed by more sniffles, as he squeezes his arms around me. "Thank you," he murmurs. "For what you did yesterday. I never would've thought Dad would..." His sentence trails off.

"His work logs surprised me, too." I retreat, finding him more composed. "He should've never put so much pressure on you. The way he used you, made you pick up all his slack, it's sick and pushed you to do things I don't think you would've ever done."

Shame clouds his features as his gaze strays to the floor. "I know..." he whispers. "I want to stop. I'm *going* to get clean."

I let loose a breath, relief washing over me, but it can't extinguish the sliver of doubt I feel. Although his intentions may be truthful, getting clean—it's easier said than done, and now he's taken on an even more stressful position. There's no convincing him to let it go, not when he's prepared his whole life for it. And in a way... I don't *want* to convince him. He's meant to be here, at this company.

I place a palm on his arm. "I'll help any way I can."

"Thank you—I mean it."

When silence settles between us, I wave a hand casually, hoping it'll splice clean through the tension in the air. "As for yesterday, I just thought if you're going to work yourself to the bone, you might as well get all the credit, whether you're CEO or not."

"Actually, about that."

My jaw drops. "You're quitting?"

"What? No!" he barks, a laugh sputtering from his mouth. "Do you think I've lost my mind?"

There he is.

I match his cocky grin. "What, then?"

He looks around suspiciously, before patting me on the chest. "Get this..." He leans in, whispering in my ear. "Being CEO is easy." More laughter.

I roll my eyes, jerking from him. "Okay, now you're head's inflated like a balloon."

"I'm serious! I hardly have anything new to learn. Dad already had me doing all his work, things I didn't even realize weren't part of the Director of Finance's responsibilities. And now that we've elected Shonda as the new DOF, I'm walking on easy street! I have one job, not two."

I blink.

Elias. Fucking. Kingston.

Perhaps the only business professional in New York City who would equate being the Chief Executive Officer of a mega-corporation with strolling down easy street. Honestly, his words are a little disheartening, knowing the challenges he endured to develop such a strong work ethic, but...

They're also brimming with hope.

My heart thunders with anticipation, as I gesture to his dark office. "Is that why you're remodeling?"

He nods. "That's right. No more pull-out couch."

Tension falls off my shoulders in one big clump. But wait —"What about the closet?"

"Yes, that'll be gone, too."

"Oh, thank God." I slump over, dramatically. "Maybe you have a fighting chance, after all..." I wink. "If you dial back on those screaming phone calls. I mean, Doris can stomach how thin your walls are, but I don't think that's the case for the rest of the floor."

A curse shoots from his lips as his cheeks stain with embarrassment. "I really wish you didn't hear all that." He pinches the bridge of his nose. "Yes, yes, I'll work on that. No more scaring the employees."

"I'm sure they'll appreciate that."

We share a smile until his fades, his gaze dropping to my box. "You know I'll always have a place for you here, Hayden. A *real* job with opportunity to grow and move up in the company. Not the hands-off bullshit Dad put you up to."

Now it's my turn to laugh. "Come on, Elias. Be real. I'd rather hike a mountain than sit in on another stuffy board meeting."

He smirks. "Thought I'd try."

"Don't get me wrong, I appreciate it, especially now that my trust fund's a goner. But don't worry, I've got a decent amount saved up."

He lifts a brow. "Why do you say that?"

"About my trust fund? It's just the truth. You think Dad will continue to support it after what happened yesterday?" I leave out the part where Elias's trust is surely safe, not wanting to tear a rift between us, when we're already mending one. Warren wouldn't jeopardize this company, his legacy, by cutting off the future of our family.

Elias shakes his head. "Didn't you hear? Dad will stand trial. Multiple cases, I'd guess, after hearing that audio clip."

"So?"

"In the case against Amber—which I doubt he'll win, not after hearing the evidence and seeing who her lawyer is—the trial will revolve heavily around his image, which is bad enough already. Messing with his child's trust fund, especially one who has close ties with the prosecution, will only make him look more guilty."

I immediately start on my rebuttal, only for a tiny sound to escape and my mouth to snap back shut. Huh, that actually makes a lot of sense. It'll probably take some time and several months' worths of bank deposits to sink in, but... I guess that's one less thing I have to fret about.

"Wow," is my only response, to which he purses his lips in a precise way that says *that's why I get paid the big bucks.*

"Well…" He pats my box. "I'd stay around to chat longer, but Doris might kill me."

I snicker. He's not wrong, there.

As he turns to leave, I snatch his arm, earning his attention. I'm not quite sure of my next words, or why I stopped him, so we stare into each other's eyes for a moment. His, a mirror of my own, but swirling with clouds that are already beginning to clear, ones I desperately hope never return.

"I know you'll lead this company in the right direction."

His teeth sink into his lip, stopping the tremble. "Thank you," he croaks out. "That means a lot." Several heartbeats pass, until he whips around, aiming for the conference room, just to stop abruptly and face me once more. "Oh, and Hayden?"

Box in hand, I lift my head. "Yes?"

"You'll find your way."

Like a crater splashing into a cool lake, his words reverberate into my gut, their innuendo understood instantly.

In life.

I'll find my way in life.

If he would've said that to me months ago, I wouldn't be so sure. But now... now my mind wanders to Juliana, musing on the immense strength she showed in that boardroom, and the patience and love she's given me over these past months. By her side, I'm a better man. Anyone could see that. Even my father—maybe that's why he wanted to take her from me. But little does he know.

No one will.

"I already have."

FORTY-SIX
JULIANA

ALL PUBLICITY IS GOOD PUBLICITY.

I've heard the old marketing adage countless times. Everyone has. Although, I never gave much thought to the saying, and always dismissed it as sounding more catchy than true.

Take, for example, the idea of one of New York City's wealthiest men plagiarizing the game I've worked five years on and flaunting it as his own on gaming's biggest stage. That would be straight out of my nightmares... and crawled into reality three weeks ago.

Now, I should be screwed, right? I mean, without my pending lawsuit, my game should be in the gutter. No one wants to play a game surrounded by controversy and ever-growing propaganda on internet forums, where allegations of who stole the game from who are being thrown left and right... *right?*

Wrong.

One-hundred-and-ten-thousand-percent wrong.

Cosmic Kitty Defense has been soaring—and I mean

soaring—on the mobile app charts to levels that make me want to happy cry, then anxiously sad cry, then vomit into a nearby toilet, only to circle back again.

Truth be told, imposter syndrome is a bitch who regularly flirts with the devils on my shoulder, especially after Dream-Scape reached out for an indie feature a few days ago—this time, for next year's convention. Determined not to make the same mistake twice, I've never responded to an email faster with an enthusiastic *YES!*

Though, I keep waiting for the comedown, a dip in sales, but the surge shows no signs of letting up. I've even seen people walking the streets playing my game, or while they're riding the subway seated two rows ahead of me. *With my own two eyes,* I've seen all this.

Pinching me isn't the right way to wake me from this dream. Frickin' slap me. Dump a bucket of water over my head, the precise temperature of a glacier, because this *cannot* be my life.

Would Cosmic Kitty Defense have achieved such popularity without the tragic events at DreamScape? Would Pixie-Plays testing out my game in front of fans have been enough to jumpstart this type of avalanche effect on its own? Maybe. Maybe not. There's no answering that, for certain, but I do know one thing.

Even though I would never, ever, under any circumstances, thank Warren Kingston for anything, I almost feel like I should—in the most smug, backhanded way possible. Not just for concocting a twisted plan that blew up in his face, and for making such a dramatic scene while being dragged out of his company that videos are now plastered across gossip news, but also preemptively for the hefty check he will write me following the verdict of our civil court case. And that's not just speculation, as Lauren has assured me...

Warren is toast.

His image. His dignity. Everything, thanks to the mountains of evidence we have against him: from those in Dream-Scape's live audience who recognized his trickery, and testimonies from my fans who have been with me since the beginning, to the digital footprints left behind on my laptop from that malicious flash drive. Hopefully, he'll end up behind bars after the criminal case, though Lauren mentioned those tend to drag on longer than civil cases.

So yes, even if I wasn't destined to become my family's first millionaire by ways of the judicial system, I may just achieve the title solely from a cutesy, most-cherished mobile game.

While these past few months may have been unconventional and chaotic, I couldn't be more grateful for the way things turned out. Foremost, for how close I've gotten with Hayden and the unique struggles we overcame together, but it's everything else, too. Helping my mom find her path toward justice, being pushed out of my comfort zone, quitting my awful job, watching my indie developer career flourish...

And getting the keys to my new apartment.

"Your view is amazing," Hayden sighs, for perhaps the fifth time since our arrival. Meandering along the wall of solid glass, his loafers echo in the empty space, and paired with that long overcoat, he looks like he owns the building.

He's not wrong. The view here is infinitely better than the one my last apartment offered—just staring straight into a brick wall, but... "You *do* realize you live in a penthouse that has an unobstructed view of Central Park, right?"

Passing the concrete column at the corner where the glass

walls meet, he hums, somehow contemplating the obvious fact. He swipes a hand through his wavy locks lazily, then sinks it back into his chino pockets, soaking in the view, as do I—though, I'm not talking about the skyline.

"I do, but there's no comparing our views of the Hudson."

I blink...

While both landmarks are highly coveted in New York City and nearly impossible to view from the same apartment, Hayden's penthouse is an exception, because of its staggering height. Certain rooms offer an amazing view of the Hudson. In fact, his studio is one of them.

"You're just blowing smoke up my bum."

He flashes me a grin, pearly-white, playful, the kind that has my knees wobbling, a feeling I pray time never desensitizes. "Now, why on earth would I do such a thing? Look around, baby. You clearly have impeccable taste when it comes to real estate."

I hold up a finger. "You mean, *Mei* has great taste."

This apartment comes with a lot of perks, namely that my best friend lives next door—literally my next-door neighbor on this exact floor. We're perfectly situated for movie nights, gossip sessions, and catching up on her new job working at a museum as a gallery assistant. Quite the upgrade over bossy Meghan, I must say.

But there are other upgrades, too, aside from the obvious things like having a dishwasher, a washer and dryer set, and a bathroom that's not *in* the kitchen. The apartment is high enough to drown out the street-level noises, and with two bedrooms, there's ample space for both a bedroom and an office.

As for the apartment building, not only are there amenities like a gym, co-working spaces, and elevators—yes, elevators, plural—capable of accommodating more than two people, it's also ten blocks from Hayden's complex. Which brings us to the most intentional of all the perks...

The opportunity to take things slow.

We talked about it, days after the commotion following the board meeting died down. Our feelings haven't changed —if anything, they've grown stronger—but that's just it. We *love* each other. That's something that doesn't come around often in life with another person, if ever. Now tag on the little fact I've never been in a relationship before... that's a lot of pressure.

What if Hayden and I—we're it? He's the only one for me, and I'm the one for him? *Forever.* Then that would mean this is the only romantic relationship I have to explore in this life-time. So, I want to do it right. No shortcuts. No skipping mile-stones, ones I can hardly name from lack of experience, which is why we haven't put a label on anything yet.

I want to wonder when he will ask me to be his girlfriend. Will it be on our third *real* date? The fourth or the fifth? And as the relationship progresses, how will it feel to cross that line and move in together? Not pressured by a contract, but because we love each other and can't stand the minutes apart.

That's what I want.

Hayden took some convincing, especially once the movers arrived for my stuff. He said if it was up to him, he'd lock me up in his penthouse so he can have his way with me, to which I—much to the dismay of literally every heterosexual woman in existence—told the billionaire's son he would do no such thing.

Begrudgingly, he agreed to take things slow on the stipu-lation we remain exclusive to one another, which I found quite amusing. Not for the obvious reason you might think—

that he's a reformed playboy, and all. No, I found the idea funny, as it was unnecessary, because label or not, we belong to each other.

Exclusivity comes with the territory.

"Fine," he says, amused, as he watches me approach the wall of glass, stopping at a safe distance. "Maybe Mei deserves some credit, but I saw those nightstands you picked out. They're fancier than any I've seen."

I glance at my bedroom, through the door left partially open. Inside, next to the pearly-white bed frame Hayden bought me the day I moved into his penthouse, are two matching nightstands. With an antique flair, they stand on delicate brass legs that complement their handles. Positioned proudly on my side of the bed is Mei's perfect vase, having finally found its worthy spot in my bedroom.

"I splurged. Consider them my house-warming gift to myself." Even though I found the refurbished pair at an estate sale, they were still two-hundred dollars each—*after* I haggled the price down. They're a luxury I could've never afforded months ago.

Turning back, I'm weightless as I study the Hudson from this height, but I regain my footing, only to wobble all over again when a warm presence envelops my backside. Steady arms loop around me, the fleece of Hayden's coat tickling my skin.

"So, you *have* put your money toward decorating, after all. Now you'll let me pay for the rest?"

I tense, meaning to turn around and argue, but he locks me into place, chuckling.

"No, Hayden. You already went overboard with your gift." In the window's reflection, I catch the ginormous flatscreen leaning against the wall, still in its box. "Just one is plenty."

"Well, what ever am I going to do about the other gifts I ordered? They're nonrefundable."

My jaw drops, lost for words. *Nonrefundable?! What a liar! Is that even a thing in this day and age?*

"It's nothing crazy, don't you worry."

"Hayden..." I warn. "What did you order?"

"Just some small stuff."

"Like?"

He hums. "Oh, you know. The usual stuff. A dining table set."

"Wha —"

"And barstools... *And* a new couch, which may or may not have come with a coffee table. I can't recall. Honestly, Jules, it's nothing to fluster yourself with. Think of it as one step above buying you some wineglasses."

"Hayden!" I screech. "We talked about this. I already have a new wardrobe, thanks to you—most of which I can't even fit in my new closet. You can't go off and slap down the funds to furnish my whole apartment."

"Oh, sure I can."

Gosh! The ego of this man.

I squirm to no use, his grasp growing tighter, until I give up and whine, "What about taking things slow?"

Soft lips brush my ear, skating a shiver up my spine. "This *is* me taking it slow," he murmurs. "You're the girl I'm desperate to impress, baby. Of course, I'm going to shower you in gifts."

My toes curl, teeth sinking into my lower lip on a giggle. *How is this my life?*

Flashing me a smile in the glass's reflection, he squeezes. "Does that sound alright with you?"

"Why do I get the feeling my answer won't change much?"

Swinging to my other ear, he whispers, "Because it won't."

I bat his arm, giggling some more, as his contagious baritone mingles with mine, chuckling over the—

Hayden stiffens behind me, his arms going slack, causing my laughter to die out as I spot what he's looking at—or should I say, *who* he sees, standing there—in the glass's reflection.

Jeremy.

My heart lurches with excitement, yet quells with anxiety. Jeremy hasn't seen us together, and if his reaction at Dream-Scape is anything to go by, then this might not bode well.

I whirl around as Hayden puts considerable distance between us, something that immediately irks me.

"Hey, Jeremy!" I say, way too chipperly for the way my brother looks between the two of us, his eyes spelling out the word *murder* every time they touch Hayden. I plaster on a smile. "I didn't hear you come in."

More silence.

Sweat nicking my brow, I clear my throat, trying again. "Oh my gosh, is that an espresso machine?!" I gasp, the sound all but genuine, when I recognize the upscale brand on the side of the box he carries, a bright red bow pinned at the top.

Color returns to Jeremy's face as he focuses on me—*thank God.* "Of course, it is. I thought the color would go great with your dishware."

"Awww, you shouldn't have." I give him a side-hug. "I know that brand. You didn't have to spend so much."

"Nonsense." His voice rumbles against me. "Anything for my little sister."

Oh, no. I hold back a sigh, watching him stare down Hayden, who's paler than a ghost and can't even meet his gaze for a split second. *Okay... maybe I should let them sort things out.*

"I'll take this to the kitchen."

I grab the box, forcing a smile that slicks right off my lips, as I round a corner. Then, I take languid steps, all the way to the kitchen. One Mississippi, two Mississippi, three... until I'm standing where my barstools soon will, unboxing my espresso machine with the urgency of a snail, taking another minute or so to appreciate the view.

That should do it.

Humming merrily, I retrace my steps, rounding a blind corner. "Wow, it's gorgeous, Jer! You couldn't have picked a better—"

I skid to a halt. *Oh, for criminy's sakes!*

In dead silence, in the *exact* spots I left them, Jeremy folds his arms across his chest, his eyes shooting bullets at Hayden, who gnaws on his lower lip so hard, I'm surprised there's any skin left.

To Hell with the nice act.

"Have you two said *anything* to each other?!"

When I don't receive any form of a response, I scoff, stepping right between the two of them. "Hellooooo..." I wave a hand, earning Jeremy's attention. "Good, you didn't fall asleep standing up, I see. How about using some words, shall we? How does that sound?"

Pursing my lips, I move over, then raise an eyebrow at Jeremy's stubborn will, a teacher scolding a student.

He sighs dramatically, looking elsewhere. "Hey."

Jesus H. Christ.

Well, luckily Hayden has impeccable social skills, so I'm sure he'll—

"Hey," Hayden greets the floor, an obvious tremble in his tone—and in his knees. He's like a shaking chihuahua moments away from standing in a yellow puddle of his own making.

"Are you guys serious right now?"

Crickets.

Un-be-lievable.

"Hey!" I snap my fingers an inch from Jeremy's nose, catching his eye. "So, this was your grand plan, after I admitted to having feelings for your best friend? To just cut ties and never speak with him again?"

"Ohh, we've spoken since then. Over text."

My shoulders release some tension. "Good, good. That's a start. It was constructive, then?" I smile, my gaze ping-ponging between them, until I spot the shadows casting along Hayden's features. *"Jeremy,"* I warn when I see his lips twitching.

"Don't worry, Sis. They were very civil, considerate conversations, and I've been meaning to catch up with Hayden here, my good buddy ol' pal, in person. I just had to take a few weeks to... blow off some steam, is all."

I blink, studying his crooked grin.

"Let me see the texts."

He snickers. "Juliana, I said don't worry—"

My hand slashes through the air, palm up. "Give me your damn phone." As I hold his stare, I anticipate a sigh, but his amusement only grows as he slips a hand into his pocket, brings up the messages, and passes it over.

Finally. Now we can get to the bottom of this—

My jaw freefalls to the floor, the instant I see the first string of text.

Jeremy: *Did you know I used to box in high school? I'm*

thinking of picking up the sport again. Maybe we can spar some-time. No gloves, of course.

"How the hell is that civil?!"

His lips tug at the corners. "Check the others. I think they were more helpful in getting my point across."

Skeptical, I read another.

Jeremy: *Just so we're clear. If you mess around with other girls while you're with my sister, I got a metal bat with your Bugatti's name on it.*

My heart contracts, as I scroll to see the rest of the text. *Awww, that's actually kind of touching. A little violent but—*

Jeremy: *... and I'll cut your balls off.*

"Jeremy!"

A laugh bursts from his lips. "Which one are you at?! Tell me, tell me. Oh, I got it! Is it the one about arson?"

My eyes bulge. ARSON?! They had a conversation that resorted to FIRE??? I scroll through, not believing my ears, except... wait a minute... hold on, that can't be...

"Why is it only you sending messages...? And why are they so frequent?" I scroll farther, adjusting my glasses at varying lengths down my nose, as if they might provide some insight into such madness. Every day, there's a new text with no response. Sometimes three or more.

Jeremy: *I've got my eye on you. If I hear you're playing games with my sister's feelings, I'll...*

"Oh my god," I mumble, swiping to the next.

Jeremy: *Just know this. If you're pressuring my sister into anything she's not comfortable with, I'll take a little night drive over to that penthouse of yours and...*

I shake my head. "Jesus, that's uncalled for."

Jeremy: *If I find out you ever lay a finger on my sister, I'll make you scream like a—*

"JEREMY BROOKS!"

His hysteria bellows through the open space, tears stinging his eyes. "I'm sorry—*oh!*—I'm sorry, that's just too funny. Look at him!" He points to Hayden, who's still in a fear-locked state.

I shove his phone into his chest. "Well, no wonder he's scared shitless!"

Anger simmers in my belly as I watch my brother wipe those tears, battling an onslaught of enjoyment at Hayden's expense. "That's just great, Jer. Instead of sitting down and talking with me over your discomfort, you harass your best friend and forbid him to date me, like I'm some child and have no say in the—"

"I didn't forbid anything."

I suck in a breath, hearing the same reaction behind me. "What?"

"Where in those texts did I say Hayden couldn't date you? Or that I disapprove?"

A little sound escapes me. *Nowhere.*

He focuses on Hayden, his expression still hard as stone. "The point of the texts was simple. I'm just letting him know what's coming his way if he slips up with you."

"Uh-uhm..." I falter, studying the hesitation on Hayden's face, the hope in his eyes, as he gapes at his friend. "I-I don't understand. So... you *do* approve?"

"Of course I do, Juliana. Hayden loves you."

Out of the corner of my eye, Hayden stumbles back, as if physically struck. And it's all I can do to just watch and stare, hand covering my mouth, words beyond me, as Jeremy approaches his best friend. His steps are hesitant at first, as if he anticipates receiving his own well-deserved verbal lashing, but then, in unison, they spring forward and embrace in a bear hug.

"I can't believe it. You... believe me?" His jaw drops, slightly agape, earning pats on his back, which are more like heavy *thuds* that rock his body.

"Yes, yes."

"What the hell, man?! Why'd you—"

"Oh, come on. You really thought I wouldn't give you a stare-down? What better way to make sure my point sticks?"

"What?! I think you took it far enough already!"

Another wave of thunderous back pats, mutual this time, as their laughter fills the air, harmonizing just like it did when we were kids.

"But Jeremy... I still don't understand. What did I do that convinced you I loved your sister?"

I smile, warmth tingling my toes.

"You should be asking what you *didn't* do."

"Huh?"

"Hayden, you haven't gone to a nightclub in two months."

I freeze, playing back those words, studying Hayden as he seemingly does the same, stiff like a board in my brother's arms. Is that right? The infamous playboy of my childhood, the heartbreaker of New York City, abdicated his title from the moment I set foot in his penthouse, beyond the conditions set forth in our agreement?

That can't be true.

Except, when Hayden looks over his shoulder, fixing those dreamy-blue eyes on me...

I know it is.

"HAYDEN, I'm serious. You *really* don't have to paint that one. It belongs in the trash."

"What? Nonsense. This is your best mug yet."

I grimace, watching him swivel it on the stand, showcasing every one of its unintentional ridges and bumps. Clad in an apron that matches my own, Hayden sits on a stool, hunched over while cinching his eyebrows tightly in concentration, brushing dollops of paint across my lopsided creation. With his magnificent art studio as a backdrop, it's like Leonardo da Vinci traded his primed canvas for a slab of driftwood.

Slapping a chunk of clay in my pottery wheel, I ease the mound to the very center, praying it sticks this time. "That's what you said about the last one—and the one before that."

"Exactly. You're improving."

I shoot him a look. "Ohhh, am I now?"

"You are!" His front teeth sink into his lip, stopping its tremble.

Despite Hayden's poor attempt at sparing my nonexistent

ego, unfortunately, I have eyes, and they can see the long row of prototypes lined up on the table beside him just fine. Somehow, their progression worsens over time, each mug sporting larger indents and more cracks than the previous.

Which is the complete opposite case of Hayden's artistic mastery, which coats my mugs in scenes of wildflowers, orange-and-red ombre sunsets, kaleidoscopes of abstract shapes, and enchanted forests like something out of *Wizard of Oz* or *Alice in Wonderland.* All right there, next to his own line of pottery. Vases, dishes, mugs, candleholders. Beautiful and perfectly symmetrical.

Even though he picked up pottery just last week.

I don't know what possessed him to put such care into mine, or to carve out a space for me in his studio, right by the window facing the Hudson with a view ten-times that of my apartment's, no matter what he claims. I'm a lost cause, whether he hires a teacher for me or not, but I'm okay with that. The quality time is what I'm after.

"Uh, huh. Sureeee."

"Trust me, Jules. That mug will top all the rest. You'll see. It'll be absolutely perfect."

My lips part. *Wait a minute. Is he poking fun at me?* I meet his eyes, finding them full of mischief. *He totally is!*

Huffing a breath, I scoot closer to my wheel, feeling the weight of his stare. Oh, great. Now I have an audience? Fine.

Using my palms, I shape the cool mound into a ball, securing it in the center. Slow and steady, I press the pedal, working the clay into a cylinder as the wheel spins in circles, humming quietly. With deliberate control, I increase the speed, sweat nicking my brow, before I sink my thumbs through the top and carve out a vague outline of a mug.

Sweeping my tongue across my lip, I secure my hands

around the whirling cone, lifting them higher and higher, elongating the mug with my movements without disturbing its symmetry.

Oh my god. I'm doing it—I'm really doing it!

Hayden's stare burns a hole in my backside as I trace back down, leaving faint rings in the clay I often see while Mei works her magic. Heart clamoring in my chest, I make a second pass, smoothing out the edges and—

My foot slips on the pedal, roaring the wheel to life.

Shit!

I gasp, releasing the pressure completely, but it's too late. I watch, in both horror and slow motion, as my first sign of brilliance breaks loose and launches across the circular platform, smacking straight into the outer barrier with a thud. It whirls around and around, each rotation growing slower, until the machine stops, leaving only silence and the sight of a half-smashed mug stuck to the wall.

Mouth agape, all I can do is stare... and stare...

"A bit like how you treat the gas pedal."

WHAT?!?!?!

I bolt from my chair as his laughs clatter in my ears. They're triumphant and endless—until I lurch over the table, oozing wet clay between my fingers. The sound of his chair skidding backward rattles through the studio, searing satisfaction through my senses.

"Oh, no—*Juliana, no.* Don't you dare—"

Recklessly, I whirl on my heel, craning my arm all the way back before hurling the ball through the air at full force. Unsure of its trajectory, I'm partially worried it'll collide into one of Hayden's masterpieces, until the goopy mess hits him square in the chest. Though a bit too high for his apron to take all of it. In fact, it only manages half.

Frozen in shock, Hayden's wide eyes meet mine as the other half slips beneath his apron, surely smearing down his front side like cottage cheese, until both clumps smack against the floor.

My hand shoots to my lips, concealing their reaction and smudging a bit of clay on them.

"Juliana..." he warns.

A small sound escapes me, hysteria gripping my insides.

"This is my favorite shirt."

Indeed. Short-sleeve and silky. Gosh, what a great color on him.

Regaining my composure, I prop a fist on my hip. "Maybe you should've thought of that before talking smack," I say with a sassy head bobble. "Quite the exaggeration, by the way. I'm an excellent driver."

Dead. Silence.

Oh, you have GOT to be joking me.

"... right?" I growl.

A hush descends upon the studio, dragging on for a heartbeat... then another... His lips twitch, the same time as my eye does.

"HAYDEN!"

I whip around, clutching another fistful of goop. Except, when I twist back, locked and loaded, I find him dashing out the door, his laughter resounding through the hallway.

TWO WOBBLY MUGS, one freshly crisp T-shirt, and twenty minutes with no messy mishaps later, I slap another mound in the center of the tray. Hunched over my station, I ease a foot on the pedal, working the clay with intention. Higher

and higher, its walls climb, forming the outlines of a mug—
one I can envision so clearly in my mind but can never bring
to fruition.

Come on, come on...

"Darn it," I hiss below my breath, as a section caves
inward, the consequence of weak walls.

Huffing a sigh, I smoosh the clay back into a ball and start
over. Even slower this time, I bring the machine up to speed,
shaping the mud into a curved dome, before sinking my
thumbs through its top. Gradually, that crater spreads,
hollowing into a symmetrical cylinder, until—

"Shoot!"

My nail breaks through the clay, splitting right through
the wall. Using my shoulder, I sweep a rogue bang away from
my face, preparing for another round. Like clockwork, I
gather the failed attempt into a mound and set it spinning
between my cupped hands, exhaling loudly when my foot
doesn't cooperate.

"Need help?" a deep voice murmurs in my ear, over the
hum of the potter's wheel. I gasp as Hayden's breath tickles
my ear and warmth envelops my backside, spreading to the
tips of my toes. I didn't hear his stool roll over here. "Hmm?
Or are you too stubborn?"

My jaw drops, tempted by a snarky comment, but I bat it
down. "Okay, fine. Maybe I could use a little help..."

"As long as you don't splatter me."

I'm about to giggle, until he reaches around me on both
sides, crowding my space even more, before his hands cup
the outsides of mine, his strong arms tracing up my own. A
tingling sensation blooms out from my center, causing my
teeth to sink into my lower lip.

"More speed," he whispers in my ear.

My toes curl as I press firmer on the pedal, spinning the tray faster. His fingers interlock between mine, guiding my hands upwards, adding pressure with a rocking motion, almost as if I'm scooping the clay to its peak. In seconds, a cylinder forms before my eyes, faster and smoother than all my previous attempts.

"Slow down... that's it... just like that."

Curse my dirty mind. Not now!

Trying to ease some tension, I squirm in my chair, but can hardly budge between his hold. Heat floods my face, as his rests above my shoulder, his cheek grazing mine. Brushing his thumbs over mine, he nudges them into the clay.

"Now push two fingers in."

My eyes bulge. *Is this for real?!*

No, no. I'm just being a perve. *This is pottery,* I remind myself as I obey—but when I do, he hums in my ear, low and brimming with praise. Swallowing hard, I push the sound from my headspace, focusing on how his thumbs guide mine along the edges, carving a trough out in the mud, while my foot work to his rhythm.

"You're such a quick learner, Jules."

Blood rushes between my thighs.

I'm doomed. My mind's in the gutter.

Soft lips brush my other ear, surging a whole new wave of confusing arousal. "Look at you, needing to wrap both fists around it."

All the air whooshes from my lungs as my foot slips off the pedal, letting the wheel die out on a silent whisper. Did he just...? There's no way I heard that righ—

He snickers.

His name shoots from my lips on a piercing shout as I whirl around and bat him on his apron, earning a string of his laughter. When I catch tears stinging his eyes, I whip back to the table on instinct, making to grab a pile of mud, intending to smear it all over his smug fa—

I freeze halfway on a gasp.

"Oh, oh my..."

Earning Hayden's attention, his chuckle simmers down my spine. "What is it, baby?" he purrs, like he already knows the answer.

"It's BEAUTIFUL!" I bolt to my feet, rolling both our chairs back a foot, as I behold my most symmetrical, smooth, glossy mug yet. "I-I can't believe it!" I exclaim, lowering my voice suddenly, when I hear it bouncing between the walls. "I mean... this mug is actually worthy of a handle."

Looking behind me, I shoot Hayden a beaming smile, finding one already lighting up his face. "Here you go," he says, handing me the metal cut-off wire, which I quickly make use of, slicing the underside of the mug, unsticking it from the wheel. Carefully, like I would my first child, I pick up the mug, presenting it in my palms.

"Wow..." is all I can muster, struck by sheer amazement, realizing the mug is more than just handle-worthy—especially if Hayden paints it. It's borderline *gift*-worthy. And I know exactly who I'd give it to.

Mei.

"See? I knew you were improving."

"Pfft." Air vibrates my lips. "Oh, please. There's no way I could've managed this without your help."

Hayden rounds the table, his features dripping with pride. "No, that was all you, baby. I just nudged you, here and there."

As I make for the table to set down my prize, my heart clenches so tightly it almost hurts, because I realize something. This is my perfect day, in each and every way, the one I would stop time for, if I could.

So, Hayden and I, we make the most of it.

Throw jazz music on. Order takeout from a place across the street. And stay in the studio until the sun arches its pink-and-purple rays across the sky, reflecting like a mirror of dreams off the Hudson below, all while Hayden paints and taps his toes to the beat of the next song. Every now and then, he saunters over and helps me sculpt another mug, his arms tickling mine as they do right now.

Gently, he guides my hands, building the mound higher and higher, before sweeping back down to smooth out the base. With a few more passes, the mug begins to take on a shape of its own, its walls forming an elegant curvature—and with it, a sort of itch forms inside me.

As the seconds wane on, it doesn't subside, and proves harder to ignore. But what is it? I shuffle in my chair, watching our hands mingle into one, focusing on the presence flooding heat along my backside. So intoxicating and cherished... so *right* in the vicinity of my own...

A chuckle rumbles behind me, one that feels like home. "There sure is a lot of huffing and puffing going on, for a girl who seems to know what she's doing now—"

"Are you going to ask me to be your girlfriend yet?!"

The wheel stops, and so does my pulse.

Dammit, Juliana, could you be any more subtle?!

Using his knees, Hayden swings my chair to face his, and sure enough, he's wearing the biggest smile ever. It only grows as embarrassment stains my cheeks and I stutter, "I-I, uhh... I meant to say..." My words fall short, stolen by the delight in his eyes.

"Ohh, my sweetest Jules. It's been five days since you

moved into your new apartment. What happened to taking things slow?"

Good question.

He grins, reading my mind. "So impatient."

"We'll still slow things down," I manage to say, but it sounds unconvincing even to my own ears. "I just... maybe I want the label sooner than later, after all."

Stealing a little oxygen from my lungs, he scoots closer. "You don't have to convince me, baby. You know I'll do anything to take you off the market—even more than you already are—but..." He glances at his palms, both coated in clay. "Do you want me to wash up first?"

"What do your hands have to do with asking me to be your girlfriend?"

"God, you're adorable." He snorts quietly as he wheels even closer. "Well, you see, I'm supposed to set the mood."

My eyes dart between his when he leans over, entrancing me with his nearness. Heart clattering, his breath tickles my mouth, as mine speaks ever-so softly. "How so?"

It's a silly question, really, and one that goes wholly unanswered as his lips crash into mine, our tongues dancing as one, before those muddy palms cup my face with achingly tender care, streaking the cool clay down my cheeks, along my jaw, and even through my hair. But I don't care, can hardly register their movements, as I sweep my own along his neck, marking his skin with the sole intention of reaching his soul.

By the time our lips part, my heart pounds with longing, overflowing with the essence of *him,* as he sweeps his thumb across my cheek, my own clay marking his strong features. And before he asks that question—that beautiful, beautiful question, the one I answer with the desire of forever—he beholds me in a way that surely only comes once in a lifetime.

Because the way Hayden looks at me...

It's like he won't get another chance to.

Perhaps, we both share an instinct, or an intrinsic type of calling, or maybe just the simple fact that...

When you know, *you know*.

EPILOGUE PART ONE
6 MONTHS LATER

"Julianaaaa, are you done with that feature yet?"

Mei's whine fails to break my concentration, as my fingers race across my keyboard. Each keystroke is silky smooth, and for once, my laptop doesn't disturb anyone around me. Granted, there's no one else here, aside from the museum handlers carrying bubble-wrapped art pieces into the storage room. Even so, they don't hear a peep from this baby.

And I *do* mean baby. This right here is the newest, most precious piece of tech I own. The Sentinel M5000. Sleek, ultra lightweight, with a sixteen-inch monitor, it makes my old laptop look like a relic from another era, and don't get me started on the processing speeds.

Well, actually, I couldn't rattle off all the technical details, apart from my personal experience running my programming suite since purchasing the laptop last month—which is, The Sentinel is fast. *Real* fast. Anything far beyond that is outside my wheelhouse.

I'm a programmer, not an electrical engineer.

Jeremy, on the other hand, lit up like a kid on Christmas

morning when he first saw the laptop, before launching into an exhaustive monologue about its specs. How many gigabytes of RAM it had, the storage capacity of its solid-state drive, the motherboard's build quality—all of which I was already aware of and could easily keep up with...

Until he broached the topic of the Central Processing Unit. Then he lost me, because my dearest brother, the over-enthusiastic engineer on Silicon Avenue that he is, didn't just gush about how fast it was, but delved into the reasons *why* it's fast —on an anatomical level. Circuits, thermal management, cache memory, *boring boring boring,* something about a Nano-Z chip unveiled at a tech conference last year, *yada yada yada,* even faster than the old generation, and *whaBAM!*

My new laptop earned Jeremy Brooks's stamp of approval.

"Hellooooo?" A palm waves in front of my monitor, blocking the view of my code. "Earth to Juliana."

"Huh?" I snap to attention, finding Mei folding her arms, a clipboard dangling from one hand.

Even though I arrived at Ascension Museum and Gallery over an hour ago, I'm still surprised by Mei's outfit—a knee-length, neutral-gray dress that conceals her dragon tattoo paired with two-inch heels and modest makeup. It's like she slipped on someone else's skin.

Who knew being a gallery assistant at a top New York City museum came with such a strict dress code? Isn't art all about self-expression?

Mei huddles close, her waist brushing my shoulder, when another pair of handlers passes through the tight space, grunting and wheezing as they balance a tall sculpture between their fingertips.

"Put that over by the wall in storage section C," she orders, earning nods from the sweat-beaded workers. "Not on the ground, like you guys did with the Baroque lounge chair, but on its respective conservation pedestal, away from employee foot traffic. Might I remind you that your laziness nearly cost the three-hundred-year-old chair a leg, and I'm not about to be blamed for it a second time."

More grunts.

She swivels back toward me, huffing a grand sigh. "Gosh, you'd think it was their first day on the job. For once, can't they just—"

Like a sixth sense, Mei's gaze snaps elsewhere, latching onto a similarly dressed girl exiting the storage room. Seemingly a few years younger than us, she carries a vase bursting with an impressive bouquet of lilies.

"Where are you taking those?" Mei's voice booms across the room.

The girl stops halfway out the door, a scowl souring her lips. "To the Main Gallery."

Shaking her head, Mei gestures toward another exit. "Angie, I told you yesterday, only orchids go in the main showroom. Lilies are for the East Gallery."

When silence crackles between them, I get the feeling the two have a longstanding history of conflict.

"Does it really matter?"

Mei taps a pencil to her clipboard, lifting a brow. "It does to our artist."

Tension coils in the air, much too thick for my liking, before the girl rolls her eyes and pushes off the doorframe, letting the door slam on its hinges. She breezes past our table, glaring at Mei. "In case you forgot, we have the same job title. You're not my boss."

"I am today."

She grumbles, loud enough for us to hear her slew of curses.

"And I better see roses in the West Gallery!"

Angie practically kicks open the door to the museum's East Wing, its weight crashing shut louder than the first.

"Fucking undergrads," Mei mumbles below her breath.

I stifle a laugh, diving back into my code.

"What's so funny?"

Darn it. "Nothing, nothing… Just that you're running this gallery like a no-nonsense hall monitor. Seems you're taking a liking to management."

"Ohhhh, no. I know what you're implying. Before you start comparing me to Meghan, I'll have you know I've been busting my butt since six a.m. Arranging transportation. Vetting caterers. Polishing frames and all the bulbs in their overhanging spotlights. Making sure the moving crew was on their A game. Assigning deinstallation duties…"

From the corner of my eye, Mei counts on her fingers, emphasizing each task. Not that she needs to. I know this showcase is just as important to her as it is to me. Not only is tonight her first time flying solo since taking her new job, but she's still in the midst of completing her PhD. Apparently, this will look good on her—already sparkling—resume before graduation.

"Hey now." I cut her rambles short. "I've helped my fair share. Maybe I'm not the one who waltzed in here at the crack of dawn, but I scrubbed those floors, didn't I? And cleaned the windows out front?" Mei's smirk widens, realizing my point. "You're not Meghan. Not even close. Anyone could— and *will*—see how much effort you put into preparing the showcase."

Her shoulders relax. "Thank you, Juliana. I really needed

to hear that. My new boss may be an improvement over our old one, but she's still type A. She'll notice any slip-up."

"Well, there aren't any," I say truthfully, noticing her fingers tapping along her clipboard, itching to skim through her checklist for the fifteenth time. I touch her arm to calm her nervous twitching. "Seriously, I mean that. Your preparation was obvious the entire time I helped—which I would continue to do until the doors open, but my stomach took over. I'm starving."

Her eyes meet my empty sandwich wrapper at the same time mine do. "Uhh, I mean, I *was* hungry," I correct, letting my laptop steal my focus yet again. "And work was calling me—specifically, this feature."

Mei smiles, looking over my shoulder. "Which is…?"

"The whisker whirlwind."

She snickers. Not how most people do, but in a way that says *God, I love your brain.* She's asked me before how I think of the feature names. My answer is always the same—I have no idea. They just come to me, usually at night while I'm trying my hardest to fall asleep. How pesky, right?

Plus, if truth be told, I'm not even that familiar with cats. We had one growing up, for a short time, while my grandparents were moving in-between apartments. His name was Ruffus, a big orange tabby who took great pleasure in shredding your toes at night if they poked out from the comforter. But that purring menace aside… my feline history is fleeting, so I'm unsure where to credit my source of clever kitty lingo.

Though, that doesn't mean I haven't thought of adopting a cat. I would've years ago, if my old apartment wasn't too cramped and didn't allow pets, and as for my new apartment, well… let's just say, it's not the monthly pet fee holding me back, rather that the adoptions would be a couple's decision and *our* kitty would be destined to be a pampered, penthouse pet, because...

I don't really sleep at my apartment much. Or *at all.*

Turns out, when it comes to Hayden, I'm terrible at taking things slow—to which he has zero complaints. I lasted maybe a month in my own apartment. Two weeks into my lease, I slept over at his place, then again, a couple of nights later... then I left my toothbrush in his bathroom and my hair-brush... then my groceries were "accidentally" delivered to his address instead of mine...

And the rest is history.

A scalding, sizzling-hot history.

It's something I can't afford to think about right now—*especially* the other night—not with my best friend standing beside me, who can read the naughty thoughts in my eyes like some scandalous gypsy mixed with a gossiping hair-dresser. It doesn't matter if she slipped on that modest dress, she's still the same old Mei. Hungry for all the details.

"It's alright." She balls up my sandwich wrapper, swishing it into a nearby trash can. "You've helped plenty, trust me, especially last night with the movers. Honestly, I know you insisted, but you shouldn't have lifted a finger today. Tonight *is* your boyfriend's showcase, after all."

I smile, pride blooming from my center, as I recall the museum's art technicians sweeping across the penthouse last night, bubble wrapping and hauling Hayden's paintings and pastels with meticulous care. They gathered most pieces from the studio, plucking others straight off the apartment walls, amassing a collection that's as impressive as it is massive. To the extent that I haven't even seen every piece yet, and they'll fill all three of the museum's galleries.

Unlike Hayden, there's no doubt in my mind bidders will

be in a frenzy over his artwork. In their eyes, he's a debut artist with a never-before-seen collection. That makes every piece even more valuable, once they're received well—which is a given.

Tonight—*Hayden's* night—he doesn't need to charm any critics. His talent will speak for him, starting in... I glance at the clock in the corner of my monitor. Twenty minutes, until the doors open.

Nerves crackle beneath my skin.

Gosh, I can't imagine how Hayden feels. I'd be with him now, if it weren't for his weekly dinner with his brother falling on today, a mere hour before the showcase. I would've urged him to cancel, but I know how important their recent bonding is to Hayden... And how much my boyfriend loves to be fashionably late.

Avoiding the daunting gaze of the clock, I submerge myself in work, click-clacking away. "I'm almost done with this feature," I tell Mei. "Don't worry, I won't miss a thing, not for the world. I'll be in that gallery from the second the doors open until they close."

"But they already did."

My fingers stall along the keyboard as my gaze looms up to her. "Huh?"

She blinks rapidly, her sass prevailing without her false lashes. "The doors—I told Angie to open them early." My heart skyrockets into my throat. "It's not an uncommon thing the gallery does, if we notice a big line outside. The West and East wings are still undergoing final touches, but... based on the crowd I saw forty minutes ago, I assume she opened the main gallery by now."

"What?!" I burst to my feet, slamming my laptop shut. "Why didn't you tell me sooner?!"

"Well, I tried, but the movers and the flowers and..."

Anxiety twists my gut into a pretzel as I hurry past her, each step toward the storage room's main exit pumping blood in my ears, louder and louder, drowning out her words, until...

All that blood simmers on a long sigh.

Oh, thank goodness.

Ambient lighting and soft chatter fill the Main Gallery, despite the impressive crowd milling about the space. Artsy types, adorned in flowy dresses, patterned scarves, and layered jewelry, others adhering to a more edgy style, flaunting leather jackets or ripped jeans, all conversing and gazing up in wonder at paintings I've admired many times before, plucked from the penthouse I now call home.

"It's amazing, Mei," I say, when she comes up next to me. "You did a spectacular job."

Eyes narrowing, she surveys the gallery, noting the caterers weaving through guests, balancing trays of champagne-filled flutes and hors d'oeuvres. "Good, it seems Angie listened, after all." She points to the orchids decorating the front entrance and scattered throughout the showroom.

I gesture toward the center of the gallery, where three moveable dividing walls stand, attached to the coffered ceiling. They're arranged in a zigzag pattern with ample space between, creating more room for paintings and natural paths for visitors to walk through. Mei must've ordered the museum handlers to roll them in while I was working.

"I love how you positioned the partition walls. They're placed perfectly."

"You really think so?"

I nod, watching warmth color Mei's features.

"Thanks." She gives me a side hug, wary of the clunky

clipboard still in her hand. "I couldn't have managed without your support today."

Yes, you could've, I nearly say, but instead offer a tender smile, knowing my best friend wouldn't accept such flattery.

For a while, we just stand in the doorway, shoulder-to-shoulder, admiring the scenery. Pride swells within me while I watch more people usher through the front doors, despite the showcase being ten minutes shy from its official start time, and art enthusiasts engage in deep conversation over Hayden's work.

Another minute passes, and an alluring melody drifts above their chatter, growing more prominent…

I listen closely to the rich sound, a harmonious blend of high notes and lower ones sustaining the elegant chords, and I'm about to compliment Mei on her soundtrack choice, until I spot the man in an all-black suit dancing his fingertips across the keys, light and effortless.

I gaze in awe, savoring the classical tune and the profound energy emanating from the grand piano. Onlookers crowd around, gawking in surprise, except for the woman in a shimmering blue dress, already leaned over the piano's lip, resting a chin on her fist and gazing longingly like the song is just for her. And by the looks of their matching corsages, it really might be.

"Wow… where'd you find him? Carnegie Hall?"

Mei follows my stare. "Actually, my friend from another major gallery who referred him to me mentioned he performs there from time to time. Guess he started picking up showcase gigs, too. He played at one she hosted a few weeks ago, but this is his first time here. His name is…" She hums, rolling her lips. *"Damien—*yes, I believe it's Damien. I hired so many professionals for this, I can't possibly remember all their names. My boss handles payroll, thank God."

I *hmph*, raising an eyebrow to the dramatic crescendo echoing throughout the showroom, which elicits a round of applause and a cautioning glance from his partner.

"Well, that Damien fellow is doing one hell of a good job."

Fortunately, the East Gallery opened moments ago, drawing the attention of numerous guests and alleviating some of the congestion in the crowded main room. I plan to follow, perhaps when Hayden decides to show up to his own event, but for now, I mosey around the Main Gallery, a glass of champagne in hand, enjoying the music and studying the paintings.

I'm not sure how long it's been since this particular one caught my eye. It's my first time seeing it, probably because it was hidden in a large stack of canvases in the studio at home. Without Mei as my artistic liaison, I stare up at the large canvas, appreciating the bright colors, the delicate brush work, and—

I lose my train of thought, as a familiar voice drifts from the other side of the partition wall.

"...and did you text Sofia to see where she's at? The doors opened fifteen minutes ago."

Lauren.

I peek through the opening between the walls, catching sight of her fiery red locks. She studies another painting beside a woman I instantly recognize—the one in a blue dress who sports a corsage that matches the pianist's. A unique shade of lilac, the flowery bundle wraps around her wrist above a gobsmackingly large engagement ring. The only one I've ever seen that rivals Lauren's.

Returning to my own painting, I can't help but eavesdrop.

"I think I sent her five already," the other girl says.

"And no reply? Weird. I wonder what the holdup is."

"Pffft, please. You already know the answer to that. Her and Ross can't keep their hands off each other. I'm sure they're doing it right now, as we speak. Maybe sneaking a quickie in the cab ride over here."

"Oh my god, quit it!" Lauren hisses, unable to stifle her laughter. "Not here."

I smile, surprised by the playful side of my family's otherwise serious lawyer.

Whenever I picture her in my mind, she's usually inside a courtroom, arms folded, staring down Warren's fleet of defense attorneys. Specifically, in civil court when the judge ruled in my favor two months back and ordered the defendant to immediately pay me restitution for his blatant acts of plagiarism.

A staggering thirty million.

Yes, *million*. Not thousand.

I still feel slightly nauseous, just thinking about it.

In the words of Hayden, watching his father crumble in his chair was in the "top five most satisfying moments of his existence." I'm sure he ranks Warren's little boardroom incident higher on said list—or maybe when Sylvia raked in half his net worth all those years ago, despite him being so young at the time.

But little does he know, none will top his father's impending criminal court sentencing. According to Lauren, he's royally screwed and will most likely never again walk these New York City streets in his lifetime, not with all the women stepping forward, voicing their own allegations against Warren. Accusations stretch back decades, sharing indisputable similarities, and took place at Kingston Entertainment, golf clubs, luxurious resorts, spas, and casinos.

Anywhere Warren touched, he was a plague. And these women—their strength and their stories—are a united front, a wave of overdue retribution, spearheaded by Lauren and triggered by my mother.

"You know I'm right, Lauren."

"Okay, fine. They're most definitely getting busy—that's why she's not texting back. But I can't be the only one still shocked over our girl finally settling down. Obviously, Damien's letting it slide and Ross is her boss and all, but... how have they not gotten caught at work? It's gone on for months."

"Come on, Lauren. It's Sofia, we're talking about. She knows how to fly under the radar."

They both hum in agreement, their tones hinting at well-kept secrets. Whatever the heck *that's* about.

Silence clouds the air around them, until Lauren's voice splices clean through. "Speaking of Damien, it seems he's backed off a bit. It's much quieter than when I first arrived. What, did he get tired?"

"You're kidding, right? Damien's fingers never get tireeee—" A gasp rings from the opposite side of the wall, and I clamp down on my lip hard, barely managing to hold back a laugh. "I-I mean... I didn't mean..."

"Jesus Christ," Lauren curses. "Yeah, you *better* rephrase that statement. That's a little TMI regarding a family member."

"I only meant... it was me. *I* told Damien to take it down a few notches."

"Did you, now?"

"Mhmmm."

In near-perfect unison, their heels clack against the ground, heightening my awareness. As they round the partition wall, I furrow my brow in concentration and study the painting before me, acting as though I've been lost in thought —certainly not eavesdropping. My artsy trance proves easy enough, except...

Aside from the soft music, I didn't realize it was *this* quiet. Nearly everyone is in the East Gallery.

"I told him he was getting carried away, like always," Lauren's friend continues. "Which is fine at Lincoln Center or Carnegie Hall, but not at an art showing, especially not one with ties to his cousin's clients. I said tonight was more about visual art."

Lauren chuckles, the sound growing louder.

Shit, shit, shit. I whip my head this way and that, in search of a solution that doesn't exist, until I just accept my fate and stare up at the exquisite painting, nursing my champagne.

"Wow, I'm sure he just loved hearing that. You telling him —" Lauren cuts off, stopping abruptly as both women cross into my peripherals. "Juliana?"

Acting confused, I turn my head.

"I knew that was you."

"Oh, hey, Lauren!" I plaster on a smile, praying she can't read my embarrassment. But who am I kidding? She's a lawyer. Of course, she can.

Her face mirrors my own. "So, uhh. Did you hear all that?"

"Oh, alright..." My shoulders deflate. "Maybe a little."

Her friend chuckles awkwardly. "Oops."

Thankfully, Lauren is quick on the rebound, acknowledging her favorite pieces so far, complimenting my dress and Hayden's unmatched talent, and introducing me to her friend, Hannah.

"I'm Juliana." I outstretch my hand, meeting her friendly, chocolaty-brown eyes, before she bypasses the handshake altogether and catches me in a hug, squeezing tightly.

"It's so nice to meet you!" Hannah retreats with a broad smile, keeping at a familiar distance. "So, your boyfriend painted all these?"

I nod, catching Lauren's smirk at my fidgety state.

"That's amazing! I'll have you know, I already placed bids on three different pieces." My eyes bulge. "Although, a girl who works here—Angie is her name, I think—told me I was outbid on all of them."

"Oh my gosh..." Excitement steals a breath from me. "Hayden will be ecstatic." *When he gets here!*

"I counter bid, of course. Still waiting to hear back. By the looks of it, there may be some deep-pocketed collectors here, but I'm not leaving without five pieces, at least. Maybe six or seven, depending on my mood."

Catching a glint of Hannah's engagement ring, looped snug beside a matching wedding band, I don't doubt her words. That diamond's not a rock, more like the tip of a mountain.

Not to reinforce the starving artist stereotype, but... she must be the wealthy spouse.

Lauren shakes her head, concealing a grin. "Gee, Hannah. How many paintings do you own? Damien's going to lose it if you shove another one above your mantelpiece. Don't think he's forgotten our antics at my family's last auction— you nearly gave him a heart attack from how much you spent."

"Yeaahhhh..." She scratches her neck. "You're not wrong."

I pipe up, "If it helps, remind him that half the proceeds are going to charity."

As soon as the word *charity* leaves my lips, both of them freeze and exchange another one of those mysterious, secretive glances. I swear I catch competitiveness gleaming in their eyes.

Clearing my throat, I glance at Hannah's corsage. "So, you came with the pianist?" I ask, stating the obvious.

"Yes, he's my husband," she says, blushing as though she's talking about a crush.

"Who's also my cousin," Lauren adds, and suddenly, the whole finger-tiredness thing makes more sense.

Yikes.

When the music switches up, I angle my head, finding a woman seated at the piano's bench instead, playing a violin. Not far from his instrument is the pianist, who laughs with a man who frankly looks out of place in the gallery.

It's not that he doesn't wear his expensive suit well—quite the contrary, actually—but the sheer size of him and the abundance of tattoos. They crawl up the sides of his neck, adorn the backs of his hands, peeking past his cufflinks, and—

Hold up. Isn't that...? I squint, making out the corsage pinned to his suit lapel, then look to Lauren's wrist, finding an identical match. No. Frickin'. Way. *That's* Lauren's husband? Now I see why Jeremy thought he was intimidating. Even so, doubt still lingers, until I catch the way she ogles him.

"Well, uhh... he's a super talented musician," I tell Hannah, before stating that her husband should consider taking the gig full time, if he hasn't already, which the duo finds amusing for some odd reason.

Secrets, so many secrets.

When another bout of silence spreads, Lauren tips back her champagne glass, gulping down the rest. And it's then I realize Hannah doesn't have a flute—something Mei would deem a crime. Apparently, art critiquing is at its finest while mildly intoxicated.

"Would you like something other than champagne?" I ask her. "My friend's running the showcase, and I think I saw some red wine in the back. I could go snag you a glass."

Hannah waves a hand through the air. "No need to trouble yourself. Thank you, though."

"You sure? It'd only take a minute."

Her teeth press into her lips. "Well, truth be told, I would love some wine, but..." She glances down, and my eyes follow hers to her stomach, where she brushes a hand, revealing a faint bump. "We're expecting."

"That's amazing!" I exclaim, almost covering my mouth in surprise. Did I really need to be so loud? But the two share a look that welcomes my enthusiasm. "I would've never guessed. You're hardly showing. How far along are you?"

"Just twelve weeks."

"So exciting. Do you know the gender yet?"

"It's a boy. The name is still up for debate. Damien likes Ethan, and my vote's for Caleb."

Despite barely knowing the woman before me, I'm filled with an inexplicable giddiness, as is Lauren, who gazes at her best friend with the same affection I reserve for Mei. "My cousin will see it your way, Hannah, no doubt."

"You think so?"

"One hundred percent."

"We're ready—we're *so* beyond ready—but it's just happened all so fast. I'm still trying to process, yet I'm so excited. Meanwhile, Damien's already planned out the nursery and bought half his wardrobe, all by the end of the first trimester. Isn't the guy supposed to be the one who freaks out? Or am I just…"

I sigh peacefully, eavesdropping once again, but this time, Hannah's voice is oddly comforting and natural, almost as if this is far from the last time I'll hear it. Lauren's, too, as I slip back into the conversation with ease, losing myself in a discussion that seemingly steers itself.

Until camera flashes on the opposite side of the partition walls steal my attention, illuminating the showroom's entrance and drawing the crowd out of the East Gallery. One by one, we gravitate toward the commotion, but I hesitate on my approach, already anticipating what I'll see before I round the corner.

A vision that evokes proud tears.

Hayden, receiving the recognition he deserves.

EPILOGUE PART TWO

I'll never grow tired of having Juliana on my arm.

And luckily for me, as of three months ago, my best friend stopped looking at me like he'd chop off said arm.

To my left, Jeremy scratches his chin quizzically and hums for perhaps the twentieth time in five minutes, his gaze fixed on the painting Juliana also admires. Sensing my irritation, she snickers, the movement squeezing my arm.

Another dramatic inhale and...

"Hmmmmmmmmmmm—"

"Bro, what is your deal?" Juliana convulses against me, shaking with silent laughter. "I already answered your questions about this one, so I don't get why you're channeling your inner Confucius. Need a gong to complete the vibe? Maybe a mat to meditate?"

I smirk when Juliana lets loose a laugh—just one, from those ruby red lips. I don't stare at them for too long, or permit my eyes to trail down the modest yet tight black dress she wears, lest I draw the attention of those around us to yet another piece of art at this showcase.

One below my belt.

"Hmmmm, yessss."

Fucking hell.

Jeremy swirls his flute by the stem, eyeing the glass, presumably searching for legs, even though he's drinking champagne, not wine. When he upturns his nose, his voice taking on a nasally tone, I instantly recognize what he's doing.

Mocking the guests.

I'd chastise him, but... they *are* a bit eccentric.

After his initial praise of my talents and an onslaught of questions, this is what he resorts to? I kind of love him for it.

He swirls some more. "Why, Hayden—Hayden *Kingstonnn,* Mr. Kingston, good sir—how very kind of you. So generous, thoughtful, selfless, considerate, and all the other words in my pocket-size thesaurus... I'd take you up on your *marvelous* offer if..."

Cringing, his deep tenor returns, as does his playful expression. "You want the truth? Yesterday was leg day. I can hardly squat low enough to sit on the toilet, let alone on some floor mat."

"Jeremy!" Juliana hisses. "So inappropriate."

His palms shoot up defensively. "Sorry, Sis. I didn't realize your boyfriend was so squeamish." My lips twitch when he nudges me.

I glance at his form-fitting attire. "You couldn't have been that sore, if you managed to squeeze yourself into that suit."

"Ahhh, you got me with that one! I'll admit it. I've been bulking hard, so this is a bit tight. But I'm serious. Yesterday's split was brutal!" He winks at me. "Just ask my man, Elias."

My man.

I'll never get used to Jeremy's new nickname for my

brother, ever since convincing him to lift weights, a feat that's more shocking than... well, *anything*. But against all odds, one month in, my brother's still going strong, adhering to Jeremy's four-day-a-week program.

"Did you ask him?" he prods again. "Huh? Maybe during your dinner tonight? Thanks for the invite, by the way." His eyes narrow into slits, half joking, half serious.

More often than not, we do invite Jeremy, but tonight was special for my brother. A celebration that I wasn't going to compromise on for the sake of appearances, even on a night like this. Because as of today, Elias is six months drug free. Not to mention, Kingston Entertainment's stocks are at an all-time high, having never trended downward since he took over leadership.

He's winning all around and was overdue for a margarita —or three. Which is why he's by far the drunkest person here, stumbling from painting to painting, smiling and snapping photos, despite the signs warning against doing so. But he's here showing support, and that's all that matters. Unlike our father, obviously, and our mother, who I didn't even bother calling, not wanting to hear her voicemail.

Although, Juliana's parents showed. They're around here somewhere, after having gushed endlessly over my showcase —and how beautiful of a couple their daughter and I make.

Amber and Raymond, Jeremy and Juliana—they're like my adopted family, and I'm grateful Elias is finally catching on to that fact.

I rest a hand on Jeremy, earning his immediate composure. "We'll invite you to the next dinner. And every one after that."

Jeremy sighs, and I feel Juliana release some tension as well, before he perks back up. "I know, man!" He pats my shoulder, his strength greater than he realizes, his gaze drifting toward a drawn-out crescendo, emanating from the piano across the gallery. "No worries, really. I was only—"

His entire body goes rigid. "Hold on..." He squints. "Is that... No, it can't be..."

Juliana whips her head, following her brother's stare. "Are you referring to the pianist?" Her brother just nods, incapable of forming syllables. "His name's Damien. That's all I really kno—"

Jeremy bolts from our vicinity, aiming for that grand piano, weaving between people like the man seated at its bench might disappear from thin air.

I blink... mimicking Juliana, before we exchange confused glances. I only shrug. "Who knew Jeremy was such a fan of classical music?"

"You should be so proud of yourself, Hayden."

As I guide us around the room still crowded with guests who shoot glances our way, I glance down at Juliana, only to find her already gazing back at me with adoration. It's the look every man dreams of and makes my heart clench every time.

"I'm serious," she presses, blushing when she notices me staring.

"I know you are, baby, and I am proud, but it's all thanks to you."

She deadpans, and *God* is it cute. Then I'm the one convincing her of my sincerity.

"And how's that?" she asks. "Every painting here is of your making, not mine."

We round a corner, exiting the East Gallery back into the main, starting up on a path we've walked several times now.

One by one, I glance at my paintings, each a testament to countless hours of work, noting the delicate white strokes at their bottom right corners that form the initials H and K. My signature still looks quite foreign to me, seeing as it's only graced the canvases for a short time, after months of Juliana's encouragement, chipping away the lies my father instilled so deeply within me.

At first, the process was gradual—sneaking out of my room at night like some meddling kid, just to sign a canvas. Just one. Then another, maybe three or five nights later. Until it all came crashing down at once and I signed every last one, so many my wrist was numb by sunrise.

I stop her suddenly in the throes of not-so-subtle onlookers who, in the wake of her beauty, may as well be the wind. Cupping her cheek, I sweep a thumb along her jawline, gazing down into her green eyes.

"That may be true, Juliana, but my paintings never would've made it to a showcase in the first place without your support. Without you, I wouldn't have signed a single one."

Emotions shimmer across her face, as she blinks to keep the tears at bay. She's quiet for a moment, before she says the closest words to my soul. "I love you."

I press a kiss to her forehead, reciprocating the sentiment on a soft murmur, while what I'd wager to be camera flashes shine past my eyelids. Juliana mumbles a curse, confirming my suspicions.

"Still not one for attention, are you, Jules?" I tease, offering her my arm once again, which she takes on instinct.

"I'm working on it."

We chuckle in unison, floating about the gallery's perimeter, until we complete our loop. "Nooow, do you want to go into the West Gallery?" Surely, she won't insist on another walk through, not when the west entrance opened over an hour ago, right...?

But against all odds, she does.

"Is that all this really is—you like going in circles?"

"Nooooo, that's not it."

My gaze narrows at her suspicious tone, contrary to her impenetrable poker face. "What's the reason, then?" Silence is her chosen response. "Juliana... Julesy-baby." She glares, but not a peep from those lips, so I soldier on. "Jujubee... Julipops... Julesy-Wulesy... Ju—"

She groans.

Thank God. I was running out of those.

"Stop it, stop it! Those nicknames are absolutely ridiculous. Have you just had those on the backburner this whole time? Fine. You want to know why I'm going in circles? It's because..."

I lean my ear close, anticipating some gossip relayed from Mei about the West Gallery, which I've yet to see.

"I'm deciding which painting to bid on."

My jaw falls slack.

"Oh, don't give me that look, Hayden."

I blink, dumbfounded. "But I let you choose the ones you wanted to keep in the penthouse after I did so. Plus, I'll paint anything you like."

She nudges me. "Where's the fun in that, huh?"

"I see how it is. One settlement later, and you're Miss Money Bags. Not that you needed it with that DreamScape feature coming up, and sticking right on target to be one of their Top Selling Games of the Year nominees. Gosh, with all those royalties, your head must be blown up like a balloon."

"That's not true!" She swats my arm in offense, while her eyes tell a whole different story. That perhaps I'm onto something.

"You sureee?" I purr in her ear, eliciting a shudder. "You know what I think? I think when I take you to another race, you'll be throwing down more cash than me."

"W-what?!" She gapes, lips sputtering. *"Hayden Kingston,"*—her sass sparks excitement through me—"I may have come across some money recently, but that doesn't make me a gambling addi—"

Noting my feline grin, she cuts herself short, returning me a flatlined look. A battle of wits that's sure to be settled later tonight. Preferably, between silky sheets. Or… elsewhere, if I'm so lucky.

"And what about *your* head?" she counters.

"What about it?"

"Between the two of ours, it's the one that must be inflated to the moon, given how every single painting of yours received bids."

She's right. Walking into this gallery tonight was like stepping into dreamland. Frankly, I didn't anticipate *any* bids, let alone a full sweep. It's something that hasn't really sunk in yet. Maybe it will in a month or two.

Or fifty.

I'll tell her all about it later, but for now… now I hit her with my signature gaze, the one formerly used to bring women of all walks of life to their knees, but is now reserved only for Juliana's pleasure.

She sucks in a breath, caught in my stare as we meander between the partition walls.

I wink. "Come on, baby. It's me, we're talking about. My ego's got no more room for inflation."

Another *whack* sounds against my suit lapel, followed up with a playful giggle, when I snatch Juliana's wrist, stopping us in front of the West Gallery. I flick my chin, gesturing to its open doors. "Are you gonna make me ask again?" I infuse a little warning in my tone.

She rolls her lips, a welcome distraction from the spike in my pulse as I await her answer. "Maaaybe…"

I chuckle low. "So that's how you want to play it, huh—" Juliana wrenches free from my grasp and bolts into the West Gallery, disappearing into the sea of people.

Oh, no, no, no…

I chase after her giggles, offering apologies as I squeeze past guests in the skinny hallway, until I break through the crowd at the heart of the small gallery. "Juliana, wait—"

But she's already there, right where I wanted her, gazing up in disbelief at the newest addition to my collection. Adorned with a gold frame, a large canvas takes up the center of the back wall, beneath rows of ambient spotlights.

I had it all planned, was going to message Mei, have her usher people out, but it seems most are doing that all on their own, recognizing the intimate moment.

"Is that… me?"

On airy steps, I approach her, until her curly locks brush the front of my suit, tickling my arms, and the top of her head grazes my chin. I murmur close to her ear, "Who else would it be?"

She leans back into me, her eyes tracing the lines of her portrait. This one took much longer than her other, and takes on a vastly different style. Most notably that it's not one particular scene or memory… but a scent.

Her signature rosy perfume, wafting through my nostrils this very instant, mingling with the real roses decorating the gallery and engulfing the entirety of the portrait's background. Clothed in a simple pair of jeans and a black tank top, Juliana seemingly lies in a bed of roses, made up of petals and pink-and-red roses, an exact match to those lined below the canvas.

Unlike the last time she discovered a self-portrait, no sappy emotions drip from her features, just... pure happiness. And somehow, it's even better. "How'd you manage to keep this one from me? It's even bigger than my birthday present."

"I have my ways."

"You matched the roses with the real ones. Wow..." Not veering her gaze, she sighs longingly and melts into my touch as I sweep a hand down her arm, leaving a wave of goosebumps. "And that necklace you painted on me is gorgeous."

I hold back a grin, my heart fluttering when I sink a hand into my pocket. "You think so?"

"Yeah. I've never seen anything like it. The attention to detail is incredible, more so than anything out in the main room."

"Sometimes, it helps to have a reference."

Her body tenses against mine, but before she can whip around, I crane my arms over her shoulders and flip open the delicate box, presenting her with a string of perfectly graded, flawless diamonds. A necklace of impeccable value, with a price tag just shy of *twenty times* that of the one I gifted her in high school.

"Hayden..." Her voice wobbles. "It's... unbelievable. I-I don't know what to say. It's absolutely beautiful."

"You don't have to say anything," I murmur, wanting nothing more than to hook the chain around her neck, anything of substantial worth to show the men of this world that she's mine.

A ring is better. For now, a necklace will suffice.

Gently, I sweep her hair off to one side. "It'll look even more beautiful on you."

Overcome with a fit of jittery excitement, she whirls around, closing her eyes. I snicker, watching her sneak a peek, confusion cinching her brow tightly.

"You have to face *away*, baby. Not toward me."

Eyes bulging, she twists back around, mumbling something below her breath, and when I loop the chain in place, a blush creeps up her neck. As I fiddle with the latch, she stares at the painting once again and gestures to the gold plaque below.

"It says this one's not eligible for bidding."

"Of course, it isn't. I'd never sell any portrait of you."

She looks to the side, catching my eye in her peripheral, a lock falling perfectly along her jaw. The irrefutable proof that no necklace or portrait will ever do her justice. "Then why bring it to the showcase at all?"

"Because, my sweetest Jules…" I hook the latch and bring my lips to her ear. "For one night only, everyone should have the pleasure to gawk at you."

THANK YOU!

If you enjoyed *Game Over,* I'd be grateful if you supported me by leaving a review. As an indie author, every review, however short, helps tremendously.

∼

Need more Hayden & Juliana?
Their FREE sexy bonus scene is in the works! Subscribe to my newsletter at **www.alexisknightly.com/newsletter** to be notified of its completion.

THE KNIGHTLY SHOP

Want a signed paperback for your shelf or book plate for the book in your hands?

Go to alexisknightly.com/shop

KEEP IN TOUCH WITH ALEXIS

Website: alexisknightly.com
Newsletter: alexisknightly.com/newsletter
Instagram: instagram.com/authoralexisknightly
Pinterest: pinterest.com/authoralexisknightly/
TikTok: tiktok.com/@authoralexisknightly
Goodreads: goodreads.com/alexisknightly
BookBub: bookbub.com/profile/alexis-knightly

Join my private Knightly Readers' Facebook Group for writing updates, exclusive giveaways and more by scanning the QR code below!

ABOUT THE AUTHOR

Alexis Knightly is an author who writes romance with angst, family drama and a heavy dose of spice. Heroes in her stories are possessive and obsessive, have filthy mouths and know exactly who they want. Happily-ever-afters are guaranteed, but not before banter ensues and flaws are conquered.

A true lover of rain, she resides in Washington State with her family, two spoiled cats and beloved boyfriend. When she's not writing, she can be found paddle boarding, binging Grey's Anatomy, trying her hardest to become a runner, or painting with a glass (or three) of wine.

Printed in Great Britain
by Amazon

44770379R00290